Looking for Fireworks

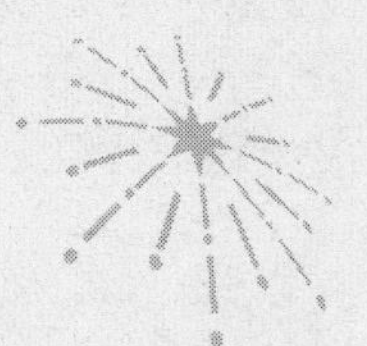

HOLLY CAVENDISH lives in Polperro, is a regular columnist for the *Western Morning News* and teaches creative writing. When she isn't writing novels, she can be found boating or riding her horse.

Looking for FIREWORKS

HOLLY CAVENDISH

PAN BOOKS

First published 2012 by Pan Books
an imprint of Pan Macmillan, a division of Macmillan Publishers Limited
Pan Macmillan, 20 New Wharf Road, London N1 9RR
Basingstoke and Oxford
Associated companies throughout the world
www.panmacmillan.com

ISBN 978-1-4472-1902-6

3 5 7 9 8 6 4 2

A CIP catalogue record for this book is available from
the British Library.

Printed and bound by CPI Group (UK) Ltd, Croydon, CR0 4YY

To my big hacking buddy – I couldn't have written this book without you x

With special thanks to Ruth Saberton

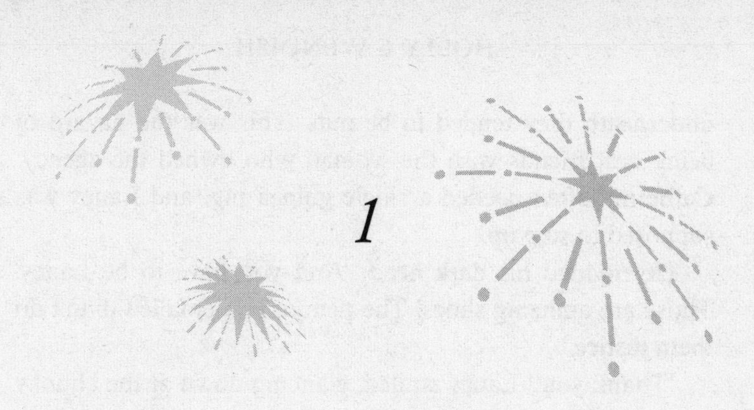

1

Is there a spark?

Laney Barwell smiled up at the handsome stranger waiting for her outside Rosalina's, Fulham's newest and coolest Italian. Wow! Tall. Dark. Handsome. As blind dates go – this one was already looking promising. This was surely the man to put the fireworks back into her love life.

OK, what did she mean, *back*? They'd not really been there in the first place, had they? Which was why she was standing on the pavement on a damp October evening with the rain wrecking an hour of labour-intensive hair-straightening and preparing to have dinner with another total stranger. Although in this case, it had to be said, a very attractive total stranger. Maybe things were looking up?

'Will Allen?' Laney asked hopefully.

Please, please don't let it be a horrible coincidence that he was wearing a red scarf, as they'd agreed in their email. After several dud dates, Laney had learned not to get her hopes up too quickly. The guys that the Catherine Wheeler Dating Agency matched her up with often adhered to 'the Snickers theory': they might look smooth on the outside, but underneath they tended to be nuts. This was the hazard of being best friends with the woman who owned the agency: Catherine often needed a single guinea pig, and Laney was supposed to step up.

He nodded his dark head. 'And you have to be Laney. Those are amazing shoes! The picture you emailed didn't do them justice.'

'Thank you.' Laney smiled, glancing down at the chunky red ankle-boots that she'd teamed with her black Missoni trousers. Sometimes her fashion sense was a little bit eccentric, but she liked to stand out from the crowd. Working in PR, she knew that it never hurt to be memorable. 'Some people think they're a bit *in-your-face*.'

'Just a bit,' laughed Will Allen, and she found herself liking the way a dimple danced in his cheek when his lips curled upwards. 'Anyway, cool boots aside, it's a pleasure to meet you, Laney. These are for you.' He handed her a beautiful posy of gerberas and kissed her cheek – just the right amount of stubble rasping across her skin to give her goosebumps. 'A bit cheesy, sorry.'

Laney made a mental note to forgive Catherine for last week's pairing with Dave from Dartford, who was only slightly less obsessed with computers than he was with the sound of his own voice. Granted, his offer to run a free defrag of her laptop was very kind, but after an hour listening to him ramble on about the merits of Windows 7 over Mac Lion, Laney's brain had needed defragging. *Maybe*, she thought hopefully as Will took her elbow and guided her inside, *just maybe there's going to be a spark with this guy?* If dating really was a numbers game, as Catherine assured her it most certainly was, then surely the law of averages meant it was high time she got lucky?

'Do you know what your problem is?' Catherine had said despairingly when Laney had popped into the agency to moan about the latest dating disaster. 'You are far too fussy. These are all seriously nice guys, if you would only give them a chance.'

'I think I'm allowed to be fussy. This is a partner I'm choosing, not a gossip mag,' Laney had said mildly, perching on the edge of Catherine's desk and peering over her friend's shoulder at the computer screen. 'Hey, he looks good. Can't you match me with him?'

'Oi, nosey. That's classified information.' Hastily minimizing the screen on her Mac, Catherine fixed Laney with a beady look. 'And, no, I can't just match you with somebody because you like the look of him. Honestly. It's a lot more complicated than that.'

'It is?' This was news to Laney. In her experience, liking the look of someone was a pretty good starting point. Maybe this was where she'd been going wrong? After all, she'd liked the look of Giles once, hadn't she?

'Of course it is.' Catherine seemed most offended. 'Honestly, Laney, you have no idea just how much work goes into making the perfect match. There are all kinds of complicated profiling and psychological testing that go on behind the scenes. You don't think I just pair people off at random, do you?'

Quite frankly, after Dave the Disastrous Date, with whom she had about as much in common as a stick of chalk on a date with a lump of Cheddar, this was *exactly* what Laney assumed Catherine did. But one glimpse of the hurt look on her friend's face was enough to make her keep quiet. Catherine's skills as a matchmaker might be on a par with those of Jane Austen's Emma, but she did mean well and she genuinely believed that true love was just around the corner for everyone who walked through the doors of the agency.

'Of course not,' Laney said, crossing her fingers behind her back and trying to recall just when Catherine had done some extensive profiling on her. Was it over the bottles of rosé they'd sunk in the Lamb and Flag on the evening that Laney and her three suitcases had made their way from Giles's flat for the last time? Or maybe just being friends for over twenty years was enough? That made some of Catherine's choices for her best and oldest friend even more inexplicable.

'I have tried, very, very hard,' Catherine said huffily. 'But you are practically impossible to please, Laney. You want perfection.'

'Of course I do. I want perfect happiness and lifelong passion. I want love at first sight. I want a fairytale romance. I want the fireworks.'

Catherine pulled a face. 'Oh, come on!'

Reaching across the desk, Laney picked up the picture in a heavy silver frame that took pride of place in the office. In it a smiling Catherine and her husband Patrick, surrounded by their three angelic-looking offspring, beamed at the camera. Catherine had married her childhood sweetheart and had been blissfully loved-up for years. Laney waved the picture under her best friend's nose. 'You're telling me this isn't the fairytale?'

Catherine sighed. 'Sweetie, let me just set you straight on a few things. The handsome prince forgets to pick up anything for dinner, hogs the duvet and sometimes looks rather too much like a frog for my liking. Marriage is blooming hard work. You need to be a little more realistic.'

Laney rolled her eyes. 'Are you sure you should be running a dating agency?'

'I'm being honest with you,' said Catherine. 'Why don't you just give some of these guys a chance? They may not make your knicker elastic dissolve, but they could be really nice once you get to know them. Real life isn't all about excitement and fireworks. Somebody has to put the bins out, you know. There's a lot to be said for a Steady Eddie.'

Laney cringed and closed her ears. No matter what her best friend might say, Laney knew the perfect relationship was out there and just waiting for her. There was no way she was going to lower her standards or settle for second best. *No way*. Her own parents had been blissfully happy. Before her mother had died, she'd never so much as heard a cross word pass between them, and they were always holding hands. She was hanging on for exactly the same.

Of course she was. Otherwise she would have stuck with Giles.

So now, as Will Allen held the door open for her like the perfect gentleman, Laney wondered if maybe this time her hopes wouldn't crash and burn? He smelled delicious, was well dressed and clearly took good care of himself. His manners were impeccable too: after he had made certain she was comfortably seated, he passed the wine list so that she could have a look. His expression was thoughtful as she considered the dizzying choice. Laney didn't have the heart to tell him that, when it came to wine, she could write her entire knowledge on the back of a stamp and still have room for the collected works of Shakespeare. Pink, fizzy and wet usually did it for her.

'I like the look of the Châteauneuf-du-Pape '97,' Will said. 'What do you think?'

What did she think? About wine? This was a first. Being a creature of habit, Giles had always tended to plump for the same white Burgundy every time they ate out (nearly always in the same French bistro he liked so much) and would have probably fallen off his seat in shock if she'd suggested something different. Not wanting to look silly, Laney pretended to be engrossed in the list while frantically trying to work out if Châteauneuf-du-Pape was red or white. Will seemed really nice and she desperately wanted to make a good impression. A first date was probably not the best time to reveal that she chose wine by price first, colour second and quality third.

'I love red wine,' hedged Laney. That was the right answer, surely?

Judging by the way Will lit up like a Christmas tree, this was certainly the right answer. Laney breathed a sigh of relief.

'You do? Me too.' He beamed. 'There's nothing better than a full-bodied red, is there? I sometimes wonder how people can drink some of these cheaper, lighter wines.'

Laney could show him *exactly* how this was done. Depending on what account she'd been working on and how demanding the client was, she had been known to cut out the middle man, forget the glass, stick her mouth beneath the wine box and turn on the plastic tap.

Probably best not to share this detail with him right now.

'In which case I'll think we'll have the Châteauneuf-du-Pape,' Will was saying. 'It's a beautiful wine, typical of the south of France, and it always makes me think of ripe plums and Mediterranean warmth. This could of course be to do with the Rhône sunshine, which adds to the full-bodied flavour. I also often detect the aroma of blackcurrants, which may be down to the quality of the soil. Yet the scent of seafood and marzipan does require a little more explanation, wouldn't you say?'

'Er, yes,' said Laney. Well, there wasn't really much she could say to this, was there? Seafood and marzipan? Really? And there was she, thinking that wine was made from grapes. She pondered on this while Will called over the waiter and placed their order, making a big deal of needing the wine to be opened at their table so that Laney could be the first to sample it.

'Lovely,' Laney said, as the waiter hovered nervously, napkin-draped bottle in his hand.

'Lovely?' Will raised an eyebrow. Holding out his own glass, he slurped back a mouthful, which he then swished around his mouth for what felt like eons. *Oh, dear Lord,* thought Laney desperately, *please don't let him spit it onto the floor.*

'I must admit, I find some of the New World wines a little rough,' Will continued, once he had – thankfully – swallowed the wine. 'I prefer the traditional ones. In my opinion, you can't beat this most famous southern-Rhône appellation. The nose and palate are replete with notes of cinnamon and clove amid the dense bramble fruit.'

And just like that he was off, faster than Red Rum out of the starting gate. On and on and on he went, as he launched into a great diatribe about grapes and soil and provenance, until Laney wanted to drown herself in claret. How was it that yet another promising date had crashed and burned even before the starters had arrived? How on earth had Will morphed from an attractive and sexy guy into a wine bore in less than twenty minutes? Was it her fault? Dave had droned on about his beloved computers. Will was clearly a wine-obsessive. And as for Giles . . .

At the mere thought of her ex, Laney shook her head, which Will took to be a comment on Beaujolais. She'd broken up with Giles six months previously after coming across a document on his computer entitled 'Laney – marriage plan'. Intrigued enough to be distracted from Facebook, she'd opened it. The document was a list, including the pros and cons for proposing to her (pro: 'Laney's not getting any younger'; con: 'home will require space for shoes'), details of where he might propose (complete with bad-weather options), links to websites for budget honeymoons and even reviews of reception venues.

Seeing the most romantic event of her life all costed out and balanced, like some kind of emotional tax return, had knocked Laney for six. What sort of a man weighed up the economic consequences of proposing to the woman he loved?

'A sensible one,' Giles had said, looking genuinely perplexed when Laney had confronted him. 'Marriage is a serious step and not to be taken lightly. I thought you'd be pleased that I'm planning our future so carefully.'

He thought she'd be *pleased*? *Pleased* to have been so coolly appraised and evaluated? Call her old-fashioned, but Laney had always hoped that, when the right man proposed, it would be because he adored her, worshipped her and couldn't live without her – not because David Cameron was introducing tax relief for married couples. Short of tattooing the definition of spontaneity onto the insides of Giles's eyelids, there wasn't anything for it but to break off the relationship. Giles was genuinely astonished that Laney hadn't been thrilled with his plans, which actually spoke volumes.

It was never going to work.

Rather like this date.

Just as Laney was trying to think of a tactful way to call time on the wine-tasting lesson, a buzzing sound came from her bag. Talk about saved by the bell. As her fingers plunged into the cavernous depths of her trusty Marc Jacobs, Laney found herself praying that this was work calling with an urgent PR emergency that simply couldn't be ignored, even at seven-thirty on a Friday. Given that her last job promoting a new digital-TV channel ended three days ago, she doubted this very much.

'Do you have to take that?' Will asked, a small frown furrowing the soft skin between his brows. 'We're having such a nice chat.'

Well, that was a new way to describe a monologue. Laney glanced at the screen, where a picture of her father, rotund and tanned from a summer spent in the garden eating his next-door neighbour's scones, was flashing at her. Now it was her turn to frown. Dad rarely called at the weekends – Fridays were generally a busy time in his B&B. In fact, he rarely called full stop. The last time they'd spoken, maybe two weeks ago, he'd felt rather under the weather and she'd been trying to bully him into seeing his doctor. Nate Barwell might only be in his sixties, but he was a widower and all alone, and Laney couldn't help but worry about him.

'Sorry, Will, but I really need to take this call,' Laney said firmly. Will shrugged, pulled a *Fine!* expression and swirled his wine petulantly.

Laney pressed the green icon to take the call.'Dad?' she said, turning slightly away from her date.'Is everything OK?'

'Now, Laney, you're not to worry,' Nate Barwell began, which instantly had exactly the opposite effect on his daughter. 'I wasn't going to call you – I'm sure you're busy – but Janet insisted.'

Janet was the neighbour with the scones and, when it came to looking out for Nate Barwell, her attention to detail made the Spanish Inquisition look slapdash.

Laney tucked the phone between her chin and shoulder and pushed a hunk of corn-blonde hair behind her ear. 'What's wrong, Dad? And don't you dare go trying to play it down or pretend everything's fine. I know you, remember?'

Nate chuckled. 'Just like your mother. I could never get anything past her, either. Now, I don't want you to worry . . . but I'm in hospital.'

Laney had the horrible sensation of descending very fast in a lift. Parents in hospital pressed all her buttons, and for a hideous moment she was eight again and sitting by the bedside holding her mum's hand, the tissue-paper skin bruised and blue from all the needles.

'What's happened? Are you all right?'

'I'll be right as rain, sweetheart. I've just had a small TIA. They brought me in as a precaution—'

'What's a TIA?' she asked. Her fingers started to pleat the damask tablecloth and suddenly the big glass of red seemed very appealing.

'It's just a mini-stroke,' Nate said nonchalantly. 'Nothing to worry about.'

'A stroke!' Laney rose from the table. 'Why didn't someone call me?'

'I'm sorry,' her dad said. 'I just know how busy you are.'

Laney glanced up and across the packed-out restaurant, where trendy couples and bespoke-suited businessmen were chatting over huge bowls of pasta and bottles of Chianti. Outside traffic bowled along Fulham Broadway, headlights beading the dusk, while pedestrians scuttled along the crowded pavements. Then she caught the eye of the impatient man opposite, who was drumming his fingers on the table and surreptitiously checking his Omega. What on earth was she doing here, in this hectic, superficial rat-race, when her father was fifty miles away in the John Radcliffe Hospital? Who cared about seafood and sodding marzipan wine when your only living relative was sick?

'I'm coming now,' Laney told him. She took her coat from the back of her chair.

'Absolutely not!' Nate cried. 'I won't hear of it. You've got your job to think about, and your house-share.'

'My latest PR commission is over and I'm due a break.'

Laney silently bid farewell to the plum job she'd just accepted, promoting a new primetime game show. 'I have money saved to cover the rent for a few months. And my housemates will understand. Some time in the country with you is exactly what I need.'

'Really?' She could hear the doubt in her father's voice. It was hardly surprising. In the past, being less than a heartbeat from the Tube and a decent coffee shop had been enough to make Laney twitchy. Her longest stint in St Pontian was probably under twenty-four hours.

'Really,' Laney said firmly. 'I'm on my way.'

Ringing off, with her father still protesting, Laney shoved the iPhone back in her bag and took a deep breath. Her pulse was galloping and she felt rather unsteady. A stroke was a serious thing. Had she been too wrapped up in her own life to notice that her father was unwell? Too busy worrying about Giles, and her futile quest for passion, to see what was really important?

Well, not any longer.

'I'm so sorry, but I'm going to have to go,' Laney told Will. 'My father's in hospital.'

Will stared at her. His eyes were now a chilly blue, like chips of ice. How come she hadn't noticed that before?

'Look, if you don't want to finish our date, at least have the decency to say so,' he said. 'Quite frankly, I think it's disgusting to use your father as an excuse.'

'Whatever,' she said and fished in her purse for a twenty to cover the glass of wine she had drunk. 'Thanks for dinner.'

Will's top lip curled as he regarded her across the table.

How on earth had she ever found him good-looking? His ears stuck out and his hairline was receding.

'Philistine!' he muttered.

'Prick!' she said sweetly. And then turned on her heel and stalked out of the restaurant, totally oblivious to the gasps and stares of the onlookers. No, she didn't give a hoot about them. All she cared about now was getting to St Pontian as soon as possible.

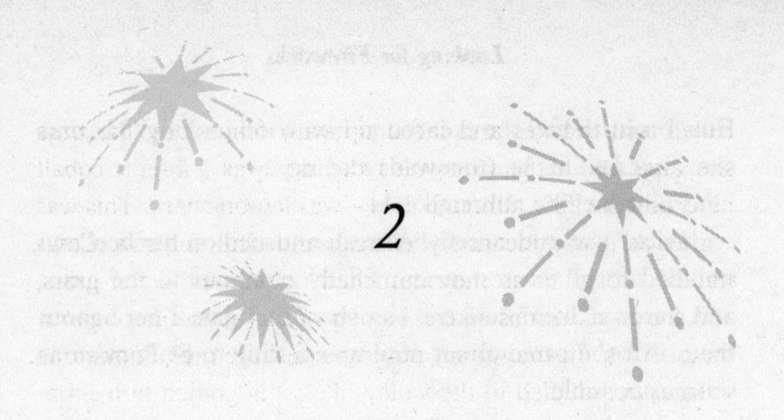

2

As she pulled her suitcase along the cobblestones that edged St Pontian's village green, Laney wondered how it was possible to travel only eighty miles from London and yet feel as though she'd arrived on a totally different planet. When she'd left Paddington the sky had been a low, leaden line above the dismal slate rooftops and a chill wind was whipping the litter into eddies. Scurrying commuters had turned their collars up against the chill and huddled into their coats as they scanned the departures board. Even the pigeons perched high in the metal skeleton of the station roof looked miserable. It was, Laney had decided as she boarded the train, the definitive gloomy winter's morning, the type that made you want to hot-foot it to Thomas Cook and book a ticket to somewhere with blue skies and icing-sugar beaches.

The train had pulled out of London and Laney had watched the city slip past her windows. As the train gathered speed, the crowded terraces soon melted away into the semis of Metroland and then into the big detached houses of Buckinghamshire. Pewter ribbon-roads became green banks, and densely crowded houses became rolling hills and pastures, frilled with hedges and laced up with fences. By the time she alighted in the Cotswolds the sky was a bright cobalt blue, and the air – although cold – was lemon-sharp. This was winter as it was meant to be: fresh and chill and raw. Cows huddled together as they munched on vibrant green grass, and the naked limbs of trees stood out as stark lines against the horizon. In the watery autumn sunshine the honey-stone village lay huddled in the valley like a big golden lion slumbering on a green pillow. Unlike London, where she would be happy to hibernate in Starbucks until the spring, here it could be fun to stomp through the winter months.

If only there was someone special to stomp with.

Laney dragged her case along the narrow pathway that led between the green and the church and eventually to her father's house. What a hike! Granted, the house stood in a peaceful spot alongside a bubbling brook and away from the road, but carrying the weekly shopping was always a logistical nightmare. And now that her father was ill, it was going to be even more complicated. How could she possibly have left him to cope on his own? And never mind the shopping; he had to cook the breakfasts for his guests, make up their rooms and do all the laundry. It was far too much for someone recovering from a TIA to cope with. Truth be told, Laney was starting to feel it might be too much for her to cope with.

Just as she was scrabbling in her bag for her keys – and wishing that she hadn't chosen one with three zip compartments – an upstairs window flew open and her father's beaming face poked out, like a tortoise emerging from a net-curtain shell.

'Laney, love. What are you doing here?'

'I could ask you the same question. Aren't you supposed to be in hospital?' Hands on hips and neck cricked, she stared up at him. It was hard to tell from a ninety-degree angle, but Nate didn't look too bad. A little pale maybe, but much better than she'd imagined.

'Ah, well, there's nothing that much wrong with me,' Nate began, but before he could continue, Janet Rolls's head popped up next to his.

'Don't listen to a word he says!' exclaimed Janet, fixing Nate with a stern look. 'The doctors were more than happy to keep him in for an extra night, but oh no, Mr I-Know-Best here wasn't having it. Somehow he managed to convince them that it was a good idea to discharge him a day early.'

'There were people there who were much sicker than me,' Nate protested.

'You've had a stroke!' Janet cried, her voice rising.

And off they went at a full-pelt bicker, framed in the window and looking so like Punch and Judy that Laney half-expected a crocodile and a string of sausages to pop up. Knowing that all this stress probably wasn't conducive to her father's recovery, Laney let herself in, dumped her case on the chequered tiles and tore up the staircase. Her father's room was in the attic at the top of the house, and by the time she had sprinted up the third set of stairs, Laney feared that she too could be in need of some medical attention. So much for all those city Zumba classes.

In the time it had taken Laney to reach the attic room, Janet had managed to manoeuvre Nate from the window and back into bed, where he was now sitting propped up against some frilly pillows with a mutinous expression on his face. The lacy duvet and bunch of flowers on the dressing table were an odd juxtaposition with the wall-mounted flat-screen television, the minimalist clothes rail and the piles of books about fishing. *Janet's work*, thought Laney with a smile.

'Tell him, Laney love,' Janet said despairingly from the far end of the bed where she was busily plumping up the duvet. 'Tell him he needs to rest. God knows, I've tried, but he won't listen to me.'

Nate rolled his eyes. 'I'm sixty-seven, not seven. And I have to get on with running the business.'

Laney perched on the end of his bed and reached for his hand. It lay in hers for a brief second, before Nate squeezed her fingers. His eyes, the same shade of green as her own, were ringed with dark shadows and as she laced her fingers through his, she felt the trembling of his hands. He was, she realized with a jolt, quite simply terrified. Since Mum had died she and Nate both had a horror of hospitals and of all things medical. It had been a long-running joke in their house that *Casualty* and *Holby City* were banned from the TV. But behind the laughter lay something more serious: the knowledge that sometimes people go into hospital and never come home.

'Janet,' Laney said, 'I don't suppose you could make us a cup of tea? I couldn't find a Starbucks nearby.'

'Fancy thinking we'd have one of those here,' scoffed Janet indulgently. 'I'll make us all a nice pot of Earl Grey, and I'll just pop next door and see if I can find some of my home-made Eccles cakes. What do you think, Laney?'

Laney thought she could feel her hips expanding at the

very idea of Janet's delicious home baking. She also couldn't help wondering if her father's neighbour's calorific snacks hadn't played a part in making Nate a little overweight too. However, since this was all supposition, and Janet really was an amazing cook, she nodded and made some enthusiastic noises, and Janet bounded from the room, a woman on a mission. Once her footfalls had receded and the front door slammed, Laney took a deep breath.

'OK, Dad, let's not beat around the bush. Just how bad was this TIA?'

Nate Barwell's gaze slid from hers like butter from a hot crumpet. 'Bad enough to have been a warning,' he said.

'A warning?'

He sighed and squeezed her fingers. 'It's all a little bit beyond me, love, but apparently it's caused by a tiny blood clot in the brain and it causes symptoms similar to a stroke. When Janet found me, I'd collapsed and I was having trouble speaking.'

Laney felt cold all over – a miracle in itself, since Janet had cranked the central heating up to tropical proportions.

'The symptoms generally go within twenty-four hours,' Nate continued, 'which is what I've found, thank goodness. But the doctors are worried it could be a bit of a forerunner to something bigger, if I'm not careful. I'm going to have some tests and I've got more drugs than Boots the Chemist. I'll need to watch my blood pressure and avoid stress. They even told me I needed to lose weight.' He sucked in his stomach. 'The cheek,' he added with a wink.

Laney's vision was blurry. 'Dad, you have to take this seriously.'

'And I will,' agreed Nate. 'But I can't abandon the B&B.'

'You don't have to. I'll help you,' Laney said firmly.

Her father's brow pleated. 'That's the last thing I'd ever expect you to do. You've got your own life to lead in London; you don't need to be stuck with an old fossil like me. And besides, Elaine Barwell, you hate the country, remember? You need to be within walking distance of Topshop, and you can't stand horses. Didn't you once tell me that you would rather eat worms than move to the countryside?'

'Dad, I was thirteen!' Laney cried, cringing at the memory of her teenage self, who had dug her heels in when her father had merely suggested the idea. 'I had a Topshop obsession, wore DMs and was in love with most of Westlife. I think I may have changed my opinion on most things since those days. Well, apart from Topshop.'

Nate laughed and squeezed her hand. 'But, sweetheart, what about your job?'

'I'm freelance. I can take time off. And we have this amazing thing called "the Internet" now.' Laney made mock quote marks in the air. 'I can work remotely.'

Her father ignored her joke. 'Could you live here?'

Laney got up, walked to the window and gazed out over the tumbled rooftops of the village where honey-hued houses dozed lazily in the autumn sunshine. Across from the house the ancient church of St Pontian stood guard over the village, cool in the yew-tree shade and surrounded by snaggle-toothed headstones. Beyond the churchyard stood two horses. Both were being ridden across the ploughed field, and one rider was an impossibly glamorous blonde who sat easily on her horse. The other was a man on a black stallion who was intent upon holding his mount in check.

Laney shuddered. She *did* hate horses. It was a real phobia. Having to bump into the big creatures, or see them on a daily basis, was a definite downside to moving to the sticks. It was true to say that you didn't see many horses sauntering down Oxford Street. And you did see a lot more shoes . . .

'It'll be brilliant,' she said, mentally crossing her fingers.

Nate was just on the brink of debating this when the thud of the front door, followed by the clatter of china and the tinkle of cutlery, heralded the arrival of Janet.

'She might be a bossy old boot, but she's a big help,' he said, with a rueful smile. 'If she hadn't had been popping in yesterday to do the cleaning, I don't know what might have happened.'

Laney nodded, making a mental note to get Janet to one side later and ask her exactly what was going on. By the time they were all tucking into treacle-sweet tea and Eccles cakes still warm from the oven, Laney had a list of questions as long as her credit-card bill and was just dying to ask them. However, Janet, it seemed, had questions of her own. And there was no fooling her, either. She might appear all sweet and pink-cheeked and harmless, but her bright eyes were as quick as mercury. When it came to Nate Barwell, very little escaped Janet's notice, which was rather comforting at times like this.

'Another cake, pet? Or maybe you'd like a piece of my fudge?' Janet shoved a plate under Laney's nose that was so crammed with sugar just looking at it made her teeth ache.

'No, I'd better not.' Laney placed a hand on her stomach.

Was it her imagination, or were her size-ten Levi's already feeling rather snug? Now she was starting to remember why she rarely visited St Pontian: all the cream teas and delicious home cooking were a mixed blessing.

'Get away, you're just a slip of a thing,' tutted Janet. 'She's got a lovely figure, hasn't she, Nate? Curves in all the right places.'

Laney laughed. Sometimes she thought she had too many curves in the right places. It was all very well being small and slight, but being blessed (or was that cursed) with D-cup boobs sometimes made life rather tricky when it came to clothes shopping.

'She's beautiful, just like her mum,' said Nate, his eyes misting slightly. 'I can't think why some young man hasn't snapped her up. That Giles needs his head checking.'

'Dad, honestly.' Laney was nipping this conversation right in the bud. 'This is the twenty-first century, remember? Women can exist quite happily on their own these days, you know. We're allowed to drive cars and vote and everything.'

'All right, all right, so your old dad's a dinosaur. I'd just like to know that you're all looked after and cared for, just in case . . .' Nate's voice quavered slightly and suddenly he looked rather frail, marooned in his cushion nest. It made Laney's eyes well up.

'My Martin is still single too.' Janet chipped in, with all the subtlety of a wrecking ball demolishing a house. 'He's a lovely boy, Laney, and a solicitor, don't you know?'

Laney *did* know. Every time she came home Janet reminded her. She'd met Martin a couple of times in the past and he'd always seemed perfectly nice. He wasn't bad-looking either, if you liked preppy guys with floppy blond hair and smart suits.

'He's just won Tetbury's Businessman of the Year award,' boasted Janet, with as much pride as if Martin had pipped Richard Branson at the post and given Alan Sugar a run for his money too, rather than probably being the only viable business in town. '*And* he's head of the village Bonfire-Night Bonanza committee.'

Laney had to bite her lip to stop laughing. Janet looked so delighted at this that Laney had to pretend she was impressed. Bonfire-Night Bonanza committee? She knew that St Pontian was pretty dead, but was November the fifth the height of the social calendar?

'You ought to spend some time together while you're in the village,' continued Janet, her eyes sparkling. 'You'd have far more in common with one another than you would with two old pensioners like me and your father.'

Nate laughed. 'Speak for yourself! In my head I'm still sixteen.'

Janet crossed her arms over her ample bosom. 'All I'm saying is that it might be nice for Martin and Laney to have a drink together one evening.'

At this point Laney decided to take pity on Janet. 'Well, why not?' she said.

She was rewarded by such a beam from Janet that she almost reached for her Oakleys. 'Wonderful.' Janet clapped her hands together. 'I just know that you two are going to get on like a house on fire. I think we all deserve another cup of tea to celebrate. I'll go and put the kettle on, shall I?' She bustled out of the room humming the wedding march.

Laney caught her father's eye and started to giggle. 'I thought I'd only agreed to go for a drink, but Janet's already picking out hats and she hasn't even reached the bottom of the stairs.'

Nate winked. 'That woman's a hopeless romantic, I must admit. Still, who knows, perhaps she's right? The love of your life could be here in St Pontian. Wouldn't that be funny?'

Laney groaned. If Nate truly thought she was about to live happily ever after with Martin Rolls, then the effects of his stroke had clearly yet to wear off. Laney had the distinct impression that in St Pontian you dated your one childhood sweetheart for years, before marrying them and living happily ever after. Catherine Wheeler would be out of business here, that was for sure. If the whole dating phenomenon was yet to make it beyond the M25, Laney was starting to wonder if agreeing to go for a drink with Martin was her smartest move.

There was only one way to find out. She just hoped she didn't live to regret it.

3

'Relax, Dad. It's only breakfast. How hard can it be?'

Laney found out the answer to that question twenty minutes later. Smoke from the toast started to billow from beneath the grill, and the fire alarm shrilled for the umpteenth time.

It was Laney's first morning manning the B&B for Nate, and things were not going according to plan. Being more of a grab-a-muesli-bar-on-the-way-to-work kind of a girl, she hadn't made a fry-up in ages, and it showed. Her timing was all over the place: the bacon was done to a crisp, the sausages were cremated on the outside and Barbie-pink on the inside, while the eggs were spitting at her viciously from the pan. And she hadn't even got started on the fried bread and baked beans yet.

With a wail of despair and a tea towel clamped to her nose, Laney braved the smoking grill tray and whisked across the kitchen with the speed of Usain Bolt, to dump it outside the back door. Leaving the top half of the stable-door open to let in some air, she yanked the egg pan from the hob and lobbed the charred sausages into the sink to hiss in the soapy water, leaping away from the hot fat as it spat at her. Good Lord! This was like a health-and-safety demonstration of what *not* to do in the kitchen.

Flapping the tea towel in a vain attempt to clear some of the smoke, Laney clambered onto the kitchen table and yanked the batteries from the smoke alarm. Enough was enough. This was not the relaxing start to the day that her father's guests were expecting. It was like a scene from *Fawlty Towers*, but she was struggling to see the funny side. Nate had built himself a really good name in the hospitality industry and his full English, made with the finest locally sourced ingredients, had earned him some rave reviews on TripAdvisor. She didn't want one breakfast disaster to ruin all of that. And neither did she want Nate to hear the smoke alarm and come downstairs to investigate.

When it came to cooking, unless it came from the M&S food hall and went *beep* in the microwave, it was a total mystery to Laney. Giles should count himself lucky that she'd never taken him up on his marriage plan. She'd have made a terrible wife. He'd probably have starved to death long ago.

Right. Deep breath, Laney told herself firmly, *and start again. You are making breakfast, not splitting the atom.* Still, at this current rate, it was just as well that she'd risen at half-six to get this show on the road. Catherine often joked that Laney needed instructions to boil a kettle.

'Should I be calling the fire brigade, or are smoke signals the latest thing in communication technology these days?'

Laney jumped at the voice and dropped a pan onto the floor, with a crash that only added to the din. She turned to see a man leaning on the half-door, smiling in at her, his hair in the soft pink sunrise the same shiny gold as the small signet ring on his index finger. Clean-shaven and wearing a freshly pressed shirt of the same denim-blue as his eyes, he looked about as far from hot and bothered as a human being possibly could. It must have been at least eighteen months since Laney had last seen him, but it was good to know that at the advanced old age of twenty-nine her memory was letting her down – if anything, he was even *better*-looking than she remembered.

'Martin.' She looked from him to the mess on the floor.

'I must say I do rather like this nouvelle-cuisine thing you have going on,' he added with a grin. 'Is this what they are doing in London now?'

'Any more comments like that and you'll end up wearing the frying pan as a hat,' Laney warned him, picking up the Le Creuset and nearly fracturing her wrist as she brandished it. 'We city folk are prone to violence.'

Martin put his hands up. 'Just teasing. I can see we have a situation here.'

'We do not!' Since it's the golden rule of PR that image is everything, Laney was not about to blow hers. However, catching the look on Martin's face as he glanced over her shoulder, she realized that she'd probably done a good job herself of shattering that particular illusion. With the smoke just clearing, eggshells scattering on the floor as if a dozen suicidal Humpty-Dumpties had taken the plunge, and the sausage pan still sizzling in the sink, Nate's lovely kitchen looked less like the set of *Masterchef* and more like something out of *Shameless.*

'OK,' she admitted. 'Maybe I'm not quite there with this breakfast just yet.'

'Maybe,' agreed Martin. The smile trickled from his eyes to his mouth, and Laney found her own lips curling upwards too. 'Call me Sherlock Holmes, because I can spot a few clues that suggest you may have quite a way before you *do* get there?'

It was a fair point. 'I need more practice.'

'Regretting turning down my mother's offer of help?' he asked.

'Your mum has been so kind already,' Laney told Martin. However, at this point, with eight hungry guests to feed and a breakfast that looked more suited to the pedal bin than the plate, she was starting to wonder if she hadn't been rather rash. 'She's helped Dad out so much. I'm sure she's got more than enough to be getting on with.'

'Not really,' said Martin cheerfully. 'Believe me, Mum loves nothing more than organizing people and getting them all sorted out. Why do you think I'm here so early? She was on the phone at the crack of dawn, giving me my orders to come over and show you the sights of St Pontian.'

'Well, that should take all of five minutes,' Laney said wryly.

'Very harsh, Ms Barwell. I think a tour of the pond, the church and the pub would take at least six. Maybe seven if we popped into the Red Lion for a swift half.'

'I could certainly do with a drink,' Laney said.

Martin glanced down at his watch. 'Hmm, flattered as I am at your keenness to accompany me to the local, I think we may be a tad early. Perhaps a cup of tea instead?'

She fixed him with a beady stare. 'Do I look like I have time to sit around drinking tea?'

'Not really,' Martin admitted. 'You look as though you've been frying yourself, never mind the breakfast.'

Peering down into the surface of a spoon and catching a glimpse of her reflection, Laney could have wept. She was red-cheeked, a stranger today to her ghds, and with a nose so greasy she might as well try frying the eggs on that. Just her luck. Her neighbour's lush, single, solicitor son turned up just when she was all flustered and sweaty? Did the god of dating really hate her this much?

'Go and freshen up,' Martin was saying gently as he reached over the door and, undoing the latch, let himself him into the kitchen. 'I'll pop the kettle on and get some of this lot sorted. No, I insist,' he added when she started to protest.

For a moment Laney hovered, undecided.

'Go.' Picking up a tea towel, he flicked it at her. 'I think you can trust me to cope with a teapot and a bit of clearing up.'

Laney didn't wait to be asked twice. If she was going to make a success of this breakfast, then she needed to get her act together. She tore upstairs to the small but pretty room that she always used when she visited her dad – he felt its view of the graveyard was off-putting for guests – where she dragged a brush through her hair, splashed water onto her hot cheeks and spritzed herself with Issey Miyake. The sharp scent made her at least smell sophisticated and had to be better than *Eau de burnt sausage*, right? She felt slightly more like her usual self, even if the reflection that floated in the age-spotted mirror was more wild-eyed and curly-haired than usual.

'*Ta-da!*' cried Martin when Laney rejoined him in the kitchen.

Laney's mouth opened so wide that she practically bashed her chin on the spotless quarry tiles. In the five minutes that she'd been gone, the room had been transformed from a disaster zone back to something out of *Country Living.* The beech work surfaces gleamed, the dishwasher was humming cheerily to itself and on the range a big pan of sausages and mushrooms was sizzling merrily. Toast was lined up in the industrial Dualit, mouth-watering bacony aromas drifted from the grill, and baked beans bubbled in the vast saucepan on top of the hob.

'How do you like your eggs in the morning?' quipped Martin, who was busily beating a bowl of sunshine-yellow yolks, pausing only to grind in some black pepper.

Taking a seat at the scrubbed-pine refectory table, she gazed around her in awe. 'Wow, Martin! I don't know what to say. This is amazing. Even Harry Potter couldn't have magically transformed things this fast.'

'I am a man of many talents,' Martin said, as he flipped umpteen golden hash-browns over. 'I also shared a student house with loads of very hungry rugby players, and cooking a Sunday-morning fry-up was par for the course.'

He might not be built like Alex Reid, but there was no denying that Martin had a good body. Slender and lithe as he was, Laney could see the definition of his chest beneath the blue shirt and, when he lifted the cast-iron pans, the muscles flexed his forearms. When he bent to place the cooked food in the warming oven, Laney couldn't but notice that the backside in those faded Levi's was firm too – not that she was really looking. No way. She wasn't checking him out – she was checking out the state of play with breakfast. As a distraction, Laney busied herself making tea. It must be the stress of the nearly ruined breakfast that was making her behave in a strange manner – she wasn't the kind of girl who went about checking out the bottoms of virtual strangers.

An hour later the guests were munching their breakfasts while Laney and Martin sat out in the garden, sipping tea and enjoying the warmth of the autumn sun. The brook burbled in the background while a blackbird shrilled to itself. In the distance a tractor crawled up a pleated plough and the bleats of sheep trembled in the air. All was peaceful and about as different from the hustle and bustle of Shoreditch as it was possible to get. For the first time since Nate had phoned her to announce his stroke, Laney felt herself relax. Maybe spending time in the country wasn't going to be quite so bad after all? If she could master breakfast without starting the Great Fire of St Pontian, then maybe, just maybe, it would all be OK?

'Thanks so much for helping,' she said to Martin. 'I owe you one.'

He chinked his Emma Bridgewater mug against hers. 'My pleasure. But be warned, I do have an ulterior motive.'

Laney's eyes widened. 'You do?'

Martin nodded, a hunk of blond hair falling across his eyes. 'Afraid so. In return for my being so helpful, I absolutely insist that you come out for a drink with me. Please, Laney, take pity on me. My mother will never stop nagging until you do.'

'So you're asking me out because your mother told you to?' Laney laughed.

He pulled a face. 'That all came out wrong, but you've seen my mother in action, you've seen how she can be. But apart from Mum, I think we could have fun hanging out. Let's face it, we under-forties in St Pontian have to stick together.'

Somehow, in spite of all her reservations about the St Pontian dating scene, Laney found herself agreeing to go for a drink with him in the Red Lion. So what if Martin didn't make her heart race and her knees weak? Maybe there was more to spending time with a man than the fireworks she was always looking for? Let's face it, she hadn't exactly been successful there, had she? He was fun, articulate, easy on the eye and he knew his way around a cooked breakfast. What more could a girl ask for?

And later on as she cleared the tables and stacked the dishwasher Laney found, to her surprise, that she was actually rather looking forward to her drink with Martin. Life in the country, it seemed, was full of surprises.

4

'Was that Martin Rolls I just saw leaving?'

A young woman teetered on the doorstep of Myrtle House, clutching a carrier bag in one hand and a bunch of flowers in the other, and cricking her neck to peer down the path as though she might still catch a glimpse of Martin's denim-clad backside.

'I thought it was his Mercedes parked across from the church,' the girl continued excitedly. 'Oh! It's brilliant that he's already been over to say hello. Janet will be over the moon.'

Laney had been living in St Pontian for less than twenty-four hours, but already she was starting to see how things worked here. There was no need for mobile phones, Twitter or Facebook: the village bush-telegraph worked far more effectively. Apparently half of Oxfordshire already knew that St Pontian's most eligible bachelor had popped over and, if Janet Rolls had anything to do with it, the other half were already waiting for their wedding invites to drop through the letter box. She felt a sudden stab of longing for London's anonymous crowds, where even her next-door neighbours hadn't a clue who she was.

'Hi, have we met?' Laney asked, while the girl chattered on, nineteen-to-the-dozen, about how marvellous Martin was. 'I'm Laney.'

'Sorry, sorry, how rude of me!' With her cheeks as crimson as her tatty fleece, Laney's visitor somehow managed to juggle her carrier bag and bouquet into her left hand and offered her right with all the enthusiasm of a dog holding a paw out for a biscuit. 'I'm Maxine Swinnerton. I live in Holly Cottage just across the green? I know your dad a bit from school.'

Laney looked at her rather blankly, because as far as she was aware Nate had been to school in the Fifties. Maxine couldn't have been much over thirty. Although the bags under her eyes and the shapeless clothes made her look ten years older.

'School?' Laney echoed, totally confused.

'Nate's one of the volunteers who helps the children with their reading,' Maxine explained. 'He's brilliant and so patient with them, especially the ones who struggle a bit. My twins, Lily and Rose, love reading to Nate.'

This was news to Laney. With a slight twinge of guilt she wondered just how much she actually knew about her father's life.

'Anyway, when I heard he was poorly, me and the other volunteers got him some bits and bobs.' Maxine held the bag out. 'Would you be able to give them to him? There's a card that the twins made too. They've been gluing and sticking since six a.m., and absolutely insisted that I brought it round as soon as possible.'

'That was kind of them to get up especially early to do that,' Laney said.

Maxine laughed. 'I can tell you don't have kids.'

Goodness! No wonder Maxine had shadows under her eyes. If Laney had to get up regularly at that time, she'd have container ships for eye-bags. Suddenly the grubby fleece and neglected roots were starting to make sense.

'Well, it's really kind of them, thanks.' Laney took the bag and card and sticky glitter instantly crusted her fingertips. Closer inspection revealed that the glitter had been stuck to the card with what looked suspiciously like Marmite. At least she hoped it was Marmite. 'I'm Nate's daughter,' she added as she tried to wipe her fingers on the tops of her jeans without causing too much damage to Calvin Klein's finest denim.

'I know. Vince – that's my husband – saw you arrive yesterday,' Maxine told her cheerfully. 'My Vince is best friends with Martin, you see, ever since school. They grew up here. And I'm second cousin to Martin on his father's side. Isn't that funny?'

Laney opened her mouth to comment, but Maxine wasn't anywhere near stopping.

'Anyway, my Vince was round at Martin's house last night, when Janet bowled up and told Martin that he needed to visit you and make you welcome to St Pontian. Vince said she was so excited you'd have thought the Queen had arrived. So that's why I was wondering if it was him I saw leaving? I was in the churchyard by the way, just putting flowers down for my nan. I wasn't spying or anything.'

Laney's head whirled. Maxine spoke as though words were about to be rationed, and it was hard to keep up.

Already the connections between various villagers were starting to tangle up like knitting.

'Sorry, you must think we're a right bunch of nosey neighbours,' giggled Maxine. 'And you're probably right. There isn't an awful lot going on here, so a new arrival in the village is quite exciting. I know, I know, we should all get out more, but the only places handy are the pub and the church. And aside from the Bonfire-Night Bonanza, we have to make our own entertainment here.'

Her giggle was infectious, and when Maxine laughed her brown eyes lost their tired shadows and shone like jet gemstones. Beneath the mumsy uniform of shapeless fleece, jeans and scraped-back hair lurked a pretty and vivacious young woman, and Laney found herself itching to do a PR job on Maxine.

'So how is Nate?' Maxine said with a worried frown.

'He's resting up, as the doctor ordered,' Laney told her. 'There's no way I'm going to let him come back down and run this place until I'm one hundred per cent certain he's well enough.'

'Does that mean you'll be staying then?'

Oh, crap! Laney supposed it did. The Internet was only so much use; she could hardly run the B&B remotely.

She nodded. 'I guess I am. For a few weeks anyway.'

Maxine clapped her hands. 'Brilliant. You're exactly what this place needs.'

'Really?' Somehow Laney doubted this. She didn't hunt, shoot or fish, which seemed to be the three main pursuits of most people in the vicinity. Nor was she exactly champing at the bit to join in the brass-cleaning and flower arranging at the church.

Maxine was looking really excited, though. 'Totally. We really need some new blood in the village, to see things with fresh eyes and give us all a kick up the bum. You need to get on one of our committees. Now my Vince, he's on the sports-pavilion committee, but there are loads of others.' She started to check them off on her fingers. 'There's the village-fair committee, the flower-show committee, the playgroup committee, the Halloween-party committee, the hunt-ball committee . . .'

'OK! OK!' Laney laughed, holding up her hands when this long list showed no signs of abating. 'I think I get the picture.'

'Oh, I forgot one.' Maxine's eyes widened. 'The Bonfire-Night Bonanza committee. Martin's on that one, and he's amazing at organizing things. He's even managed to persuade Toby – that's the guy who runs Middlehaye Farm – to stable his horses for the night and donate a pig for the hog roast. And Martin's going to give all the proceeds from the Bonfire-Night Bonanza to the sports-pavilion committee, which—'

'Vince runs, I know.' Laney interrupted with a smile.

Maxine tugged at the end of her ponytail. 'I know I go on about him far too much, but honestly, Laney, I just adore my husband. He really is the love of my life and I guess I'm such a hopeless romantic that I want everyone to be as happy as we are.'

Laney raised her eyes to heaven, or at least to the black beams of the kitchen ceiling. 'You have to meet my friend Catherine. You're both so in love you make it sound like a communicable disease.'

Maxine chuckled. 'A sensible woman. I'm sorry if I've been less than subtle by dropping all those hints about Martin. It's just that he's such a lovely guy, and I think you and he could have a really nice time together.'

Laney composed her features into an innocent expression. 'Martin? Who's that? Have you mentioned him at all?'

'Very funny.' Maxine whacked her on the arm.

There was something about Maxine's round smiley face, all bright and hopeful like a child's, that just cried out to be liked. The young woman was as open as a Wikipage.

'If I told you that Martin and I are going out for a drink together at the pub, would you be pleased?'

'Oh, my God!' Maxine leapt up as though she'd been poked in the bottom. 'There's me wittering on about him all afternoon, and you've already gone and got yourself a date.'

'It's not a date!' Laney said quickly. 'It's just a drink. Don't get excited.'

But she might as well have been speaking to the white-washed wall, for all the notice Maxine took of this. Excited beyond belief, she continued to sing Martin's praises so highly that Laney half-expected the heavenly host to descend and join in too. By the time her new friend left to collect the twins from drama club Laney felt exhausted. Attacking the ironing pile was a rest after being in the full flow of Maxine discussing St Martin of Rolls. As she pressed a particularly frilly pillowcase, Laney wondered if he'd wear his halo on their date.

Date? Er, she meant *their drink.*

Later that afternoon Laney found a small tea shop and was glad to see they offered lattes. She took five minutes for a call to Catherine. Outside the light was fading from the sky and the street lamps were pooling Tango-hued light across the pavement. Above the higgledy-piggledy rooftops the sky was becoming inky-dark and sprinkled with stars, which glittered like the card Maxine's twins had made for Nate. While she sipped her drink Laney watched people scuttle by, collars turned up against the chill and their hands pushed deep into their pockets. The cold in Oxfordshire had more of a bite to it than the toothless London damp, and it was a relief to warm her fingers on the chunky mug.

'How's your dad?' Catherine was asking. In the background Laney could hear Peppa Pig asking George where Daddy Pig was, while Patrick – Catherine's husband – was wondering aloud who had the Sky remote control. Somehow Catherine was managing to tune all this out and have a conversation. Her friend was the queen of multitasking.

'No stress,' she explained. 'That's what the doctor said.'

'So what about the B&B? Who's going to take that on?' There was a heavy pause before Catherine said, 'Oh Laney, tell me you haven't—'

'What choice do I have?' Laney crumbled her cinnamon muffin between her fingers. Suddenly her appetite had vanished. Along, it seemed, with her career, her social life and any chance of romance.

'But, babe, maybe don't take any more bookings at the B&B? At least not until he's better, anyway. Now, before I go, I have to know: have you bumped into any hunky farmers yet? Been up to bad stuff in a barn? Or snogging in a cow-shed? I know what goes on in these rural hideaways. It's a hotbed of passion and intrigue.'

'You've been listening to *The Archers* for too long,' scolded Laney. 'So no, for the record, I haven't kissed any farmers in the past *twenty-four hours*. I must be slacking.'

'I'm disappointed, young lady.' Catherine tutted. 'Your report will read *Must try harder*.'

'Sorry, Miss. However, I *am* going for a drink tonight with a single and very eligible solicitor. Will that do?'

The whooping down the phone confirmed that it would. 'That's my girl. A date already. Go, you!'

'Obi-Wan has taught you well,' Laney heard Patrick say.

'It's not a date,' Laney shouted so that Patrick could hear. 'It's just a welcome-to-the-village drink with the next-door neighbour's son. To be honest, C, I'm not really sure it'll ever be more than that. Martin's a lovely guy, but there really aren't any fireworks there.' *Just a lot of spitting fat and burnt-sausage smoke,* she added silently.

'Don't you start all that fireworks nonsense again,' Catherine warned. 'Give the poor man a chance, Laney. All this spark-stuff is beginning to sound like an excuse not to get close to anyone, if you ask me.'

'I didn't ask you,' Laney said. 'And anyway that's total

rubbish. I'm not afraid of getting close to anyone. I was with Giles for ages, wasn't I? We nearly got engaged.'

'You nearly got engaged, but you didn't, did you?' Catherine pointed out with faultless (if irritating) logic. 'And while we're on the subject of Giles, what exactly was wrong with him anyway? He was a nice guy, kind, had a good job, not bad-looking and was quite entertaining, in his own way. I could go on . . .'

Laney exhaled slowly. Catherine was right. Giles was all those things and more. He'd make a perfect husband for somebody, just not for her. Of course he was nice and good company, but surely there had to be more to a lifetime of love than just 'good' and 'nice'? That was hardly the stuff of great literature. Would Juliet have killed herself for love if Romeo was merely *nice*? Or Cathy have been quite so devoted to Heathcliff if he'd been *good*? Hardly. So what was wrong with holding out for a grand passion? The kind that made your nerve-ends fizz and your insides turn to melting ice cream? Catherine could say whatever she liked on the matter – Laney knew what she wanted.

Once Catherine rang off, with Patrick and the children calling out their love too, Laney sat for a long time staring into her cooling coffee. The warmth and fun of Catherine's home, with its close family ties and the bond between Catherine and Patrick, was something Laney cherished. At the same time it threw into sharp relief what was missing from her own life. Giles had offered her all that. Was Catherine right? Should she have settled?

Laney took a deep breath. Perhaps the answer to all these questions was a resounding *yes*? If so, then perhaps it was time to listen to her head rather than her heart and admit that grand passions only belonged in novels and films. Real life was much more mundane than that. After all, Romeo and Juliet never had to do the washing or put out the bins. And Heathcliff would have been a menace with a Hoover.

Maybe it was fate that she was meeting Martin Rolls for a drink this evening?

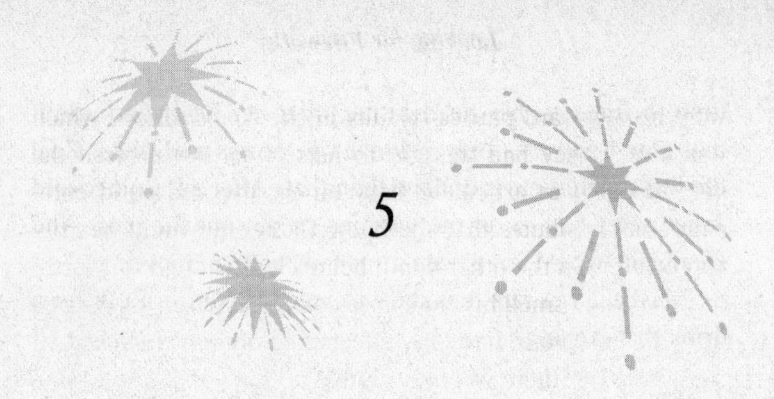

5

'Here we are, one glass of Pinot. And just in case you feel the urge, a packet of pork scratchings too.' Martin deposited the spoils of his trip to the bar on a table and grinned at Laney over the top of his pint. 'Who says we don't know how to live it up in St Pontian?'

Laney laughed. 'Cheers. Who needs pretentious champagne bars anyway?'

She had been pleasantly surprised with her evening so far. Martin had collected her from Myrtle House and, like a perfect gentleman, escorted her over the river and around the green to the pub. Dressed in dark-blue Levi's, tan Cat boots and a leather jacket that was just on the right side of worn, he looked urbane and trendy. His blond hair was neatly cut and his chin dusted with just enough stubble to be fashionable rather than merely unshaven. As they walked she'd tucked her hand into the crook of his arm and they'd chatted away easily, as though they'd been friends for ages.

They'd talked about Janet and Nate, speculating on the possibility of something going on between them, before turning their attention to the village and its inhabitants. There were no awkward pauses or lulls in the conversation, which was nice, Laney had thought to herself as they entered the pub. Martin was articulate, easy on the eye and good company – all attributes that she knew Catherine would heartily approve of. On the other hand, being close enough to Martin that she could smell his expensive cologne and see his clipped nails didn't seem to have any effect at all on her. He ticked all the boxes. But there were absolutely no fireworks.

It was weird. Here she was, with an attractive, single man – the kind of guy whom girls in London would kill to get a date with – and it was as if her sex drive had gone into hibernation.

Just her luck.

Since Catherine's warning that she didn't give men enough of a chance was still ringing in Laney's ears, she was determined to make the most of this night out. She did give people a chance. Of course she did. It wasn't her fault that most of the men Catherine had set her up with were single for a very good reason. And as for Giles, she'd given him sixteen whole months of her life, and if that wasn't giving a guy a chance, she didn't know what was.

And tonight she was feeling generous. The pub was surprisingly tasteful, with not a horse brass or toby jug in sight. Instead the bar area had been whitewashed and had bright prints of local scenes dotted across the plain walls. The beams were painted black and were used as a makeshift menu, with chalked-on names of dishes scrawled across them in italic script, while white fairy lights were looped across and strung over the bar. The furniture was made from chunky wood and looked homespun and clean, and in the enormous chimneyplace a fire crackled merrily. Locals stood in a huddle at the bar chatting amongst themselves, their attention only leaving their pints when they caught sight of Martin and Laney arrive.

'It'll be all around the village now that I'm with a mysterious beautiful blonde,' he told Laney with a grin. 'And what they don't know now, they'll make up later.'

And sure enough, although she was sipping her drink and warming her feet by the fire, Laney was very conscious that she was being observed by the group of people drinking at the bar. She was glad she'd worn her favourite trusty magenta Diane von Furstenberg wrap dress and chunky Rocket Dog wedges. The dress was close-fitting and showed off her curves, while the colour made her skin look like peaches and picked out the bright-green flecks in her eyes. Her hair was loose and straightened, which was a vast improvement on the last time Martin had seen it, and she'd taken great care to apply just enough make-up for a quiet evening drink. Catherine couldn't possibly accuse her of not making an effort.

However, if Martin had noticed the lengths she'd gone to in order to look good this evening, he didn't mention it. *Playing hard to get, maybe?* she wondered. Instead he was busy gossiping about all the other people in the pub, filling her in on who was who, or who was with whom, and even who was with whom but shouldn't be. After about ten minutes Laney's head was whirling, because this was like trying to follow all the plot lines from *EastEnders*, *Corrie* and *Emmerdale* at once. In fact it was harder than that, because if she got all this confused she might make some seriously awkward mistakes.

'Sorry, I'm banging on.' Seeing her confused expression, Martin was instantly contrite. 'You've only just arrived. You don't need to know who everyone is, or who was blamed for stealing the maypole in 1897.'

Laney laughed. 'It's a lot to take in. In London I go into a pub and don't know anyone.'

'Well, that will never happen here,' Martin said. 'And even if you haven't the foggiest who *they* are, they will all know who *you* are. And I'm afraid you may have just totally blown your street-cred by having a drink with me.'

From the evil sideways look that a bottle-blonde by the bar had just given her, Laney totally doubted this was true. She suspected that being seen in the Red Lion with the local solicitor had actually made her street-cred rocket. It was just a shame that the fireworks weren't also rocketing.

Aware that Laney was rather lost when it came to local gossip and intrigue, Martin steered the conversation away from St Pontian and back to the wider world. He had studied law at UCL and done his articles with a law firm in Cheapside and was only too happy to tell anecdotes about his time in the city.

'I must admit I miss the Tube,' he sighed, fixing her with his twinkling smile. 'There was something about travelling on the Underground that really appealed.'

Laney, who only two days before had been playing sardines on the District Line, wasn't quite so sure. 'Why don't you squeeze yourself into a cattle van? It would probably smell nicer.' Being five foot three, she tended to find her face jammed into someone else's armpit with alarming regularity. *Not* having to travel on the Underground was one of the things she wouldn't miss about London life. She was just launching into the horrors of Tube strikes and signal failure when a squat man, shoehorned into a Man U strip a good three sizes too small and with the beetroot-red complexion of the bar-stall sportsman, waddled up to the table and cut across her.

'Sorry to interrupt, love,' he said, looking quite the opposite, 'but I really need a word with Martin.'

Martin caught her eye and winked. 'Urgent village business, I expect. It couldn't possibly wait until my friend's had another glass of wine and I've finished my pint?'

The small plump man visibly puffed himself up. 'It certainly couldn't. This is important. Martin, mate, the fireworks have arrived. And as head of the Bonfire-Night Bonanza, you haven't got time to be in here drinking. You need to be checking that they're all stored properly. There are certain health-and-safety regulations that must be adhered to, you know.'

'Or else there might be the most terrible explosion? Roman candles and silver rain everywhere? Or will the sports pavilion turn into one enormous rocket and zoom off into outer space?' Martin raised an eyebrow, and Laney found herself trying not to giggle. 'Will we have to plead poverty and borrow a tent from the Scouts for the annual cricket-club tea?'

'You can joke all you like, Marty,' said the plump man, looking affronted, 'but someone has got to take responsibility for those fireworks, and the last time I looked at the committee list, that someone was you.'

Martin rolled his eyes at Laney. 'See? I did warn you what it was like here. Life in the fast lane. I daren't even finish my drink. The village could be destroyed in an explosion of Chinese pyrotechnics, if I don't get to the sports pavilion within the next sixty seconds.'

Laney liked Martin's dry sense of humour, even if his chubby friend wasn't quite so amused.

'Well, far be it from me to keep you out drinking, Mr Rolls,' she said. 'I couldn't live with myself if the village saw its annual big display three weeks too soon.'

Martin pulled a linen hanky out of his jeans pocket and made a big show of mopping his brow. 'Phew! What a relief. Laney Barwell, you're the best.'

'Laney Barwell?' The other man's eyes widened as he looked from Laney to Martin and back again. 'Nate's daughter?'

Wow! This must be what fame was like. *Eat your heart out, Katie Price*, thought Laney. *And I haven't even had to get my boobs out.* Placing her wine glass on the bar mat (embossed with the legend 'St Pontian Ales – a saintly brew'), she held her hand out and smiled. 'I certainly am. What's your name?'

'Oh, I'm so sorry, you must think I have absolutely no manners, what with butting in and then not introducing myself.' Flushing the same colour as the football strip he was poured into, the man leaned across the table and, narrowly missing her glass, clasped her small hand in his clammy paw. Years in PR had taught Laney self-control that was second to none, and she continued to smile sweetly while resisting the urge to snatch her hand away and wipe it on her dress.

'My wife will kill me for being so rude,' he continued, beaming down at Laney. 'She's been singing your praises over at ours.'

'Told you,' Martin said, giving her a nudge.

Laney caught his eye and wanted to giggle.

The stranger, though, was still pumping her hand with great enthusiasm. 'I'm Vince Swinnerton,' he announced proudly. 'Maxine's husband?'

It was just as well that Laney was sitting down. She couldn't have been more surprised if the Loch Ness monster had done the conga through the bar with a few of its pals. *This* was Vince? From the way Maxine had talked about her husband, Laney had been expecting some kind of cross between Brad Pitt and James Bond. This portly guy with a receding hairline and health-and-safety obsession was the antithesis of both. Wow! Love really was blind.

Hmm. Maybe Catherine did have a point about her being picky . . .

'Of course,' Laney said, recovering her surprise with the swiftness and ease that had made her one of the best PR girls around. She leaned across the table and gave him a kiss on both cheeks. 'I'm delighted to meet you, Vince.'

Vince went an even deeper shade of Man U crimson. One plump hand touched his cheek. 'All that London kissing stuff. I'm a married man, I'll have you know!' Vince looked wrong-footed and flustered. He turned back to Martin. 'Anyway, mate, what about those fireworks?'

Martin looked sadly down at his empty pint glass. 'No peace for the wicked. Ah, well, I guess that's what I deserved for choosing law. Laney, is it OK with you if we go and check these fireworks out?'

Outside the wind was gathering force, hurling itself through the trees and whistling down the chimney. Laney looked longingly at the flames dancing in the grate and thought how nice it would have been to have curled up with another glass. On the other hand, a brisk stomp over the green to the sports pavilion would probably help to work off a few of those pork scratchings, cream teas and Janet's Eccles cakes.

Wrapped up warm in coats and scarves, they set off across the village for the sports pavilion, taking a detour via Janet's house so that Laney could borrow some wellies.

'There are no pavements in the country, my love,' Janet insisted when Laney baulked at the cat-sick yellow monstrosities that Martin dug out from the boot room. 'You don't want to ruin your pretty shoes in all the mud.'

Laney really didn't. So she borrowed a pair of Martin's thick hiking socks, tugged on the hideous wellies and thanked God that she wasn't setting out to impress anyone.

The sports pavilion might, from its glamorous name, have conjured up images of men in clotted-cream sweaters playing long games of cricket in buttery English sunshine, but in reality it was little more than a glorified hut in the middle of a quagmire. By the time Vince had unlocked the doors and cranked up the ancient fan heater, Laney was freezing cold and covered in so much mud that she felt like an extra from *War Horse*.

'Here, have this.' Martin undid his scarf and wound it tenderly about her neck. As he did so, he was so close that Laney felt his warm breath flute against her cheek and his soft smiley mouth was only inches away from hers. It was possibly the closest she'd been to a handsome single guy for quite some time, and she was very disappointed to discover that her pulse rate remained steady and her knees didn't show the slightest sign of trembling. It was totally frustrating – like getting a free pass to Cadbury World and developing a sudden aversion to chocolate.

'Right,' said Vince, appearing with a clipboard and pen tucked behind his ear. 'I'll read out the list of contents and, Laney, you can check them off. Martin, you take this measuring tape and work out exactly the proximity to the exits, so that we are storing these fireworks correctly.'

Martin saluted. 'Aye-aye, Captain.'

So for the next (very dreary) ten minutes Vince read out a list of fireworks in a monotone, and Laney dutifully ticked off each individual Roman candle and traffic light. How Vince could make something as magical and as exciting as fireworks become so totally and utterly boring was a mystery, and probably some kind of weird talent. Matched only by the amazing fact that such a dull man had managed to capture the heart of a funny and vivacious girl like Maxine.

Maybe Vince has hidden depths? thought Laney as she checked off firework number 122. Perhaps she should just settle for the fact that Cupid really did work in mysterious ways?

'OK, all the measurements are done,' announced Martin, bounding back into the room and flinging an arm around Vince's shoulder. 'Can we go back to the pub now, boss?'

Vince shook his balding head and peered closely at his clipboard. 'I'm not convinced we're storing them right. Health-and-safety regulations state they should be at least ten metres apart from heated appliances. This fan heater is only six metres away.'

'We only turned it on because it's freezing in here,' said Martin patiently. 'We'll unplug it and turn it off when we leave.'

Laney was impressed with his tolerance. She was cold and thirsty and, quite frankly, felt like telling Vince exactly where he could stick his clipboard. There was something about his obsessive attention to detail and planning that reminded her of Giles, and it wasn't a happy comparison.

'Oh no, you've forgotten to put this box away.' Vince swooped down on a box of fireworks that lurked behind a pile of cricket stumps. 'It's not on the list, and that's going to really upset my system. We'll have to start again.'

Laney would rather eat the fireworks than go through this rigmarole for a second time. 'If it's not on the list, maybe it's a freebie,' she said, desperate for a little excitement. 'How about we set this box off?'

'Great idea!' cried Martin, his eyes lighting up just like a November the fifth bonfire.

'No way,' said Vince, looking horrified. 'We haven't risk-assessed them. We don't even know if—'

'Live a little dangerously, mate,' urged Martin, scooping up the box and heading for the door. 'Coming, Laney?'

Laney didn't need asking twice. She giggled like a school-girl disobeying the rules and sprinted after Martin.

Together they stepped out into the darkness and made their way across the inky-dark cricket pitch. Crouching down, Martin put the firework on the ground. 'Stand back,' he whispered. He lit the blue touchpaper of a fountain and darted backwards, grabbing Laney's hand and pulling her further back.

Laney held her breath, excited to see what would happen next. Martin looked at her with wide eyes. They smiled at each other as the fuse fizzed away. Could this be . . . a moment?

The fuse reached the firework and . . . coughed. Then spluttered. A few sparks dripped from the sides, before it fizzled out and gave up completely.

Crumbs! She hoped that wasn't some kind of metaphor.

Their smiles turned to cringes.

'That was pretty useless,' said Martin. 'I hope the rest aren't the same. I'll try another, shall I?'

She nodded. 'How about a Roman candle?'

He smiled. 'Your wish is my command.'

He grabbed another from the box and lit the fuse. They took a few steps back and this time the firework didn't disappoint. Myriad sparks flew into the air like the plumage of a phoenix: red, turquoise and gold.

Laney gasped and clapped her hands. What was it about fireworks that always made you feel like a child? Was it the wonder of the colours against the pitch-darkness? Or maybe it was just the excitement of not knowing what was to come next?

The fireworks banged and shrieked. They were glorious.

'The dud was just a one-off,' said Laney. 'These are lovely.'

Martin gave an exaggerated sweep along his brow.

'Let's try another,' he yelled.

He started merrily letting off fireworks, right, left and

centre. Away from the action, Laney tucked her hands into her pockets and huddled down into her jacket, enjoying her own private display, until the sound of boots striding through the mud made her start. Spinning around, she saw a man loom out of the shadows, his eyes like wet molasses, glittering with anger, and the expression on his sharp-cheekboned face as dark as the night-time sky. He hadn't spoken a word, but already Laney felt his anger crackle from him like static and her heart started to beat faster. She didn't think she had ever been so aware of another person's physical presence.

Just as the stranger rounded the corner of the pavilion, another firework flew up into the sky and for a split-second lit up the darkness. Behind him the world was filled with silver and blue light, which lit the planes and angles of his chiselled face and settled on the grim line of his mouth. Hair as dark as ebony curled around his head and was briefly lit up like a halo in the glittering fantail of sparks.

Were all these fireworks a sign? Surely it was just coincidence. But when he turned to face her, his dark eyes were full of the reflected fireworks and she found that her words had suddenly fled. She searched for something to say. She couldn't wait to find out if this gorgeous man matched up to his grand entrance.

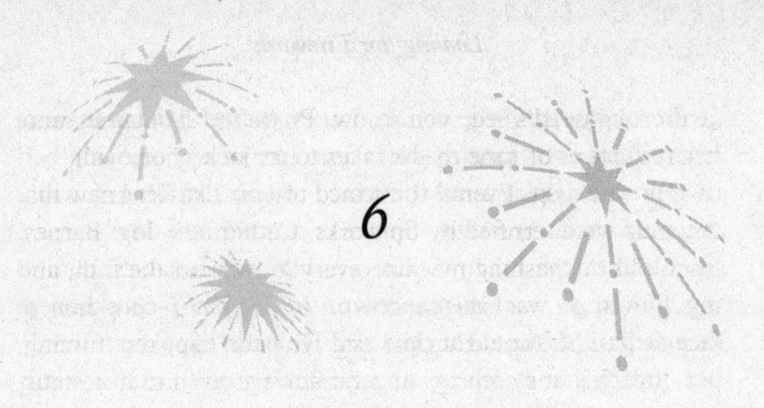

6

'Hi,' she said, finding the words before he mistook her for a statue.

The man – tall and broad-shouldered – was so swathed in shadows that it was hard to make out his face. However, there was no mistaking the fury that emanated from every one of his body cells, and when he finally opened his mouth it was to shout.

'What the hell do you think you're doing?' he yelled.

Laney was shocked.

'What sort of idiots let fireworks off in the countryside? My horses are absolutely terrified.'

Laney put her hand to her mouth. 'I'm really sorry,' she began. 'I never thought—'

The man clearly wasn't in any mood to hear about what Laney may or may not have thought, and cut straight through her apologies. 'The least you could do is call and give me a warning. I'm responsible for the safety of these horses. Right now they're spooked, and galloping up and down the paddocks like lunatics. It doesn't take much to snap a thoroughbred's leg, you know. Probably about the same short amount of time that it takes to make a phone call.'

He was right. Even a confirmed townie like her knew that animals were terrified by fireworks. Catherine's dog, Barney, shook like a washing machine every November the fifth, and by Diwali it was in meltdown. *How could I have been so thoughtless?* She could understand why the man was fuming. But still, he was coming on a bit strong, given that he must have known it was an accident.

'Shit! Toby, I am so sorry. This is totally my fault.' Martin stood at Laney's side, his hand clasping her elbow in a comforting gesture. 'I'm the idiot who never thought this through, and I totally apologize.'

The man glowered at him. As he moved into a square of light pooling from the pavilion doorway, Laney could see that his sharp-cheekboned face was pale with anger and a muscle ticked in his cheek. Dark eyes flashed at her from beneath a thick mane of ebony curls. In spite of feeling strangely compelled to look at him, drinking in every detail as though his features were iced water on a summer's day, she was glad to have Martin standing beside her. This character looked every bit as explosive as the rockets and bangers she'd just been watching.

'I can't apologize enough,' Martin said, smacking the palm of his hand against his forehead. 'I hope there's no harm done?'

The man exhaled slowly. 'Luckily not. But there could have been, and that's the point. You need to plan these things carefully. Not just go right ahead and have an impromptu fireworks party when the mood takes you.'

'Toby, mate, I am so, so sorry.' Vince scuttled over, wringing his hands and looking the very picture of contrition. To Martin he added, 'What were you thinking? Have you any idea just how much red tape and health-and-safety paperwork there is to organize a fireworks display? It takes hours – *hours* – to arrange!'

Laney looked back and forth between the arguing men.

'I do know,' Martin said gently. 'I am head of the committee, after all. I'm afraid I just got carried away.'

'You have responsibilities.' Vince's voice was getting shrill. 'You'll get the whole display banned at this rate. What will happen if Toby complains to the parish council?' Eyes wide, Vince rounded on the stranger. 'Are you going to complain? Will you lodge a complaint? What can I say to persuade you not to?'

For one awful moment Laney thought Vince was going to throw himself on his knees and plead and, by the horrified look on his face, this Toby character clearly thought the same.

'Look, no harm's been done *this time*,' he said gruffly.

Vince looked as though he was going to weep with relief. 'Thank you. Thank you.'

Toby shrugged. 'I'm not against a bit of fun. Just not when it endangers my animals.'

Martin nodded. 'You're spot on, mate.' Smiling down at Laney, he added, 'I think it must be the excitement of having a city girl with me.'

Toby didn't say anything, but the expression on his chiselled face suggested that he didn't think this was necessarily a good thing. Taking the initiative, Laney stitched her best PR smile to her face and, holding out her hand, said brightly, 'I'm Laney Barwell. Nice to meet you.'

'Toby Woodward.' Her hand was engulfed in his gloved one. For a few seconds her fingers rested, all curled and safe, in his palm, before abruptly being released. Her pulse skittered. All he had done was take her hand. What was going on? It must be the drama of defusing a ticking farmer.

'Toby runs Middlehaye Farm,' Martin said, blissfully oblivious to Laney's break-dancing heartbeat. 'He breeds pigs. They made the pork scratchings we had earlier.'

Toby rolled his eyes. 'That's not the most glamorous description of me, but better than "pig man", I suppose.'

'If it makes you feel any better,' Laney said, looking up at him from under her eyelashes, 'the scratchings were delicious.'

Toby smiled back – and *wow*! As his wide, sexy mouth curled upwards, it was like the sun breaking through stormy skies, and she found that she was smiling back at him.

'Look, I'm very worried about the fact that we haven't packed these away properly,' interrupted Vince sternly. 'So let's do that now, shall we?'

Laney was suddenly disappointed. She had an urge to rebel against the strictness of Vince's rules. Impulsively she turned to Martin. 'Would it be very awful if we had one last firework? A quiet one this time? Like a Catherine wheel?'

'I don't think so.' Vince crossed his arms across his portly chest. 'There's been enough trouble caused by those tonight, hasn't there, Toby?'

Toby frowned in an exaggerated way, and it made Laney want to rebel even more – just to annoy him.

'As long as it doesn't fly or explode, I don't think this kind man can object, can you?' she said

'Well . . .' he started, clearly searching for an excuse.

'Brilliant!' she said.

Unable to help herself, Laney dragged Martin to the box and they fetched a round Catherine wheel and fixed it to a gatepost. As she helped to hammer in the nail, she said, 'My best friend is called Catherine Wheeler. She's never forgiven her parents for that.'

'Parents, eh?' said Vince, blowing onto his fingers in an attempt to warm them.

Laney dug her hands into her coat pockets and found herself wishing that Toby would object, just so they could continue their argument. But she reined herself in. Confused and rather alarmed, she tried to focus on Vince's long-winded tale about how and why he was named after Van Gogh, but was so aware of Toby standing only inches away that she just couldn't focus. When she looked up, his dark-eyed gaze was resting on her, as though he wasn't quite certain what to make of her. Her cheeks warm, Laney forced herself to stick up her chin and smile triumphantly.

'Right. That's it,' Martin announced proudly, plucking a box of matches from his pocket and lighting the blue touch-paper. 'Here we go.'

As Martin leapt back, the Catherine wheel started to whirl and fizz, sending a fantail of yellow and scarlet sparks into the inky night. Round and round it went, dazzling them and showering the damp grass with bright sparks. Laney clapped her hands together and gasped, Martin whooped and even Toby dragged up a smile. Only Vince tutted and shook his head, muttering dark warnings.

The Catherine wheel gained momentum, spinning around with all the enthusiasm and energy of Kylie in her golden hot pants. It was wild and slightly out of control. Laney had to pretend the way it was wobbling wasn't making her nervous. Suddenly it worked its way free of the pin. Laney gasped. But before anyone could react, it hit the ground in a shower of sparks, then started freewheeling down the hill . . .

Down the hill and straight towards Toby Woodward's farm.

'Loose firework!' cried Martin.

'Get the fire extinguisher!' Toby yelled, setting off after it.

Laney's heart was in her throat. She ran too, desperate to stop anything bad from happening.

'We'll have to fill in loads of paperwork if there is any damage,' Laney heard Vince wail. 'I'll find an incident report sheet.'

While Vince dithered by the pavilion and Martin dived inside to yank the fire extinguisher from the wall, Laney and Toby tore down the hill. All the treadmills, spinning classes and gym workouts were nothing compared to actually having to run across fields and tear down a lane. Faster and faster went the Catherine wheel, spraying the frozen earth with fiery sparks. With her breath coming in short, painful gasps, Laney raced after Toby as they chased the runaway firework through the driveway and into the farmyard.

Seconds later it crashed into the gate of a barn, sending piglets scattering for cover in a cacophony of squealing and outraged grunts.

She felt terrible. Because of her childish urge to do something naughty, she'd endangered living creatures.

'Grab a bucket,' Toby shouted over his shoulder as he headed into the pig pen.

Laney searched for a bucket.

He shouted again as Laney dithered, 'By the wall on the left. There's a water trough there. Hurry!'

Although her lungs felt as much on fire as the renegade Catherine wheel, she raced across the farmyard, snatched the bucket and plunged it into the ancient granite trough, scarcely noticing how the icy water bit into her fingers and sloshed over her legs. Nothing mattered more now than flinging the water over the firework, before it had a chance to catch the straw alight. Bucket aloft, she hurled the water with all her might, leaping back when smoke rose and the flames hissed. Toby was still grabbing the animals and carrying them out as Laney raced back to the trough and refilled her bucket, just to make certain the fire was gone.

She stamped on the straw to catch any sparks, then stood doubled up, with her hands resting on her knees, gulping greedy lungfuls of sharp air and watching Toby scooping up piglets, which he tucked under his arms.

Toby placed the last piglet into a separate pen and watched it limp away. Laney felt awful. She still couldn't speak, for she was too busy trying to catch her breath. Now that the adrenalin was subsiding, she was very aware of her cold wet clothes plastered against her legs, of her fingers more frozen than anything Captain Birdseye could make and of her hair, now resembling a tangled mane. Toby Woodward, she noticed, seemed hardly breathless at all. In fact he'd even taken off his coat and was working in a T-shirt, which clung to the contours of his chest and showed off the muscles in his arms.

Laney gulped and forced herself to look away. It was probably just as well she'd practically dunked herself in the water trough.

'Is everything OK?' Wielding a fire extinguisher like Luke Skywalker with a light sabre, Martin raced into the yard, skidding perilously on a pile of manure and almost catapulting himself into pig pen. 'Is there a fire?'

'We're fine.' Shutting a gate firmly, Toby spun round to face Martin. 'No thanks to you and your fireworks.' His mouth was set in a tight line. Laney's heart sank. He was furious.

'I'm so—' Martin said.

'All your *sorrys* won't help my pigs. They're really distressed.' Toby ran a hand across his face. 'There's one that's limping now, so I'll probably have to call the vet. I should have stuck to my guns: fireworks are a liability. And so are you.'

Martin looked mortified, and Laney's heart went out to him.

'It was an accident,' she said gently, slipping her arm through his and giving it a squeeze. 'It wasn't Martin's fault the Catherine wheel came loose.' To Toby she added, 'We'll do what we can to help.'

Toby fixed her with a granite-hard look, his gaze straying to her arm linked through Martin's. Something flickered in the depths of his eyes, but was gone so fast that Laney barely had time to try and register what it was. 'No, thanks.'

'Come on, that's not fair.' Laney wasn't having this. Toby hadn't objected to the Catherine wheel, had he? 'It was an accident. Now you're refusing our help? Well that's—'

'You can help by staying away from me, my animals and fireworks,' he said curtly. 'City folk clearly don't understand country ways.'

And with that, he turned on his heel and stalked away in the direction of his farmhouse, leaving Laney open-mouthed. *What a rude, ignorant man.* How dare he try and blame her for the accident and make it sound as though to come from the city was a bad thing? At least she had manners.

Fuelled by outrage, Laney stepped forward to follow Toby and give him a few home truths, but Martin caught her sleeve.

'Don't,' he warned. 'Give Toby some space.'

'He's got enough space between his ears,' fumed Laney. 'How dare he? He was as keen to light the Catherine wheel as we were.'

'Hmm, somehow I doubt that,' Martin said. 'I think you can be pretty persuasive when you want to be, Ms Barwell. And that's a compliment, before you get mad at me too. There aren't many who can talk Toby Woodward round, that's for sure.'

Laney stared after Toby's retreating back, rigid with anger as he slung his jacket over one strong shoulder. As his bicep swelled, her mouth dried.

Martin sighed. 'Toby's OK, once you get to know him. He's just devoted to his animals, that's all.'

'Which is why he turns them into sausages?' Laney said sceptically.

'He's complicated.' Martin took her hands in his and chafed them gently. 'And you're cold. I need to get you home and thaw you out. Come on.'

As they walked back across the village towards the B&B, the air sweetly heavy with the tang of wood smoke from Agas and fires, Martin took Laney's hand in his, warming her chilled fingers up, before giving her his gloves. Then they crossed the frozen ploughed land with their hands still linked and their breath rising into the star-freckled sky like incense. The silence was comfortable, and although there were no weighted moments or heart-stopping smouldering stares, Laney thought there was probably a great deal to be said for light-hearted and *un*-complicated.

'Thanks for a fun evening,' Martin said when they reached the B&B. Leaning forward, he gave her a gentle kiss on the cheek and Laney caught the delicious tang of A*Men. Mmm. That had to be an improvement on *eau-de-pig-pooh*, surely?

'And there was I, thinking life in the country would be boring,' she admitted, smiling up at him.

'That's just a vicious rumour. And now you've had your initiation, how about joining the Bonfire-Night Bonanza committee?' Martin raised an eyebrow. 'It will be a walk in the park after today.'

Laughing, Laney couldn't help but agree. Once Martin had gone, she leaned against the Rayburn, unwound her scarf and thought about how the boy-next-door might prove to be exactly what she needed. Gentle, funny, urbane and about as moody as a sunbeam. Much easier than smouldering tempers and brooding, dark good looks. Honestly, what on earth had she been thinking, to imagine that she'd seen *signs* when she saw fireworks explode over Toby's head? The house-wine in the pub was clearly stronger than she'd thought.

Catherine was right. The idea of love at first sight was ridiculous. She wouldn't be making that mistake again.

7

'I'm so sorry. I hope I haven't held you up?' Breathless from sprinting across St Pontian, Laney tugged off her gloves and then unwound her scarf. It was toasty inside the pub, and since the Bonfire-Night Bonanza committee had hunkered down right by the open fire, she would soon be cooking. Already warm from her journey, she was starting to regret dressing in a cream cashmere jumper and thick woollen trousers.

'Not at all.' Martin smiled warmly at her and Laney thought how nice he looked this evening, in a red shirt that made his hair shine like newly minted pound coins. 'You make yourself at home while I go and fetch you a drink. Glass of rosé?'

'Please.'

While Martin busied himself going to the bar, Laney shrugged off her jacket and smiled a shy hello to the other villagers, who were crammed around a table, backsides perched on various stalls, barrel seats and benches.

'Laney! Come and sit here.'

Maxine Swinnerton, looking delighted, waved at Laney

over the table. 'Shove up, Julie,' she said cheerfully to a large middle-aged woman, who good-naturedly shifted her bulk further along the bench and heaved her bag onto the table. Drinks and chins wobbled for a moment, before all subsided and Laney was able to squeeze herself into position.

'Thank God you're here,' Maxine whispered. 'I love Martin to pieces, but some of his committee look like they want to burn me on the bonfire whenever I try to make any suggestions. Just because we've done things a certain way since the year St Pontian himself was living here doesn't mean we can't have some changes, does it?'

Actually Laney wasn't totally convinced that she and the bonfire committee were particularly well suited. After the incident with Toby and his pigs – or 'Roast Pork Night' as Martin had duly christened it – she was rather wary of the whole business. Toby's angry face, silhouetted against the light of the Catherine wheel, was an image she was trying very hard to forget.

Laney was just about to try and explain this to Maxine, who was now chattering away nineteen-to-the-dozen about something the twins had done at school, when the tapping of a teaspoon against a pint glass, accompanied by uberloud throat-clearing, announced that Vince wanted to make a start.

'We can't sit here gossiping all night,' he said sternly to Maxine, who instantly stopped mid-flow. 'There's an awful lot to sort out.' Reaching into his bag, Vince pulled out a sheaf of papers, which he doled out to the people at the table. The heading was 'Agenda', and Laney's heart sank into her Dubarry boots. This list made *War and Peace* look like a pamphlet. What she had hoped might be a light-hearted night out, where she might get to meet some new friends, looked in danger of becoming a lengthy and officious grind, thanks to Mr Health-and-Safety Vince.

'Hold on, wait for me,' Martin called. Back from the bar, he handed Laney her glass of wine, gave Maxine a bottle of something that was an evil-looking blue, and then squeezed himself onto the bench.

A pretty redhead, with curves that a Kardashian would envy, smiled at him and said, 'As if we would start without you, Mart.'

'Thanks, Isla, at least somebody cares whether I am here or not, to chair my own meeting,' said Martin, giving her a wink.

Vince flushed. 'I was just trying to keep up on schedule. Babysitters aren't cheap, you know.'

'Mate, I'm teasing you,' Martin said gently. Peering at the agenda, he read aloud, 'Item one, lighting of the fuse.'

Maxine nudged Laney. 'Here we go. They'll argue for hours now over the slightest detail. I hope you're prepared for a long night.'

'We need a celebrity to light the fuse,' Vince explained. 'That would be a real draw, and we'd make a lot more money. Then we could build the extension we need to the sports pavilion, and hold two events in the same venue. We don't want another episode like we had last year, do we?'

There was much murmuring of agreement at this.

Bemused, Laney raised her hand. 'What exactly happened last year?'

Maxine cringed and drew a line across her neck. Laney guessed there was more to this story.

Isla tossed her mane of glossy auburn waves back from her face and threw a pointed look at Vince. 'It was booked – weeks in advance – for a pony-club committee meeting. But Vince decided to hold the cricket-club AGM there instead.'

'Now, you just wait a minute. That AGM was in the diary long before you decided to hold your meeting,' Vince said hotly.

'We checked the diary and it was empty.'

'You looked at the wrong page,' Vince insisted. His face was red and his eyes bulged like golf balls. 'Do we need to run through the diary formatting system again?'

'Darling, watch your blood pressure,' cried Maxine in alarm. To Laney she whispered, 'He takes it all so much to heart.'

So Laney could see. Wow! She could hardly believe people would get so worked up over a sports pavilion. Suddenly Toby Woodward's outburst about his pigs didn't seem quite so over-the-top after all. Not that she was thinking about Toby Woodward. No way.

'That confusion caused a village feud,' Maxine told Laney.

'A feud? More like a war,' commented the barmaid, a tall slim girl with very dark hair, who seemed hauntingly familiar. As she collected glasses she added, 'My brother wouldn't drink here, because he didn't know what side he was supposed to be on.'

'Mine of course,' said Isla, with a pout of her bee-stung lips.

'Mine,' said Vince, glowering at her across the table, 'if he wants to be in the cricket team next summer.'

'Toby won't have time for cricket; he'll be far too busy with the farm and taking me to horse shows,' said Isla firmly. 'There's no point me getting Guinness this fit, if I can't go out and compete on him. And Tobes promised that he'd tow the trailer.'

Laney shook her head. Working out who was who, who was with whom and related to whom in this village was like playing human sudoku. She hoped she hadn't said or done anything that could have been really embarrassing or landed her in hot water. Of course a guy as attractive as Toby Woodward would be married. And Isla, with her moss-green eyes, flame-red hair and incredible curves was the perfect foil to his dark good looks.

'You must be Toby's wife,' Laney interrupted, looking for a wedding ring, but Isla's hands were in her pocket. 'I met him the other night. I am so sorry about the pigs. I never intended that Catherine wheel to run away. I hope everything is OK now?'

The barmaid's eyes widened. 'That was you? Toby was fuming for days. He's hardly talked about anything else, has he, Isla?'

Isla had turned pink. 'No, and if I hear that firework story again, I'll drown myself in a water bucket.' As she spoke she twirled a lock of hair around her forefinger and looked down at the table.

'Yeah. He was seriously annoyed with *you*,' said the barmaid with a cheeky grin. Eyes the same colour as wet peat met Laney's. 'I'm Alyssa Woodward, by the way. Toby's sister.'

Oh no! She'd only just arrived and she'd upset half the village. 'I am sorry,' she said. 'It was an accident.'

Alyssa raised an eyebrow.

'And it was my fault,' said Martin, stepping in. 'It was my bright idea to have an impromptu display.' He glanced down at his watch and sighed. 'Now, can we please get back to business? A celebrity to light the fuse.'

Maxine clapped her hands. 'Laney, you're from London. You must know loads of celebs. Prince Harry parties all the time, I've seen it in *Heat*. Do you know him?'

Laney looked over and saw the expression on Maxine's face. Her tongue firmly in her cheek.

'Seriously, though,' Maxine continued, 'you worked in TV. Do you have any contacts?'

Laney found that she was the focus of attention of every person at the table, all of whom had their eyes trained on her expectantly. Everybody clearly thought that when she was not in Oxfordshire angering pig-farmers and their wives with pyrotechnics, she was living it up with the stars.

'Well, I have met a few celebrities,' she said gently, 'but that was work, and their numbers were all held by the company I was freelancing for. I wouldn't say I was on friendly terms with any A-listers.'

'What about asking Zara Phillips?' wondered Isla. 'She's fairly local, and maybe she would help out? Toby knows her a bit from when he was eventing.'

'Kate Moss lives in the Cotswolds,' chipped in Vince. 'Maybe she would do the honours? That would make my day.'

'Blood pressure!' warned Maxine again.

'I only have eyes for you, my sweet,' said Vince hastily.

'Kate Moss would be a great choice,' Laney said excitedly.

'She's really cool, so would go down much better, image-wise. Let's show everyone that there's more to life in the countryside than women going everywhere in jodhpurs and being obsessed with horses. I mean, how clichéd is that?'

'Thanks a lot,' huffed Isla. Getting to her feet, she grabbed her Toggi jacket from the back of her chair and glared at Laney.

Now that Isla was standing, Laney could see that her curvy body was clad in skin-tight cream jodhpurs and that the T-shirt beneath her swelling breasts was emblazoned with a glittery image of a rather bilious-looking pink pony. She looked as if she'd strolled right out of the pages of a Jilly Cooper novel.

'So sorry for being a cliché,' Isla hissed.

Laney did a mental face-palm.

'I only meant that it would be nice to do something different,' she said, reaching out to touch Isla's hand. 'I didn't mean to upset you.'

Isla snatched her hand away. 'Just because you've come from London doesn't make you better than the rest of us,' she said.

Laney was horrified. 'I would never, ever think that.'

However, Isla wasn't listening. Muttering that they could forget their stupid committee, she stormed her way through the pub and slammed out of the door. Moments later an engine roared into life and the tail-lights of a four-by-four could be seen sweeping out of the car park.

'I am so sorry,' Laney apologized to Alyssa, hoping she'd pass it on to Isla. 'That was stupid and tactless of me.'

Alyssa grimaced. 'She's a bit sensitive at the moment.

There's . . . well, there's stuff going on. I'll explain to her that you didn't mean to upset her.'

'But she's horsey,' wailed Laney. 'And I just really insulted horsey people.'

'Most of us round here ride,' said Martin kindly. 'It's what we do.'

'Maybe you should try it?' Alyssa suggested. Digging into her bag, she pulled out a dog-eared business card with *Toby Woodward: Livery* written on it and a mobile number. 'Tobes has horses on livery, and he's dead patient with beginners.'

Laney's heart started to thump and she could feel the colour drain from her face.

'Hey, you've gone a really funny colour.' Martin took Laney's hands in his and looked at her intensely, his eyes filled with concern.

'Is she going to faint?' Maxine was asking.

'I've got smelling salts somewhere,' chipped in Julie, hauling her massive handbag onto the table and burrowing inside.

'I'm fine,' said Laney. Taking another deep breath, she gave them a weak smile. 'Look, this is going to sound absolutely ridiculous to all of you, but I have an intense phobia of horses.'

'Really?' asked Martin.

Laney nodded. 'I was bitten by one when I was eight, and I am absolutely terrified of them now.'

'Bloody hell!' said Alyssa. 'You do know we have fields full of them here, don't you?'

Everybody stared at her with a mixture of pity and curiosity. Laney didn't blame them. When she said it aloud it sounded totally ridiculous, even to her, as well as completely illogical. But then what did logic have to do with a racing pulse, a hammering heart and an all-consuming, paralysing terror? Nobody looked stunned if you said you were scared of spiders, or wasps, or even dogs, but somehow whenever she mentioned that she was scared of horses it was as if she'd said something terrible. Equinophobia wasn't really much of an issue in London – give or take the odd police horse, quadrupeds were few and far between. However, here in St Pontian she was starting to see that it could be rather tricky.

'Horses can be very dangerous,' Vince kindly pointed out. 'The health-and-safety legislation for equine businesses is very complicated, for that exact reason.'

'They kick and they smell,' said Maxine, wrinkling her freckly nose. 'And I, for one, am not a fan. But I am a fan of white wine. How about we get a couple of bottles and then attack this agenda? Our babysitter is booked for one more hour, so we ought to get stuck in.'

Everybody decided this was a great idea and it was amazing how, after several bottles of wine, they seemed to fly through the agenda. An hour later Martin was walking Maxine and Laney home – Vince was keen to stay for one more drink – and was very happy with what they had achieved. The giant Bonfire-Night Bonanza was going to be a huge success.

'Home safe and sound,' Martin said as they crossed the narrow bridge to the B&B. His hand in the small of Laney's back guided her through the darkness, and while she fumbled for her keys he shone the light from his mobile phone to help her. He really was the sweetest, most helpful guy.

'Well, goodnight,' Martin said, leaning forward and brushing her cheek with his lips. 'It's been great fun. Thanks for all your help.'

'Hmm,' said Laney. She wasn't sure quite how much help she'd been, upsetting Isla and then distracting them all with phobia talk for half the night, but it was kind of him to try and make her feel better. Martin was a genuinely nice guy. She just wasn't used to them, that was all. An endangered species.

'I seem to drag you out to the oddest things,' he said, gently pushing a strand of her hair back from her face and smiling down at her.

For a moment Laney wondered if he was going to go for a full-on snog. She seriously couldn't tell. There were no butterflies fluttering in her tummy and her heart wasn't skipping a beat. He could be about to discuss the weather or jump her bones, she really didn't have a clue which.

'So how about we go out for dinner instead?' Martin was asking. 'Just a quiet restaurant, some good food and hopefully some even better conversation. What do you think?'

'I think it sounds lovely,' Laney said truthfully.

'And this time I promise there will be no horses, no shouty pig-farmers and definitely no fireworks.'

Definitely no fireworks? But that's what she was looking for.

She supposed there was only one way to find out for sure. Perhaps the dinner date would be the time to ask some of these questions and see if she could find the answers? There was no rush in any case, she told herself, as she made her dad a hot drink and counted out his tablets. From the look of exhaustion on her father's face and the worried expression on

Janet's, she was going to be living in St Pontian for some time yet.

She just hoped she would be as successful at avoiding horses as Martin seemed to be at avoiding kissing.

8

Running a B&B is far from glamorous, Laney thought as she scrubbed the charred bits on the frying pan and slopped water into her Marigolds. Up at the crack of dawn to get breakfast started, she had already served six fry-ups with all the trimmings, smiled and chatted with the guests, stripped beds, changed sheets and loaded the dishwasher. And all before nine-thirty in the morning. Her nails were wrecked, she was living in jeans, and straightening her hair was a thing of the past. But at least her dad was able to rest.

And she hadn't poisoned any guests yet, Laney reflected with a smile, as she attacked the grill pan with her scourer. She might have wild curly hair and be in need of a manicure, but at least there hadn't been any culinary disasters. She had Martin to thank for that, because he had popped over on several more occasions to lend a hand and gently point her in the right direction. Each time she saw him Laney warmed to him even more. What wasn't to like? He was good fun, kind and helpful, and they chatted away like old friends as they cooked together. She was really looking forward to their meal too. Maybe getting away from the village and their parents would be the springboard to moving the relationship to a different level? Perhaps she would feel less inhibited and more romantically inclined towards him if they were on neutral territory?

Up to her elbows in soapsuds, Laney was so deep in thought that the sharp knock on the door made her jump. She hoped it was Martin again, offering to help with the washing up.

'The door's open,' she called. 'Come in and put your rubber gloves on.'

'I'd rather not, if that's all right with you. Yellow isn't really my colour.'

Laney froze. The only sound was the popping of the soap bubbles. That wasn't Martin's voice. That deep timbre with its slightly mocking overtones belonged to somebody quite different, somebody she had been trying very hard not to think about.

She turned round slowly to see Toby Woodward.

'You did say the door was open,' he said.

Splash! The grill pan slipped from Laney's fingers and back into the sink. Soapy water sloshed over the draining board and slopped onto the quarry tiles.

'Sorry, I didn't mean to make you jump.' Toby stepped from the open doorway and into the kitchen. In the low-ceilinged room he seemed very tall and broad. Even though the kitchen table stood between them, every cell in her body was quivering.

'I didn't realize it was you,' said Laney, hoping her voice didn't sound as shaky as it felt.

'So you don't want to see me in rubber gloves?'

Laney gulped. Toby was dressed in overalls and boots, his dark curly hair caught up at the nape of his neck with a leather cord, but now she had an image of him dressed in a great deal less – save for a pair of rubber gloves. Maybe she should run the cold tap and plunge her head under it? Her face felt hotter than the Rayburn.

Luckily for Laney, Toby didn't appear to have mind-reading skills and, while she busied herself emptying the sink and stacking the plates, he was peeling off the top half of his overalls to reveal a tight white T-shirt that was clinging to the taut muscles beneath. Good Lord. It was like having a 3D *Hunky Farmers* calendar.

'I don't mean to sound rude, but what are you doing here?' Laney asked, wondering if she was in for another telling-off and wishing to goodness that she wasn't wearing her father's terrible apron.

Not that it actually mattered what she looked like. This was the rudest farmer in the Cotswolds, not Brad Pitt. Although it had to be said that, with the morning sunshine burnishing his hair and picking out the amber flecks in his eyes, Toby Woodward could probably give Brad a run for his money. And, like Brad, he was married.

'I'm here with your logs,' Toby told her, jerking his head towards the window. Peering through the smeary glass – another chore for her list – Laney saw his battered truck parked on the far side of the brook, piled high with wood. 'For the fire?' he added when she looked a bit blank. 'I do a monthly delivery to quite a few houses in the village.'

'Right. OK then.' Uncertain as to how to respond, Laney just stared at him. She couldn't help it. He looked so out of place in the twee kitchen. Dragging her eyes away, she said quickly, 'Can I help?'

Toby shook his head. 'Nah. You'll get filthy. And besides, I have a system going. I'll carry them over and stack them for you too, seeing as Nate's out of action. How is he, by the way?'

That was the million-dollar question. The quick answer was *Going out of his head with boredom.* Seriously, Nate was starting to drive Laney nuts, because – like a teenager gone wrong – he refused to do as he was told and continually tried to sneak downstairs to do some work. Only this morning she'd caught him setting the tables for breakfast.

Still, there was no need to bore Toby Woodward with all her worries. He was probably only being polite.

'He's getting there, thanks. He just needs to keep his feet up for a bit longer.'

'That won't be easy for Nate,' remarked Toby. 'He never stops. Give him my best, won't you?'

'Of course,' Laney promised, surprised that Toby seemed to know her father so well. Nate had never mentioned him, or at least she didn't think he had. To be honest, she kind of tuned her father out when he was talking about the village. It had always sounded like something from a George Eliot novel, but now she was living it, Laney wished she'd listened a bit harder.

'And do one more thing for me?' Toby added.

'What?'

His eyes held hers for a moment. Then glittered with amusement as they swept down over the ridiculous cutout-bra-and-suspenders apron: Nate's idea of a joke.

'Would you mind removing that apron? I'm finding it rather distracting.'

Face as red as the lingerie on her pinny, Laney yanked it off. She could hear Toby chortling as he sauntered up the path to his truck.

Of all the cheek! Face still flaming, Laney stuffed the apron in the bin. *Thanks a bundle, Dad.* Why he couldn't have a striped butcher's apron like a normal father, she really didn't know.

She busied herself scraping frying pans and trying to chip off cremated baked beans from saucepans so that she wouldn't be distracted by the sight of Toby Woodward carrying logs up the path. She was certainly not watching the way his strong and well-muscled body made light work of stacking the wood. *Certainly not.*

By the time Toby had finished his labours and popped in to collect the money, Laney had cleaned the surfaces, stacked the pots and pans, brewed fresh coffee and had also managed a swift trip to the bathroom to tone down her flushed cheeks and drag a brush through her hair. She wasn't sure quite why, but there was something about Toby Woodward that made her nerves jangle like Janet's windchimes. It was probably because of the fireworks incident. After all, he was a rude, grumpy pig-farmer.

'All done,' Toby said, sticking his head around the kitchen door. 'I'll be on my way.'

His hair was springing in dark ringlets out of the leather cord that bound it, and he looked hot – in every sense of the word. No wonder he was so toned. Lugging half a ton of firewood was more of a workout than prancing about on a treadmill. Disloyally, Laney recalled how Giles had jogged around the common now and then and made it as far as the gym's snack bar. Toby had a physical job, Giles worked in an office. It was hardly fair to compare them.

'Would you like a drink?' she said. *Where did that come from?*

He glanced at the kitchen clock and shook his dark head. 'Thanks, but I'd better be on my way. There's a lot to get on with at the farm.' He shot her a look from beneath coal-dust lashes. 'There's traumatized pigs that need counselling.'

He was laughing at her. And there she was, agonizing about it all. In fact Laney cringed every time she thought about the runaway Catherine wheel and the terrified piglets.

'Sorry,' said Toby, seeing her face fall. 'That was mean of me. The pigs are fine, I promise.'

'I'm so sorry . . .' Laney buried her face in her hands.

'It's fine.'

She heard footsteps crossing the stone floor and minutes later strong hands, roughened from outdoor work, had taken hold of hers and peeled them away from her face. Looking up, Laney saw that Toby was smiling down at her. Goodness, when he wasn't glowering, his eyes were all twinkly and, from the merry way they crinkled at the corners, it was clear he was no stranger to smiling. She'd obviously really annoyed him the last time they met.

'Honestly, Laney, there's no harm done,' Toby assured her.

'Wasn't one injured, though?' This had been playing on Laney's mind. She knew they were livestock and not pets, ultimately destined for sausages and chops, but even so she hated to think that one of the piglets could have been injured. She was probably just a sentimental townie – she ate meat after all – but she'd never actually met her burgers or sausages before. It made her see things in a very different light.

'Well, yes, but she'll survive,' admitted Toby. Seeing the stricken expression on her face, he added quickly, 'Look, if you've not got anything planned, why don't you come up to the farm with me and see for yourself?'

Apart from a rather urgent date with the Hoover, Laney had absolutely nothing planned. Her friendship with Maxine was growing, and they sometimes made a circuit or two around the duck pond if she was about between school runs, but that was it. Her social life hadn't so much shrunk as totally disintegrated. You knew things were bad when a trip to a pig farm was the highlight of your week.

So that was how Laney came to find herself clambering into Toby's ancient truck. Shoving aside a pile of *Horse & Hound* and stowing his plaid jacket into the footwell, Toby grinned and said, 'Your carriage awaits.'

'Why, thank you.' Hopping in, Laney found herself sitting higher up than she was accustomed, and as they drove the short distance to the farm Toby pointed out all kinds of local landmarks and chatted away about his work. Gone was the moody guy of the other evening, and when he described his Gloucester Old Spots and Tamworths he seemed to fizz with energy.

'You seem really passionate about your pigs,' Laney commented as they rattled over a cattle-grid. She hoped her boobs weren't bouncing too much in today's scooped-neck top. Not that Toby would have noticed anyway. Not when his wife had such fantastic boobs.

'Yep, I suppose I am. Far less trouble than people, in my experience,' he said thoughtfully. 'And when you've had enough, you can turn them into dinner.' He laughed.

'How can you bear to do that?' Laney shook her head. 'Don't you get fond of them?'

Toby looked surprised. 'I suppose so, but ultimately the luxury-food market is what they're destined for. My pigs are rare breeds, and if I wasn't raising them for market – me and other farmers like me – they would have died out a long time ago. We raise them organically, feed them well and, for the most part, they're as happy as, well, pigs in muck.'

Laney had to admit it made the circle of life sound much more civilized.

'They're butchered locally too, so they don't have to endure a long, stressful journey. I can promise you, Laney, everything is done here to ensure they have a good life. I truly believe that there has to be some humanity and compassion in farming.'

Wow! That had to be the longest speech she'd heard Toby make yet. It was impressive too, and everything he said made sense.

'So, no meat industry, no pigs?' she asked, as Toby steered his truck through a very narrow gateway and into the farmyard.

'You've got it. Farmers don't breed them for decoration. The countryside is a business, every bit as economically driven as the city,' Toby explained. 'That's what city people sometimes forget, I think. The countryside for them is a place to relax and have holidays. But for those of us who live here, it's work. The fields, the livestock, the fences – none of it tends itself.'

Laney nodded. This certainly made sense, and she was impressed with Toby's spiel. She might feel more at home in Selfridges and Waitrose, but he was obviously totally at one with nature. From the ease with which he manoeuvred the massive truck, to the way he leapt from the cab and shooed away a flock of mean-looking geese, Toby was comfortable here. And, Laney recalled with a rumble of her tummy, the sausages she'd sampled had been amazing. The man was clearly on to something. He had a fantastic product, lived in a beautiful place and had the dark good looks of a Hollywood action hero . . .

Then it hit her. *This man is marketing gold.* He would look amazing on television. Like Jamie Oliver crossed with Hugh Fearnley-Whittingstall – only sexy. Suddenly the PR part of Laney's psyche, which had been slumbering for a few weeks, jolted bolt upright.

'What magazines do you advertise in?' she asked as they crossed the yard. Although it was only mid-morning, Toby had obviously been hard at work before he left for his log deliveries, because the yard was immaculate, with not a stick of straw out of place. It was really pretty, Laney thought in surprise. Not muddy or smelly at all. The farmhouse was picture-postcard perfect, all mellow honeyed stone, mullioned windows and smothering ivy. Imagine all this packaged up and tied into the organic produce, a TV show and cookbook.

Toby was looking at her blankly.

'Magazine adverts? For your produce? You must know the kind I mean: glossy aspirational ones for country-style living or good food?' Laney pressed on. 'Who does your website? Have you optimized your Google searches?'

Toby's brow creased. 'Christ, I feel a complete Luddite! I'm rather embarrassed to admit it, but we don't have a website. And I've never advertised anywhere. We just tend to sell through the local farm shops and pubs or word-of-mouth, and that does the trick.'

'But your meat is fantastic!' Laney cried, catching his arm. Beneath his overalls his biceps felt like rock. She let go swiftly. Oh, dear Lord! *Your meat is fantastic?* That sounded like a line from a corny Seventies soft-porn film.

Wasn't this the part where he'd make a comment about being well hung and then drag her into a barn? Mortified, she hardly dared look at him, but fortunately for her Toby wasn't thinking along the same lines. Instead he seemed absolutely chuffed to bits.

'We use old family recipes,' he explained with that smile that lit him up from the inside, 'and hundreds of years of local knowledge. I'm really glad you like them.'

'I certainly do. And so will loads of other people, if they get the chance to sample your stuff.' Laney's mind started whirring. 'Look, tell me to butt out by all means, but I work in PR and I think I could really help you put Middlehaye Farm on the map. Build your brand. A bit like Innocent did with their smoothies.'

'Really?'

She nodded. 'Yes, really. I think you've got something really special here.'

Toby blushed.

'I'm around for a few months, so I'm more than happy to give you a hand with some marketing and publicity ideas,' she continued. 'My last few jobs were all in television, so this will be a good way to diversify my portfolio. And I'll do it for you for nothing; it's a way of making up for the chaos I caused the other day.'

Toby laughed. 'I told you, that's all forgotten about now. But I won't pretend I couldn't do with some help, raising our profile and playing the media game. I'm just a simple farmer, see.' He put on a fake farmer voice. But with his sculpted cheekbones, dark eyes and tall, rangy body, Toby was about as far from being *just a simple farmer* as it was possible for anyone to be. Unless it was one from a sexy Land Rover advert.

Laney smiled. 'Just leave it to me,' she said.

Toby nodded, but Laney could tell he didn't really think she was serious. Just wait. In a few weeks he'd be amazed. Middlehaye Organic was going to hit the big time. By the time she'd finished, it would be right up there with Prince Charles's Duchy Originals. Just thinking about this exciting project gave Laney goosebumps.

At least she hoped it was thinking about the project that was giving her goosebumps.

The next hour passed really quickly as Toby gave her a tour of the farm. By the time they reached the cobbled stable-block Laney's head was swimming with all the information. Breeds of pigs, sheep, ratios of feed to body weight, government quotas, organic status stipulations – it just went on and on. Whoever knew there was so much to farming? Toby was fascinating, and knew so much that Laney could have listened to him all day. As they chatted she made mental lists of all the contacts she was going to pursue and composed umpteen pitches. She couldn't remember the last time she'd felt this excited about a project. Maybe this would be the making of her career?

'So that's it really,' Toby concluded, smiling down at her as he bolted the barn gate. 'Just the stables to go and your tour will be complete.'

Laney felt a jolt of fear. 'Stables?'

'We do some livery. It brings in a bit extra. We've all had to diversify, especially after the foot-and-mouth.' He slid open the heavy wooden door. 'Come inside and meet the crew. Belle would love you to give her a carrot.'

Laney was rooted to the spot. Feeding a horse, placing her hand near those huge yellow biting teeth, had to be right up there on her list of top-ten worst things to do. Her heart began to pound beneath her ribs and her mouth was drier than the straw in Toby's barn.

'She's a good old girl,' Toby was saying over his shoulder as he strode into the American barn. 'Used to be a show jumper, until she fractured her pedal bone and put an end to all that.' A grey mare put her head over a half-door, whickering delightedly when Toby stroked her nose and scratched behind her ears. 'Now she lives a life of luxurious retirement. We may put her in foal next spring to one of the stallions at the point-to-point yard. I think she'll throw a pretty foal. What do you think?'

Laney couldn't think. She could hardly breathe.

'Laney?' Abandoning the horse, Toby rejoined her, his

brow crinkling with concern. 'Is something wrong? You've gone a very funny colour. Are you feeling ill?'

She took a shaky breath. 'I know you'll think this is ridiculous, but I'm terrified of horses.'

'Really?' asked Toby.

'Yes,' she said with a wince. 'I was bitten by one when I was a kid, and now . . .'

Placing an arm around her shaking shoulder, he said, 'I pass out at the sight of blood. Everyone has something they don't like.'

Laney shook her head. 'It's more than not liking something. It's an absolute dread. I feel sick just thinking about stepping into that barn. If I actually had to go near a horse, let alone feed it, I think I'd die of fright.'

'OK, we won't make you do anything like that,' said Toby, giving her shoulder a comforting squeeze. 'But horses are a major part of life here, and feeling like this can't be very nice for you.'

She hung her head. 'I know. It makes no sense.'

He took her hand in his. 'How about you just come inside and stand next to me while I give Belle a carrot? I promise she won't come anywhere near you.'

Laney swallowed. She'd rather eat grubs on one of those gross reality-TV shows. Like it or not, though, she was living in the countryside now and it was time she tried to get over this.

Dredging up every drop of courage she possessed, she nodded.

'Well done,' said Toby, and he led Laney into the American barn and up to Belle. Standing behind him, still trembling,

Laney watched as the horse searched Toby's pockets, its liquid-chocolate eyes lighting up when he produced a titbit. Being close enough to smell the horse's oaty breath made Laney feel quite giddy, but as Toby crooned to the animal she felt herself start to – if not *relax*, exactly – become far less tense. There was something really touching too about the way Toby related to the horse; he was so calm and gentle that it was impossible not to be soothed by him. Close up, Belle was also far from the teeth-snapping, hoof-stamping monster of her memories. In fact, with her delicately boned face, silvery coat that was almost lilac in places, and nose as pink as the underskirt of a button mushroom, she was actually rather pretty.

'Do you trust me?' Toby whispered.

She nodded. It made no sense, for she barely knew Toby Woodward at all, but something deep within Laney trusted him implicitly. Holding her breath, she let him take her hand and lay it against Belle. Warm fur, soft as velvet, brushed her fingertips when Toby moved her hand to run it down the horse's neck. She could feel his breath warm on the nape of her own neck. Laney shivered.

'Hello?' The barn door slid open. 'Toby? Is that you?'

As her eyes adjusted from the gloom of the barn to the brightness of the autumnal sunshine outside, Laney saw Isla striding towards them. Dressed in tight cream jodhpurs and shiny black boots, she looked as if she'd just stepped from the showring. Suddenly Laney felt like she'd been caught in the act.

Toby dropped Laney's hand and stepped away. 'Isla. I thought you weren't riding until this afternoon?'

Toby's response just made it worse. Laney couldn't blame Isla for throwing such an evil stare her way. If she'd walked in to find her husband virtually holding hands with another woman, she would have felt the same.

Isla shrugged. 'Changed my mind. Guinness! Hey, boy!' She clicked her tongue, and right on cue a glossy black horse peeked his head over the door of the stable next to Belle. With a cry of fear, Laney shot backwards.

'God, chill out! You'll scare him,' said Isla scornfully, taking in the terror on Laney's face. 'Guinness doesn't bite, you know.'

That's where you're wrong, thought Laney, while her heart did a street-dance routine that Diversity would envy. She still had the scars to prove that horses could bite. And blooming hard, too. Though Laney knew it wasn't really the bite that had caused her phobia. It was what happened afterwards.

'Anyway.' Her green eyes narrowing, Isla stared hard from Toby to Laney. 'What's going on? You two look very cosy.'

'I was giving Laney a tour of the farm,' Toby said evenly.

'Right,' said Isla slowly, but her expression said something quite different, and the look she gave Laney should have laid her out on the well-swept floor. 'Since when did you have such an interest in agriculture?' she asked Laney. 'You said jodhpurs were a terrible "cliché".'

'I'm going to give you guys a hand with PR,' Laney told her, choosing to ignore the jibe because, in Isla's case, she suspected the green eyes were metaphorical as well as literal. 'And it's been fascinating to see a real working farm.'

'Yes, I don't suppose you get much understanding of

country life in *the city*.' Isla spat the last two words. 'You have to be born to it really.' Turning to Toby, she said, 'I think Guinn overreached quite badly yesterday in the field. Do you think I should have turned him out in his boots?'

Toby shrugged. 'Possibly. Did you wash it?'

'Yes, and I purple-sprayed it too, but I'm really worried. Could you watch me trot him up and down the yard and see if he's sound?'

'Sure, in a bit. Let me just finish telling her about Belle,' said Toby. To Laney he continued, 'She has the nicest nature, and I think a foal out of her would be a lovely way for the owner to feel that some of her sweet temper and talent lives on. What do you think?'

Laney opened her mouth to say that she thought it was a lovely idea, but before she could draw breath Isla butted in.

'Toby, I think I'm going to add a feed-balancer to Guinn's dinner. He needs a bit more condition, don't you think?'

'Good idea,' said Toby, tossing the words over his shoulder, then turning back to Laney. 'I wish you could have—'

'And also have you heard him cough?' persisted Isla. 'I tried soaking his hay, but to be honest I think I might switch to haylage. Is it really that much more nutritious?'

Toby walked towards Isla. 'I'm not too sure . . .'

Laney left them to it. She made her way back outside into the warm October sunshine. The words washed over her head in a tide of equine-related linguistics that she had no way of understanding: '*coronet bands*' this, '*Speedi-Beet*' that, '*miscanthus*' the other. They might as well have been speaking in a different language. And even though she had touched Belle's neck – albeit with Toby's strong hand to guide her – Laney had a sinking feeling that this was one language she would never be able to understand.

She was out of place in St Pontian. And Toby Woodward was married and out of reach.

9

'Dad! You're meant to be resting.'

Laney couldn't believe it. She'd only been away for a couple of hours, but in her absence Nate had been extremely busy. Not only was a *coq au vin* bubbling away, but the carpets were looking suspiciously well vacuumed. And as if that wasn't bad enough, Vince was ensconced in the sitting room in the middle of a heated debate.

'Hello, love. I didn't think you'd be home for a while,' her dad said, looking so sheepish that it was surprising a shepherd and a collie dog didn't saunter through the sitting room.

'Obviously.' Hands on her hips, Laney fixed her father with a stern look. Talk about role reversal. Who was the parent here?

'We were just having a bit of a discussion about the sports pavilion,' explained Vince. 'Your dad's on the committee, and there just happen to be a few urgent bits of business that need clearing up.'

Vince and his bloody sports pavilion. You would think it was the Brighton Pavilion, the way Vince talked about it, not a wooden structure with a tin roof. When she looked at

Vince, who was now flipping through an enormous black lever-arch folder marked *Minutes*, she realized that in St Pontian such things as committees and village feuds mattered very much indeed.

'Vince, I think I need to explain something,' Laney said gently. Looking at her father she continued, 'Nate might tell you that he's fine, but the reality is that unless he avoids stress and takes it easy, he's right in line for another stroke. And it could be a *serious* one this time.'

Laney's dad hung his head. 'I'm sorry to have worried you, sweetheart. I just want to be up and running again.'

'And you will be. But only if you listen to what the doctor says,' Laney screeched in despair. Nate was so stubborn that she might as well be talking to the wall. In fact the wall would probably be more attentive. To Vince she said, 'Please, try not to stress Dad out with things that really aren't important.'

That was the wrong thing to say. Even the thinning sandy strands of hair on Vince's head seemed offended. 'Our sports pavilion *is* important, thank you very much. The upcoming Bonfire-Night Bonanza is all about the pavilion. And there's an awful lot of people round here who think so, even if you don't.'

Oh, Lord! Now she'd upset Vince, who had folded his arms defensively and was looking very put out. Taking a deep breath and drawing on all her reserves of tact from ten PR years' worth of smoothing ruffled feathers, Laney said, 'Why don't I take Dad's place on the committee until he's well enough to return? I can bring the minutes home and have a chat with him about them.'

Vince narrowed his eyes as though sizing her up. What a cheek! She'd organized parties for major publishing houses, orchestrated the launch of a top celebrity's perfume, and once she'd even escorted George Clooney to a premiere (OK, to his car, but hey, it was *George Clooney*), so she could probably just about handle the pressure of the sports pavilion. Still, not wanting to upset Vince any further, Laney merely waited and just smiled so sweetly that it was a miracle her teeth didn't rot.

'Well, maybe we can give it a go, but on a strictly trial basis,' Vince said eventually, and after much internal struggling. 'Just until your father's better, and not with his decision-making capacities, obviously.'

'Obviously,' said Laney. The man was infuriating. Maxine deserved a medal.

'If it is all too much for you, though, Nate, you really must say,' Vince added as he shrugged on his coat. 'And don't forget what we were talking about earlier too. I meant what I said; my offer still stands.'

Nate seemed to sag even deeper into his armchair and ran a weary hand across his face. 'I'll think about it, Vince, I promise you, but please give me some time.'

Eh? What was this all about? Perplexed, Laney stared from her father to Vince and back again. They *had* been discussing something when she arrived, and whatever it was had upset her dad.

'What's going on?' she demanded.

'Vince has made me an offer on the B&B,' said Nate.

'A fair one too. And if you're really serious about cutting down on the stress, you ought to consider it.'

Laney could hardly believe what she was hearing.

'You've got a bloody cheek,' she hissed as she shooed Vince to the door. 'Coming round here and trying to make offers to my father in his weakened state. What sort of opportunist are you?'

Vince shrugged. 'Business is business, Laney. You understand that. Besides, I made a good offer.'

'I don't care if you offered him a million pounds and a lifetime of back-massages. He doesn't need this right now.' Laney was so incensed by Vince's brass neck that it was amazing she didn't explode, and leave just Janet's comedy wellies standing smoking in the porch.

'Then you'll probably agree that the last thing he needs is the stress of running a bed-and-breakfast,' Vince shot back as she bundled him out of the front door. 'See you at the next meeting,' he called over his shoulder. 'Don't be late. You're only on trial, remember. And I've got a big agenda.'

'And don't I know it!' Laney muttered as she slammed the door. Honestly. Vince didn't so much take the biscuit as the entire tin.

Back in the sitting room, Nate was slumped in his chair looking grey with exhaustion. Another blot in Vince's very blotted copybook, as far as Laney was concerned.

'You know, love,' he said, looking up and giving her a watery smile. 'Maybe Vince has a point?'

'Vince has a bloody nerve.'

Nate sighed. 'You said it yourself – the B&B is hard work. I can't expect you to stay here and take it on. Maybe it is too much for me?'

'Dad! I didn't mean that it would be too much indefinitely.' Laney was horrified to think that her constant concern for her dad could have led him to draw these conclusions. 'When you feel stronger, we can think about employing somebody else to help out. And don't think you can get rid of me that easily.'

'You've got a life of your own to lead.' Nate shook his head. 'I know how much you love London, and that's where you should be, not buried in the middle of nowhere with your old dad. You've got a great career too, and I'm very proud of you.'

There was a lump in her throat the size of a football. Laney didn't think she'd ever before heard Nate say that he was proud of her. They hadn't ever really had the sort of relationship where feelings were readily discussed. Not even when Mum died. Of course she *knew* he was proud of her, had sort of just assumed it, but to hear him say it meant a lot.

'Don't worry about that,' she told him firmly. 'I've already picked up a job here.'

Her dad raised his eyebrows in surprise.

'I'm marketing Middlehaye Farm for Toby and Isla Woodward,' she said in a *So there* tone of voice. 'So I can help you *and* develop my business.'

'Toby and Isla Woodward?' he said, looking confused. 'Isla isn't married to Toby.'

What? Had her dad not fully recovered from the stroke? Toby and Isla not married?

'Toby is single?' She hated the way her voice came out in a choke.

'Yes,' he said. 'I think he and Isla were together at one

point – and she might wish it was still that way. But Toby hasn't been with anyone for a while now.'

He took off his glasses and rubbed his eyes wearily, which made Laney realize that Toby Woodward wasn't exactly the point of this conversation.

'Are you okay, Dad?'

'I don't know, love,' her dad said with a sigh. 'Maybe I should take Vince up on his offer. Then you could go home and not have to worry about me.'

'Of course I worry about you. You're my dad.' If he hadn't been so frail and exhausted, Laney would have shaken him at this point. 'We are not about to quit and give up. Having this place and living in St Pontian was always your dream, and Mum's.' She crossed her arms and gave him her most determined look. 'I'm having a lot of fun here.'

That was sort of true, wasn't it? Martin was sweet; Maxine, in spite of being married to Vince, was great fun; and Toby – well, she hadn't made up her mind about Toby yet. However, obsession with committees aside, life in the countryside wasn't nearly as dull as she'd assumed.

'So, no arguments, OK? I'm staying put and we are *not* selling up.'

Goodness, just listen. She sounded like a stroppy teenager. This was the effect that her dad was having on her. In a minute she'd be sticking JLS posters on her wall and moaning about how unfair everything was.

Her father closed his eyes. 'You sound just like your mother. And one thing I always knew with Jenny was that when she made her mind up, there was no changing it. You've got her stubborn streak, that's for sure.'

'So listen to me then,' she told him firmly. 'Now, you go and have a lie-down while I make a cup of tea, and no more arguments, all right? None of this is doing your health any good.'

He smiled. 'OK, boss.'

Was she like her mother? wondered Laney as she leaned against the windowsill and looked out at the fields while the tea brewed. She didn't think that her mum had been stubborn, but then she'd only been eight when she'd died. Sometimes she panicked because she couldn't remember her mum very much at all, just blurry images like faded Polaroids in an album. Long, curly blonde hair a bit like her own, soft cuddles, and one bright memory of being sung to sleep when she'd been poorly. Sometimes Laney would catch the scent of Coco and, no matter where she was, be transported right back to another lifetime, when her hand was held in Mummy's and the world was a safer, happier place. Other times, though, she would smell hospital antiseptic and be right back by the bedside, that hand of her mother's now frail and her skin tissue-paper-thin.

Laney blinked away the tears that suddenly blurred the view.

Squaring her shoulders, she turned her attention back to making the tea: strong and sweet, just the way Dad liked it. She was more determined than ever that she would do all she could to help the one parent she was still lucky enough to have. And if that meant stepping back from her career and staying in the countryside, then it was a small sacrifice to make. Taking care of her father and his business were all that mattered.

The fact that Toby was single didn't matter at all.

10

To: editor@westerndailynews
Cc: tobyfarmer2@yahoo.com
Bcc: catherinecupid@catherinewheelermatches
Subject: Feature Article

Hi Amanda,

Thanks so much for getting back to me this quickly.
I really appreciate it.

As we discussed earlier, the focus of the article will be Toby Woodward and the rare breeds he raises at Middlehaye Farm. The slant to take on this piece could certainly be how farmers are having to diversify in this tough economic climate. Mr Woodward currently produces organic sausages and meats, which are sold locally for commercial and domestic use.

I look forward to meeting your reporter. I also hope that the staff at the WDN enjoyed the pork-and-mustard sausages on sticks that we sent.

Yours sincerely,
Laney Barwell

'Well?' Laney asked, leaning back in her chair after reading this email through for what had to be the millionth time, and wedging her mobile between her chin and her shoulder. 'What do you think?'

'I think I need to meet this Toby character and see exactly what all the fuss is about,' Catherine told her. 'Is he good-looking? Is he single? Eligible?'

Honestly! Talk about living and breathing your job. While her friend continued to fire off hundreds of questions about this latest client, Laney rolled her eyes at her reflection. To be fair, Toby was very attractive, and she could certainly admire him in an aesthetic kind of way – just as she might a nice painting or a sculpture. And now it turned out that he was single as well. However, there was no way she was telling Catherine this. Her best friend would have them engaged, married and expecting their first baby before she'd even finished the sentence. She was like Jane Austen's Mrs Bennet, only armed with the Internet and a dating database.

'He's OK, if you like dark, brooding farmers,' Laney hedged.

'Who doesn't like dark, brooding farmers?' Catherine screeched, making Laney's eardrum ring. 'Striding across the cornfields looking all windswept and moody? What are you thinking, wasting time sitting down and writing emails about sodding sausages? Put your wellies on, girl, and *get in there*.'

'Babes, Toby is a livestock farmer. He doesn't grow corn,' said Laney mildly. Stretching her cramped arms, she returned to her position of crouching over the Mac at the kitchen table and turned her attention back to the screen. Clicking out of the email, she opened iWeb and the home page of the website that she was building for Middlehaye Farm. A funky logo framed the page, designed by a graphic-artist friend who'd owed her a favour for getting some free Take That tickets, although rather than the eye being drawn to this, it was Toby's dark gaze that pulled you in. There he was, leaning against a gate and glowering into the camera with such smouldering intensity that Laney had been amazed her little Kodak didn't catch light. Behind him were the rolling Cotswolds hills and the farmhouse, slumbering like a golden princess on a background of green velvet. She hadn't been wrong: Toby and his farm were a marketing dream.

'I hate having my picture taken,' he had muttered, looking just like a rebellious schoolboy when Laney set up the pose. 'Can't we just have a few of the pigs? That's what we're selling, after all.'

'No, it isn't.' Standing on her tiptoe (goodness, he was tall), Laney had reached forward and brushed the windblown curls out of his dark eyes. 'People actually don't want to think about where their lovely sausages really come from. We're selling a lifestyle here: the country life.'

'Some lifestyle to aspire to,' said Toby, leaning against the gate while Laney clicked away. 'I've been up since four a.m. shovelling crap and feeding piglets. It's a good thing they can't scratch-and-sniff this picture.'

Laney giggled. As he looked every inch as if he'd just stepped from the pages of an advert for Musto, she was pretty certain that lots of the women who saw this webpage would be dying to scratch-and-sniff Toby Woodward. And he smelt delicious, for the record.

'Who cares what he farms, if he's sexy and single?' Catherine went on.

Sexy? Oh, all right then, Laney thought – and she opened iPhoto and scrolled through all of her images of Toby – he wasn't *bad.* As Catherine chattered on, she looked through all the shots she'd collected. There he was cradling a piglet in his arms and smiling right into the camera, his teeth almost shockingly white against his dark skin and stubble; and here he was in another shot with his arm slung over Belle's neck. Laney peered closer. Was it her, or did that horse look smug?

'OK, Toby is attractive,' she admitted. 'And although he's not married, he's not quite single, either. Isla hangs around him like she is his guardian angel – warding off evil vixens.'

Catherine scoffed. 'If he was serious about her, they'd have made it official years ago.'

'They're really well suited, with all the horsey stuff they like to do. And besides, she's a gorgeous curvy redhead. Honestly, Cat, you should see her. She looks like an erotica cover girl – all tight jodhpurs, immaculate make-up and long black riding boots. I couldn't compete with that.'

'Do you want to?' said Catherine instantly.

Looking at her reflection in the kitchen window, Laney pulled a face at herself. Today was a working day and so she'd skewered her blonde mop on top of her head with a Bic, hadn't bothered with make-up and was wearing a tatty pink hoody, flowery shorts and an ancient pair of Uggs, which in terms of odour could probably give Toby's pigs something to aspire to. London Laney had left the building.

'No,' she said firmly. 'I really don't. Toby's a nice guy, but, apart from already being under someone else's thumb, he's really not my type. For one thing, he's country-born and bred, and for another – like most people around here – he's obsessed with horses. I hardly think he'd want to be involved with a girl who has a ridiculous equinophobia.'

'Sweets, you have got to get over this,' said Catherine gently. She sighed. 'You know it isn't really about horses, don't you?'

Laney *did* know, but she wasn't prepared to start talking about the inner workings of her psyche right now, and certainly not without an alcohol fix.

'I've been working on it,' she said. 'Toby's got this horse on livery – Belle, she's called – and I've actually patted her a couple of times now.'

'Laney, that is *fantastic*!' Catherine was being genuine. She's seen Laney's phobia in action. 'I knew I had a good feeling about this Toby fellow.'

'Yes, he's a *good* client, makes *good* sausages and is being a *good* help at easing me into living in a place where horses seem to pop up just about everywhere,' Laney agreed. 'But I am not, I repeat *not*, interested in him in any other way.'

'Methinks the lady doth protest too much,' Catherine murmured.

'Well, you *methinks* wrong.' Clicking out of the photos, Laney got up from the computer and walked to the window. It was a lovely autumnal day with honeyed sunshine spilling across the fields and making the river glitter like a Swarovski showroom. Maybe she should stretch her legs and go for a walk. Martin's car was parked outside the church. Maybe they could take Janet's Labrador for a walk across the stubble fields?

'I'm spending a bit of time with Martin, remember?' she reminded Catherine. 'He's really sweet, and much more my type than a farmer would be.'

'Hmm.'

'Hmm? What's that supposed to mean? I thought you'd be pleased that I'm going places with a good-looking, brainy solicitor? He's got a Mercedes and he's really sweet.'

'I am pleased. However, I want you to be happy. The question is: do you want to bonk his brainy brains out?'

'Who said romance was dead?' Laney shook her head. 'It's early days yet. Too soon to think about *bonking*, as you so tastefully put it. What are we anyway – fifteen?'

'Then you don't,' said Catherine bluntly. 'When I first met Patrick I couldn't sleep for thinking about just how much I wanted to be with him. It was like being plugged into the mains. I thought I'd *die* if I didn't get to sleep with him.'

Laney remembered this well. Catherine had been unbearable. Luckily for her, though, Patrick had felt exactly the same way, and for a few months they'd been joined at the tongue as if they'd been welded together. At least it had been worth the emotional highs and all the adrenalin. Nine years and two children later they were still the happiest couple she knew.

Which then begged the question: *Did she want to bonk Martin's brains out?* He was kind, he was funny, he was generous, he was easy on the eye, but . . .

'Well?' said Catherine.

Oh, for goodness' sake. This was ridiculous. This kind of talk simply wasn't dignified for women pushing thirty. She respected Martin, and he respected her. They were having an old-fashioned courtship, that was all, and that was probably how things were done in the countryside. Why did it all have to be about sex? That would come later.

'Besides,' Laney continued after repeating this train of thought. 'You're the one who's always saying that I'm stupid to be looking for fireworks. You're the one who says that the spark can grow.'

'Yes, but,' she heard a hesitation from Catherine that she hadn't heard in ages, 'I'm not hearing anything about this Martin that makes me think there'll *ever* be a spark. When you talk about this Toby character, though . . . How would you have felt if Toby had grabbed hold of you in his barn, pulled you against him into the straw and had his wicked way with you?'

'I think you need to work for Black Lace,' Laney told her. However, this image was now seared onto her mental DVD player and her face felt quite flushed. What would it be like to feel Toby's strong hands around her waist and the muscles of his torso against her chest? She gulped. She'd never know, that was for certain. Time to change this conversation before Catherine got well and truly carried away, and she herself was totally unable to look Toby Woodward in the eye.

'So shall I send this email or not?' she asked.

'Yes, yes, if you really must change the subject,' Catherine said. 'But don't think I'm fooled: I'm a professional, remember?'

Laney pressed *Send*. 'Let's hope this is the start of great things for my first solo client.'

'Oh! I meant to tell you, Patrick says he's had an idea that might be useful,' Catherine remembered. 'He was at school with that TV chef, Julian Matlock. Have you heard of him?'

Laney certainly had. Julian Matlock, with an erupting temper than made Vesuvius look half-hearted, was compulsive viewing. His latest show was high in the ratings and his current cookbook was number one in the bestseller list.

'Why don't we get Patrick to send Matlock a sample of Toby's sausages and see what he thinks?' continued Catherine.

'That's a brilliant idea. Thank you. I'll get right on to it.' Fired up and – thank God – distracted from images of being ravished in a hay barn by Toby Woodward, Laney jotted the idea down in her notebook.

Catherine cleared her throat and Laney knew something was up. 'Um, Laney,' Catherine started. Something was *definitely* up. 'I saw Giles yesterday . . .'

Laney held her breath. Was Giles married to someone else already?

'. . . and he was looking like a wet weekend—'

Their conversation was interrupted by a knock on the door and Martin poking his blond head round. *Phew,* thought Laney. The last thing she needed was to hear about how miserable Giles was without her. There were only so many guilt trips that a girl could take. She'd need a season ticket at this rate.

'Sorry,' he mouthed. 'You're busy, I'll pop back.'

'No! No!' Laney felt her face do an impression of a Ketchup bottle. She hoped he hadn't overheard any of her phone call. To Catherine she said, 'Cat, I'd better go. Martin's here.'

Her friend giggled. 'All of these men desperate to spend time with you. And now here's brainy Mercedes-Martin, bang on cue. Maybe the time for being gentlemanly is over? Hope so. For your sake, sweets.' And, in between giggles, she rang off, promising to call again soon.

'I'm not interrupting anything, am I?' Martin asked, gesturing to the Mac. 'Are you working?'

'No, not at all.' She smiled up at him. With his open face and twinkly eyes, he was nice-looking. So what if she didn't want to jump his bones? Catherine had been twenty-one when she'd met Patrick. You behaved differently in your early twenties, didn't you? This was a mature relationship, a friendship that would hopefully grow into something deeper and more lasting. Relationships didn't have to be all about sex.

While she made a pot of coffee Laney chatted to Martin about Nate, the cheek of Vince's offer, and her ideas for marketing Middlehaye Organics. (Catherine's suggestion that maybe it should be renamed Well-Hung Meat she kept to herself.)

'This is a great idea. Toby's products are amazing,' Martin said excitedly. 'Thanks, just what I needed.' He smiled as she handed him a coffee. Taking a sip, he added thoughtfully, 'Tell me to butt out if you like, but I know some people who would love to help.'

'Really?' Somehow Laney doubted it – solicitors knew more about the law than PR, in her experience – but it was sweet of him to offer. *See.* This was what a real relationship was about: mutual respect and trust.

'Do you want to bonk his brains out?'

She shook her head. *Get out of my head, Catherine.* Nodding at something he'd said, Laney tried to imagine Martin leaping up from his seat, dashing the Mac and her paperwork onto the floor, and taking her there and then on the kitchen table.

And failed miserably.

Instead all she could picture was him strolling through a National Trust property in his cords and shooting jacket. The height of excitement might be a cream tea somewhere. Not that there was anything wrong with that. She loved cream teas. In fact, she would concentrate on thinking about eating one, rather than on that disturbing image of Toby Woodward in the hay barn. They sipped coffee and talked about the fast-approaching Bonfire-Night Bonanza – Martin had made a website for it and had put out feelers for a celebrity guest. Laney tried her hardest to concentrate on all of Martin's good points: his easy conversation, his merry eyes, his good-humoured laughter, but her thoughts kept slipping away from him and back to that hay barn, like a bead of condensation on a glass. Bloody Catherine!

In despair Laney suggested that they went for a walk. Fresh air and exercise were what she needed, and more time with Martin. Martin who was kind, and clever, and attractive. And much more her type than a bad-tempered, horse-loving, sort-of-attached pig-farmer.

So what if he didn't make her go weak at the knees just yet? When he did finally kiss her, then the fireworks would go off, and it would be more than worth the wait.

11

After walking four miles with Martin, Laney was no nearer to getting to the bottom of how he might feel about her or, more importantly, how she actually felt about him. They hiked to the top of Green Lady Hill, where they shared a KitKat and admired the view, but the conversation never progressed beyond the safe topics of people they knew and the plans for the Bonfire-Night Bonanza. On both the climb up and the descent there were more than ample opportunities for Martin to have indicated that he wanted to be more than just her good friend. There were gates to climb and stiles to negotiate, both of which would have given him a great excuse to have lifted her up or given her a helping hand. Likewise, when the path narrowed and twisted its way back through the woods, he could have stood a little closer, even taken her hand, and she wouldn't have thought it out of place. But Martin chose not to do any of these things, instead keeping up a constant cheery dialogue and, apart from steadying her when she tripped on a tree root, made no real effort to get close.

Maybe I've lost it? wondered Laney, once they'd parted

company. Maybe she was metaphorically over-the-hill, as well as literally. This thought made her feel more than a little depressed. She hadn't exactly wanted Martin to rip her clothes off, but it might have been nice to have some indication of how he felt about her. A girl liked to be wanted, after all.

She stood on the bridge that spanned the brook between the street and her father's house and watched the water beneath burble over the pebbles. A lazy trout basked in the shadows, but – sensing her gaze – flickered away like quicksilver, a bit like the way her thoughts kept skittering away from Martin.

Laney glanced at her watch. Ten to four. The sun was well on its way to the horizon, sickly yellow in the pale wash of the sky. There were no guests at the B&B today. Nate and Janet were playing bridge and Laney had already prepared Nate's dinner. She could go home and do a little more work on Toby's website, but the thought of having to spend another hour gazing at his dark, hawk-like profile was unsettling. Maybe she should pop into the pub and see who was about?

Pop into the pub? Laney gave herself a mental shake. Drinking at four p.m.? Was this what it was coming to? The next thing would be joining her dad for bridge or even, God forbid, starting up her own committee.

'Hello.' Maxine, holding the hands of two very cute children, had paused on the pavement and was smiling at her. 'I thought it was you, Laney. What are you doing there all alone?'

Laney smiled back; she couldn't help it because Maxine

looked so colourful in her trendy multicoloured velvet hat and chunky ethnic-print coat. The twins were dressed like mini-me versions and even sported the same bright-green frog wellies.

'Theme-day at school,' Maxine explained, seeing where Laney was looking. 'Pied Piper. Easy enough to do – better than the last time, which was the flipping Romans. Vince freaked when he realized how many bed sheets I'd wrecked.'

Laney could just imagine. There'd probably been some kind of health-and-safety issue too, knowing Vince. It was lucky she hadn't seen him since the other day, because if she had, he'd have been facing a few health-and-safety issues of his own.

'I've just been for a walk with Martin,' Laney told her and Maxine raised her eyebrows. 'Just as friends.'

'Shame,' said Maxine. 'Martin's a honey and you two look good together. You'd have lovely-looking kids, like Botticelli angels.'

Personally, Laney thought that, given the current rate of progression, her ovaries would have long given up by the time she and Martin got around to having kids. 'I was just on my way home,' she said. 'Do you want to come in for a cup of tea?'

'I'd love to, but unless I get these two back and stuffed full of E-numbers within the next five minutes, there'll be hell,' said Maxine. 'How about you come too? If you can cope with the chaos, that is?'

For a brief second Laney was torn. She was still furious with Vince for being so tactless with Nate, and had deliberately been keeping her distance until she cooled down. Did

Maxine know? Was she part of it? Her merry freckled face was so honest and friendly that Laney could hardly believe it of her, yet on the other hand she was Vince's wife, and loyal to a fault.

'M-u-u-m!' One of the twins tugged Maxine's hand. 'I'm hungry.'

'Me too,' said the other.

Maxine rolled her eyes. 'Told you. Half-starved, these poor kids. Let's get going, I think there's a chocolate cake somewhere.'

The twins whooped with glee at this, and in spite of her misgivings Laney found herself laughing and agreeing to join them. Ten minutes later she was sitting at the table in Maxine's cheerful kitchen with her hands wrapped around a chunky ceramic mug, munching on a piece of cake that probably contained all her calories for the month. As the twins squabbled, Maxine refereed with a good-natured cheerfulness whilst at the same time making pizza, feeding the pets and chatting to Laney.

'Impressive,' she observed. 'You make an octopus look clumsy.'

Maxine shrugged. 'Years of practice. When Lily and Rose really want to, they get me running around like R2-flipping-D2. Throw Vince into the equation, and my skills are really tested. You know what? Take my advice: stay single and never have kids.'

But she was laughing as she said this and, looking around the kitchen, at the colourful pictures Blu-tacked onto the walls, the crammed family calendar and the wellies lined up by the door, Laney knew Maxine didn't mean a word of it.

From the cat slumbering on the windowpane, to the colouring pencils that had rolled across the quarry tiles, every inch of this place, and of Maxine, was devoted to the family.

'Wouldn't you have found it hard to look after the kids and run the B&B?' Laney asked, glancing at Maxine to register her reaction. 'I can see how good you are at spinning plates, but surely that would be an awful lot to take on?'

'What B&B?' Maxine's brows furrowed. The perplexed expression on her face instantly revealed that she didn't know anything about what Vince had been up to. Laney heaved a mental sigh of relief. Although she hadn't known Maxine long, she had really warmed to her, and it had been disappointing and hurtful to think that there might have been an agenda behind her friendship.

'Vince wanted to buy my dad's place,' Laney said, not caring that she was probably dropping Vince in it.

Maxine stared at her. 'Laney, either I'm being really thick here or you're not making any sense at all. What on earth makes you think Vince wants to buy the B&B?'

Laney said gently, 'Because I was there when he made my dad the offer.'

Maxine sank onto a chair.

'Dad was really upset,' Laney told her. 'I'm afraid I shouted at Vince a little too.'

'I'm not surprised,' Maxine said, still frowning. 'What was Vince thinking of? How very odd.'

'Odd! That's an understatement. You really had no idea?'

Maxine shook her head. Two bright spots of colour were burning in her cheeks and her eyes were dangerously bright. 'I know you haven't known me for very long, Laney, and you have absolutely no reason whatsoever to believe a word I'm saying, but I promise you I didn't have a clue. If I had, I would have told Vince it was tactless and insensitive. I wouldn't want Nate upset for the world, especially when he's been so unwell.'

Vince really was a piece of work. 'But he's your husband. Surely he'd run a decision this huge by you?'

'Oh, he probably did tell me and I had my head buried in one of my trashy novels,' Maxine said, trying to laugh it off. The catch in her voice, though, told a very different story. 'He always tells me I never listen to a word he says.'

Personally, Laney didn't blame her. If she were married to Vince Swinnerton, she'd literally try and bury herself so deep in trashy novels that he couldn't find her ever again. Still, it was probably best to keep thoughts like this to herself.

'We've been together for so long,' Maxine continued, mashing her cake with the edge of a teaspoon. 'He probably thinks that I can read his mind.'

It was on the tip of Laney's tongue to say that this wouldn't take long, but she bit her lip. She'd got off on the wrong footing with Vince and, if somebody as sweet as Maxine loved him, the guy must have some redeeming qualities.

'So how long have you guys been a couple?' she asked.

'Well, I remember a few dinosaurs roaming around at the time.' Maxine's face screwed itself up as she tried to remember. 'We were seventeen, and I'd known Vince for years. His family lived three cottages down, and we used to play together as kids. We hung out a lot – pony club, gymkhanas, young farmers, you know the kind of thing.'

'Not really,' said Laney.

Maxine smiled. 'Anyway, we just hung out as friends, and I fancied him like mad.'

Laney had to stifle a smile.

'Don't look so surprised. Vince was *gorgeous* when he was younger. Everyone fancied him. He had this amazing mane of white-blond hair, and an earring too. When he got his motorbike and leathers, I thought I would die of excitement every time I looked at him.'

Vince had had a *motorbike*? Laney couldn't have been more surprised if Maxine had told her he'd driven a Space Shuttle. Motorbikes weren't exactly for the safety-conscious.

'My friends told me to give up on him,' Maxine continued dreamily. 'Vince was a year older than me, and he always had a girlfriend. He was way out of my league too. Even hotter than Leonardo DiCaprio.'

So that was it. Whenever Maxine looked at Vince – grumpy, pedantic, slightly overweight Vince – she saw the boy he had once been, the Jack to her Rose. Personally, Laney would have jumped . . .

'I didn't stand a chance, because I was always just plump-and-plain Maxine; his good friend, the one he liked to talk to, the one girl he hadn't ever had to impress. We'd still hang out and chat, and I'd dream that one day he'd see me for who I really was, because that's what happens in all the books, isn't it?'

Laney nodded. She'd read a million books with that particular storyline. In her experience, they were all from the fiction section.

'Anyway, it was the St Pontian summer ball, and I was all

resigned to sitting on the edge. Then Vince walked over with a white rose and asked me to dance. *Me!*' Maxine clasped her hands, and Laney saw again the girl she'd once been: short, shy and overlooked, until her hero strode across the dance floor to claim her, just like a scene from a movie. 'It was like we were the only two people on the dance floor. And, when he finally took me in his arms and kissed me, well, I thought I'd burst with happiness. It was the most romantic thing that had ever happened to me. Country boys like Vince, and Martin, aren't given to showy displays of romance and affection. They don't like to show emotion.'

Toby Woodward had shown emotion all right, the night of the escaping Catherine wheel. There was passion there and a hidden depth, Laney thought with a shiver. Then she wanted to kick herself for letting her thoughts wander back to Toby. It was Martin she was supposed to be thinking of.

'Anyway, all those years and a set of twins later, we're still together,' said Maxine, rather defensively. 'I know he isn't always easy, and he doesn't look much like Leonardo any more, but I love him.'

Laney was touched by her loyalty. 'Even Leonardo doesn't look much like Leonardo any more,' she pointed out and they both laughed.

'Look,' Laney said, 'I don't know what Vince was up to that day, but I'm willing to think he may just have got carried away.'

Maxine nodded like the Churchill dog. 'Oh yes. That sounds like Vince. He'll get a mad idea in his head and then he just won't let it go.' But she didn't look sure. With all his health-and-safety obsessions, Laney doubted that Vince ever did anything without double-, triple- and quadruple-checking first. 'Oh, Laney, I really hope this won't stop us being friends. It's been lovely having you in the village. I'd hate us to fall out over a silly misunderstanding.'

Laney wasn't convinced how much she had misunderstood Vince trying to bully her father into selling the business, but Maxine was so sweet and looked so sad that her heart went out to her.

'Of course we won't fall out. Look, why don't you both come over for dinner?' she suggested. 'We can clear the air a bit. And I know Dad could do with some company. How about next Tuesday?'

'I'd love to.' Maxine's face lit up like the Oxford Street Christmas lights. 'Oh! Vince probably won't be able to make it. He's got the short-mat bowls committee on Tuesdays.'

The excitement never ended.

'Well, how about you let me know what night you can make, and then we'll sort something,' said Laney finally, when after looking at the calendar it soon became apparent that Vince was a very busy man indeed. 'Or maybe we could get a takeaway?'

'Bless you – a takeaway. Where from?' laughed Maxine. 'I think maybe we had better just meet at the pub.'

Laney didn't really want her father in the pub, with all the temptations of pork scratchings, alcohol and cheesy chips. These things did not bode well for his cholesterol levels.

'I'll cook,' she said firmly. 'You just tell me when you can make it.'

'And let's invite Martin too. And his mum,' Maxine said with a grin. 'It can be a triple date!'

Great. Dating with her dad and Vince – the world's most annoying man.

Bidding Maxine farewell, she crossed the village green. Martin was nice, but the thought of a meal with him and all the others hardly filled her with excitement. Maybe if it was just the two of them in a quiet romantic bistro? she thought. A bottle of wine, some seafood, some candles? That could be good.

The only problem was that every time she tried to imagine Martin moving in for a kiss, Laney saw Toby Woodward instead. Toby with his dark, intense eyes, sharp-cheekboned face and strong, sinewy arms . . .

Toby who was her client, was with Isla, and was totally not her type at all.

That Catherine Wheeler had a lot to answer for. The sooner Martin made his move, the better. These thoughts were starting to get rather worrying.

12

'I knew I should have worn my tracksuit bottoms and not these jeans.' Maxine pulled a tortured face at Laney. 'I can't eat another thing. I am absolutely stuffed.'

'Not even the rest of this tiramisu?' Laney asked slyly, pushing it across the table. 'It's really good.'

For a second Maxine looked torn as her tight waistband and her desire to sample the creamy dessert wrestled with one another. The dessert won.

'Oh, go on then, I can probably make room,' she said, leaning over and plunging her spoon in. 'Mmm, mmm. Oh, my God, this is heavenly! Definitely worth putting on a few pounds.'

Laney laughed.

It was Tuesday evening and the two girls were sitting in the pub by a blazing log fire. Between them was a bar table covered in empty dishes, the scraped-clean plates and bowls the only evidence of the lasagne, garlic bread and drunken-pork casserole that had been served up an hour before. Now they were full and warm, and looking forward to one more glass of wine before Maxine had to head back to relieve the babysitter. Vince, as usual, was at a committee meeting.

'I'm glad we made this a girls' night,' Maxine said, licking her spoon.

Laney nodded. 'I don't think my dad or Martin would have enjoyed hearing your childbirth story.'

'Wimps! They think they're big strong men, but nothing compares to the agony of labour,' Maxine said stoutly. 'And I know that Vince wouldn't have enjoyed hearing about George Clooney half as much as I did.' She leaned forward and fixed Laney with a piercing gaze. 'Are you sure you didn't sleep with him?'

'Sadly, George was the perfect gentleman. Besides, I was with my ex, Giles.'

'Ah yes, Giles,' said Maxine thoughtfully. Over their meal Laney had told her new friend all about her relationship with Giles, and why she'd felt it had to end. 'So you wouldn't cheat on him even with an A-lister?'

'Actually, no, I wouldn't.' Laney was adamant on this score. 'What's the point of being with somebody, if you don't put your heart and soul into it?'

'I'd never cheat on Vince,' said Maxine. 'And I know he feels the same way. But George Clooney – well, maybe I'd have to ask him for a hall pass. I'd do the same if he ever met Kelly Brook.'

'Sorry to interrupt, but are you all finished?' barmaid Alyssa asked.

'Yes, thanks,' Laney said, smiling up at her. Now that she knew Toby and Alyssa were related, she could see the resemblance. Both were tall and lean, with chiselled cheekbones and thick, glossy hair even darker than the mahogany bar. In contrast to her brother, though, Alyssa had lighter eyes and a less intense manner.

'It was a shame we couldn't have the sausages,' Maxine said. 'I love those. Especially with the cheesy mash. Why were they off the menu?'

Alyssa shrugged. 'No idea. Tobes said he'd run out, which is a first. He's probably just too busy hanging out with Isla and her horse to bother bringing any over.'

'Guinness is a beauty.' Maxine looked thoughtful. 'Will Toby ride him at the Fairford point-to-point this year, or will Isla do it?'

'Isla, I should think, with Toby training her. They're thick as thieves with it all at the moment,' said Alyssa as she stacked the dishes up her arm. 'To be honest, I was relieved when she moved Guinness from my yard and took him to Toby. I love my brother, but I don't really need to hear his praises sung morning, noon and night.'

As Maxine and Alyssa chatted about horses, Laney stared into the fire and reflected on the fact that this was a major part of country life that she was going to have serious problems getting her head around. Toby and Isla shared this passion for horses, and it obviously brought them closer together. It was just as she'd said to Catherine: he had *country* running through him like seaside rock, while – much as she was enjoying St Pontian – she herself was still a city girl at heart. Martin straddled both camps with ease, which made him far better suited to her.

Actually, thinking about Martin, she wondered where he was tonight? He'd said that he'd had a prior engagement in

Bath, but hadn't said what it was. Sometimes he could be quite mysterious. Slipping her phone from her bag, Laney sent him a quick text, hoping that he'd had a nice evening and inviting him to join her and Maxine for a drink, if he was back in time. There – she was making an effort. Catherine would be proud of her. When she looked up again she was taken aback to see that Toby had arrived and, judging from the glowering look on his face, he wasn't very happy.

'Isla isn't here,' his sister told him over her shoulder as she carried the plates to the kitchen. 'She said she'd be up about half-nine, if you wanted to meet her.'

'I haven't come here to see Isla,' Toby said shortly. Scanning the room, his gaze alighted on Laney and he nodded grimly. 'I've found exactly who I'm looking for.'

He had? Suddenly Laney was regretting the garlic bread and the spinach cannelloni. And why on earth was she wearing her baggiest, most unflattering smock top? He was looking absolutely gorgeous in faded jeans, Dubarry boots and a battered Barbour. The scarlet scarf slung around his neck accentuated the darkness of his colouring and, unfortunately, also seemed to announce the kind of mood he was in. As Toby marched towards her Laney's stomach lurched. He looked really, really angry. She racked her brains – come on, little grey cells, what have you done that might have annoyed him this time – but no, she couldn't think of anything. Maybe it was just a bad day at the farm?

'Hi, Toby.' Maxine, as much use at sensing moods as Laney was at ignoring them, gave him a bright smile. 'Just the man I was talking about. Do you know that I couldn't have your lovely sausages tonight? They've sold out.'

'Actually, yes, I did know,' said Toby. Turning to Laney, he slammed a letter down in front of her. 'I take it this is your doing?'

The letter only just missed the remnants of Maxine's chocolate-fudge cake. Picking it up, Laney saw the headed paper.

'This is from Julian Matlock,' she gasped. *Wow! Well done, Catherine and Patrick*. Sending the produce had been a long shot but maybe, just maybe, it might get them somewhere.

Toby crossed his arms and fixed his burning gaze on Laney. 'I know. Read on.'

'Julian Matlock, the chef? *Cooking on Gas* and *Cheating Eating*?' Maxine's eyes were big blue circles. 'Oh, wow! I love him.'

'Me too.' Alyssa said. 'Don't tell my Steve, but I *would*!'

'Glad you're all so impressed. Maybe I should have been a celebrity chef and not a farmer?' said Toby drily. To Laney he said, 'It seems that Mr Matlock has a fan club. Why don't you tell them what he has to say?'

Laney scanned through the letter. With every word she read, her heart beat a little faster. This was great. No, this was better than great. This was *amazing*. *Incredible!*

'Don't keep us in suspense,' pleaded Maxine.

'Julian Matlock has written to Toby to congratulate him on his range of organic sausages. He says they are excellent, and quite simply the best sausages he has ever tasted. Which they are, of course,' said Laney warmly. This was all fantastic news. Why Toby was looking so irritated, she had no idea. 'Julian Matlock says that from now on he will be selling –

and selling only – Middlehaye Farm sausages in his three restaurants.' She looked up. 'Oh, my goodness. This is brilliant. He says that he's telling everyone about your produce, and that he's going to mention it on his show and in his column. Toby! This is the break that we've been hoping for. Why aren't you jumping for joy?'

Toby closed his eyes. 'Why didn't you run this by me?'

'Because it was such a long shot that I didn't want to get your hopes up,' Laney cried in frustration. 'I couldn't have imagined in a million years that this would happen.'

'No wonder the pub couldn't get any sausages,' breathed Alyssa.

'Orders are up three hundred per cent,' Toby told her.

'That's good news, isn't it?' asked Maxine.

'It says here that he wants you to come to London for an interview,' Alyssa said, peering over Laney's shoulder at the letter. 'Wow! He wants you to appear on his show. That's bloody amazing. Please take me with you!'

Laney felt jubilant. This was it. She'd known Toby would be television gold. She just never dreamed it would happen this quickly.

'I hate London,' Toby said shortly. 'I've got absolutely no desire whatsoever to go prancing around with celebrity chefs and TV crews. I'm a farmer and, strange as it may sound, I actually need to be on my farm, taking care of my animals.' He huffed like an old-fashioned steam engine. 'The sows are farrowing any minute. There's no way I can leave.'

'Surely somebody could help?' Laney was taken aback. She'd been so excited about the potential that linking up with Julian Matlock could offer that it had never occurred to her this might pose a problem. And it was only a problem according to Toby. Suddenly furious, she glared at him. Talk about ungrateful!

'I could help with the farm, and Steve would give a hand,' Alyssa offered, but her brother shot her down in flames.

'Don't be so ridiculous. Neither of you knows the first thing about pig-farming, and besides you've got your hands full with the livery yard.'

'Surely it's a good thing that Julian Matlock likes your sausages?' ventured Maxine. 'Doesn't that mean everyone will want to buy them, and then you'll sell loads?'

'It would be, if we had enough sausages,' Toby said slowly, as if explaining something to the village idiot – a job that he probably thought Laney should apply for. 'Unfortunately I only have a finite supply. I only have so many pigs, so I can only make so many sausages. Do you understand? And I don't want to be rushed into expanding the business, either.'

'Can't you breed some more?' Laney asked. She betted Richard Branson never talked like this.

Toby gave her a withering look. 'Good idea. I'll just go and magic some up, shall I? Let me explain how this works. I need a sustained breeding programme. I need to introduce new bloodlines. Pigs need time to gestate. These things can't happen overnight. This is a farm not a . . . not a shoe shop. I need to do some careful thought and planning.'

There it was. The dreaded P-word. What was it with men and their desire to plan everything? Hadn't they any idea what spontaneity meant? Toby Woodward was as bad as Giles – yet another man who couldn't appreciate living in the moment and being creative.

'I'll help you with it.' Laney raised her chin and stared him straight in the eye. 'Whatever you need doing, I can help.'

'And you're an expert on breeding livestock too, I suppose?' He laughed rudely. 'No, thanks. Your help has caused me enough headaches already. All my local customers are furious. Don't you understand? You haven't helped me *at all*. In fact, you've made things about a hundred times more difficult.'

'You horrible, ungrateful . . .' Laney was about to call him a 'pig' when she realized he'd probably like that. 'Insufferable man! I've got you the best publicity ever – publicity that could be worth far more than flogging a few sausages to local pubs – and *this* is how you thank me?' She stood up and pushed her stool back so hard that it tumbled over and walloped Toby in the shins. Not that Laney cared. She only wished it had hit him somewhere even more painful.

'*You're* angry with *me*?' Toby looked perplexed. '*I'm* the one with umpteen customers breathing down my neck and a load of nosey journalists on the phone. I thought you were a PR *consultant*? Forgive me, but if so, when did I miss the *consulting* part of this process?'

Right. That was it. She'd heard quite enough. Laney wasn't so much seeing red now as every shade of crimson, magenta and cerise in the colour spectrum. She'd been working really hard for Toby Woodward, and this was all the thanks she got? Well, sod it! And sod him too. She'd had quite enough of ungrateful, pedantic, unspontaneous men to last her a lifetime.

'Stick your PR job,' she told him. 'And stick your sausages

too. Preferably where the sun doesn't shine. If my help's so awful, then fine, do without it. You're on your own.'

Snatching up her bag, Laney shoved past him and stormed out of the pub, leaving Toby staring open-mouthed and furious behind her.

13

'Laney! Wait!'

She was storming across the village green like a paratrooper while Maxine was panting as she tried to keep up. Laney took pity on her and stopped. Slightly overweight, Maxine was already hampered by her high-heeled boots, which insisted on impaling themselves in the squidgy grass. By the time she caught Laney up, her face was puce and her breathing ragged.

'Sorry.' Laney paused by the duck pond and kicked at the grass verge with the toe of her boot. If only it were a voodoo-verge and Toby-bloody-Woodward was grabbing his head and screaming somewhere. 'I just needed to get out of there.'

Clutching the stitch in her side and struggling to catch her breath, Maxine bent double for a moment.

'Did you hear what he said?' fumed Laney. 'How ungrateful can you get?'

Maxine collapsed onto a bench, but Laney was far too wired to sit down. Instead, as her friend got her breath back, she paced and relived the conversation of a few moments earlier. How could he be so scathing? The Julian Matlock connection was the sort of PR link you prayed for, and could really put Middlehaye Organics in the collective consciousness. But oh no, for Toby Woodward it was an inconvenience. She was rushing him.

Rushing him? Toby needed to light a firework underneath himself, if he wanted to launch his business right into the twenty-first century. Well, from now on that was it – she was through with small towns and small-town mentalities. She'd ring some of her old London contacts and see if they had any freelance work for her. If Toby Woodward wanted to be left alone, then left alone he would be, to wallow in muck with all the other pigs.

'Laney? I said are you all right?'

Maxine's voice interrupted Laney's train of thought and for a split-second she was startled to find herself on the green, rather than in the pub rowing with Toby.

'I'm fine,' she said, even though she was shaking from head to foot. 'Sorry if I caused a scene in there. It was just that I'm so furious. Can't he see what a fantastic opportunity this is for him and his business? Not even so much as a *thank you* for all my hard work. His pigs have got better manners than he has.'

Maxine laughed. 'Don't take it personally. Toby's always been a man of few words.'

Laney did take it personally. Very personally. 'He should be on his knees thanking me.'

'Toby Woodward isn't like that.' Maxine patted the bench. 'Here, sit down a minute. All this pacing is making me feel exhausted.'

Laney sat next to her, but – still agitated – her fingers

drummed on the arm of the bench. She couldn't remember the last time she'd felt this infuriated. Even when she'd seen all of Giles's notes and the carefully debated pros and cons of getting married, she'd only been mildly pissed off. If she was honest, it had been the get-out clause she'd been waiting for. He certainly hadn't been able to get to her like Toby-bloody-Woodward.

'I'm really surprised at Toby,' Maxine continued thoughtfully. 'He's not usually one to make his feelings known, especially in such a public way. When his engagement broke up, he was really in pieces. I think he gave up with women at that point. He's usually one who plays his cards really close to his chest.'

'Toby and Isla were engaged?'

'No, no. Isla and Toby have been on-and-off since school. Me and Vince used to double-date with them for a while.' She put her arm round Laney conspiratorially. 'Toby was engaged to some American for a bit. We were all surprised, because she didn't seem his type at all. He was bonkers about her, but I don't think she could handle life as a farmer's wife and she didn't stay long. When it didn't work out, he was right back to his normal grumpy self – only worse. He never, ever shows how he feels.'

'So tonight was the exception to the rule? Am I supposed to feel lucky?' Laney pulled a face.

'Not lucky, but maybe you should feel unusual? Alyssa was gobsmacked. She said she's never seen her brother behave like that before.' Maxine's eyes widened as a thought occurred. 'OMG. It's like something out of a novel! A stormy and passionate relationship, where the hero and heroine think they hate each other, but their true emotions are the exact opposite.'

'Maxine, please.' Laney mimed a vomiting gesture. 'I think it's safer to say that Toby is a private man, who hates the idea of a celebrity circus and wants to be left in peace. My setting the opposite in motion has really pissed him off.'

As the words fell from her lips, Laney realized that actually perhaps Toby did have a point. Much as it irked her, perhaps she should have asked him first, before she went steaming ahead with her own ideas? Maybe he did have a point about not being consulted?

But Maxine wasn't listening. She was far too busy losing herself in a romantic fantasy. 'You're like Lizzie Bennet and Mr Darcy. He's brooding and proud and private, but secretly in love with you.'

Laney laughed out loud at this nonsense. 'He's not brooding, he's just miserable. I know, how about we ask him to strip off to his breeches and a shirt and jump in the village pond? Maybe when he comes striding out, all damp and dishevelled, I'll realize that my feelings have changed and I am totally and utterly in love with him after all?'

'That's it, take the mickey,' said Maxine huffily. She crossed her arms and fixed Laney with a steely look. 'I'm telling you, I read a lot of these books and I know a tortured romantic hero when I see one.'

Since Maxine was married to Vince, Laney decided not to listen too hard to anything she might have to say. Steering the conversation round to less emotive matters, she allowed herself to be persuaded to go back to the pub for one last drink before Maxine had to return to the twins. Reassured to learn that Toby had also stormed out, Laney decided she probably deserved a brandy. She ordered herself one and took a table by the bar.

'Talking of romantic heroes and your love of reading,' she said to Maxine as they clambered up onto bar stalls and ordered their drinks, 'why don't we start a book group?'

'Oh yes. Great idea.' Maxine's eyes sparkled at the thought. 'It could be like a committee all of our own.'

'No, it couldn't.' Laney's mind was made up. She hadn't lived in St Pontian for very long, but already she'd had enough of committees, and the petty rules of the people who ran them, to last her a lifetime. Possibly two. 'No rules. No leaders. Just a group of people who meet once a week to talk about books, eat some nibbles and have fun.'

'It's a great idea.' Maxine reached into her huge handbag and – after removing a packet of tissues and a glittery hair-slide – located a notebook. 'Right. Let's get planning.'

Pleased to have a distraction from the altercation with Toby (the image of his angry face seemed to have frozen in her mind like a broken Sky+), Laney threw herself into deciding what books they should read, where they should meet and what format the gatherings should take.

'We'll have to hold it on Thursdays,' Maxine said. 'Vince is about then, and you're free too.'

Laney nodded. 'Thursdays are good for me.'

'But Thursday is craft-committee night,' called Alyssa from the far side of the bar, where she was unloading glasses from the dishwasher and eavesdropping.

'Alyssa's the head of the craft committee,' Maxine whispered to Laney.

Laney shrugged. 'There are only so many days in the week,' she said. 'People will have to make a choice, I'm afraid. I'll pop a notice on the village noticeboard and post a few fliers around, so that everyone knows it's on.'

Alyssa slammed the dishwasher door shut so hard that the glasses on the shelves rattled in terror.

'There you go again,' she said, rounding on them so swiftly that Laney almost toppled off her bar stall. 'Interfering and doing things without asking people.'

'That's not fair, Alyssa. Laney was only doing her job for Toby,' said Maxine hotly. 'She doesn't know him, or how private he is.'

Alyssa's dark eyes flashed. 'Because she never bloody thought to ask. Just like she never asked about having a book committee—'

'Book *club*,' Maxine corrected her.

Alyssa sighed. 'Fine – book club – on the same night as craft committee.'

'I don't need to ask your permission to start a book club,' Laney said. What was it with people here? It was like primary school, a pathetic *if you're her friend, then you can't be my friend* mentality.

'Probably we'll only have a few people turn up anyway. Not everyone likes reading,' pointed out Maxine diplomatically, but Alyssa wasn't in any mood to be placated. Being stubborn and bloody-minded clearly ran in the Woodward genes.

'Well, Isla holds the keys to the village noticeboard and she won't give them over to you.' Hands on her hips, Alyssa glared at Laney. 'So you'll have to stick your posters somewhere else, won't you?'

'Fine. Not a problem.' Laney was tempted to stick her tongue out because of the childishness. Instead she finished her brandy and placed the glass on the bar with a thud. Her head was starting to ache. 'Time to go home and rescue the babysitter, Maxine.'

'Nobody will come anyway,' Alyssa sneered as Laney and Maxine headed outside. 'They like the craft committee. Who wants to read boring books? Nobody, that's who.'

'Well, we'll just have to see about that,' Laney said, 'won't we?'

And with that parting shot, Laney left the pub for the second time. She was through arguing with the Woodward siblings for one night. Now she'd made an enemy of Alyssa. And over a book club. It was absolutely ridiculous. The sooner Nate was well again and she could go back home to London, the better.

⁂

The next morning Laney deleted her prototype website for Middlehaye Organics, emailed some of her old contacts in PR and then busied herself stripping beds, doing the laundry and checking that her dad had everything he needed. After lunch Maxine popped over with some posters and fliers she'd made to promote the book club, and the two girls spent a happy hour stomping around the village delivering their leaflets. Armed with drawing pins, they left no telegraph pole, bus stop or useful fence post unadorned. If nobody came to the book club, it wouldn't be for the lack of advertising, that was for certain.

There were almost as many posters for their book club as there were for the Bonfire-Night Bonanza. It clearly was the thing that St Pontian was most proud of.

'It's a shame we can't use the church noticeboard,' said Maxine sadly when, after finishing the modern estate behind the ancient Norman chapel, they approached it. 'It's where everyone puts their notices.'

'I'll pin one to the frame,' Laney decided. 'That way at least some people will see it, and maybe Isla will open up the board and display it properly? You never know.'

'She won't,' said Maxine in a matter-of-fact tone. 'She's thick as thieves with Alyssa.'

Laney supposed this was to be expected. Isla was Toby's girlfriend after all, and practically one of the Woodward family by all accounts. Not that she had been asking around or anything. Who Toby chose to date was of absolutely no interest to her. Resigning herself to the fact that Alyssa and Isla probably wouldn't be inviting her for tea any time soon, Laney pinned the poster to the board so that it covered the Bonfire-Night Bonanza notice, as clearly everyone knew about that already. There! Now everyone who passed would know that this Thursday was the first gathering of the St Pontian book group. All they needed to do was bring a bottle and some ideas for reading matter over to Maxine's house. Simple.

'Hey! What do you think you're doing?'

A clatter of metallic hooves against tarmac started the familiar sickening sensations in Laney's body. She turned to see Isla and Toby on two horses. The sight of the beasts made her head spin.

'Well? What are you playing at?' demanded Isla, pulling Guinness up so hard that sparks flew from his hooves.

They must have been galloping recently because his nostrils were blood-red, egg-white foam frothed around his mouth and Guinness was clearly in no mood to stand still. Sidling from side to side and rolling his eyes, the horse danced about like a creature from Greek mythology. Not that this seemed to bother Isla, who sat him easily, with her reins held in one gloved hand. The smell of hot horses filled Laney's nostrils and the world dipped and rolled.

'We're putting up our posters for the book group,' Maxine said, jutting her chin up in a determined manner. 'Have you got the keys for the board? It's locked.'

'I'm not giving them to you. Stand still, Guinness.' Isla looked down at them contemptuously. 'There's a clash of activities that night. I suggest that if you really want a book club, you change your days.'

Laney's heart was racing, but she was determined to stand her ground.

'Can you dismount . . .' she found it hard to speak, '. . . so that we can talk, please?' she asked, hardly able to hear her words over the rushing of her blood.

'Don't be ridiculous.' Isla brought her whip down on Guinness's shoulder. 'I said *stand*.'

Guinness flinched and Laney recoiled.

'He's hotted up from blasting through the woods. The worst thing you can do with a wound-up horse is get off. Don't you know anything?'

Not about horses, no, and neither did Laney want to. Just being this close to one was enough to turn her legs to boiled string. 'Please get off,' she begged. 'Please.'

'What's going on?' Toby rode over. He was astride a huge coloured cob, all heavy feathered feet, shaggy mane and bright-blue eyes. Like Isla's horse, his was excited from its ride, but Toby stilled it easily with soft hands on the reins and a smoothing of the neck. 'Steady, Apache,' he said gently, more gently than Laney had ever heard him speak to a human. 'Whoa there, girl.'

Now there were two horses. Laney felt her throat closing.

'Laney and Maxine have taken it upon themselves to stick posters all over the village. They've started a book group and have been trying to use the village noticeboard without asking me,' said Isla.

'My God, what a heinous crime,' drawled Toby. His eyes, dark and mocking, met Laney's. 'Making more executive decisions, Ms Barwell?'

'We just wanted . . .' But Laney trailed off as Toby's horse took a step closer. She felt her legs start to quake. Clutching the noticeboard so hard that her knuckles glowed chalky-white through her skin, she pleaded, 'Please, Isla, if we're going to discuss this, could you tie them up somewhere else? I really don't like horses.'

'You can't seriously be scared of Guinness and Apache?' Isla curled her lip scornfully. 'What a hoot! That's absolutely ridiculous.'

It might well be ridiculous to Isla, but at this point in time Laney couldn't have cared less. She really was terrified. In a moment she would not be able to breathe. Then she'd pass out. And there was no way Laney was going to pass out in front of Toby Woodward. She'd rather drown herself in the village pond, thanks.

Turning to Toby – who knew how afraid she was of horses and who had been so sweet with Belle – she pleaded, 'Toby? Please?'

But Toby didn't look at all sympathetic. His face, shadowed by the peak of his riding hat, was set and unsmiling, with not so much as the merest trace of the gentleness that she'd seen there before.

'The horses aren't hurting anyone,' he said curtly. 'They're a part of life here, Laney, just like farming, and village communications. I suggest you get used to it.'

Even though every cell in her body was screaming at her to run, she was determined to get into the noticeboard and prove her point. 'Give . . . me . . . the . . . keys . . . please.'

'Isla decides what goes on the noticeboard,' Toby said coldly. 'Like I decide what goes on at my farm, and you decide what goes on in your business. That way, everyone knows where they stand.'

He was taking Isla's side? Even though she'd told him just how frightened she was?

'Put your notice somewhere else,' said Isla, looking jubilant.

Laney wished she had sufficient oxygen to wipe the smile off Isla's face by telling her that Toby wasn't backing her out of loyalty, but because he had a score to settle with Laney. Isla looked so smug, perched high up there on Guinness, that Laney wanted to grab her by her Horseware gilet and give her a good shake. Sadly, that would have to wait for another, horse-free time.

'I have to go,' Laney gasped.

And, with trembling legs and racing pulse, she turned away from them both and walked as fast as she could towards home, with Maxine scuttling behind her, then helping her along. But no matter how far she walked or where she hid, Laney knew there was no escaping her phobia of horses.

And no escaping either, it seemed, the icy contempt of Toby Woodward.

14

'Well, I think a book group is a lovely idea,' Janet Rolls said staunchly as she rolled pastry over the floured worktop. 'My friend Sandra in Chipping Norton goes to one and she loves it. They read *Titus Groan* last week.'

'Goodness!' Laney was taken aback. Working her way through the Gormenghast trilogy wasn't *quite* what she'd had in mind when she'd suggested starting a book group. More like a few chick-lit novels, with a couple of thrillers and the odd classic thrown in for good measure. 'Maybe we should start with something a little shorter?' she suggested. 'Until we know how much time people have to do the reading.'

'Fair enough, love.' Rolling the pastry back into a ball, Janet attacked it afresh. 'Always roll your pastry three times before popping onto the pie dish,' she said when she saw Laney watching. 'That way the crust rises a treat.'

Laney stored this little snippet away. It was Tuesday evening and she and Janet were making steak-and-ale pies for the freezer. Or rather Janet was making steak-and-ale pies for the freezer and Laney was watching in awe. Pies that didn't come from M&S? Wow indeed!

'Isla and Alyssa aren't very keen on the idea, though.' Laney rested her elbows on the kitchen table and cupped her chin in her hands. 'They still won't give me the keys to the church noticeboard.'

Janet tutted. 'Those two have been Queen Bees around here for far too long, in my opinion. Their noses are probably well and truly put out of joint, having a beauty like you arrive on the scene.'

Laney laughed. 'Hardly.'

'Now, my girl, don't you dare start putting yourself down. You're absolutely gorgeous, and they both know it. Look at you, with all those lovely golden curls, nice figure and beautiful skin. No wonder they've both been behaving like proper madams.'

Bird's-nest hair, unseen by Toni & Guy for way too long, and a body that is feeling far too squashed in its size tens is more the case, Laney thought ruefully.

'My Martin thinks you're wonderful,' Janet said. 'And he is never wrong.'

Martin thought she was wonderful? That was news. He played his cards close to his chest in that case, because so far Laney hadn't noticed anything special about his attention. He sent the odd sweet text or funny email, but so far the bouquets of red roses and declarations of undying love had been missing.

Which was fine. Being friends was fine.

'Toby Woodward doesn't think I'm wonderful.' Laney picked some crumbs of pastry from the table and rolled them between her fingers. The expression of scorn on his face when she'd run away from the horses was driving her insane, as was their unresolved argument. As hard as Laney tried not to think about Toby, her rebellious mind kept returning to him with alarming regularity. It was probably just wounded professional pride, but it was still very disturbing. Toby was a mood-vacuum – every time she thought of him, Laney ended up feeling annoyed.

'Toby Woodward is a very silly boy,' said Janet staunchly. 'You worked really hard to help his business and, if he doesn't appreciate it, then that's his loss.'

'I know, I know.' Laney squashed the pastry ball flat. 'But, Janet, you should have seen the expression on his face when I ran away from the horses. He thinks I'm pathetic. Maybe I am? Who's afraid of horses?'

'Lots of people. Horses bite and kick and smell.' Janet draped the pastry over the pie dish, cut off the extra with a knife and started to crimp the edge with her fingers, while Laney watched in fascination. 'Spiders, however – what do they do apart from spin webs and eat nasty flies, hmm? Yet nobody thinks any less of somebody for being frightened of a spider. Your phobia makes a lot more sense on paper.'

On paper maybe, but in St Pontian it made no sense at all.

Janet popped the pie into the Aga, then sat down at the table.

'Tell me to mind my own business if you like, love, but why do you think you're so scared of horses? Have you always hated them?'

Laney sighed and shook her head. Where to begin? 'I used to love horses when I was little. I had hundreds of My Little Ponys and I was always pestering my parents for riding lessons. One day they gave in and took me down to the local stables for a look. I was so excited.'

She closed her eyes. The memory was so vivid that she could almost be transported back there again. The warmth of the spring sunshine on her face, the sour smell of muck mingling with the sweetness of hay, the ponies looking over the half-doors, Mum and Dad holding her hands . . .

'While my parents were chatting to the instructor I found a piece of carrot on the ground.' Laney wound a curl around her forefinger as she spoke, an old nervous childish habit. 'I picked it up and decided to feed it to one of the ponies. I was only eight, and I had no idea that you had to feed horses by putting food on the palm of your hand. I used my fingertips and of course I got bitten. It wasn't the pony's fault, it was an accident, but my finger was broken and I had to go to hospital.' She held up her hand to Janet. 'Look, you can still see the bump where they had to set it.'

Janet's kind was all sympathy. 'Poor you. No wonder you don't like horses.'

Laney shook her head. If only this had been the end of the story. She would willingly have suffered ten such injuries.

'We went to the hospital for an X-ray and to have it set. Which was quite exciting for an eight-year-old. Or at least it was until my mother collapsed.'

Janet's hand flew to her mouth.

Over twenty years later Laney could still recall the scene as though it was only yesterday: Mummy crumpled onto the floor like a rag doll, Nate's cries for help and the running of medics. She'd stood on her own, with her hand in a sling, and watched them lift Mummy onto a trolley and wheel her away.

'That was the day we found out that my mother had ovarian cancer,' she said slowly. 'She'd been tired, but we really had no idea. By then it was stage three and inoperable. She died two months later.'

The kitchen was as still as someone holding their breath. The only sounds were the gentle burble of *The One Show* from the residents' sitting room and the hiss of the pie cooking in the Aga.

Laney's throat felt tight with unshed tears. 'Since then, it's weird, but I haven't been able to look at a horse without my heart racing and feeling as though I can't breathe.' She gave Janet a watery smile. 'You probably don't need to call in a psychologist to tell you why.'

'You poor love. No wonder you get yourself in such a state.'

'Obviously the horses have nothing to do with Mum getting cancer.' Laney shrugged. 'I probably should have had counselling or something at the time, but Dad was in no state to think about anything like that. He was absolutely in pieces. He's never got over losing Mum. They were the perfect couple, and I don't think anyone could ever come close. That's why he's never been involved with anyone else. He never will.'

'Never?' Janet asked.

'Never.' On this score Laney was certain. 'They were everything to each other. Dad only moved here because it had been Mum's dream to live in the Cotswolds. He always thinks of her, even after all this time.'

Janet looked down at the table. For a moment she seemed to be struggling with something and her mouth quivered. Then she took a shuddering breath and looked up. Goodness, were those tears in her eyes? Laney was touched by her neighbour's depth of feeling.

'I can't try and understand how awful it must have been for you and Nate.' Janet reached out and took Laney's hand in her own floury one. 'But I'm here for you both now, if that is any help.'

'Of course it is. I don't know what Dad or I would have done without you.'

'Believe me, it's my absolute pleasure,' said Janet with feeling. 'After my husband walked out, I don't think I'd ever felt so alone, especially with Martin all grown up and gone. Having Nate to talk to and spend time with has been a great comfort to me.'

The two women smiled at one another across the kitchen table. It had been years, Laney realized with a shock, since she'd been able to have a real heart-to-heart like this. There was something about Janet Rolls that was so warm and comforting you just wanted to pour out all your troubles so that she could make them better. It was bit like talking to a mum.

'Get on with us.' Janet fished into the pocket of her pinny for a tissue and blew her nose loudly. 'What a pair! And as for that Toby Woodward, don't you be taking to heart anything he does or says. He's been a right old misery guts since his fiancée left him. None of us can do or say anything to put a smile on his face. That sulky madam, Isla Birch, is welcome to him.'

Laney opened her mouth to say that Toby wasn't always

sulky and cross. When he'd stacked the logs that day and shown her around the farm he'd been great company, and his crinkly smile had been infectious. Then she recalled how taciturn he'd been in the pub, and how unsympathetic he'd been yesterday, and her heart hardened. There was no defending the indefensible.

'But this horse phobia is going to be a real issue, living here,' Laney said sadly. 'Everyone rides, the hunt meets at the pub and even Martin enjoys point-to-pointing.'

'Only because he likes to think he can pick a winner,' Janet said, winking. 'And he likes being with you, so he's obviously good at it.'

Laney blushed. 'Do you really think he likes me?' she asked.

'Of course he does.' Janet looked taken aback that Laney should be in any doubt. 'Why else would he spend so much time with you? He sees you all the time, doesn't he?'

Er, no, actually. Where Janet had got this idea from was anyone's guess. Martin and Laney had probably spent only a handful of hours together since she'd arrived in St Pontian. Laney was just about to ask Janet exactly what she meant when her mobile alert beeped. *Sports-pavilion committee meeting* read the screen. Oh, Lord! She'd totally forgotten, and now she was running seriously late. Vince would pop a blood vessel.

Kissing Janet fondly and calling a cheery farewell to Nate, Laney set off for the pavilion. It was busier here than in London. Maybe she'd go and visit Catherine in the city for a rest? Laney crossed the village and when she saw a sporty Mercedes parked outside the church her heart lifted. Martin was here. Of course. She'd forgotten that he was on this committee too. There were so many that she was starting to lose count.

Maybe tonight was the night they would finally get everything in the open and move things forward? She hoped so, especially after hearing what Janet had to say about how much he liked her. Perhaps Martin was just shy? Maybe it was time she grabbed fate by the balls and made the first move? It was high time she had some romance in her life.

15

'I'm so sorry I'm late.'

Red faced because she really hated being late and making a spectacle of herself, Laney squeezed into the only vacant seat remaining in the sports pavilion. The meeting was already in full swing, and while she wrestled herself out of her duffel coat and scarf – it had suddenly turned very cold, cold enough for snow, in Janet's opinion – she listened to Vince listing the merits of spending what was left of the funds raised by a raffle on buying some new commemorative plaques. This idea was being hotly debated by Martin, the heat of the argument provided by the flagon of mead they were all working their way through. A mugful was placed in front of her and just the smell of it was enough to make her tipsy.

Oh well, Laney thought as she took a swig, *in for a penny, in for a pound.* Perhaps if she got sufficiently drunk the evening would pass more quickly? Glancing at the agenda, she certainly hoped that would be the case. If ever a cure for insomnia was required, this would be it: rugby vs football. What colour for the changing-room repaint? Who was responsible for cleaning the loos? *Yawn-city.* She was starting to regret her impulsive decision to take Nate's place.

There were no other women present on this committee, which probably accounted for the boys'-club atmosphere in the room. Several older gentlemen looked rather put out to have somebody with ovaries present, and when Vince had explained that she was standing in for Nate, one elderly gent with a handlebar moustache and nose like a cauliflower suggested that they held his place open until he was better, and that Laney joined the craft committee instead?

'That's Sir Henry Callington,' Martin whispered into Laney's ear. 'Total old fossil, but he owns half the village.'

Big deal, thought Laney. Seeing that St Pontian was smaller in size than her local Waitrose, this hardly put Sir Henry on a par with the Duke of Westminster. Anyway, who cared what he owned? He was still a sexist pig.

'Much more your thing than this sport business, m'dear. You don't want to worry yourself with that,' Sir Henry continued. 'You could make something pretty to cheer your father up, if you join the craft committee. Or how about the baking circle?'

Laney's eyebrows shot into her fringe.

'Capital idea,' chimed in another old duffer, and a few of them nodded in agreement. Laney glanced at Vince for some support, but he was suddenly totally engrossed by his agenda.

OK. She was on her own then.

Emboldened by the mead – and her naughty streak – Laney said sweetly, 'I'm sure my father would be far more cheered up if we started a women's five-a-side team. Or how about mixed aerobics? That could be a lot of fun.'

The elderly gentleman looked horrified at these suggestions.

'Do women play football?' Sir Henry spluttered, his face turning puce. 'Aerobics? Leotards? In the cricket pavilion? Never.'

'Not active enough for St Pontian?' Laney widened her eyes innocently. 'Well, there is pole-dancercise, which is supposed to be very good for suppleness, but I can't say I know much about it. I think fitting a pole in here would be pretty tricky,' and she sussed out the space by looking up to the ceiling and down again. 'But I guess we could give it a go.'

Sir Henry nearly choked on his drink. Martin's shoulders shook with silent laughter.

Vince shot Laney a very black look. 'We're deviating from the agenda.'

'Sorry. I was only teasing,' said Laney. Goodness, but this mead was strong, it was as if her tongue was running away with her. 'Seriously, while Dad is sick, why don't you look at my being here in a more positive light and take some feminine input on board? You want the sports pavilion to be used by more people and generate an income, so why not try and attract more women? Perhaps we could find a Pilates instructor to do a class a week, or maybe a yoga teacher?'

'Those are great ideas,' said Martin. He gave her a warm smile and Laney's heart lifted.

'Kindly save your ideas for Any Other Business, please,' said Vince pompously. Clearing his throat loudly, he continued. 'If we could return to the agenda and item two, the raffle money, what I propose is as follows . . .'

While Vince read out his proposals, Laney tuned out and

imagined soft lighting, yoga mats and some deep relaxation. Hmm. It could work. Stomping through the woods was all very well, but it didn't tighten all the spots that a girl needed tightening. If she ever did get up close and personal with Martin, she wouldn't want any wobbly bits to horrify him.

'So I therefore conclude that we spend the funds on a brass plaque to commemorate this year's twenty-fifth anniversary of the pavilion,' finished Vince proudly. 'Are we agreed?'

'No, we're bloody well not agreed,' said Martin, frowning. 'That raffle was a general raffle organized by the whole village, and the funds were for general use. At no time was it specified that we'd allocate them solely to the sports pavilion. We need to use a chunk to pay a celebrity to come and light the bonfire, remember? That's the draw we need, to attract lots more visitors to our November the fifth celebrations. If we're going to break even, we need outsiders to come.'

'So you literally want the money we raised to go up in smoke?' Vince said. 'Very beneficial to the village.'

'And a metal plaque is beneficial?' countered Martin.

'It's part of history. In years to come, people will look at it and know who we were and what we did.' Vince puffed out his chest. 'I would have thought that appealing to posterity was important.'

'It'll be melted down or nicked,' Martin said bluntly. 'Let's think about what people need now, rather than what they might want to see in a hundred years' time. If we make some money on the Bonfire-Night Bonanza, then maybe we could put it towards putting on a Christmas party for the elderly again.'

'Perhaps if you spent less money on the fireworks –

which, may I point out, will cost thousands and be over in less than ten minutes – maybe you could still throw a Christmas party for the pensioners?'

'And if you weren't so health-and-safety conscious, maybe we'd have more money in the first place, rather than wasting it all on insurance?'

Crumbs! Martin and Vince were really going for it now. As the debate continued, they started to insult each other in the personal way that only old friends really can. When Vince started mocking Martin for his arty-farty, poncey fireworks fetish, Martin pushed back his chair and stormed out. For a moment everyone froze. Moments later the throaty roar of the Mercedes could be heard as Martin tore off down the road.

Turns out Martin gets passionate after all, thought Laney.

'Maybe we'll go on to the next item?' Vince said when an awkward silence fell. 'Item three: under-fifteens football fixtures.'

The rest of the meeting passed in a rather dull and uneventful way. After Martin's stormy exit, Vince seemed subdued and nobody else was really in the mood for a debate. By nine p.m. everybody had sloped off, leaving just Laney and Vince to clear away the chairs and wash up the glasses.

'Maybe the mead wasn't such a good idea?' Vince remarked as they stacked the seats against the side of the room. 'People tend to lose all rationality when there's booze involved.'

Laney wasn't having this. It was one thing rowing with Martin, but quite another to accuse him of being drunk and irrational.

'You said some pretty hurtful things,' she pointed out. 'And Martin wasn't even drinking. It wasn't the alcohol that made him tear off like that. It was you and what you said to him.'

Vince looked confused. 'What did I say?'

Lord, the man was a sensitive as a house brick! Leaning against the chair stack in order to take a breather, Laney said, 'All that stuff about him being a big girl's blouse, with his love of pretty fireworks? And I don't think he was very happy, either, when you called him Arty-Farty Marty.'

'But I've always called him that. Arty-Farty Marty was his nickname at school. He had a few others actually, but I won't go into those right now. Why on earth would he take offence at that? It's only schoolboy stuff.'

'Maybe because you're not at school any more?' Laney pushed her curls back from her hot face. 'Look, Vince, I know I haven't been here very long, but I am quite good friends with Martin and he might be a bit of a joker on the surface, but underneath he's really sensitive.'

'You and Martin, eh?' Vince raised his eyebrows.

She flushed. 'It's nothing like that. We're just friends.'

'Really? Well, he's a fool.' Vince looked at her appraisingly, and Laney felt awkward being the subject of such scrutiny. How much mead had he drunk this evening? Quite a lot, judging by those crimson cheeks and that sweaty brow.

'Call him and apologize,' she suggested. 'Martin thinks the world of you and he'll hate the fact that you've fallen out.'

He nodded. 'I will. God – sorry if I caused a scene on your first night. I don't know what got into me. I'm not usually one to row. It must have been the booze. That and the stress at work. I think maybe the pressure is too much.'

'Maybe we should risk-assess *you* before the next meeting?' she teased.

Vince hung his head. 'I know you all think I'm a bit of an old fusspot, with my health-and-safety concerns, but the thought of something going wrong and my being to blame is a terrible burden to bear. It's all I think about at work, and I'm sorry if I carry it home with me. It's boring, I know.'

'We all know that you're only trying to do your best,' said Laney kindly.

'I am. I really am.' So grateful was Vince for Laney's sympathy that he clutched her hands in his own clammy paws. It took all her effort not to recoil. 'All I ever try to do is my best for everyone. For my clients, for the village, for Maxine.'

'Of course you do,' said Laney, wondering when she had inadvertently signed up for the counselling committee. 'Maxine knows that. She adores you.'

'You think?' Vince laughed bitterly. 'That's news to me. All I ever hear about is what the twins need, what jobs I need to do in the kitchen, and how unfair it is that she never gets to go out. So I work even harder, take on more overtime, and what then? It's moan-moan-moan about how we never spend time together any more. So then I have a brainwave that we could run a B&B, so that we could work together and see each other more, and guess what? That's wrong too, because I never ran it by her first and I upset your dad. I can't win!'

Blimey. That was quite a speech. Who would have guessed that puffed-up, self-important Vince had so many self-esteem issues running beneath the surface?

'We've drifted apart,' he finished sadly. 'I don't think I'm what she wants any more.'

'I'm sure that's not true,' Laney said gently. 'However, rather than talking to me about it, don't you think you should be having this conversation with Maxine? If you tell her how you feel, I'm sure you'll be able to sort all this out. In fact, I think—'

Suddenly Vince didn't seem too interested in what Laney thought. Before she realized what he was doing, he'd lunged across and planted his lips on hers in a sink-plunger kiss. For a split-second Laney was frozen with horror. Then all her natural instincts kicked in and she shoved him away so violently that he careered into the stack of chairs.

Thud! Thump! Wallop! Chairs tumbled down on top of Vince, who yelped and squeaked with every one. Good! Laney could only hope this would knock some sense into him or, even better, clout him on the bonce so hard that he forgot all about his crazy behaviour.

'What the bloody hell are you playing at?' Laney cried, wiping her mouth with the back of her hand. Yuck! Talk about slobbery.

'I'm sorry. I'm sorry!' Cowering beneath the heap of tumbled chairs, Vince made a pitiful sight. 'I don't know what got into me.'

'Total insanity, that's what! You're a married man, remember? And your wife is my friend.' Furious beyond words, Laney glowered at him. How dare he? And what a hideous position he'd now put her in with Maxine.

'I know, I know.' He buried his face in his hands. 'You

were being so sweet to me, so kind, and for a crazy moment I thought . . .'

He'd thought what exactly? Sickened, she couldn't bear to hear any more.

'I felt sorry for you. I was being sympathetic. Since when did being a listening ear mean sticking your tongue down my throat?'

'It doesn't. But you were holding my hands!'

'Because *you* grabbed them!' Laney closed her eyes in despair. 'Vince, whatever you may have thought, that was not a come-on.'

'I know, I know. It was a moment of madness, that was all. It was the drink. I wasn't thinking properly.'

Laney thought this was probably the understatement of the year.

'In fact I can promise you one hundred per cent that I've never done anything like this before. I've been with Maxine for years and I've never been unfaithful. You have to believe me.'

Actually, Laney did believe him. Vince seemed genuinely upset, and he had drunk an awful lot of mead. On the other hand, neither of those things excused what he had done.

'Please don't tell Maxine. She'd be so hurt,' Vince pleaded. 'There's no point upsetting her over what is just a silly drunken kiss, is there?'

'Let's get one thing straight. You kissed me. I had absolutely nothing to do with it *whatsoever*,' Laney said, not liking the implications here.

Vince closed his eyes. 'But we were here on our own after the meeting. I'm not sure Maxine would see it that way. This is a small village. Things are very easily blown out of all proportion.'

Shooting him a look like a bullet, Laney stormed out of the pavilion and into the inky night. The cold air was a balm to her hot cheeks, but nothing could soothe the frantic whirling of her thoughts. As she stomped across the village green, not caring that the mud would probably be wrecking her favourite suede boots, all Laney could think about was the horror of the past ten minutes.

To tell or not tell Maxine, that was the question. The trouble was that Laney had a horrible feeling that whatever course of action she decided upon would only end in tears. On the one hand, she liked and respected her new friend and didn't want to keep any secrets from her. On the other, Maxine would be devastated, and Laney really didn't want to hurt her over something so meaningless.

Bloody Vince and his clichéd midlife crisis. Laney felt like bashing her head against the village noticeboard in frustration. Something told her that no matter what decision she made, she wouldn't be able to win.

And that was not a happy thought.

16

'This is fantastic,' whispered Maxine, tipping yet another packet of Kettle Chips into a bowl and fetching more dips from the fridge. She could hardly contain her excitement and did a little skip across the kitchen. 'I never imagined that so many people would come! We should have started a book group *years* ago.'

Laney smiled, partly because her friend's enthusiasm was just so contagious, and partly because she was also thrilled by the response. In spite of being banned from the village noticeboard, having their posters *mysteriously* covered over with more adverts for the craft committee and the impending Bonfire-Night Bonanza, and Alyssa's negative comments to all and sundry, Maxine's small sitting room was crammed with women keen to get reading. Far more wine-drinking and eating of nibbles had gone on than intense literary debate, but it was early days. The fact that more than ten people had chosen to come was encouraging in the extreme. And if they never ended up talking about books, then so what?

'It's brilliant,' she agreed. From the sitting room came the excited burble of happy nattering women, punctuated by the odd laugh and the munching of food.

'To think I was worried nobody would come,' Maxine shook her head in wonder. 'You were worried too, weren't you?'

Actually yes, Laney had been worried. Very worried. But not about the book club. Instead she'd been terrified of arriving at Maxine's and bumping into Vince. Just the mere thought of seeing him again made Laney want to curl up and die, and she'd almost wept with relief when Maxine told her that Vince had gone out for a drink with Martin.

'Apparently they had some silly falling-out at the meeting,' Maxine had explained while she and Laney set up the sitting room for the book group. 'Vince said that Colonel Browning brought some of his home-made mead over and everyone got a bit plastered.'

'Hmm,' Laney had said. Unsure whether or not to remind Maxine that she had taken Nate's place on this particular committee, she'd chosen to keep quiet. Whether or not this was a mistake would remain to be seen, but Laney was doing her very best to put last Tuesday evening out of her mind. Sadly, this was easier said than done, and she had a nasty feeling it was going to cost a lot in very expensive therapy.

Maybe *that* was what Vince could spend the raffle proceeds on.

'Vince never could hold his drink,' Maxine had laughed. 'I've told him to take Martin out and apologize for whatever it is that he's done. Good friends are hard to come by, and far too precious to lose.' She'd paused from mashing up avocados for a guacamole dip and had given Laney such a sweet smile that her heart had twisted. 'And I'm including you in that, Laney. I know we haven't been friends for very long, but already I know we're going to be really good pals. You can just tell with some people, can't you?'

Laney had nodded, but she'd felt terrible. Would Maxine feel the same way if she knew that only two days ago her husband had been kissing her? Totally unwelcome and unreciprocated as that kiss was, she was really afraid Maxine might not view it in the same light. That was why she'd decided not to say anything. It wasn't from any desire to protect Vince – being drowned in mead was too good for him, in her opinion – but because she really liked Maxine and couldn't bear the thought of losing her friendship. In the two days that had passed since the sports-pavilion committee meeting, Laney had relived that excruciatingly awful kiss so many times that it now spooled before her vision like some hideous video-nasty. Surely the guilt of not telling Maxine was written all over her face? If only she had left after Martin went. If only it had never happened.

But happened it had, and she supposed she would just have to deal with it.

'Now all we have to do is decide what we ought to read. I think maybe we should start with the latest Philippa Gregory? Or perhaps *Pride and Prejudice*? That's always good fun.' Maxine chattered away cheerfully as they returned to the sitting room. 'Then we could watch all the different film versions and compare.'

'Compare what? The pertness of Darcy's bottom?' Alice Rogers, the red-faced and weatherworn wife of the Master of Hounds, was suddenly all of a quiver, just like her husband's pack when on the scent of a fox. 'Oh! That could be a lot of fun. I was going to suggest we read *Riders*, but I'd much rather watch movies and gawp at hot young men.'

This was all getting a little off-topic. Jane Austen would be spinning in her grave.

'Why don't we begin with something fun and modern?' Laney suggested gently. 'How about the latest Sophie Kinsella, just to get us started? It should be easy to get hold of too.'

Everyone nodded and thought it a great idea. Great presumably because, with this decision out of the way, they could get on with the serious business of eating and drinking. This was fine by Laney. Sipping her glass of white wine and nibbling some mini bruschettas, she reflected that if it hadn't been for feeling so guilty about bloody Vince she'd be having a great time.

'So, Laney,' said Alice, peering over the top of her third glass of Chablis. 'What's this I hear on the grapevine about the divine Toby Woodward losing his temper with you in the pub the other day?'

There was no need for a village noticeboard in this place.

'It was nothing. Just a misunderstanding about some PR,' Laney said swiftly.

'It didn't sound like nothing to me. I heard he got quite heated, which isn't like our Toby at all. He's normally quiet and deadly, that one,' Alice said. 'You should see him on the field. Nobody rides with the guts and determination of Toby Woodward – nothing ever fazes him. I think you've got right under his skin.'

The other women in the room murmured and nodded

their agreement. Laney sighed inwardly. They hadn't even read a word of romantic fiction and yet already everyone was slipping into Mills & Boon mode. Maybe she should cancel the chick-lit and suggest some Stephen King instead?

'That's not the case at all,' she said firmly. 'I'm sure he's very happy with Isla. They have a lovely time riding out together and talking horses.'

Alice Rogers snorted just like one of her horses. 'Isla Birch has hands like cast-iron. That will never last, mark my words.'

'Are they still together?' Jane Thorne, who worked in the post office, looked confused. 'I thought that fizzled out years ago.'

'You know young folk here. On-off. On-off. Like a whore's drawers,' boomed Alice.

Laney snorted her Chablis so hard that her eyes watered.

'They are always together these days, so I think they're on again,' Maxine said, curling up into the giant beanbag and sipping her drink thoughtfully. 'But if they weren't, who knows? I think he does have a soft spot for Laney.'

Laney rolled her eyes. The only soft spot was in Maxine's head, if she really believed that.

'How on earth do you draw that conclusion?' she asked. 'You saw how unhelpful he was when I asked him to move the horses away. Hardly the action of a besotted suitor.'

'That proves it.' Leaning so far forward that she almost toppled off the sofa, Alice fixed Laney with a beady look. 'That nasty woman he was engaged to – couldn't ride for toffee, either – was a dreadful townie.'

'She was an agent from New York,' Maxine filled in when

she saw Laney looking even more bemused. 'Anna Somebody-or-Other. Anyway, she was researching her family tree and ended up in St Pontian, and finished up in Toby's home. They were chalk and cheese, which is probably why it never worked out.'

'Which is why he'll be extra-harsh on you when you show anti-countryside tendencies,' finished Alice triumphantly. 'He daren't allow himself to fall in love with another beautiful city woman.'

My God, what was in this wine? Had they all gone stark raving mad, or had all the fresh air and ozone got to them? Laney didn't think she'd ever heard such a load of old twaddle in her life. Number one: she was far too short and curvy to be considered beautiful. And number two: Toby Woodward was most definitely not in love with her.

'I hate to burst your romantic bubble,' she said firmly, 'but it sounds as though I'm as different to Toby as this Anna-woman was, and he is certainly not my type. In fact, I think he's one of the rudest and most arrogant men I've ever met.'

'Which is where the chemistry comes from.' Alice, who had to be pushing fifty on a good day and with the wind behind her, smacked her lips. 'Hmm. He's as tasty as the meat he produces.'

There was much laughing at this, and the conversation moved on to a rather bawdy discussion of who they would and wouldn't sleep with, if their lives depended on it. None of this meant much to Laney – she had yet to meet Nick the farrier and Alex, who did hedging – but at least it meant the pressure was off her for a minute.

'I'm so glad I was young when I met my soulmate.'

Maxine sighed. 'It certainly makes life a lot easier. I can't imagine not being with my Vince, and I know he feels the same way about me.'

Oh, Lord! Cringing, Laney tried not to listen as Maxine sung Vince's praises. Now she felt worse than ever about that kiss. Thank goodness Maxine had no idea. She might not be quite so gushing about her relationship then.

'I don't believe Vince is such a paragon,' Alice Rogers said. 'Tell me he doesn't fart and snore, and drop his dirty socks on the floor?'

Maxine flushed. 'Well, yes, but—'

'And does he watch sport when you'd rather see a chick-flick? And does he spend more time with his committees than he does with his family?' Alice was as relentless as a waterfall. 'And what was the last compliment he gave you? Hmm? Not one about your cooking, either, before you tell me how much he loves your apple crumble. One about *you*. He should adore you.'

'Alice!' Jane looked shocked.

'What?' Alice sloshed more wine into her glass. 'Oh, come on, don't be so coy, girls. What's said in the book group stays in the book group. If we're going to get to know each other, we might as well start now. I'll get the ball rolling. Charlie and I always do the deed on a Sunday afternoon, after church and before evening stables. It's another chore ticked off the list for us both, so that we can crack on with the week! So, Maxine, when did you and Vince last spend hours in bed because you wanted to be there, and not because you needed to sleep?'

Maxine's full mouth trembled. 'I can't remember. But

we've got twins and we're really busy. We can't spend all of our time snogging like teenagers, you know. I'm a mum, and I'm so flat out with the girls that it's hard sometimes to fit Vince in as well. And he's really pushed at work, so it's the last thing he wants to do when he gets home.'

This was too much information. Excusing herself, Laney went to the bathroom and ran her hands under the cold tap for a few moments. Vince had said that Maxine didn't have time for him and that he was really stressed at work. Maybe he had been telling the truth?

By the time she returned to the sitting room, Maxine, her tongue lubricated by a bottle of wine, was admitting that she and Vince had been having problems. They never talked any more and, what with their respective committees and looking after the children, rarely spent any quality time together. They hadn't made love for months. The women all offered reassurances that Maxine and Vince were the best-suited couple they knew, and Alice, sobering up by now, pointed out that all marriages go through rough patches.

'My Charlie even had a fling with one of the girl grooms,' she said gruffly. 'I wasn't happy about it, but we got through it, and now I wouldn't be without him for the world.'

'I know Vince would never do that,' said Maxine firmly. 'He's not the kind to cheat.'

Laney swallowed. Her whole body was trembling with horror, her heart pounding like something out of an Edgar Allan Poe novel. Oh God, Maxine must never find out about Vince's kiss. *Never*. It would break her heart.

Fortunately the conversation turned to other topics, and Laney was able to busy herself by clearing away. By the time the last of the women had staggered out of the door she was feeling slightly calmer. Vince would never breathe a word, and she certainly wasn't going to be spilling the beans. Everything would be fine. Maybe she could offer to babysit so that Vince and Maxine could spend some time alone. Yes. Laney brightened at the idea. That was exactly what she was going to do.

'That's really sweet of you. Thanks, Laney, you are such a star,' said Maxine when Laney suggested this. 'I don't know what came over me, coming out with all that personal stuff. Whatever must the others think?'

'With the amount they've all knocked back, I'd be amazed if they remembered any of it,' Laney replied.

Maxine handed over Laney's coat. 'Well, in spite of my confessional moment, I really enjoyed tonight. I can't wait for next week. I'm going to pop into Oxford tomorrow and buy that book. Or maybe I'll even download it to my iPad.'

Laney wound her scarf around her neck as she stepped onto the doorstep. Although it was only half-ten, a heavy frost was already icing the village green. Bright stars sparkled in a sky as dark as Toby Woodward's curls.

'Actually, Laney, before you go, there is something I need to ask you. Something I have to know.' Maxine's face was serious as she spoke.

Laney gulped. Did Maxine know? Did she suspect?

'It's about Vince,' she said.

Laney held her breath.

'I need you to be honest, no matter how much you think it might hurt me.'

Laney's blood was ice in her veins. She tried to speak, but her words were as frozen as the silent village.

'If he tries to make another offer on the B&B, will you let me know?' Maxine continued, blissfully unaware of Laney's racing heartbeat and weak legs. 'I think he might be buying because he's planning to leave me.'

Laney opened her mouth to explain that Vince only wanted the B&B as a way of spending more time with his wife, but thought better of it. After all, Maxine would want to know how on earth she knew this, which would take some explaining. Instead she promised to keep her friend aware of any developments.

'Of course I'll tell you,' she said.

Was this lying by omission? Laney wondered miserably as she crossed the village. Hands plunged deep into her pockets and her breath rising like smoke, she looked up at the stars and wished on the brightest, most sparkly one that Maxine and Vince could sort their problems out.

She only hoped that by keeping silent she wasn't adding to them.

17

Laney was up early the following morning and, unlike some members of the book group who were staggering round the village looking rather the worse for wear, her head wasn't too sore. She was still stressed about the whole Vince and Maxine business, but unfortunately that couldn't be cured by swigging Resolve and gulping down a couple of Nurofen. And she was still desperately worried about her father's health, and this business was only adding to it, not distracting her from it.

Quite what she could do Laney was still frantically trying to figure out. She was convinced that the two still loved each other, and that each was feeling equally undervalued. All she had to do was work out a means of getting them to realize it. She was no psychologist, but Laney had watched enough *Oprah* and *Jeremy Kyle* to know that when people felt neglected, they often did very daft things indeed. And she was certain that Vince's bumbling pass at her and his obsession with health-and-safety fell firmly into this category.

All she had to do was find a way to get them talking again and recapturing the old feelings.

Hmm. It would probably be simpler to split the atom before lunchtime. Still, Laney was determined to come up with something.

After boiling an egg for Nate's breakfast and giving him strict instructions not to move from his armchair, Laney set off for the village shop. Three guests were booked in that evening and she wanted to make sure the cupboards were stocked, a substantial meal prepared and nothing left to chance. If the B&B was to keep its excellent reputation, then nothing short of perfection would do, and Laney was nothing if not a perfectionist. Luckily the local grocery shop was surprisingly good, and by the time she was strolling back up the main street she was struggling to carry a basket crammed full of crusty bread, fresh eggs and locally grown produce. No Middlehaye sausages were available – surprise, surprise! – so she plumped for chorizo instead. Toby was obviously still having issues meeting the demand for his products, even if the thank-you card had yet to arrive . . .

Tortilla española tonight, Laney decided as she left the shop. One thing she could just about manage to make on her own. With the home-made apple pie that Janet had brought over, and thick yellow cream from the local dairy farm, it should be a good meal and up to Nate's high standards. Vince would have a long wait if he thought she was about to give up and sell the business.

The frost of the previous evening still lay thickly on the grass and a fried egg of a sun hung just above the church spire, as though trying to do a balancing act. The village was bustling with people going about their daily business, and Laney called a cheery 'Morning' to everyone she met. This had to beat being on the Tube, where if anyone spoke it was usually because they were a psycho. *Yes*, Laney decided as she peered into the window of Isla's gift shop, *life could be a lot worse*. It was good to slow down for a bit. It was also good to spend time with her father. It was lovely to actually sit and chat to him and have an insight into his world. Having lost one parent already, Laney was determined to make the most of Nate.

The door of the gift shop opened just as Laney was dithering on the brink of going inside. She really wanted to buy some postcards to send her friends in London, but wasn't sure whether Isla would welcome her, after Book-Groupgate. Hampered by her basket, Laney couldn't step aside quickly enough, and Toby Woodward, walking backwards because he was calling instructions to Isla about a dressage test, cannoned straight into her. The basket dropped to the ground with a thud and the heart-plummeting splat of eggs.

'Goodness, I am so sorry,' Toby apologized, crouching down to retrieve runaway apples and oranges. 'I didn't see you there.'

Laney glanced down. She was wearing a bright-red padded coat and couldn't have stood out more if she'd tried.

'Well, of course I saw you,' he continued hastily as he crammed the produce back into her basket, 'but not quickly enough, obviously.'

'Obviously.' Laney dug her hands into her pockets and let him scrabble around on the pavement. There was no way she was going to help. Not after his scene the other day.

'I was just . . . Isla was just . . .' Toby trailed off as he scrabbled about, rescuing runaway mushrooms. His glossy dark head was only inches away, and Laney suddenly found she had the most terrible urge to wind her fingers into his curls. Appalled, she made her fists into balls and dug them even deeper into her pockets. 'I wasn't paying attention, I'm afraid. Sorry.'

'Sorry?' Laney raised her eyebrows. 'Did you just apologize to me?'

Toby stood up and gave her a rather sheepish look. 'I think we've got off to a bad start. I'm not normally so rude. And I know you only meant to do me a favour by contacting that celebrity chef. I love the peace of the farm, and I try to run it as my father would have wanted. Dad knew how he liked things – small and properly done by the family – and I'd hate to do anything he might not have approved of. It sounds stupid, I know, but keeping the farm as it is, that's like a part of him.'

Laney said nothing. She didn't need to because she recognized that bleak look in Toby's eyes. She saw it in her father's whenever he talked about her mother.

He sighed. 'I guess what I'm trying to say is that I'm just no good at handling sudden pressure and change. I'm afraid it may have sent me into a slight panic.'

'*Slight panic?*' She shook her head. 'Total meltdown more like.'

Toby laughed. 'OK, OK. Yes, it was a meltdown. I'd never seen orders like it, and I felt under huge pressure to expand and make changes. But that's probably a good thing. It's too easy in St Ponty to be lulled into a rut. Even if it is a very nice rut, don't you think?'

His eyes, the same rich brown as soy sauce, held hers.

Laney had the oddest feeling that Toby was trying to say something, but quite what she wasn't sure.

He cleared his throat awkwardly and handed her the basket. 'Christ, what a mess! My clumsiness has broken all your eggs. Why don't you hop in the truck with me and pick some more up from the farm?'

'It's fine. I'll just go back to the shop and get some more.' There was no way Laney was going to risk being responsible for upsetting the balance of Toby's farm any further. Knowing her luck, one of Nate's guests might turn out to be a world-famous omelette chef, who would henceforth refuse to cook with anything other than Middlehaye Farm eggs. That would probably send Toby into meltdown too.

'You absolutely will not. I broke the eggs and I insist on replacing them. My hens are laying like crazy, so you'll be doing me a favour. I promise that you won't ever have tasted anything better.'

Toby placed his hand in the small of her back and propelled Laney along the street towards his truck. She tried to protest, but her vocal cords were having an uncooperative moment. Her legs, it seemed, were in on this too, because they just wouldn't turn around. Almost before she knew it, Laney found herself perched in the passenger seat of the Toyota, next to a snoozing springer spaniel.

'That's Jerry,' Toby said, putting his hand underneath the slumbering canine and sliding him over to free up some space.

'Jerry Springer!' Delighted, Laney couldn't help laughing and Toby joined in.

'Alyssa's idea of a joke. He's her dog really and getting on a bit now, aren't you, boy?' he told Laney, fondling the dog's ears affectionately. 'Alyssa runs the livery yard side of the business, and she's flat out at the moment getting ready for hunting season.'

Laney looked at him blankly.

'Fox hunting?' Toby explained. 'That starts in early November, and lots of our livery customers pay her to get their animals hunting-fit. That was another reason why I couldn't go to London – Alyssa will be far too busy to help me with the farming.'

'I don't know much about rural life,' Laney admitted as Toby drove them along the main street, before heading up the steep and wooded lane that led out of St Pontian.

'And you're not big on horses, either.' He turned his head and gave her a thoughtful look from beneath thick, sooty lashes (*wasted on a man; if I'd been blessed with lashes like that, I'd save a fortune on mascara*). 'Which is why you were so odd, when Isla and I saw you by the church noticeboard.'

She was about to tell him exactly what she thought of Isla and her petty village politics, but then thought better of it. No man wants to hear his girlfriend being disrespected, however much she might deserve it. Toby was with Isla, so presumably thought the sun shone out of her jodhpur-clad behind. Laney chose to say nothing, but sighed and let her fingers smooth the silky-soft dome of Jerry's head.

'I'm sorry I wasn't more help with the horses,' Toby said. He changed gear as he swung the truck into the farmyard. 'I was . . . angry.'

'With me?' she asked.

Cramped between the gearstick and the dog, Laney felt

her cheek was so close to Toby's lips that she could sense his breath warm against it. Her mouth dried and her heart was doing a weird pogo underneath her padded coat.

Finally Toby shook his head.

To keep calm, Laney concentrated on stroking the dog. 'It helped when I stroked Belle,' she told Toby, 'but I'm no way cured.'

It had helped, too, having Toby by her side that day, but there was *no way* Laney was telling him that.

Killing the engine, he said, 'Well, let's work on that, shall we?'

Flinging open the driver's door, Toby leapt out and beckoned Laney to follow. Moments later she was striding across the farmyard in his wake, trying very hard not to plaster her knee-boots with mud and muck. She soon gave up, though, when Toby sploshed through the muddy gateway that led to the paddocks. Maybe she ought just to admit defeat and go around in wellies like everyone else here? What was the point of clinging on to London fashions? *I might as well buy a boiler suit and give in,* she thought.

Picking up the scarlet head-collar draped over a wooden stake, Toby ducked beneath the strand of electric fence that marked the first paddock. At the far side Belle was grazing contentedly by the stream, all cosy and plump in her funky checked rug. Her breath was rising in misty plumes and every now and again she snorted happily.

Even so, Laney felt her heart start to race. She tried to think of her breathing and control it.

'Come and say "hello",' said Toby.

On hearing his voice, Belle looked up, her liquid-brown

eyes bright with curiosity, and her nostrils flared when she whickered a greeting. Beautiful as the horse was, with her flowing silver mane and intelligent head, Laney felt the old familiar hand of panic squeeze her heart.

'I . . . I can't,' she whispered.

He held out his hand. 'Of course you can. Come on, it'll be fine.'

As if in slow motion, Laney stretched out her hand. Toby's fingertips brushed hers.

He smiled and nodded at her, curling his large hand around her smaller one. Her hand in his felt so safe and so natural that she probably would have followed him anywhere. Like someone in a dream, she allowed him to lead her across the paddock, where the only sounds were their boots crunching over the frozen grass and the gentle champing of the grazing horse. The glittering sun balancing on the blackthorn hedge made the grass sparkle and seemed not to care that it might be punctured by the sharp fronds. Belle, hoping for treats, abandoned her grazing to join them and stood patiently while Toby caught her. Laney's hand, freed from his while he buckled the head-collar, felt oddly lonely.

'Come on.' Toby held his left hand out to Laney again. With his forefinger tenderly tracing the curve of her thumb, he walked the length of the paddock, with the horse on the far side. Although her heart was racing, there was something so soothing about being beside Toby that after a few minutes Laney's pulse began to slow. Instead of the leg-weakening panic, she started to feel almost peaceful. The burbling of the stream and the soft hoof-beats lulled her, as did the rhythmic caress of Toby's finger against her palm and the gentle way he crooned to the mare. Round and round the paddock they walked, until Laney was no longer aware that Belle was only feet away.

'Well done,' said Toby when they paused by the gate. Smiling down at Laney – a real smile that crinkled the corners of his eyes and lifted everything in that sharp-cheekboned face – he said, 'Want to give her a treat before we let her go?'

For a second she dithered. Toby was delving in the pocket of his Barbour and Belle nudging him impatiently. After watching how gently the horse took a treat from his hand, Laney nodded.

'Well done, you,' said Toby. 'Now hold your palm flat, thumb in, and just let her do the rest.'

Balancing Laney's hand on top of his, Toby placed a treat in her palm. Laney pushed away memories of the moment when the horse bit her all those years ago, and concentrated on the present. Seconds later Belle's velvet muzzle had scooped it up. She smiled up at Toby, her eyes wide with excitement.

'I did it.' She exhaled a shaky breath.

'Of course you did.' He smiled back and this time when her heart skipped a beat it wasn't from fear. 'Do you want to try again?'

She nodded. And sure enough Belle took another treat, looking absolutely delighted at the way the morning was progressing. After four more, and with a face that ached from smiling, Laney agreed that maybe it was time to stop. She could feel the adrenalin working its way round her system and needed a break.

'Let's stop feeding her up now,' Toby said as he removed the head-collar. 'She's not allowed to be ridden these days, and she'll get fat.'

'Tell me about it,' Laney sighed, glancing down at the red Puffa jacket. It was hardly the most flattering garment in the world. In fact, what on earth had got into her to wear such a monstrosity? She must have been living here too long. If she wasn't careful she would be wearing overalls soon.

'Don't be ridiculous,' Toby said softly. He was still holding her hand and he tightened his grip, pulling her closer and trapping her fingers against his heart. Even beneath the waxed jacket Laney could feel it beating. As she looked into his dark eyes she saw her own reflection in those inky depths, small and wide-eyed. Mesmerized, she couldn't look away. Even when Belle snorted and pawed the ground she didn't flinch.

'You're—'

Toby stopped speaking as three large vans pulled into the yard, spraying mud everywhere as they screeched to a halt.

'What the hell is going on?' Toby dropped her hand, and now his eyes were narrowed suspiciously. 'Do you know anything about this?'

'No.' Laney was stung by the assumption that the chaos in the yard was her doing. Slamming doors and hooting horns did not mix well with animals. Jerry was barking like crazy, pigs started snorting and even the mild-mannered Belle shied away. 'Stop blaming me for everything. Why do you always have to think the worst of people?'

He shrugged. 'I'm not usually wrong. People tend to let you down, in my experience.'

Laney sprang away as though scalded. So people all let him down, did they? 'With an attitude like that, I'm not surprised,' she said coldly.

He shrugged. All their previous closeness seemed to melt away like the frost in the sunshine, and Laney suddenly felt chilled to the bone beneath her layers. Jolted back to the present, she followed him as he strode to the gate, her breath sharp in the cold air and aching with a curious sense of disappointment. Why this was she didn't know. Toby Woodward was spikier than a sea urchin, so she really oughtn't to be surprised.

In the farmyard van doors were flying open and what seemed like hundreds of people were spilling out onto the cobbles. Were those cameras? And why did that man have a light meter? And what on earth was a make-up crew doing here? Were they lost?

Confused, she watched as the third van opened its doors and a man who looked suspiciously like Martin got out.

No hang on, scratch that. This man didn't look *like* Martin. This man *was* Martin.

'Laney.' With a broad grin and a wave Martin sprinted across the yard. 'Hey, you,' he said, kissing her on the cheek. 'Isn't this a surprise?'

'It certainly is,' said Toby darkly. Two girls in ridiculously high heels, and showing so much midriff that they were in danger of getting frostbite, were screaming with delight as they saw the piglets, while a guy who made Gok Wan look butch squealed when he stepped in some muck. 'My Kurt Geigers! OMG!' he yelled.

Rounding on Martin, Toby demanded, 'Martin? What's happening?'

'It's publicity,' Martin said proudly. 'But really you should thank Laney, not me. She inspired this.'

'I did?' Laney was confused. 'How?'

'You were talking to me about getting some free publicity,' Martin said, looking a bit hurt that he wasn't quite getting the ecstatic reception he'd anticipated. 'I said I had some contacts.'

Laney remembered this conversation. She also remembered thinking that his off-the-cuff comment probably wouldn't amount to much. Three vans and one very annoyed Toby later, she was starting to regret this.

'Well, one of them, my uni friend Camilla, works for *Country Life Style*. I told them all about the farm and Julian Matlock, and they want to run a feature on Toby. Isn't that brilliant news?' Looking utterly delighted with this coup, Martin beamed at Toby and Laney. 'This is the kind of exposure you can never buy. The editor has even visited Julian Matlock's restaurant specially, and she's raving about it. Wait until she writes this up. You'll never look back. Middlehaye Farm will be huge!'

Laney didn't dare catch Toby's eye. Now that she knew him better, she was horribly aware this was exactly the kind of thing that the intensely private farmer hated. No wonder he looked horrified. If he thought she'd planned this all behind his back, he'd never forgive her.

Suddenly the thought of this upset her very much indeed.

'So,' continued Martin, clapping Toby on the back and propelling him towards the Gok Wan lookalike. 'This is your big moment. They've come to interview you and do a photo-shoot. Isn't that the best news ever? Now off you go to hair and make-up, and stop looking so fed up.'

The look on Toby's face said that he was *seriously* fed up. And this time Laney could see why.

18

'Just give it a try,' Laney said to Toby. 'I know how much this farm means to you and I promise I won't let any of this get out of hand.'

Toby looked doubtful, which was fair enough. Already the farmyard was a hive of activity with photographers setting up shots. The journalist who was going to interview Toby was champing at the bit and the stylists were eager to get going. *Out of hand* was probably exactly what it looked like to him.

'Within a couple of hours all of this will be gone again,' she promised. 'And it will seem like a dream.' She waved her hands around for dream-like effect.

'A bad one,' muttered Toby.

Laney sighed. Although she wished Martin had run this by her, she was secretly thrilled that *Country Life Style* had decided to run with the story. With the glamour of *Tatler*, the beautiful photography of *Country Living* and the class of *Country Life*, the magazine was the must-have read for anyone who aspired to rural ways and the so-called simple life. The classifieds section of the paper bulged with adverts for tweed, designer furniture and stunning properties where the well-heeled could bake their bread, do some cross-stitch and cook the organic produce they had sourced from the local farmers' market. In short, it was the perfect vehicle in which to market Toby and his products, and she couldn't have done better if she'd tried.

If Toby would only listen to her and stop looking like a wet weekend, then maybe, just maybe, they would get somewhere.

'Look,' she said gently, slipping her arm through his and steering him away from the hustle and bustle of the photo-shoot, 'please trust me on this. I know how you want to stay true to the values that your dad stood for.' Laney understood why Toby would want to do something for his father. She was worrying about her own dad too. 'I totally respect that, and I promise that, whatever happens, you'll be well and truly in the driving seat when it comes to growing the business.'

Toby ran his hand over his face. 'I just don't know, Laney. This really isn't me.'

'Walking next to Belle really wasn't me, either,' she reminded him. 'But I gave it a go because of you.'

A ghost of a smile played across his mouth. 'And it wasn't so bad, was it?'

She recalled the roughness of Belle's mouth on her palm; the sensation of Toby's hand enclosing hers.

'It wasn't bad at all. I gave it a chance, and you were right. So *please* do the same for me?' She wiggled her eyebrows in an effort to persuade him. 'Think of it as a chance for you to put your dad's philosophy out there and start to educate people about good food and good animal husbandry. When people buy your produce they're not only buying meat – they're buying into your ideologies.'

'Wow!' Toby stared at her. 'You really believe in this, don't you?'

Laney nodded. For some reason that she couldn't quite put her finger on, she really did. Somehow Middlehaye Farm had sneaked its way into her heart. With the right marketing, he'd have the success he deserved.

Toby exhaled slowly. 'Then maybe it's time I stopped being so stubborn and let you do your job? Trust is a two-way thing after all.'

'So you'll do it?' Laney hardly dared hope.

He smiled, that slow smile that lit up the depths of his eyes and softened the sharpness of his face. 'If you can bring yourself to walk near Belle, I think I can brave a few journalists.'

Laney stood on tiptoe and kissed his cheek. The stubble rasped against her lips and for a split-second she wanted nothing more than to rub her cheek against it. Then she mentally shook herself. What was going on? She needed to be professional here. Toby was her *client*.

And if he wasn't? asked a little voice in her head.

Leaving a very worried-looking Toby in the capable hands of the stylist and make-up crew, Laney wandered over to Martin.

'Thanks for doing this,' she said. 'I owe you one.'

'You owe me loads.' He laughed. 'Not at all, it's a pleasure. Besides, I've known the Woodwards for years and it's nice to be able to lend a hand. They had a really tough time when their dad died. I handled the estate, and I'm sure Toby won't mind me saying that it was touch and go whether or not they'd be able to keep it.'

'That bad?'

Martin nodded. 'Foot-and-mouth wiped out the dairy and beef herds in 2001,' Martin explained. 'Then there were death duties to pay, and all the testing to get organic status. Toby really had to think on his feet to get this place up and running. The rare breeds, the livery yard and the original produce lines were all part of that. He couldn't bear to lose this place because it's been in the family for generations.'

Laney glanced round. The farm was beautiful. Set amid the rolling Cotswolds hills and deeply wooded valleys, it was breathtakingly lovely. No wonder Toby was so protective of it. She hoped now more than ever that the publicity they achieved would really help him get the business off the ground. Whether or not he expanded it, or just reinvested the money so that Middlehaye Farm became a River Cottage-style enterprise, didn't really matter. She just wanted him to have proper recognition.

'Well, thanks all the same,' she told Martin. 'I don't know what I expected, but it certainly wasn't this.'

He grinned. 'I'm surprisingly cultured for a country boy, aren't I?'

She held up her hands. 'Guilty as charged. I was prejudiced.'

'We don't all chew grass, say "Oo-ah" and read *Farmers' Weekly*,' he teased. 'Anyway, talking of culture, I was wondering if you fancied coming to a gallery opening with me? On Friday? It's a friend of mine I've known for years. He's opening a small gallery in Chipley-under-Wychwood.'

At last! Martin was asking her on a proper date. And about bloody time, too. Catherine was starting to ask far too many awkward questions about why he hadn't made a move, and Laney was struggling for answers. It was a big relief that he had finally asked her out.

More than a relief, she told herself firmly, she was very pleased. Of course she was.

'I'd love to come,' she said warmly.

'Great.' Martin looked happy. 'Nick normally has champagne on tap. I'll drive, so—'

'Laney! Darling!' A loud shriek pierced the air. 'I can't believe it's you. And who is your yummy friend?' Like a heat-seeking missile, a glamorous blonde was making a beeline for them. Her gooseberry-green eyes out on stalks at the sight of Martin, she kissed Laney firmly on both cheeks, before stepping back and appraising her. 'Interesting coat, sweetie. Is it Dior?'

Laney laughed as she kissed her back. 'Primani, I believe, darling. But never mind my coat, Selina. What are you doing here?'

'I'm a stylist on *Country Life Style* now, darling. No wonder you've left London for the sticks.' She widened her eyes at Martin. 'The men here are seriously gorgeous.'

'Martin, this is Selina White. Selina, this is my friend and neighbour, Martin Rolls,' Laney said, deciding that introductions were needed. Martin was looking rather nervous as Selina took his hand and checked him out through narrowed eyes. And so he should. Selina, who was great fun and one of the best stylists in the business, was such a man-eater it was a wonder she hadn't sprinkled salt and pepper over Martin, tucked a napkin into her plunging neckline and sat down to gobble him up.

Martin dutifully air-kissed Selina. Her huge satellite-dish-style earrings nearly put his eye out as he dodged her glossy lips.

'Selina and I used to work together,' Laney explained swiftly. 'We did several big campaigns. The last one was an aftershave launch for Matthew Fox, wasn't it, Sel?'

'Hmm, Fox by name, fox by nature,' said Selina, practically licking her lips. 'We did the Peter Andre one too. Wasn't that dreadful Vanessa Evans with us then?'

Laney shuddered. 'Don't remind me. She truly was the boss from hell.'

'Nearly as bad as Pippa Menzies Johns?'

'Eugh! I wonder whatever happened to her? Darling, she was foul.'

It was so easy to slip back into London mode, thought Laney wistfully as she and Selina chatted away about mutual friends and colleagues. The *darlings* and *OMGs* slipped from her tongue with ease, and for a moment she was part of that scene again, rather than the girl in the ugly red coat who needed her roots doing and a good manicure.

'I can see you girls have got loads of catching up to do,' Martin interjected politely. 'And I've got loads to do back at the office. I'd better get on and walk back to the village. Lovely to meet you, Selina. Laney – I'll call you about that gallery opening. It's black tie, OK?'

She smiled. 'Fantastic. I'm really looking forward to it.'

Martin smiled at Selina, then turned and walked off down the path.

'Well, well – you are a dark horse,' said Selina as they both watched him go. In the sunlight Martin's blond hair glinted and he certainly cut a dashing figure in his dark Paul Smith suit. Laney felt a twinge of pride.

'How long has this been going on?' Selina asked.

'He's just a friend, Sel,' protested Laney. 'There's *nothing* going on.'

Selina raised her perfectly threaded eyebrows. 'A friend who's taking you to black-tie events? That's my kind of friend. If he throws in a good shag as well, then perfect.'

The thought of doing anything that personal with Martin was so alien and just, well, just plain odd that Laney laughed. She was pleased to be going on a date with Martin at long last, but she wasn't sure she was ready to be that intimate with him just yet. The fireworks she was hoping for seemed to have a very long fuse, but she was sure Martin would light it eventually.

She turned the conversation back to old friends and acquaintances from the London PR scene, and thankfully Selina was happy to be distracted by this. By the time Toby appeared for the photo-shoot they were so deep in reminiscences that it took a moment for Laney to register exactly who she was looking at.

'Jesus!' Selina grabbed hold of Laney's arm so hard that her Rouge Noir nails dug into her arm. 'Who is *he*?'

Laney's mouth fell open. She simply couldn't help it, because Toby looked absolutely gorgeous. Gone were the tatty clothes and tousled curls of earlier, and in their place was a Prussian-blue cashmere sweater and soft faded jeans that clung to the lean lines of his muscular legs, which tapered down into Dubarry boots. A checked Henri Lloyd coat was slung across his broad shoulders and a scarlet scarf wound around his strong throat. His hair fell in glossy waves to his shoulders and flopped over his forehead, its darkness even more marked in contrast to his pale skin and dark eyes. Somebody had given him a shave, and now the bones of his face stood out in the bright autumn sunshine, sharply enough to ski off.

'That's Toby Woodward,' she said slowly.

'The farmer? Great. The one time I decide to let my junior take over and that's what she gets.' Selina shook her head ruefully. 'He's gorgeous.' Glancing at Laney, she added with a wink, 'Darling, don't drool.'

Laney swallowed. If she was drooling, she really couldn't help it: Toby looked incredible. His tall, rangy body moved with a panther-like grace and, as he posed for the pictures, he looked so at ease and at home that she already knew every shot would be amazing. He'd always been attractive, but with this little bit of added gloss he was icecap-meltingly hot.

'I think I need to buy myself a place in the country,' Selina was saying thoughtfully as they watched Toby pose by the five-barred gate. 'I'm starting to see the attraction.'

The shoot took just over an hour, during which time Toby posed with pigs, horses and hay bales. Laney watched and was impressed by the good-natured way that he took direction. Selina – chihuahua tucked under her arm and busy adjusting a collar or scarf every now and then – was positively purring with pleasure. This was, she told Laney, front-cover material. And a look that she'd designed and coordinated appearing on the front page of *Country Life Style* was fantastic for her profile.

'I had a feeling he'd be good,' Laney admitted.

'Good?' Selina's neat eyebrows shot into her fringe. Peering at the Mac that Selina had balanced on the side of a water trough, Laney could see the photos they'd taken. Toby was a natural.

'Laney, you have a product there that will sell itself, if you place it in the right arena. He makes RPattz look plain.'

The camera loved him. Toby's wide-spaced eyes gazed warmly from the screen and his smile was so sweet that Laney felt her teeth rotting. These were stunning shots. With Toby as the face of Middlehaye Organics, the produce would fly off the shelves.

If he wasn't snapped up as a supermodel first.

'How did I do?' Toby asked nervously, looking over her shoulder once the final shots were completed.

She showed him the Mac, and when he saw the shot of himself holding a piglet he grimaced.

'God, I look like a total plonker!' was his verdict.

It was the injured piglet, Laney realized. She'd privately nicknamed it Applesauce, but didn't dare tell Toby. She'd almost died of mortification earlier, when she thought he'd overheard her talking to it.

'You look fantastic,' she told him sternly. 'Ditch the Barbour and wellies, I say.'

He stuck out his tongue at the next shot of him leading Belle, clad in white breeches, black boots and a green Musto sweater. 'Who seriously wears gear like that around a farm?

Those boots would be trashed in seconds. Christ! I hope none of the local farmers see this lot. They'll die laughing.'

'Afraid of losing your field-cred?' teased Laney.

Toby pushed the curls back from his face. 'Something like that.' He peered closer and shook his head. 'Green wellies and a tweed jacket? I look like some soft city person's idea of a farmer.'

'That's exactly the look I was after, so thank you,' said Selina crisply. Stepping forward, she held out her hand. 'I'm Selina, stylist-in-chief at *Country Life Style*.'

This should be interesting, Laney thought as the two shook hands. Selina was the most citified person she knew. With her Louboutins, her handbag dog and her designer clothes, she was never happier than when drinking Cristal in a smart bar or driving her convertible Audi through Piccadilly. Whereas Toby was a self-confessed loather of all things urban. It was like having two opposing magnets meet. Would they repel or attract?

'Well-behaved little dog,' Toby was saying, gently caressing the chihuahua's bony head with his large hand.

Selina visibly melted. 'He's called Louis, and he's my absolute baby. Mummy just adores you, doesn't she, sweetie?'

This was no understatement. Louis had his own wardrobe, dietician and even a baby stroller, to rest his little legs on the odd occasion when Selina took him to the park. Luckily, though, Toby didn't know any of this – Laney had a strong suspicion that he'd be highly scornful; after all, Jerry Springer slept in a barn and earned his keep by guarding the farm. Toby had charmed Selina by talking about dogs, so he could be at ease in any company. That was worth knowing. From a PR perspective, obviously.

'Listen,' Toby said to Laney, once Selina had reluctantly left to help pack away, 'I've been thinking, and I owe you an apology.'

Laney widened her eyes. 'Just the one?'

'OK, perhaps I owe you several,' he admitted, 'but how about, for starters, I say sorry that I wasn't more appreciative of everything you've done so far. I might be a simple farmer, but I'm not an idiot, and I am aware just how much good publicity is worth. What you've done for the farm – with Julian Matlock, and now with this shoot – is probably above and beyond anything I could have ever imagined. It knocked me for six, and I didn't handle it well.'

Laney could tell her face was turning red.

'If I've been a pig-headed pig-farmer, then I'm truly sorry. Would you let me buy you dinner on Friday to make amends?'

Laney was taken aback. Toby was asking her out?

'As a thank-you,' Toby said gently when she didn't respond. 'You can choose the venue, but I'm warning you, unless it's Julian Matlock's place, we'll be hard pushed to find Middlehaye sausages.'

The thought of going out for dinner with Toby was appealing, as was the idea of trying Matlock's lauded menu, but the thought of eating out with another woman's man made Laney feel distinctly uncomfortable.

'Won't Isla mind?'

He shrugged. 'I'm sure she'll be fine.'

Laney hesitated. There was the oddest fizzing sensation in the pit of her stomach, a bit as if she was a bottle of Coke that somebody had been shaking up. Did that mean she liked Toby more than she ought to?

Alarmed by this thought, Laney said quickly, 'That's really kind of you, but it's totally unnecessary. I'm only doing my job.'

'And you're doing it brilliantly too, in spite of being hampered by me. As you refuse to let me pay you, you can at least let me buy you dinner.'

For a moment she was torn, wanting more than anything to spend time alone with Toby, but knowing in her heart that it was a really bad idea. He was more addictive than any drug, and potentially equally dangerous. It would do her absolutely no favours. She was in danger of feeling more, whereas he saw her purely as a business contact.

Go! cried her heart.

Don't be ridiculous! yelled her head.

Then, luckily for her head, Laney remembered that she was already busy on Friday. Martin had asked her to accompany him to a gallery opening, hadn't he?

'I'm actually out on Friday night,' she said.

'Out?' Toby's dark eyes held hers. 'Is it important? Can't you reschedule?'

She swallowed, suddenly nervous. 'Not really. I'm on a date.'

His face didn't flicker a muscle, but the air suddenly crackled like static. 'Anyone I know?'

Laney nodded. 'I'm going to a gallery opening with Martin.'

'*Martin Rolls?*'

A strange expression momentarily flickered across Toby's

face, before it was abruptly shuttered again. *How weird*, thought Laney. For a second he'd looked almost startled. Charming! Was it really that incredible that a man wanted to take her out?

'Right, well – good. That's fine,' Toby said swiftly, digging his hands deep into his pockets and looking away. 'No problem, Laney. I hope you have a wonderful time. With Martin.'

She stared at him. 'I'm sure I will.'

'Excellent,' said Toby. For a second he looked as though he was about to say something else, but then the moment passed and he just sighed instead. 'Well, look, thanks once again for today. I do appreciate it. Now, if you'll excuse me, I think I'd better get changed before I wreck all these designer threads. Time for me to be a humble pig-farmer again.'

And just like that he was off, striding away with such speed that Laney almost toppled backwards. A hand reached out to steady her and, turning round, she saw Selina also staring after Toby. Raising her Chanel shades, the stylist watched him cross the yard and go into the house, slamming the door with such force that the windows rattled.

She whistled and fixed Laney with an inquisitive look. 'Well, well, well. I don't know what that was all about, but it seems you've really upset our resident hunky farmer. What on earth did you say to him?'

Laney was perplexed. Had Toby Woodward got upset because she turned him down? Did that mean . . . Laney had too much to think about, worrying about her father's health, to work out what this might mean. However, at the very idea that Toby might like her, something inside flickered into life.

19

Martin looked great, really handsome in his dinner jacket and bow-tie, thought Laney as they entered the art gallery. She felt proud to be on his arm and he was certainly attentive, finding her a drink, introducing her to people and filling her in on who was who. Everyone seemed to know him, and she was pretty soon overwhelmed with names and introductions. Her head swimming, she accepted a glass of Moët and listened in as Martin chatted away easily.

It was Friday evening and the small gallery in the pretty Cotswold town of Chipley-under-Wychwood was packed to the gills with well-dressed people sipping champagne and munching on canapés. The elegant crowd wouldn't have looked out of place at a smart London gathering, and Laney was very glad that she'd worn her trusty DVF black dress. Teamed with funky silver Mary Janes, matching chunky bracelet, and with her hair straightened to within an inch of its life, she felt that she wasn't letting Martin down.

The gallery consisted of three interlinked basements that stretched beneath a pretty Georgian-style town house. Recessed lights threw clear beams down from a white ceiling and bounced from the wooden floor with migraine-inducing intensity. It was as smart as anything Laney had seen in Knightsbridge, and she was impressed by the sympathetic way in which the traditional brickwork and features had been blended into such a light and modern space. The artwork was also an interesting mix of old and new. The walls were covered in paintings that ranged from traditional oils of Cotswold landscapes and pastoral scenes to primary-coloured splodges that could have been finger-painted by four-year-olds. The middle of the space was filled with sculptures: a monstrous papier-mâché-and-wire lobster loomed over the gathering, dwarfing the headless torso that appeared to be made from tin foil, and *almost* detracting from a huge steel phallus. All that was required was an unmade bed and a cow in formaldehyde and she could be in Tate Modern.

'You seem to know everyone here,' she remarked to Martin, once the local town councillor and his wife whom they'd been chatting to drifted away to admire the next painting. Laney was taken aback at just how busy it was. The mix of people here was certainly eclectic: from landed gentry, to pop stars, to writers – everyone seemed keen to look at and discuss art. There wasn't a jodhpur in sight. Again Laney suspected that she'd been guilty of stereotyping and generalizing. Of course people outside London enjoyed culture.

Martin shrugged. 'What can I say? I've lived around here for most of my life, give or take a few years at uni and doing my articles. I'm Cotswolds-born and bred. In fact,' he added with a wink, 'I probably have *Made in St Pontian* stamped on my backside.'

Encouraged, she laughed and slipped her arm through his. 'Is that an invitation?'

Unfortunately for Laney, this flirtatious remark went right over Martin's head. If indeed he even heard it, above the shrill tones of the small, plump man dressed in the most extraordinary purple turban and gold kaftan.

'Marty! Darling! I'm so glad you could make it to my little soirée. And you look absolutely divine in that suit. Ooh, I could simply gobble you up!'

'Of course I made it, Nick, I wouldn't miss it for the world. You've done a fantastic job,' Martin told him, raising his glass. 'I just know this is going to be a huge success.'

'Darling, I just hope success isn't the only *huge* thing I come across tonight,' he wheezed, digging Martin in the ribs with a pudgy elbow. 'What's the point of having all these *gorge* young men about otherwise?'

Goodness. It's like bumping into a Cotswolds version of Alan Carr, thought Laney with a smile as the man fussed over Martin, flicking lint from his suit and making wicked comments about some of the other guests. If she'd known who they all were, it would probably have been very amusing, but instead she felt rather lost. Sensitive as always to her feelings, Martin placed a hand on her shoulder.

'Sorry, I've been most remiss about making introductions, haven't I?' he said. 'Laney, this is my very good friend, Nick Scott. He owns this gallery and is also an extremely talented sculptor.'

The man turned the same hue as the papier-mâché lobster. Peering short-sightedly at Laney through trendy wire-framed glasses, he asked, 'And who's this delightful creature?'

'This is my friend Laney Barwell.'

Nick's face contorted into an exaggerated expression of surprise. '*Girl*friend?'

'Friend,' said Martin firmly. He and Nick exchanged a look that Laney couldn't quite fathom. Maybe Nick was really good friends with Martin's ex? That would explain why he was sizing her up so intently. Maybe he was making comparisons? Instinctively she sucked in her stomach. Then she relaxed again because, now she came to think of it, Martin had never mentioned an ex. Nick was probably just extremely short-sighted.

Laney held out her hand. Nick took it and kissed the knuckles flamboyantly. 'Charmed to meet you, my angel. Any friend of Marty's is a friend of mine. Have some more champagne.'

Laney held out her glass as a waiter passed by. Biscuity bubbles burst across her tongue and, sipping the drink, she tuned out Martin and Nick, who were discussing some conveyancing issue to do with the gallery, and glanced around the crowded room. She nearly spat out her drink when she locked eyes with Toby.

What on earth was he doing here? An art-gallery opening was the last place on earth she would have had expected to see him. He was almost unrecognizable in a suit and tie, and although he wasn't as dressed up as some of the guests, he looked a million times sexier. She smiled at him and Toby smiled back; a slow smile that lit his eyes and made her heart flip over slowly.

Uh-oh. This wasn't good. This wasn't good *at all*.

She was just about to make her way over when Isla

stepped into view, threading her arm through Toby's as she stood on tiptoe to whisper into his ear. Instantly Laney felt underdressed. The DVF might be an old faithful, but Isla had really pulled out the stops this evening and looked absolutely stunning in a green silk evening gown that clung to her curves and showed of her Cheddar Gorge cleavage to perfection. Her red hair was coiled into snaky ringlets that tumbled across her creamy shoulders and, when she tilted her head back to laugh at something Toby said, they brushed the small of her back.

Toby and Isla were definitely On. And no wonder! When she wasn't dressed in riding kit and being a total bitch, Isla was gorgeous.

'Laney!' Toby waved at her across the room. 'Come and have a look at this sculpture. Isla and I are having a bit of a disagreement.'

Excusing herself from Martin and Nick, she wove through the crowd and joined them in front of the giant phallus. Goodness, it was complete with veins and everything. Then she looked at the price tag and nearly choked for the second time that evening. Was the artist having a laugh? If so, he'd be laughing all the way to the bank, if somebody actually bought it.

'It's art,' Isla was saying, her hands on her hips as she faced the sculpture. She took a step back and narrowed her eyes thoughtfully. 'I see it as a post-feminist comment on the patriarchal nature of twenty-first-century society.'

Laney was sure it had great biological accuracy and scientific merit – but *art*? She wasn't convinced that she'd want it in her front room.

'It is?' Toby frowned, then shook his head. 'No. Sorry, Isla. It still looks like an enormous cock to me. I must be missing something.'

'You are. The entire point.' Isla rounded on him. 'Honestly, Toby, look *harder*, can't you? It's a comment on subjugation and phallocentric order.' She tossed her hair in frustration. 'Sometimes I wonder why I spend so much time with such a philistine.'

It was on the tip of Laney's tongue to say *Probably for his phallocentric qualities*, but Isla didn't look in the mood for a joke, so she kept quiet. Muttering about how hard it was to appreciate fine art when everyone else just didn't understand it, Isla stropped off to go and appreciate the giant lobster.

'That's probably a comment on the inner Piscean nature of a frustrated inland society,' remarked Toby idly. A champagne glass dangled between his fingers and his dark hair fell over one eye. Laney fought the urge to reach forward and brush it back.

'It could of course just be a giant lobster,' she said thoughtfully.

'What? Straightforward art? Whatever next!' Toby took a sip of his drink and returned his concentration to the sculpture in front of them. 'What do you think of this fine specimen then?'

'I think I'd run if it came near me.' Oh, crap! The words were out of her mouth before she could stop them. Then she caught Toby's eye and they both burst out laughing.

'I would say it was bollocks, but there aren't any,' he said.

'But what about Isla's feminist theory? Don't you think there's anything in that?'

'Nick sculpted it, and he's about as feminist as my prize boar,' joked Toby. 'So no, absolutely not. If anything, it's a total fantasy on his part, unless his latest boyfriend has hidden talents,' he added. 'More likely it's his idea of a joke, judging by the price tag.'

'I think I'll move on,' Laney said. There was only so long she could stand and chat about willies with Toby Woodward. Any longer and she'd be telling him that this was the closest she'd come to one for ages. It was time to go and look at some rural oils. That was far safer.

'Good idea,' agreed Toby. 'It's enough to make a guy feel inadequate.'

They moved on to look at the next exhibit, which just so happened to be a triptych of semi-naked nymphs. Nymphs, that was, with boobs that would put Jordan to shame, and hair that wouldn't have looked out of place on a WAG.

'Christ!' Toby covered his eyes with his hands. 'I've never seen so much naked flesh at one party. It's like being in the Playboy mansion.'

'Now it's my turn to feel inadequate,' sighed Laney.

'Hardly,' Toby said softly. 'You're beautiful.'

Laney's eyes widened. Was he taking the mickey? Glancing up at him from under her eyelashes, she saw that he was staring at her with that same intensity he applied to everything he did. His hand reached up and tenderly brushed a lock of hair behind her ear.

Laney swallowed. The place on her face where his fingers had brushed her cheek tingled.

'Toby, don't,' she said.

'Sorry. I didn't mean to offend you.' He looked away.

'You didn't, not at all,' Laney said, placing her hand on his arm. 'It's just that I don't think you should say things like that. Not when you're with Isla.'

'With Isla?' Toby frowned. 'I've told you I'm not with Isla.'

'But . . . everyone says you are – or that you will be.'

He sighed. 'In that case, *everyone* is wrong. We're just good friends, that's all.'

Laney glanced across the gallery. Isla was standing next to the headless torso talking to a balding man. Her laugh was loud and sounded forced, and there was much tossing of her hair. Every so often she glanced in Toby's direction just to gauge his reaction. There wasn't one. He was far too busy talking with her. Maybe she'd been wrong all along and they really weren't a couple. At this thought her heart lifted like a hot-air balloon.

'We were together for a while when we were very young,' Toby continued, leaning forward so that Laney could hear him above the murmur of voices and chink of glasses. The scent of his aftershave made her senses reel. 'Then for a bit in our early twenties. But we're much better as friends. She keeps Guinness at the farm, and I give her some instruction. Everyone in St Ponty might want us to get back together, but it's never been on the cards, and that's all there is to it.'

Somehow Laney doubted that Isla saw things quite this way, but she felt like turning cartwheels to learn that he was properly single. She hadn't realized just how much the thought of him being with Isla had troubled her.

'So then,' said Toby, with that crinkly smile.

'So then,' she echoed, smiling up at him in return.

The air between them was so charged with electricity that Laney thought it could have powered St Pontian for a month. Her every nerve-ending was tingling.

'There you are.' Martin joined them, shattering the atmosphere and making Laney step hastily away from Toby. Martin put his arm on hers and pulled Laney towards him. With a jolt she remembered that *he* was actually her date for the night.

'Sorry if I neglected you. Nick does like to go on.'

'Toby and I were discussing sculpture,' Laney said.

'Don't you mean the post-feminist comment on the phallocentric nature of society?' Toby corrected.

'Nick's prick?' Martin asked with a grin. 'It is rather a talking point.'

That's one way of putting it, Laney thought.

'How's everything going with the Bonfire-Night Bonanza preparations, Martin?' Toby asked.

Laney wondered if he was about to make a dig about the disaster with the Catherine wheel, but the look on his face was open and genuine.

'Good, thanks, seems all to be going to plan. Vince has the health-and-safety more than covered, so it's just up to me to make sure everyone has a good time.'

Toby laughed. 'If it's anything like last year, it'll be great.'

'It'll be better than great,' Martin said. Then his tone changed. 'Can I steal Laney away from you? I've got a few people I want to introduce her to. They might be useful PR contacts.'

Laney saw Toby looking at Martin's hand on her arm and felt uncomfortable all of a sudden. This was madness. Martin was her date. She was supposed to be thrilled that he was starting to get closer.

'Of course,' said Toby. 'I'll see you both later.'

She stepped away, but it was too late – Toby had slipped back into the crowd and minutes later Isla was glued to his side. He may not have thought they were together, but from the way she wound her arms around him and flicked her hair back from her flushed face, Laney could see that Isla thought very differently.

What was more, the black look that she threw Laney across the room said very clearly that she should keep her hands off.

20

'And then he did *what*?' Catherine asked incredulously. 'Am I hearing you right?'

Laney tucked the phone beneath her chin and lay back on her bed. While her best friend exclaimed and exhaled, she studied the ceiling. Goodness, but it could do with painting. Maybe that was something else she could help Nate with. The whole place could do with freshening up.

'He did nothing,' she said when Catherine finally paused for breath. 'Martin dropped me home after the gallery opening, kissed me on the cheek and then drove away.'

'He didn't even ask you if he could come in for a *coffee*?'

Laney laughed. 'No. I think we can safely say that, when it comes to me, *coffee* is the furthest thing from Martin's mind.'

'Then he's an idiot,' said Catherine loyally.

'No, he really isn't, Cat. Martin's a really nice guy, and I think you'd like him if you ever met. I just need to face the fact that, to coin a phrase, "He's just not that into me".'

'More importantly, are you that into him?' asked Catherine. 'Were you disappointed?'

Laney paused. Trust her friend to ask the questions she hadn't been brave enough to ask herself. She'd been so busy trying to figure out what Martin was thinking and looking for that she'd not thought too hard about her own feelings.

Last night, after they'd driven the six miles back to the village, Laney and Martin had chatted away in their usual friendly way, discussing everything from Nick's interesting taste in sculpture to how amazing Isla looked. Jazz played softly on the stereo, the sky was sprinkled with stars as cold and bright as diamonds and, when Martin pulled up by the river, she'd thought that maybe this would be the moment he chose to kiss her. It was classic date etiquette after all. However, Martin had seemed oblivious to all this and had just pecked her on the cheek and thanked her for a lovely evening. This was a clearly a hint, Laney had thought to herself as she climbed out of the car. As the tail lights of Martin's Merc faded into the darkness she'd been mystified, a little miffed that he was so obviously immune to her charms. But *disappointed*?

Laney searched her heart and knew the answer was a resounding *no*. She liked Martin a great deal and thoroughly enjoyed his company, but the spark really wasn't there. It never had been.

She exhaled slowly. 'No, I guess not. He's lovely, but you know those fireworks I always go on about?'

Although she couldn't see her, Laney knew that Catherine was rolling her eyes.

'Those bloody fireworks,' her friend muttered.

'They're important to me. How can you possibly have a relationship if the chemistry isn't there?' protested Laney.

'And they weren't there with this Martin character, were they?'

'Not even a squib, let alone a damp one,' Laney admitted. 'What's wrong with me, Cat? Maybe I should have stuck with Giles after all?'

'Absolutely not. Giles wasn't right for you, and neither is this Martin character. And anyway, Ms Barwell, you aren't being one hundred per cent honest with me, are you? I suspect there have been plenty of fireworks exploding for you. Just not with the people that you've told me about. Am I right?'

Laney closed her eyes and recounted the first time she saw Toby: crossing the field in front of the sports pavilion, fireworks cascading down around him. Just the memory made her stomach do an impression of a pancake on Shrove Tuesday.

'I think you've got feelings for this Toby character, haven't you?' Catherine pressed on.

Laney said nothing, but just the mention of his name was enough to make her pulse skitter. It was a sensation that Giles, for all his careful planning and diligence, had never once made her feel.

'Haven't you?'

Laney gulped. She couldn't deny it any more. Toby Woodward was all she could think about. Last night, once Martin had driven away and she'd gone to bed, Laney had lain awake for hours reliving their conversations and trying her hardest not to think about how it might have felt to have *his* hand on her arm.

'Yes,' she whispered, and it was such a relief to finally admit it that she could have wept.

'I knew it.' Catherine's whoop of excitement down the phone nearly deafened her. 'God, I'm good! I'm not a match-maker for nothing. So what are you waiting for? Go for it, girlfriend. The sexy farmer wants a wife!'

'Calm down. He might not even be interested,' protested Laney.

'You won't know until you try, will you? Stop messing around and just go for it and shag his brains out,' was Catherine's advice.

'I hope that isn't the kind of advice you give your clients.'

'Maybe it should be? Then they wouldn't waste so much time. Seriously though, babe,' at this point Catherine's voice took on a serious tone. 'Time isn't elastic. Don't spend another second thinking about someone you're not really interested in and who clearly isn't that bothered about you.'

'Don't hold back, will you?' said Laney.

'In my experience there's really no point messing around with these things. You either want to be with someone or you don't, and if you really wanted to be with this Martin, then you would be by now. It's so flipping obvious that you like this Toby character.'

Laney was surprised to hear this. She thought she'd been pretty measured in her descriptions of him and was pretty sure she'd only mentioned him once or twice.

'After all,' continued Catherine, 'you never stop talking about him.'

Oh! Maybe not then.

'He is rather yum,' Laney confessed, thinking back to the photo-shoot.

'And so are you. Laney Barwell, stop being such a chicken

and tell him how you feel. Faint heart never won fair farmer. Why don't you say something at the big bonfire-party thing?'

Laney found herself promising her friend that she would get her act in gear and speak to Toby at the bonanza.

'You may as well have some metaphorical fireworks to go with the literal ones,' were Catherine's parting words.

Wouldn't that be amazing, Laney thought with a delicious shiver of anticipation. It was high time she had some sparklers in her love life.

But apart from having to figure out what to say to Toby, she had to let Martin down. Although she still wasn't quite sure whether he fancied her, he had been a good friend since she had arrived in the village and Laney would hate to hurt his feelings. He had never shown her any indication that he felt anything towards her other than friendship, but that didn't necessarily mean that he wasn't going to be upset. For all she knew, Martin might be really shy and just have been building up the courage slowly.

Very slowly.

In any case, no matter what Martin's feelings might be, Laney knew she couldn't hide from hers any more. She liked him very much as a friend, but no matter what she did there would never be any fireworks. Not even so much as the fizz of a struck match. When she thought of Toby Woodward, it was a very different matter. The whole of China couldn't manufacture enough.

'Good idea of yours to meet up for food,' Martin said later that evening when he joined Laney at the bar. 'Saturday nights are for being sociable, aren't they? Not staying in watching *Britain's Got Talent*.'

As Laney paid a sulky-faced Alyssa for their drinks she couldn't help thinking that watching wannabes prance around with performing pets was probably a more cheerful prospect than sounding the death-knell on her fledgling relationship with Martin. As usual he was very affable, and while they sat down and waited for their food they chatted away easily.

'Besides,' he said, taking a sip of his pint, 'with the Bonfire-Night Bonanza coming up, I won't have time for socializing any more. The head of the committee is a very busy man.'

Laney laughed at his fake pomposity. There was absolutely no tension or sexual vibe at all, she realized. At no time did his thigh rest against her own or his fingers brush against hers, which took some doing, because the pub was packed and they were squashed next to one another on a banquette and enjoying a tapas-style sharing platter. She might not be in Derren Brown's league when it came to reading minds, but Laney was pretty certain Martin would be fine.

But even though she was convinced that his feelings for her were nothing more than friendly, it still took several glasses of wine before she felt brave enough to broach the subject.

'It's great that we're such good friends, isn't it?' she said cheerfully.

Martin, who was busy texting on his iPhone, looked up briefly and gave her a warm smile. 'Absolutely. Without you, I'd be stuck indoors with a pile of briefs to wade through and half an eye on some tragic stage act, for entertainment.'

Laney set her glass down and took a deep breath. It was time to lay it on the line. 'I'm really glad we're friends, Martin. I'd hate for that to change.'

'Of course it won't change. We get on very well.' He was still engrossed with his phone. *Who is he texting with such urgency?* wondered Laney. *Is it another woman?* If so, that would be great.

'We do, don't we? Which is why I think we should just stay as friends. Nothing more.'

There. She'd said it. Laney steeled herself for a response.

'Absolutely. Of course we should be friends.' Martin looked up from his iPhone with a puzzled expression. 'I don't know what you're so worried about, Laney. We've never had a cross word, so I can't think why we'd fall out. Unlike Vince, with whom, if he continues to email me any more of these sodding health-and-safety documents, I will undoubtedly fall out.'

Oh no! Martin was getting totally the wrong end of the stick. How could she make it really clear? Jump onto the pub table, do a tap dance and start singing 'I don't fancy you' at the top of her voice?

'What I mean to say is that I don't think I'm ready for a relationship yet,' Laney said. 'With anyone.'

'That's fair enough,' said Martin, one eye still on his mobile. When the text alert chimed, he snatched it up as though his life depended on it. 'About time she got back to me.'

So there was a woman! Laney felt relieved. Much as she didn't want to be with Martin, there was a small part of her that would have felt hurt and rather insulted to have been rejected for no reason.

'Anyone nice?' she asked.

'Depends on your definition of nice, I guess, but yes, I think so.' Martin scanned the text and then beamed at her. 'I've *finally* managed to find us a celebrity to light the St Pontian bonfire.'

Now that was good news. Laney loved celeb gossip and was a fully subscribed member to *Grazia*, *Heat* and all the glossies.

'I don't know if you follow rugby at all,' Martin continued, 'but Tana Heretini has recently signed to Bath on a season's transfer from the All Blacks.'

Laney wasn't a rugby fan, but she'd heard of Tana Heretini and the All Blacks. This guy was both local and international – perfect for this kind of event.

'That was his agent's assistant, confirming that he's more than happy to do the gig.'

'Fantastic news!' Laney was genuinely delighted for Martin. For one thing, it was a relief for him. She knew that he had tried so hard to find a celeb, but all the TOWIEs and A-listers he'd contacted had been less than keen. Tana Heretini, with his shaved head, rippling muscles and strong limbs inked with mysterious tribal tattoos, was a true find. Since his arrival in the UK he'd done the chat-show circuits, several magazine spreads and had been papped with an entire galaxy of soap stars. Although she didn't follow rugby, Laney would have to live on Mars not to know who Tana Heretini was.

'It is, isn't it? His being there will be a huge draw. Maybe this will be a record year?' Martin couldn't have looked happier, his grin spread from ear to ear and his eyes sparkled.

She chinked her wine glass against his. 'This is going to be the best Bonfire-Night Bonanza ever.'

'I think we need more than wine to celebrate this. Hang on while I fetch some bubbly,' said Martin. Leaping up from the seat he strode to the bar, iPhone still in hand as he texted like crazy.

He had taken her news well, she reflected with relief. Maybe he'd never seen her in a romantic light after all? Had she been reading his signals all wrong?

Laney gulped and drained her wine glass. She hoped she wasn't as bad a judge of body language as all that. If bonfire night was going to be the night when she told Toby Woodward how she felt, then she'd better not get confused then too. No. That couldn't be the case.

Being rejected by Toby was a scenario Laney simply couldn't bear to contemplate.

21

The evening of November the fifth couldn't have been more perfect if Martin had managed to arrange the weather, as well as everything else. The daytime had been one of those perfect crisp late-autumn ones. The sky was a bright Wedgwood-blue, the mud frozen underfoot, and the trees and hedgerows draped with lacy spiders' webs.

All day long the villagers of St Pontian had worked to build the bonfire, and by the time the light started to seep from the sky and the sun was little more than a scarlet finger-nail above the plough, a huge pile of wood and scrapped furniture dominated the village green. Around the edge of the green were the striped awnings of stalls erected for the evening. One would sell hot spiced cider, Maxine had told Laney earlier, another would be a barbecue and the third would sell old-fashioned cakes and sweets. The display itself was set up in a field across from the church; safety-first Vince had put them far enough away to ensure that no rogue rock-ets and bangers would endanger the crowd, but, because the land rose in a series of gentle folds, just the right distance to afford the perfect view.

The clocks had gone back only a week before, and now inky darkness stole over the rooftops by five o'clock. The horses in Toby's paddocks huddled in their rugs and stood in muddy gateways, and it really felt as though winter was arriving. Although it was barely a week into the new season, already Laney's inner dormouse had kicked in and for the last few days she'd found that she was longing to curl up and hibernate. It was hardly life in the fast lane. She found herself drawing the curtains by four, switching on the lamps in the B&B and joining Janet to cook up pots and pots of stew laden with stodgy dumplings and buttery mashed potatoes. After supper it was time to curl up in front of the wood burner and snooze through an evening of television, before staggering off to bed. It felt as though somebody had pulled her plug out, and she wondered how she ever coped with all the socializing she'd had to do as a PR girl. Life in the country had a rhythm all of its own, that was for sure.

It said a lot about the Bonfire-Night Bonanza that the excitement in the village had the power to entice Laney from the snug house, wrap up warmly in her thickest coat and take herself down to the green. Janet had spent all afternoon baking jacket potatoes, cooking sticky honey-and-mustard sausages and boiling up a big vat of tomato soup. All this was to be carried across to the green by Martin and placed in a makeshift tented kitchen, where she would dish it up after the display. Laney's mouth was watering just at the thought. Maybe she'd start her diet *after* November the fifth?

'Everyone will be ravenous,' Janet had explained when Laney expressed surprise at the vast quantities of food being prepared. 'Believe me, we make good money from selling grub. Because we all usually spend the day helping to build the bonfire, people will have an enormous appetite. You'll see. Everyone gets involved in the Bonfire-Night Bonanza. They come from miles around.'

Janet hadn't been mistaken. As Laney had helped to put up stalls and carry equipment from her neighbour's house to the green she'd bumped into shopkeepers, builders and village folk bustling round with wood and junk, while their children made guys, excitedly competing to make theirs the best, so that it could take pride of place right on the top of the bonfire. Usually the head of the Bonfire-Night Bonanza committee had to judge – no easy task, Martin pointed out. Forget *Strictly* and *The X Factor.* The Best Guy competition was really serious stuff. Proud mums and dads got most upset if they felt their child hadn't been given a fair chance. Luckily for Martin, this job would fall to Tana Heretini today, which meant, he said with a look of relief, that he wouldn't be a hate-figure in the village for the next six months.

The celebrity rugby hero was due to light the fireworks at seven, but the village bonfire began at half-six and Laney was planning to be there for the very start. Up in her bedroom vantage point, where she was dithering over quite what to wear, she could see that although it was only a quarter to six a steady stream of people was already flowing into the village. Committee members in fluorescent tabards stood outside the pub and around the green, rattling collecting buckets and directing people to the best places to watch. The buzz of excitement was palpable, and Laney found herself feeling excited too. As she pinned her curls up onto the top of her head with a glittering clip, she reflected that she'd never felt this jittery about attending film premieres and smart parties.

But then Toby Woodward hadn't been attending any of those, had he?

I feel like a fourteen-year-old, thought Laney in despair. Her bed was piled high with the contents of her wardrobe. Although the mound of clothes could probably have been used by NASA to get man to Mars, she couldn't find anything to wear. Not one thing. She twirled in front of her mirror and frowned at the reflection peering back at her. The little black dress teamed with suede knee-boots and chunky silver jewellery might have seemed a great idea when she was planning an outfit to impress Toby, but in reality she looked ridiculously overdressed. And wait a minute. Turning sideways, she scrutinized her profile critically. Was that a tummy bulge? She *knew* she'd been eating far too much of Janet's wonderful food.

With a howl of despair she tore the dress off and ripped out her hairslide. So much for planning a knock-him-dead outfit to test Toby's apparent interest. She'd been through just about every dress and boots combo that she owned, and each outfit looked more out of place than the last. What might have done the job in a Shoreditch bar or a Kensington restaurant would just look plain ridiculous here. At this rate she'd be going out in her pyjamas.

OK, breathe, Laney, breathe. The answer has to be staring you in the face.

Opening her wardrobe again, just in case the *sexy-outfit* fairy had made a delivery in the past sixty seconds, she regarded the contents with a sinking heart. Short skirts, strappy shoes and scoop-necked tops were more likely to get her a night in casualty with hypothermia than be the means of securing a night of passion. Defeated, she hurled herself backwards onto the clothing mountain. Maybe the key was not to make any effort at all, but to just go as herself – or the St Pontian version of herself. If Toby Woodward liked her, then he would like her regardless of what she was wearing.

Cheered by this thought, Laney spent a further ten minutes rehanging her clothes, before digging out her favourite vintage Levi's and teaming them with a long-sleeved white T-shirt with a heart motif and her chunky Cat boots. With this ensemble over her best peach-silk La Perla set, she felt far more relaxed and comfortable. A Nivea face wipe removed her carefully applied make-up and in its place went a slick of lip gloss and some mascara swept over her top lashes. There was no need for blusher, because her cheeks were already pink and her eyes brighter than anything Optrex could invent. As she brushed out her curls and left them to tumble loose around her shoulders, Laney realized that she hadn't felt this wired since . . . since – well, *ever* actually. None of her London dates, so carefully selected by Catherine, had ever managed to make her feel so giddy with longing and so totally, utterly and terrifyingly alive.

Not that Toby was a date, she reminded herself sternly as she spritzed Angel behind her ears and onto her wrists. There was nothing to say that he would be at all interested in her. She had nothing concrete to judge this by, no solid evidence whatsoever – just the strongest and most inexplicable gut feeling that they were meant to be together. It had no logic.

They were from opposite worlds, infuriated one another and probably had absolutely nothing in common, but when she thought about him all of these things were immaterial; she wanted nothing more than to be close to him.

Laney just hoped that he felt the same way. All the signals seemed to be there. He'd invited her out, had held her hand so tenderly when she was afraid of Belle and had gone out of his way to make it clear nothing was happening between him and Isla. She was sure that he felt the same way.

'Nothing ventured, nothing gained,' she said to her reflection, who regarded her doubtfully.

And with this pep-talk in mind she grabbed her leather jacket and red cashmere scarf and hurried downstairs. All this messing about with her clothes had taken far too long and it was already six-twenty.

Laney had agonized about whether to let her dad go too. He'd pleaded with her like a grounded teenager and she'd finally relented, made him promise to wrap up warmly and to let her know if he felt ill at any time. Nate and Janet had then scurried from the house, in case she changed her mind.

Finally ready, Laney locked the B&B, wound her scarf around her neck and headed towards the green. She could almost taste the sausages, the aroma of which was drifting in the air, and the small car park was already jam-packed and the buzz of excitement was palpable. All around was chatter and laughter. The people who owned houses facing the green were having their own parties in their gardens with friends and family, settling onto their terraces to watch the show, glasses of mulled wine in hand. Some children were waving sparklers around and drawing their names in light so bright that it almost hurt her eyes to look, while others were busy putting the finishing touches to their guys.

'Join us!' called Maxine when Laney passed her cottage. 'We've got Pimm's Winter. You know you want some.'

Laney laughed. 'More than you know. Maybe in a bit?'

'Don't be too long – some of the book-club girls said they'd pop by, and you know how they like a drink,' warned her friend.

Promising to stop by after the display, Laney continued on her way, marvelling at just what a good job Martin and his committee had done. The stalls were doing a roaring trade and everywhere she looked villagers were munching Janet's sausages and drinking soup or having a go at the tombola. There might not be the designer fashion and fancy canapés of the London gatherings she was used to, but the atmosphere and goodwill here beat those hands-down.

It didn't take Laney long to spot Toby. He was crouching down by the bonfire and attempting to light it with a spluttering Zippo. Every now and then a spark or two would fantail up into the darkness before fading away. Toby, dark head bent over his labours, was cursing.

'Man make fire?' Laney teased.

He looked up and smiled. 'Man make hash of it,' he said.

And suddenly every Mills & Boon cliché Laney had ever read came out to play. Weak legs, watery knees, racing heart – you name it, she had it.

She had it *bad*.

Toby flicked the lighter again and this time there was nothing at all. Pulling a rueful face, he said, 'Maybe I should have been a smoker? At least then I'd have a decent lighter. This thing of Alyssa's is hopeless.'

'How come you got landed with this job? I didn't think you were on the Bonfire-Night Bonanza committee?' Phew, at least her voicebox was still working, she thought as she squatted down beside him.

'I haven't a clue. Martin was supposed to be in charge of the pyrotechnics, but he's busy entertaining the celebrity guest.' Toby flicked the lighter again. 'Damn it!' He checked his watch. 'It's quarter of an hour behind schedule already.'

'Here, let me have a go.' Gently she prised the lighter out of his hands and shook it, before coaxing out a blue flame. Seconds later the bonfire was starting to crackle, and fire was licking a path through the twigs and dry wood.

'A woman of hidden talents,' Toby remarked admiringly as the flames took hold and started to whoosh through the pile of timber. The winning guy, perched aloft on a rickety old chair, started to smoulder.

'A woman of a misspent youth, more like.' Laney passed the lighter back. 'My Zippo is the only thing I missed when I quit.'

They stood side by side and watched as the fire leapt higher and higher. But she was more aware of the man standing next to her than of the rising flames in front of her. As the guy caught alight and the watching crowd cheered, she thought that she knew exactly how the guy felt: if Toby so much as brushed his arm against hers she was certain she'd spontaneously combust. Just the thought of being any closer to him made goosebumps ripple all over her. In fact, just thinking about how it might feel to have his skin against hers made even her goosebumps get goosebumps.

'You're cold. Come here.' Toby, noticing her shiver, put his arm around Laney and pulled her close. He was so tall that her head didn't reach past his shoulder, but instead she found she nestled perfectly in the crook of his arm, with her head resting against his heart. She gulped. He was so warm and strong and smelt delicious. She didn't think she'd ever felt so safe and so at home in her entire life.

Everything about Toby Woodward felt right.

'Better?' he asked, his lips pressed against her temple.

Laney really couldn't speak because her voice had curled up and died with joy. Better? That was an understatement.

Tuning out the tannoy's announcement that Tana Heretini was about to light the fuse and begin the display, she could think about nothing more than how wonderful it felt to be held by Toby. When she felt his lips stray from her cheek to the corner of her mouth, it was the most natural thing in the world to turn her head and kiss him.

When it happened, the magic of it made her almost dizzy with joy. She felt his lips on hers and the strength of his arms as they closed around her. His mouth tasted of the cold, and of the night and of bonfire smoke, and it was the most delicious sensation imaginable. She never wanted him to let her go.

Above them the frosty night sky was suddenly filled with the brightest of fireworks. Golden stars, peacock-blues and silver sparkles lit the velvet-smooth night while the sparks from the bonfire fantailed into the dark. Whizzing noises, explosions and loud bangs filled the air. As Laney kissed

Toby back, winding her fingers into those thick curls and loving the feeling of his mouth on hers, she knew for a total certainty that at long, long last she had found the man who made fireworks explode in her heart and soul.

It was wonderful. Magical. Incredible.

And she never wanted this kiss to end.

22

'Hey!'

A hand grabbed Laney's shoulder and abruptly she was yanked away from Toby's lips.

'What do you think you're doing? Get off my brother.'

For a moment Laney was dazed, for being transported so swiftly from the heaven of being in Toby's arms to the reality of being on the village green was something of a shock, and her head seemed to spin. If it hadn't been for Toby steadying her, she would have crumpled onto the frozen grass. Alyssa, breathing heavily and eyes glittering like wet coal, was glowering at Laney. With her hands on her hips and her chin tilted defiantly, she didn't seem to care that she'd so rudely interrupted a tender moment.

'Alyssa? What's going on?' Toby glowered at his sister.

'Nothing,' hissed Alyssa. 'Just stopping you making a big mistake.' There was such loathing in her voice that Laney shrank back. This book-group grudge was getting seriously out of hand.

'I think I'm big enough and ugly enough to make up my own mind, thanks,' Toby said coldly.

Alyssa just curled her lip scornfully. 'That's because you don't have a clue about her.'

'Hey!' said Laney, leaping to her own defence.

However, Alyssa wasn't finished. 'I saw you kissing Vince in the sports pavilion the other evening.'

Laney felt the blood freeze in her veins.

'Bored with him now, are you? Thinking that it might be fun to have a crack at my brother?'

Now Laney's head really started to spin.

'That's shocked you, hasn't it?' sneered Alyssa. 'Did you think you could keep it a secret? Maybe next time you and Vince want to meet somewhere, perhaps you should lock the door, or maybe book a hotel?'

'I—' started Laney, but Alyssa wasn't going to give her the chance to finish.

'The sports pavilion is used by everybody.' She stared at Laney smugly. 'Including the craft group.'

'Is this true?' Toby asked, his dark eyes pinning hers.

Laney's heart thudded with dread. She opened her mouth to try and explain, to tell him what had really happened, but Alyssa was too quick for her.

'Of course it's true! I saw them. They were so engrossed that they didn't even notice me. I'd left my phone behind after craft group, and there they were. It was disgusting. He's a married man.'

Laney's stomach was in freefall. 'It wasn't like that,' she whispered.

Toby's mouth set in a harsh line. His hand on her wrist tightened its grip to an iron bite.

'Is it true?' he repeated, his eyes boring into hers.

Laney could hardly breathe because the tide of nauseated horror sweeping through her was so overwhelming. Silence stood between her and Toby like a third person. For a second she struggled to answer, as though caught in the coils of a bad dream.

'No,' she said, when she finally found her tongue.

'Are you sure about that?' Toby demanded. 'Your face looks pretty damned guilty.'

'No! I mean, yes. I mean . . .' she said desperately, aware that she was *sounding* pretty damned guilty. 'He kissed me and—'

'What?'

A wail of despair cut through the charged atmosphere. *Maxine.*

To her horror, Laney realized that Maxine and Vince had been standing by them to watch the fireworks. She'd been so caught up in the heady joy of kissing Toby that she simply hadn't noticed. To be honest, the world could have ended and she wouldn't have been any the wiser – that was how thrilling and just how all-consuming his kiss had been.

'Vince, tell me that never happened,' Maxine gasped, her eyes wide with disbelief.

Vince said nothing. His mouth just swung open on its hinges.

Maxine looked from her husband to Laney and shook her head. 'You were supposed to be my friend,' she said, her voice breaking. 'How could you?'

With a sob, Maxine spun around on her pink-wellied heel and plunged into the crowd of people still oohing and aahing over the fireworks display.

'Maxine! Wait!' Laney cried despairingly, but it was too late: her distraught friend had vanished into the press of bodies. For a split-second Vince dithered, frozen with horrified indecision, before following in her wake and calling for Maxine to wait.

Toby dropped her wrist and pulled away. 'It looks clear enough to me,' he said coldly.

'It isn't. It didn't happen like that,' stammered Laney. She met his intense stare. Saw the thick black lashes framing his dark eyes, the strong profile, the razor-sharp cheekbones and that set, ruthless mouth. Icy tears froze on her cheeks before they could even fall, because his look of disappointment broke her heart.

'I didn't kiss Vince,' she whispered brokenly. 'He kissed *me*.'

Toby wasn't listening. Instead he gave her a dark, twisted smile and shook his head wryly.

'Is this some kind of sick challenge? Come down to the country and see how many local boys' hearts you can break? First Martin, then Vince and now me? You must be very proud of the scalps you've collected. Maxine's distraught, thanks to you and your games.'

This was a nightmare. 'No, no!' Laney tried desperately to make him understand. 'It didn't happen the way you think it did. And nothing has ever happened with Martin, I promise. We're just friends.'

Alyssa snorted rudely. 'Yeah, right.'

Toby shook his head. As he stared down at her, she met the full force of his gaze and saw such loathing there that she recoiled. 'You're just the same as all the rest, aren't you?

I can't believe a word you say. Don't bother to lie any more. I don't want to hear it.'

Suddenly Laney had had enough of all this. She was being judged and sentenced without even being listened to. Everyone was jumping to conclusions – the wrong conclusions – and it was horribly unfair. Toby had turned his back on her now and was looking at the podium instead, making it blatantly clear that their conversation was over. Well, it wasn't. How could he go from kissing her as though she was the most precious thing in the universe to loathing her, in just moments? He couldn't turn his feelings off that quickly. All that was in her had responded to him, and from the moment that his lips had touched hers Laney had known beyond all doubt that Toby Woodward felt the same way. It denied all logic. It made no sense. Yet there was no avoiding it: they had a connection that dissolved the memories of anything else that had come before.

'Why won't you listen to me?' she cried, grabbing his sleeve and trying desperately to pull him round to face her. 'Vince was drunk and made a pass at me. I swear to God that nothing more has ever happened.'

However, Toby's attention couldn't have been further away from Laney, and her frantic explanations seemed to slide from his hearing like oil from water. Shaking her off distractedly, he stepped away, apparently transfixed by the podium where Tana Heretini was addressing the cheering crowd and telling them how impressed he was with the display. Were they ready for the second part? The crowd cheered and called out a resounding *yes!* A honey-blonde stood at the sporting star's side, prompting him every now and again, and patting him encouragingly on his huge muscled arm.

Alyssa followed her brother's gaze and her mouth opened. 'Anna Marsh?' she breathed. 'What's that bitch doing here?'

A muscle started to leap in Toby's taut cheek and, if anything, his mouth set in an even grimmer expression.

'I have no idea,' he said flatly.

Anna? Laney glanced across at the woman. Slim and perfectly groomed in tight designer jeans, smart boots and a silver jacket that hugged her slender frame, she looked every inch the chic city girl. No old jeans and boots for her, for she was dressed in full urban rural style. As though sensing their scrutiny, the woman looked up and, when her gaze alighted on Toby, her lips curled into a delighted smile. Raising her hand, she waved at him and, looking like a man in a dream, Toby raised his hand in return. Then it dropped to his side. There was a tense set to his mouth and, when he turned to Laney, his eyes were deliberately blank.

'It's been an interesting evening,' he said, and his tone was hard. 'If you would excuse me, there's somebody I need to speak to.'

He turned his back on her and strode away in the direction of the podium. Moments later the crowd had swallowed him up. Laney's blood ran cold. Anna? Wasn't she the fiancée who'd broken Toby's heart? Distraught, and convinced that everyone was looking at her and whispering, she plunged her hands into her pockets and hung her head. How on earth was she going to put this hideous mess straight? Somehow she had to make Maxine realize that nothing had ever happened between her and Vince, but that would be easier said than done, when all the evidence pointed to the contrary. And as for Toby, how could she ever explain that she wasn't just toying with his emotions, when even she could see just how bad it looked?

In her pocket was her mobile, and Laney curled her hand around it. Mobiles really were comfort blankets for adults. Just one press of the speed-dial button and she could be talking to Catherine, sobbing her heart out and getting sympathy and advice. For a second Laney was about to make the call, before she remembered that Catherine had taken the children to Battersea Park to enjoy a fireworks display. It wasn't fair to disrupt her best friend's family time just because she was having a crisis. Besides, deep down something was telling her this was one mess that only she could sort out.

With impeccable timing, the heavens decided that right now would be a great time to open. Pathetic fallacy swung into action, for just as Laney was toying with the idea of calling Maxine there was an enormous clap of thunder and torrential rain fell from the sky. People shrieked and began to scatter like ball bearings as they ran for cover. On the podium Tana stood for a moment in confusion, before Martin jumped up and ushered him to shelter. No sign of the mysterious Anna, however, and as Laney made her way to join Martin underneath Janet's stand she was tortured by images of Toby gallantly sheltering his ex beneath his Barbour. Maybe he'd even take her home to dry off? Run her a bath, hand her a towel and then . . .

Oh no! Laney almost howled aloud at this idea. She couldn't think this way; it would drive her mad. She'd have to do one thing at a time, preferably before she was driven out of the village for being a husband-stealing harpy or maybe burnt at the stake. Rumours had obviously spread even quicker than a trend on Twitter, and by the time Laney joined Martin she'd had so many cold looks that she practically felt frost-bitten.

'This is a disaster,' Martin said when she joined him. Rain hammered like gunfire on the canvas roof and they huddled together sadly watching the green clear.

'What are you going to do?' Laney asked. There didn't seem to be much point in carrying on with the second half of the display now. Everyone was inside drying off and even the bonfire, which had been a raging ball of flame only moments before, was struggling to stay alight. It was all rather metaphorical.

He shrugged. 'Pack away, I guess. We'll have to cancel the rest of the display. I suppose I'd better resign myself to getting drenched collecting back whatever fireworks I can.'

'I'll help.'

Martin looked surprised. 'Really? Aren't you going to Maxine's for the fireworks supper?'

Laney had been invited and, until the events of earlier, had been fully intending to join in what was rumoured to be one of the best parties of the year. Hmm, maybe not. Something told her that Maxine and Vince wouldn't be welcoming her with open arms now, even if they were still in the mood for a party after Alyssa's revelations.

'No, I'll give you a hand,' she said.

Call it penance, call it distraction, call it anything you like, thought Laney as they headed out to collect the fireworks; at least out in the pouring rain she could be guaranteed not to bump into any other villagers. She didn't think she could bear any more evil looks and whispers. Getting soaked to her knickers and contracting pneumonia was a small price to pay for some space while she figured out how to put this mess right.

She just hoped that she would manage to think of a way.

23

It was the morning of November the sixth and Laney looked over the village green for what had to be the hundredth time, but there was absolutely no sign of Toby. Lots of people had come to help with the tidy-up, but none of them were talking to her. While she stuffed rubbish into sacks and piled up plastic seats she had plenty of time to think about what she wanted to say to him. She'd lain awake for most of the night too, reliving the scenes of the evening before, and had started the day gritty-eyed and with a thumping headache. If only Toby would show up. She knew if he just gave her a few minutes she could make everything all right.

By eleven o'clock Laney was ready to abandon all hope of seeing him at all. He must really hate her to keep his distance. Well, either that or he was rekindling his romance with his very attractive ex-fiancée – a thought that made Laney feel like drowning herself in the village pond.

It was a damp and gloomy morning with a mizzling rain that beaded her eyelashes, made her mascara run and turned her hair into mad Medusa ringlets. The sparkling frosty world of yesterday had turned into a grey and sodden mush, which suited Laney just fine because it matched her mood exactly. She didn't think she'd ever felt so totally and utterly miserable. Nobody was speaking to her and so she worked alone, with only her whirling thoughts for company. She'd tried to strike up a conversation with a couple of the girls from book group, but after getting just monosyllabic responses Laney gave up. Everyone, it seemed, had made up their minds that she was to blame. Even Vince – whom she was desperately avoiding – seemed to be more popular than she was this morning, which was unfair in the extreme. This was all his fault, and Laney felt like running him through with her litter spike.

I'm the tarty woman from the big bad city come to tempt their men away, Laney thought wryly when she saw Isla and her friends whispering. Maybe she should just hang a red light outside the B&B and be done with it? Or perhaps somebody could brand her with a scarlet letter? Or, for pure devilment, perhaps she ought to take to wearing fishnets and stilettos every time she left the house. They might as well enjoy their stereotyping.

'You're doing a great job.' Martin joined Laney and gave her a warm smile. Her heart lifted because it was such a relief to be with someone who didn't think she was St Pontian's answer to Belle de Jour.

'Thanks,' she said, smiling back. 'We're nearly done, aren't we?'

Martin nodded. 'I think so. Come and join us in the pub for a drink and a sandwich? The Bonfire-Night Bonanza committee has got some loose ends to tie up and you'll catch your death of cold if you stay out here much longer.'

She grimaced. 'Believe me, that would be a happy release. Anyway, thanks all the same, but I don't think the rest of the committee will be overjoyed if you rock up with me this morning.'

'Laney, I don't know what's been going on,' Martin said gently, placing a hand on her shoulder, 'but one thing the law has taught me is that there are always two sides to every story, and I'm not about to start judging anyone. You're my friend, my very good friend, and if the others have an issue with that, it's their problem.'

She looked at him doubtfully. 'St Ponty is a goldfish bowl, and right now I feel like the only fish.'

'It's a one minute wonder; they'll all be gossiping about someone else tomorrow,' he said sagely. 'Come on, you know I'm right. Don't let the bastards grind you down and all that.'

She couldn't help laughing. Martin had such an easy way of putting everything into perspective. Abandoning her rubbish sack, she tucked her arm through his and followed him across the green and into the pub. The murmur of chatter paused when she entered and Alyssa's glare could have frozen molten lava, but Martin squeezed her hand between his arm and side and whispered, 'Don't worry, they've not used the ducking stool for years,' which made her smile.

'I don't know what you've got to laugh about,' snarled Alyssa as she grudgingly poured them both a half. 'Not after what you've done.'

Laney sighed. 'Alyssa, I promise I haven't done anything.'

Alyssa crashed their drinks onto the bar. Lager slopped onto the bar towels. 'I don't want to hear your pathetic excuses. You should be ashamed.'

'That's enough,' Martin told her and his tone of voice said quite clearly that he would not be argued with. Alyssa looked taken aback, and suddenly Laney realized just how formidable an opponent he would be in court. Martin might look affable and be polite and gentlemanly, but there was a core of steel that ran beneath the blond good looks and charming manner.

'We're here for a drink, not to be harangued by the staff,' he said firmly. 'So keep your opinions to yourself.'

'Sorry,' muttered Alyssa, but the evil look she threw at Laney could have laid her out on the floor.

'Wow, remind me never to piss you off,' Laney remarked as they made their way over to the big window table where the rest of the Bonfire-Night Bonanza committee had gathered.

Martin winked. 'Beneath this polite and friendly exterior beats the heart of a ruthless dictator. Watch and learn, baby!'

He was in an amazingly good mood today, Laney reflected, seeing that the display had been ruined last night, half the fireworks were left over and they'd hardly made any money because everyone had left early. In fact Martin's good humour was such a contrast to Toby's smouldering wrath that she almost wondered if she'd made the right choice. Then she relived their kiss again, her hand rising fleetingly to touch her lips wonderingly, and knew that there had never been a choice. It had always been Toby. There was something unsettled between them that lay beyond all reason. For a while her mind had denied it, but her soul had always known.

There were a few icy looks thrown in Laney's direction when she joined the other committee members, but she was getting used to this now and managed to rise above it. Martin clearly took no nonsense, and everyone there respected him far too much to make a scene. Vince, seated at the far end of the table, threw her a pleading look, but Laney pointedly ignored him. Mr Swinnerton had caused her enough trouble for one lifetime, thanks.

'The money we took on the door didn't cover the cost of the fireworks, let alone everything else. We were expecting to make most of the profit from the beer tent and stalls. So we've actually lost money and half of the fireworks are still left,' Martin concluded after explaining the state of play. He ran a hand through his floppy blond fringe and looked thoughtful. 'I'm open to suggestions as to what we can do to rectify this. We need to make back at least a grand to break even.'

There was much tutting and sighing and pulling of faces at this news.

Tentatively Laney raised her hand. 'May I say something?'

'If you really must,' said Nancy the shopkeeper, looking as if she was sucking the particularly acidy bit of an acid drop.

'You're not even on this committee,' said Alyssa, who was hovering behind Vince as she collected glances. 'So, no.'

Martin gave her a steely look. 'Aren't you supposed to be at work?' To the others he said cheerfully, 'As chair, I'm happy to open this to the floor. All ideas are welcome at this point, unless any of you have got a few grand to chip in?'

Unfortunately nobody had, and most of them suddenly found their drinks extremely fascinating.

Taking a deep breath to steady her nerves (which was ridiculous; she'd spoken in front of big groups of high-powered corporate captains of industry, so to be this shaky about speaking in front of a few locals was surely not an issue), Laney said, 'I'm on the sports-pavilion committee—'

'Yeah, we know all about you and the sports pavilion,' sneered Alyssa.

Vince turned puce and buried his face in his hands.

Choosing to ignore all this, Laney pressed on. 'Why don't we raise some funds by having a Winter Ball, maybe at the beginning of December? How about on St Pontian's Day? That's the second, isn't it?'

'It is.' Martin looked at her thoughtfully. 'Go on, Laney.'

'Well, I was thinking that maybe we could use the remainder of the fireworks and have a display then, as a celebration?' Warming to her theme, and noticing that people were actually listening to her, she carried on. 'And how about we hold a dance in the pavilion? A bit like a prom where everyone dresses up, has some food and does some dancing? We could charge an entrance fee and raise some money that way.'

'That's a great idea.' Martin beamed at her. 'Well done, Laney! What do the rest of you think?'

'It is a good idea,' admitted Nancy grudgingly.

The other committee members nodded and murmured their approval. A vote was held and it was unanimously agreed that a Winter Ball was exactly what they would do. Vince – in his capacity as chair of the sports-pavilion committee – immediately started to think about all the health-and-safety implications. He looked so worried that, if she hadn't wanted to throttle the guy, Laney would almost have felt sorry for him.

Martin turned up the full wattage of his smile on her and for a moment she basked in his admiration. 'That's all agreed then. Well done, Laney.'

'What brilliant idea has she had now? Throwing your car keys into an empty pint glass?'

Martin swung round. 'What on earth—?'

'Nice to know who my friends really are,' Maxine said bitterly from behind him. They'd all been so engrossed in their plans for the festival that nobody had noticed her arrival. She looked terrible; her eyes were red from weeping and ringed with dark circles. The normally smiley mouth drooped downwards, and even her usually bouncy hair was lank and lifeless. Laney's heart twisted. She couldn't bear to see her friend so unhappy.

'Maxine, this is just a misunderstanding,' she began, but the younger woman held her hands up and shook her head.

'I don't want to hear a single word from you,' she spat. 'I wish I'd never set eyes on you . . . you home-wrecker!'

'I haven't done anything,' Laney gasped, stung by the venom in her voice. 'This is a misunderstanding. You've got it all wrong.'

'Oh, I have, have I?' Maxine put her hands on her hips and glowered across the table. 'Tell me exactly what I don't understand about another woman kissing *my husband*. Are you going to deny that's what happened?'

'Yes! No!' Laney was so confused. 'It wasn't the way you think it was.' She stopped for a split-second to gather her thoughts. This was the moment when she could tell everyone the truth and make it clearer than clear that it was Vince who'd made a drunken pass at her. Vince was totally to blame for this mess and it was time everyone knew it.

'Well, go on then, amaze me,' said Maxine coldly. 'Tell us all what really happened, why don't you?'

The pub was silent save for the ping and jingle of the fruit machine by the door. This was it. Time to clear the slate. Then Laney caught sight of Vince, and the desperation on his face stopped her in her tracks. If she told Maxine the truth, then Maxine would hate Vince even more, wouldn't she? She might never forgive him and what would happen to their marriage and the twins then? It was too a high price to pay for Vince's drunken moment of midlife-crisis madness. No matter what the cost to her own happiness and reputation, she couldn't do that to a marriage.

'Nothing happened,' she said quietly. 'It was just a stupid thing. It meant nothing.'

'It meant something to me!' screeched Maxine. Her face twisted with fury, she rounded on Vince. 'All those years I gave you. Two children! I made us a home! All the nights I stayed at home lonely so that you could go out, and this is what I get? How do I know that you really were at committee meetings when you said you were? How do I know you haven't been out shagging half of the Cotswolds?'

'Babe, I haven't. I never looked at anyone else,' Vince protested, but Maxine was having none of it.

'Until *she* showed up, right?'

'No, no! It isn't like that.'

Maxine's face was contorted with anger. 'Do you know what?' she said slowly, looking from Vince to Laney. 'You're welcome to one another. Vince, you've got an hour to pack your things and get out of my house. I never want to see you again!'

With this parting shot she stormed out of the pub, slamming the door so hard that the ancient building rattled. Vince was frozen for a moment, then suddenly leapt to his feet and tore after his wife. Everyone in the pub watched this drama unfold with open mouths. Once Vince had left the whispering began. Laney was under such scrutiny that she felt like a germ on a microscope. When Oscar Wilde said that the only thing worse than being talked about was not being talked about, he'd clearly never lived in a small Cotswolds village.

Martin tipped back his chair, clasped his hands behind his head and regarded her with concerned blue eyes.

'The time for worrying about being nosey is long past, I think,' he said slowly. 'You and I need a proper talk.'

Laney hoped he would live up to his promise and take her side.

24

Laney was barely conscious of the walk back to the B&B. Promising Martin faithfully that she would put the kettle on and tell him everything he wanted to know, she had left the pub as quickly as she could. The atmosphere there was so thick you would have needed a chainsaw to cut it. Even before she shut the door she could hear the sharpening of knives ready to be plunged into her back.

I've been an idiot, she chided herself, as she crossed the narrow bridge over the river and up the garden path. *I should have been honest with Maxine from the very beginning. All I wanted to do was save her from being hurt, and what have I done instead? The exact opposite. There's no way she'll believe me now.*

In silence she let herself into the house, intending to go upstairs for a shower and some quiet time, to ponder exactly what to do to put things right. Instead she was met by Nate, flushed in the face, breathless and in a state of high excitement.

'Are you OK, Dad?' Laney asked, a pang of worry hitting her.

'Laney! There you are at long last. You'll never guess

what's happened,' he exclaimed, rubbing his hands together in glee. 'We've got some guests.'

Laney relaxed and shrugged off her damp coat and scarf, hardly ecstatic at this news. 'That's great, Dad,' she said, pleased for him at least, 'but don't overdo it.' Guests were always welcome news in the quiet winter season, but did he really need to be so excitable? Stress of any kind wasn't good news for a man who had the potential to suffer from strokes.

'No, you don't understand. These aren't any old guests.' Nate grabbed Laney's hand and tugged her after him towards the guests' sitting room. 'Come and meet them.'

Realizing it was going to be a while before she could have some much-needed solitude, Laney followed Nate.

Waiting for Laney in the sitting room was a pair of guests whose arrival certainly raised her blood pressure. Sprawled in one of the armchairs, which looked liable to buckle at any second, was Tana Heretini. Laney blinked. Had the stress of today taken more of a toll than she'd realized? Or was rugby's golden boy really sitting in their front room?

'Tana, Anna, this is my daughter Laney,' Nate said proudly. 'Laney works in PR.'

Laney had been so focused on Tana, who had risen to his feet now and crossed the room in two strides of his giant-redwood legs, that she had failed to notice the slender blonde standing by the bay window. It was the same girl she'd seen on the podium yesterday; the girl whose presence had made Alyssa gasp and the colour drain from Toby's face.

'Great to meet you,' Tana said, pumping Laney's arm up and down as he shook her hand. Goodness but he was tall, like a creature from another planet. She barely came up to his chest and he seemed to dwarf the room – Gulliver in a Lilliputian guest house.

'Nice to meet you too,' Laney said, smiling up at him and getting a crick in her neck. 'My dad here is a huge rugby fan. You'll have made his week.'

'Week? Decade more like,' chortled Nate.

'I'm Anna Marsh.' Once she was released from Tana's paw, the blonde stepped forward and shook hands too. Her nails, Laney noticed, were beautifully French-manicured, without so much as a chip in the pearly pink polish. Rather like her own nails used to be, when she lived in the city and could afford a weekly trip to Nails Inc. Anna's hair too was a perfect shade of honey-blonde and fell in a shimmering sheet to her shoulders. Teamed with immaculate make-up, a stylish designer suit and a gym-honed body, there you had it: the ultimate successful city-girl chic.

I looked a bit like that once, thought Laney wistfully as they exchanged small talk. Anna was beautiful. No wonder Toby had been smitten. What on earth had gone on between them to cause things to end so badly? They must have made a stunning couple.

'Anna's an American,' Nate said helpfully when there was a pause in the conversation.

Laney smiled at Anna, who smiled back. The expression didn't quite meet her eyes, which were the same chilly blue as an arctic sky.

'Thanks, Dad, but I think I'd managed to work that one out for myself.'

'I'm a sports agent,' Anna explained, 'based in New York.

I spend a lot of time flying over the Atlantic. I'm representing Tana and we just got him signed to the Bath Barbarians.'

'She's like Jerry Maguire, but prettier!' boomed Tana. 'She's awesome.'

Anna inclined her perfect blonde head. 'Thanks, Tana, but I'm not sure I deserve such praise after booking us into that appalling hotel last night.'

'Which is why we're here, and not in some God-awful hole in town.' Tana paced to the window and looked outside. Turning round to beam at Laney he said, 'This little village is so . . . *real*. I said to Anna that I had to stay here while she finds me something long-term.'

'Can we get two rooms?' Anna was tapping away on her BlackBerry, a small frown of concentration plating her brow. 'I think five nights will do it. Tana's got *Jonathan Ross* and *A Question of Sport* on the eleventh, so we'll need to be in London then.'

'Of course.' Nate looked as though he was going to explode with joy. Laney made a mental note to check his blood pressure the first opportunity she got. He'd better not get any silly ideas into his head about going for a kickabout with Tana. 'We'll book you into our two finest rooms for as long as you need, won't we, Laney?'

Laney nodded. There was absolutely no reason why not. Having a celebrity guest would only add to the reputation of the B&B – especially if they got a photo – and the money was always welcome. If she felt slightly intimidated by the aura of power and success that Anna exuded along with her Chanel No. 5, then that was her issue to deal with. Besides, maybe it would do her good to see at first hand the kind of woman Toby Woodward was *really* attracted to? So much for all that about hating the town and loving the country. He couldn't have found a more citified woman to propose to if he'd tried.

'Hello! Laney? Nate? Where are you folks hiding out?'

Martin's amused tones caused Laney to look up from filling in the booking log. Of course, he'd said that he would come over for a talk. No doubt he was dying to know exactly what had gone on between her and his best friend. Her heart quailed. He'd turned out to be such a good friend, and she didn't think she could bear to lose him too. Not for the first time she felt glad that the boundaries of their friendship had never been blurred.

'We're in the front sitting room!' she called. 'Come on through.'

'Oh, I'm sorry to interrupt when you've got visitors,' said Martin when he joined them. 'Shall I come back?'

'Not because of us, mate,' said Tana cheerfully. 'We met last night, didn't we? You're the guy who organized the fireworks. Great night, loved it.'

Martin swelled visibly with pride. 'Thanks. I only wish I could have organized the weather. I would have made more time then to welcome you and have a chat.'

Tana nodded his shaven head. *Does it hurt to tattoo your scalp*, Laney wondered? 'Yeah, that was a pity. I spotted you from the podium and saw you make a run for it. You should be a fly-half.'

Tana was like a tall, tanned sunbeam, Laney observed. His good humour was infectious, and within minutes he and

Martin were chatting away like old friends. She didn't think she'd ever seen Martin laugh so much as when Tana told him that his name was Maori for 'little man'. In fact he seemed to find everything that the burly New Zealander said highly fascinating. She would never have had Martin pegged as a rugby guy, which just went to show that you never could tell.

Anna, who had been following this exchange with a very peculiar expression on her face, finished tapping away on her BlackBerry and looked up.

'Tana, I hate to interrupt, but we need to unpack our things and then get over to BBC Thames Radio. You're going on their drivetime slot, remember?'

Tana rolled his tawny eyes. 'Jeez, and there was me thinking I was in the UK to play rugby.'

'Afraid not,' said Anna crisply. To Nate she said, 'Would you be able to show us to our rooms? We really need to get going.'

'Absolutely.' Nate was nodding like the Churchill Insurance dog. 'Follow me.'

Anna stalked out of the room after him, her perfume drifting in her wake.

Tana pulled a face.

'She works me bloody hard . . . and for some reason I pay her for it. Maybe we'll catch up soon? Go for a beer?'

Laney was just about to say, 'Yes, great idea,' when she realized that Tana was actually speaking to Martin. Oh well, they probably wanted to talk about rugby and girls and boy-stuff. In any case, something told her that she'd have her work cut out with Anna. Used to city standards and boutique hotels, the woman had the potential to be a very demanding customer, and Laney had absolutely no intention of giving her anything to complain about.

'I didn't realize it was that woman when I booked Tana,' said Martin, whispering in case Anna was still in earshot. 'I only ever spoke to her secretary. Toby must hate me for bringing her back here.'

Laney didn't reply. Toby wasn't the only one who didn't like Anna sniffing around.

'But how are you doing?' Martin asked, once they were finally alone in the kitchen with two enormous mugs of tea and a plateful of Janet's biscuits. He pushed a couple towards her. 'Here, get these down you. Choc-chip cookies cure all ills, in my experience.'

She grimaced. 'No, thanks. Then I'll be fat, as well as public enemy number one.'

'Drink your tea, take a deep breath and tell Uncle Marty all about it,' he advised. 'Obviously I've already heard Maxine's version, the village version and of course my mother's version, but I'd far rather hear yours.'

So, over a mug of PG tips so strong that it could have arm-wrestled Tana Heretini and won, Laney told him absolutely everything. Martin was so quietly onside and so genuinely sympathetic that before long she was sobbing into a heap of kitchen towel. He was so great at listening – having to deal with divorce cases must have taught him a lot about how to handle emotional women.

'So that's it,' Laney hiccupped, dabbing her eyes with a piece of Bounty. 'Everything was going so well, I really loved it here, and now it's all gone horribly wrong. The Vince-thing will make everyone hate me. Maxine really hates me.'

'Sweetheart, I'm sure she doesn't.' Martin reached across the table and took her hands in his. 'She's hurt and confused and furious with Vince, but she doesn't hate you.'

'What could I have done?' She raised her drenched eyes to his. 'It was such a stupid thing to happen, and I didn't want to hurt her further by telling her, if she would never find out.'

'You did absolutely the right thing.' He squeezed her hand. 'Look, I've known Vince for a very long time and, no matter what women think, men do actually sometimes confide in one another. Vince is having a really hard time at the moment. He hates his job, feels old and fat, and the more he tries to gain control of his life, the more pompous and silly he seems. Underneath all the health-and-safety bollocks is a really cool guy who loves his wife and kids.'

Laney recalled Maxine's story about how motorbike-loving Vince had been the Brad Pitt of St Pontian. Now it was more like *arm*pit. What on earth had happened?

'Life,' said Martin gently when she voiced this train of thought. 'Responsibility, mortgages, shopping, bills. All those things have got in the way. He got drunk, you were sweet enough to listen, and in a moment of stupidity he tried to be seventeen again. That's all.'

The relief made Laney's legs feel like cotton wool. 'That's exactly it. Oh, Martin, how come you get it, but the others don't?'

'Because I am a genius.' He winked. 'And because this is juicy gossip, so everyone wants to have their say. Look, I can't promise anything, but I'll try and talk to Maxine.'

She gave him a watery smile. 'That's not the worst of it.'

Martin's eyebrows dived into his floppy fringe. 'It isn't? What else have you done? Shagged the vicar? Swum naked in the pond?'

'Nothing quite that bad, but pretty bad.' She dropped her gaze. 'I got a bit carried away by the atmosphere and the fireworks. Oh, Martin, I kissed Toby Woodward.'

'Of course you did.'

Her head shot up. 'What?'

Martin leaned back in his chair and raised his eyes to the ceiling in despair. 'Laney, I'm not head of the Bonfire-Night Bonanza committee for nothing. I know fireworks when I see them, and they've been exploding between you two since the night we had a runaway Catherine wheel.'

Laney was shocked. 'Wha—'

He smiled at her. 'You need your eyes tested. Why do you think Isla was such a bitch about the book group? She could see from a mile off how Toby feels about you and it made her jealous. And why do you think he was always making such a fuss about Julian Matlock and those bloody sausages? It was just an excuse to see you.'

'But . . .' She stared at him, her heart rising with hope, like one of Janet's Yorkshire puddings.

'And then there was the way he couldn't keep his eyes off you at Nick's gallery opening. Isla had more flesh on display than the cast of *TOWIE*, but Toby only had eyes for you.'

Was this true? Had Toby truly had feelings for her from the moment they'd met? If so, how lovely was Martin not to have been jealous or annoyed or think that she'd wasted his time?

When Laney remembered how they'd parted, recalled how

Toby's expression had changed when he saw Anna, her hopes crumbled into dust. He would never forgive her for this Vince-business.

'If there *were* fireworks between us, they've been well and truly rained on,' she said sadly. 'Toby probably wants me tarred and feathered and held in the stocks, or whatever it is people in the country do.'

'You're pretty quick to judge him,' Martin said. 'How do you know what he thinks or feels, unless you ask him? Country people and town people aren't so very different, in my experience. Maybe it's time you looked at the way you see us, rather than stressing about the way you think we view you?'

And with this comment he got up, ruffled her hair affectionately and refilled the kettle.

'I think we need another cup of tea while you think that through,' he said. And really there was no arguing with this. Martin was, Laney realized with a jolt, absolutely right. She needed to stop judging by appearances. She'd been wrong about Toby, wrong about Vince and wrong about Martin's intentions.

Just what else she might have got wrong didn't bear thinking about.

25

It was early morning, just gone eight o'clock, and Laney had set off to the village noticeboard to cancel the book group. There seemed little point in continuing it now. She doubted anyone would want to come anyway and it was highly unlikely that Maxine would be up to having people round – and there was no way she would want to see Laney.

Of course the noticeboard was locked – she'd never expected anything different – but Laney wasn't going to seek Isla out to ask for the key. Instead she'd made a laminated note, which she was going to tape to the glass.

Just as she was almost breaking her teeth by trying to bite off a chunk of Sellotape, Maxine walked past and tutted loudly.

'You know you're not supposed to do that,' she said. 'Then again, since when have you ever cared about silly things like rules?'

Laney sighed.

'Or silly things like loyalty. Or marriage vows?'

Laney removed the tape from her mouth and defiantly secured the notice to the glass. After her talk with Martin the day before she was less inclined to beat herself up. She'd not done anything wrong and was in the right frame of mind for setting the record straight, but when she turned round she saw that Maxine was with her daughters. She bit back the words that bubbled up like lava within her and took a deep breath.

'Maxine, I'm sorry for what happened. I do care about you, and I'd never do anything to hurt you.'

Maxine's top lip curled. 'Yeah. Right.'

Laney sighed. 'Look, you don't believe me. That's fair enough, and I get it, but maybe you should speak to . . .' She cleared her throat and took a sideways glance at the children, who were pulling fluff out of each other's hair, so Laney continued, 'some of the *other* people involved? Then you might just find out that *those people* care about you more than you think.'

Maxine's voice rose by several decibels. 'I hardly think *those people* give a . . .' She too took a sideways glance at her children. 'Give two hoots about me, after what *they've* done.'

'I don't want you to hate me, but I'm not surprised if you do. There are more important *things*,' Laney nodded again towards the twins, 'to consider. Just open the lines of communication,' she said wearily.

'She's right, Mum, you need to talk to Dad,' piped up one of the twins, tugging Maxine's sleeve.

Maxine couldn't have looked more shocked if her daughter had offered to pay the mortgage for a month. 'Were you listening?'

She rolled her eyes like an early-onset teen. 'Talk to him. He's really sad.'

'Daddy is *not* sad,' Maxine growled.

'He is,' said the other twin. 'He's been sad for ages.'

'And he's really sad at sleeping on the couch,' added her sister. 'He told me.'

'That's enough, girls!' Maxine's eyes were suspiciously bright. 'Don't you dare talk about our personal affairs in the street. You're making us late for school.' Tugging them after her, she marched off, but before she turned the corner she called over her shoulder, 'Just mind your own business and stay away from me.'

Well, that went really well, Laney thought. It was hopeless. No matter what she said or did, Maxine was determined to think the worst. Martin had promised to speak to her, but quite frankly Laney wasn't going to hold her breath. Her former friend had a very stubborn streak and she was starting to realize that Vince, annoying though he was, probably hadn't had the easiest time, either. The couple had been together for so long they'd forgotten why they'd fallen in love in the first place. They were both as bad as each other, and their marriage needed a rocket up its backside. If she could think of a way to help, then she would do all she could, but that was easier said than done when Maxine hated her.

So much for the simple life.

Back at the B&B, Nate was presiding over the cooker and peering into the grill pan with a bemused expression.

'I know I cooked the whole packet of sausages,' he said when Laney joined him. 'That means Tana's eaten all eight.'

'He is an athlete,' Laney pointed out. 'I guess all that rugby must build up an enormous appetite.'

'But an entire packet of sausages?' Nate shook his head. 'That's hardly healthy.'

'You're a right one to talk about healthy eating. Who was it again with the sky-high cholesterol count?'

He held his hands up. 'Guilty as charged. I'm a reformed character now, though. Yoghurt and granola are more my thing these days.'

'Just as well, seeing as our celebrity guest has eaten everything else,' she grinned. 'Go and have a rest, Dad, you've done quite enough today. I'll clear away.'

In the dining room Tana was still tucking in, his plate piled with toast and jam.

'Great breakfast,' he told Laney.

'Glad you enjoyed it.' She couldn't help but smile. And wow! Laney didn't think she'd ever seen the breakfast buffet looking so depleted. Not bad going for just one guest. The place she'd laid for Anna was still pristine, which wasn't really much of a surprise. You didn't get a figure that slender by pigging out on a full English.

'So, what's it like living here?' Tana was asking as he mopped his plate with a piece of buttered toast. 'Everyone seems very friendly. Is it a good place for me to buy a house?'

Laney thought for a moment. Until the falling-out with Maxine she'd been very happy living in St Pontian. OK so it didn't have the bright lights and amenities of the city, but this was more than compensated for by the stunning countryside and generally simple way of life.

'Yes, it is,' she told him. 'If you get involved – maybe join a couple of the committees or something – you'll make friends really quickly. The sports-pavilion committee would be over the moon to have a celebrity member.'

He nodded thoughtfully. 'Who's on that one? Anybody I'd know?'

Laney considered this unlikely, since Tana had only arrived a couple of days ago, but since he was her guest she humoured him.

'Well, there's me and dad; Henry Overton, who's lord of the manor; Jason Leck, who teaches at the primary school; Martin Rolls—'

'Martin Rolls? Isn't he the guy I met yesterday? The solicitor?'

'That's him.'

'Sounds like a great crowd. Sign me up,' said Tana. His plate was empty, so he snatched a croissant and smothered it in jam and butter, before biting into it with relish. While he proceeded to demolish everything in sight, Laney stacked the dirty plates and they chatted about the Winter Ball. Tana thought it was a great idea and had loads of suggestions, even offering to donate a pair of tickets for the rugby World Cup as a raffle prize.

'Tana. There you are!' Anna strode into the dining room. 'Come on, we don't have a second to waste. We're on a tight schedule today.'

She was clad in full running regalia: iPod, Reebok Runtones, headband, pace-watch, wrist weights and of course designer shorts and vest. Her face was flushed and she'd obviously been further than just down the stairs. Laney was inwardly amused. People's eyes must have been out on stalks when Anna ran through the village. The members of the local running club wore tatty trainers and still swore by their Walkmans.

'Sorry, doll, I was just having some extra fruit,' said Tana.

As if by magic his plate had vanished and in its place was a bowl piled high with grapefruit and blueberries. Eh?

'I'm so sorry if it was demanding of me to ask your father to cook egg-white omelettes and steamed spinach,' Anna continued, contorting her body into some weird kind of yoga stretch, 'but Tana is an athlete and his body is highly tuned. His coach has put me in charge of his very specific nutritional requirements.'

Laney didn't dare look at Tana. 'No, that's absolutely fine. No trouble at all.'

Standing on one leg and twisting the other around her calf, Anna went on, 'I mean, this village was always stuck in the Dark Ages, and I can't see that anything has changed. No coffee shop, nowhere to buy protein shakes, nowhere was open at six a.m., no Wi-Fi. God, the list is endless! When I asked a local about the nearest gym he directed me to some God-awful shed with a dumbbell in it.'

'That'll be the sports pavilion,' Laney said.

'Whatever.' Anna uncoiled one leg and then repeated the exercise with the other. She looked like a constipated ostrich. 'Now, sports stuff aside, Laney, where can I get a gluten-free birthday cake around here? It's my birthday very soon and I have an intolerance.'

It sounded very much to Laney as though Anna had intolerances to many things, and not just wheat. Still, it was her job to keep the customer happy, so she suggested Tesco.

'Tesco?' Anna's pretty nose wrinkled with distaste.

'It's very unlikely you'll find gluten-free products in the village,' Laney said patiently. 'It's only a small place.'

Anna rolled her eyes. 'Jesus! This country! No wonder the economy's on its knees. Where the hell am I supposed to go now to find protein shakes? Tana has to have them.'

'I can probably manage without,' said Tana hopefully, but his agent rounded on him with such fury that he shrank back. *Wow!* thought Laney. *If Anna can reduce a six-foot-four giant rugby player to a quivering jelly, she must have made mincemeat of Toby. No wonder he was so scarred.*

'You most certainly can *not*. That thing,' she pointed at his torso, 'is your temple!'

One that worshipped fry-ups and toast. Laney hid a smile because Tana looked so sheepish.

'I'll pop to the village shop in a minute and see if I can find those protein shakes you need,' Laney said soothingly, while Anna faffed about touching her toes and stretching out her calves.

While she had her back to him, Tana made vomiting faces at Laney and mouthed, 'Thanks for not telling her about the sausages.'

She winked at him. Anna was a total food-and-exercise Nazi. She wanted her client to be a perfect specimen in order to parade him around. Poor Tana.

Leaving Tana to his orders, Laney cleared away the rest of the dishes – including a breakfast plate that had *mysteriously* appeared on the seat of a dining chair. Once the dishwasher was humming away and a big vat of French-onion soup was bubbling on the Aga, she pulled on her jacket and set off to the village for the second time that day. This time there was no sign of Maxine, but several villagers stared at her as she crossed the green.

The village shop/post office/newsagent was fairly quiet when Laney arrived. Nancy – the rotund woman who ran it – was reading a copy of *Take a Break* behind the counter and absent-mindedly munching her way through a bar of Dairy Milk. When Laney asked her whether she stocked protein shakes for athletes, she sighed wearily and dragged herself away from what was obviously a very gripping true-life story.

'Not you as well. That whiney American woman was in here earlier demanding exactly the same thing. We're a shop, not a blooming chemist.' Nancy narrowed her eyes. 'She was right rude to me as well; nigh on blamed me for the global recession. We're only a small village shop. Not bleeding Harrods.'

Laney could well believe it. She cringed when she recalled how scathing she had been about the village shop's lack of items that she'd taken for granted when she lived in London. She just prayed that she hadn't been as rude.

'The nerve of that woman in any case, turning up here as bold as brass after everything she's done,' fumed Nancy. 'After the way she treated poor Toby, too.'

Laney was just plucking up the courage to ask Nancy what had really happened between Toby and Anna when the bell signalled the arrival of another customer.

It was Vince.

'Oh, Lordy,' breathed Nancy, perking up like a sniffer dog scenting a stash of drugs. 'This could be interesting.'

There was no way Laney was going to stick around to provide Nancy with a virtual-reality version of a true-life drama. She'd only wanted to do some shopping, not star in St Pontian's answer to *Jeremy Kyle*.

'Excuse me,' she said to Nancy and exited the shop as quickly as she could. Maybe she'd moved so fast that she'd been little more than a blur and Vince hadn't recognized her?

'Laney! Hey, Laney! Wait up. I need to talk to you.'

Fan-flipping-tastic. This was all she needed – bloody Vince causing a scene in the street. Already she could sense the net curtains twitching in the cottages near the village shop. Did he really have to shout?

'Laney, wait,' puffed Vince. When he reached her he bent double for a minute and rested his hands on his knees as he struggled to get his breath back.

'Go away!' Laney looked around frantically. Already the postman and several old biddies were watching them.

Vince straightened up. *He looks terrible*, Laney thought with a jolt. All the confident swagger had fizzled away, and beneath several days' worth of stubble his skin was grey.

'But I need to speak to you.' He fixed her with a look of sheer desperation. 'I'm so sorry. It was a stupid drunken moment, and I can't tell you how much I've regretted it.'

'That makes two of us,' she said.

He glanced down at his tatty scuffed trainers. 'I dragged you into my midlife crisis. I wish I could explain why I did it, but I can't.'

He was so contrite. So much more likeable without the usual arrogance and swagger. In spite of all the trouble he'd caused – not least the terrible falling-out with Toby – Laney started to pity him.

'I've made the biggest mistake of my life. Maxine hates

me and she won't listen to a word I say to her.' He raised his eyes to hers. They were bright with misery and red-rimmed from grief. 'I thought I was losing her before all this happened. And now that I really have lost her I can't bear it.'

'Vince, I'm sure you haven't lost her. Just tell Maxine all the things you told Martin: about how you don't feel loved any more, and how you worry you're not the man you were.'

He swallowed. 'Martin told you that?'

'He had to do something, to stop me beating you to death with my handbag,' Laney quipped.

'It makes me sound kind of pathetic, doesn't it?' He hung his head.

'Not pathetic, Vince, just human. Tell Maxine how much she means to you.'

He nodded. 'The trouble is I'm not very good at all that romantic stuff. What should I do?'

Now that was the million-dollar question. *Grovel* was probably the right answer, but it probably wasn't what he wanted to hear. He looked so desperate, and earlier on Maxine had looked exactly the same. Short of banging their heads together and locking them up in a small confined space, there wasn't anything else she could think of.

Unless . . . unless . . .

'Bear with me, Vince,' she said slowly. 'I think I might just have an idea.'

26

'Laney, what are you up to on Thursday night?' asked Martin, as he bowled into the Barwells' kitchen.

Laney was standing at the table preparing vegetables for the raw platter that Anna was insisting Tana ate for dinner. He was still consuming sausages and junk food at an alarming rate, but so far Anna hadn't caught on. She hadn't actually been around that much and always seemed to be off to meetings. Laney just hoped she really was flat out with business matters and not rekindling her romance with Toby. She didn't think she could bear that.

Laney hadn't seen him since their ill-fated kiss, but he still filled her every thought.

'Hello? Earth to Laney.' Martin waved his hand in front of her face. 'I just asked what you're up to on Thursday.'

'Sorry, I was just trying to remember whether it was George Clooney or Brad Pitt I was seeing that night,' she joked, but her heart was sinking. Surely he wasn't asking her out? She'd thought they'd agreed just to be friends?

'Don't worry, you can still hang out with your Hollywood A-listers. It's more of an alibi that I need.'

'An alibi?' Laney put down her chopping knife and stared at him. 'I hope it's not anything illegal?'

Martin grinned. 'Don't worry, I'm not about to rob the post office or anything. I'm just going somewhere and I'd rather my mum didn't know about it.'

Laney was intrigued. 'What on earth are you up to?'

'Nothing that my mother needs to know about.' He reached out for a piece of carrot and chomped on it. 'She's far too nosey. But if she thinks I'm with you, she won't ask any awkward questions.

'I'm not sure. I don't want to lie to Janet.' Laney didn't like the idea of being caught up in any kind of deceit. Look what had happened when she'd tried to protect Maxine by not telling her about Vince's drunken pass.

'You won't need to. I'll just lead her to believe we're out together.' He reached out and grasped her hands. 'Please, Laney. This is really important to me.'

Goodness. She didn't think she'd ever seen Martin so passionate about anything. Whoever he was meeting so secretly obviously meant a great deal to him. In spite of her reservations Laney was intrigued.

'You're not seeing a married woman, are you?' she asked.

'Definitely not. I promise.' He paused and for a moment looked as though he was about to say something, but thought better of it. 'It's just early days, and I don't want the whole village talking.'

This was something Laney totally understood. 'All right then,' she said reluctantly. 'Tell Janet we're out. I'll think of somewhere to go so that I don't bump into her.'

'Brilliant!' Martin's face lit up like the Harrods Christmas-window display. 'Thanks, Laney. You are a star.'

'And in return for so shamelessly using me as an alibi, you have to tell me any gossip. Deal?'

'Deal.' Martin shook her hand and then the conversation turned to other things, but Laney couldn't help wondering just what he was up to and with whom. He must be going out with some radically unsuitable woman – someone Janet really wouldn't approve of. Janet had been extremely frosty with Laney until Martin had explained what had really happened with Vince, so she could well imagine how hard she could make it for her son, if she disapproved of his choice.

Maybe Martin was seeing Anna. This thought perked Laney up. Janet really disapproved of 'the American woman' – everyone did – and was bound to be horrified if her son became romantically involved with her. Maybe Anna had been sneaking off to spend time with Martin? Which meant that she wasn't seeing Toby. Which meant that things were looking up.

⁂

When Thursday finally arrived, Laney decided to hide indoors with a good book and a bar of chocolate. She wished she could have continued with the book group because it had been so much fun. She'd really felt as though she'd been making friends and settling into the village.

At least she'd have a quiet evening. Anna was out at yet another very important business meeting, and Tana had also gone out.

Everyone was out except for her. Laney was starting to

think she'd never go on a date again. Maybe she ought to just admit defeat and book herself into the nearest convent?

'No book group tonight?' Nate asked when he saw Laney in her Uggs and trackie-bottoms combo.

She shook her head. 'I cancelled it. After all the stuff with Vince, nobody would want to come, would they?'

Nate sighed. He'd heard the story and had felt desperately sorry for his daughter. 'You should have had more faith in people, darling.'

'Everyone thinks the worst of me. I just couldn't bear the thought of setting up the room and then have nobody turn up.'

'You should count on your friends,' he sighed. 'But, like your mum, there's no arguing with you, is there? Me and your mum always used to squabble and she always had the last word.'

Laney was surprised. Her parents never got angry with each other. 'I don't remember you two ever arguing.'

Her father laughed. 'Of course we did. Every couple does. Your mum would get into a right old state about something, but if I tried to help she'd go mad. It used to drive me round the twist. I never met a woman so stubborn.'

'I guess I always saw you guys through rose-tinted glasses,' Laney said. 'I thought everything was perfect.'

'Come here, you.' Nate folded her into a hug and kissed the top of her head. 'I adored your mum, but no relationship is perfect. There are always issues and misunderstandings – it's how you deal with them that makes the difference.'

Laney rested her head against her father's chest and, just for a few minutes, she was a child again.

'Darling, I know things haven't been the easiest for you here,' Nate continued, 'and I can't tell you how much I appreciate you giving up your own space to come here and look after me. If you feel that you want to go back to London, then don't let me keep you. I'm feeling so much better. On the other hand, if you want to stay, then there's always a place for you. And lots of people who love and care for you.'

She hugged him back. 'Dad, I wouldn't have had it any other way. I know I might have been like a fish out of water when I first arrived, but that's changed. Thing is,' she stepped back and smiled up at him, 'I think maybe the time has come to go back to London.'

'I'll miss you.' Nate's eyes were suspiciously bright.

'I'll come back and visit,' she promised.

Nate settled down in the sitting room to watch television and Laney curled up with her book, but try as she might she just couldn't concentrate. Even the chocolate failed to cheer her up, and instead she found her thoughts drifting back to Toby. Placing the book on the arm of her chair, she closed her eyes and indulged herself by reliving their kiss for what had to be the thousandth time.

Toby was so handsome that he took her breath away. She saw again his sculpted face, high cheekbones, finely chiselled mouth and those compelling dark amber-flecked eyes. With that strong profile, he drew all eyes to him and made her feel so safe and protected. How good it had felt to be held in his arms and to feel the strength of those wide shoulders. To think that she might never be that close to him again made her want to howl.

Laney opened her eyes and it was almost a shock to be back in the sitting room, rather than outside in the smoky darkness and wrapped in Toby's arms. Her novel was good, but romantic fiction certainly didn't come anything close to the reality. She sighed. It was half-past seven, the book group should have been in full swing, and yet here she was hanging out with her dad and *Grazia.* Maybe she should boot up her laptop and start checking out the train times to London?

She didn't know whether to be excited or heartbroken. Either way, it was clear that she couldn't carry on like this. It was time to take control and get her own life back. She could still run Toby's PR campaign from London, and she might even be able to utilize some better contacts. Not that she was thinking about Toby any more. Just as she was moving on from St Pontian, so she would also be moving on from him, which was probably a very, very good thing. Even if it felt as though her heart was breaking.

27

Laney was finding it impossible to concentrate. The train-timetable website kept crashing and every time she thought she'd booked a ticket the payment screen sent her right back to the beginning. After three attempts she gave up. Maybe fate was trying to tell her something?

The doorbell chimed. Laney glanced at her watch. It was twenty to eight – there was no way Martin would be here to tell her all about his top-secret date, and Janet was out with the craft committee. Someone looking for a room, maybe?

Minimizing Facebook, and knowing that Nate was bound to have nodded off in his chair, she went downstairs to answer the door. To Laney's great surprise Isla and Alyssa were on the front step. Bracing herself for a big shouting match, she opened the door. Might as well get it over with.

'Hello. Sorry we're late. Have you started without us?' said Isla, stepping forward and thrusting a bottle of wine into Laney's hands.

'We just had to make sure that everyone knew that the craft committee wasn't on this week,' explained Alyssa. 'We figured that we all deserved a break, after making all the banners for the Bonfire-Night Bonanza.'

What on earth is going on? Laney thought, while wine and giant bags of Kettle Chips were piled into her arms. They pushed past her and into the corridor.

'We've come for book group,' Isla explained. 'It is still on Thursdays, isn't it?'

'It was . . . but I cancelled it,' Laney said. 'I stuck a notice on the village noticeboard.' On the *outside* of the village noticeboard.

'Oh, that!' said Isla airily, with a toss of her auburn curls. 'I took it down.'

Laney stared at her. 'What? Why?'

Alyssa cleared her throat. 'Because we realized that we might have jumped to conclusions about you and been a bit unfair.'

A bit?

'And then when Vince told us what really happened, we felt awful,' Isla said, her cat-green eyes wide. 'He's such a muppet. Snogging somebody else to make Maxine jealous was never the way to get her to jump his bones. All it would take was a bunch of flowers and a night out of the village to do that.'

Alyssa winced. 'It'd take a head-and-brain transplant to get me to shag Vince.'

'Wait a minute.' They were talking so fast that Laney felt confused. 'Vince told you about what he did?'

'He's told loads of people,' nodded Isla.

'He feels a prat, and he's really sorry for letting us all think badly of you.' Alyssa smiled at Laney and there was something so familiar and dear about the expression that she couldn't help smiling back. 'I'm sorry I was a bitch!'

'It's a small village and people get paranoid.' Isla tucked her hair behind her ears and looked a bit shamefaced. 'When you arrived, all glamorous and sophisticated, a few of us felt insecure.'

'Me? Glamorous and sophisticated?' Laney could hardly believe what she was hearing. She shook her head. 'Hardly. I was terrified because I didn't know anyone. And I was so out of place.'

'Don't put yourself down,' said Alyssa. 'You're gorgeous, and you were a threat. When all that stuff about Vince came out, it just scared everyone even more.'

Laney was stunned. Sophisticated? Gorgeous? A threat? This wasn't quite how she viewed herself.

'Then when I saw you kissing my brother I was furious,' Alyssa recalled. 'The last thing he needs is to get his heart broken by another city girl like Anna. I couldn't stand the thought of you getting your claws into him.'

There's no chance of that now, thought Laney.

'I had hoped he and Isla would get back together,' continued Alyssa, 'but that was never going to happen.'

'I hang out loads with Toby and he's lovely, but there's no spark,' Isla sighed. 'On paper it's all there, but the bottom line is that he doesn't fancy me.' She looked sad, but stiffened her upper lip and continued, 'If we were together it would only be as a compromise and because it made practical sense.'

'When Anna arrived back, I realized just how much nicer you are than her,' admitted Alyssa. 'If I can't have Isla as my sister-in-law, then I'd much rather you were with my brother. He seems to really like you.'

Laney's head was whirling like the runaway Catherine wheel. So many things of which she had been certain were being swept away. Her parents' perfect marriage, Isla and Toby's relationship, Vince being horrible – none of this was real. It was all based on assumptions that she'd made. She gulped. *What else have I been wrong about?*

Both girls were smiling at her nervously. It had taken a lot of courage for them to come to the house and apologize. Alyssa's warm words had certainly brought a lump to Laney's throat. Nate had been right – it was possible to find friends in unexpected places.

Inviting the girls in, she opened the bottle of wine and, sitting around the kitchen table, they chatted about the whole Vince and Maxine problem. What could they do to bring the couple back together?

'I had an idea the other day,' Laney said. 'It might work, but it's a bit of a gamble.'

Isla leaned forward. 'Go on.'

'Well,' Laney said slowly, because ever since she'd bumped into Vince she'd been thinking long and hard about this, 'I think we've all been looking at the problem the wrong way round. Rather than worrying about Maxine wanting Vince, we need to think about finding her a way to feel good about herself again.'

'You're right,' Alyssa nodded. A flashback of the sensation of dark curls beneath her fingertips almost floored Laney and she had to take a deep breath. She couldn't keep thinking about Toby, especially if he was back with Anna. It would drive her mad.

A broad smile spread across Isla's face and her eyes sparkled like summer rockpools. 'I think I've got it,' she said, 'It's high time Cinders went to the ball! How do you fancy a girls' night out?'

⁂

'What do you want? Can't you see I'm busy?'

Maxine was standing in the doorway, a half-eaten Snickers in her hand and with her hair scraped back from her face with an elastic band. She was wearing a baggy tracksuit and her face was blotchy and make-up-less. To say that she was horrified to see them was an understatement.

'We've come to cheer you up,' announced Isla, bouncing past her and into the cosy kitchen. 'I've got face-packs and straighteners and nail varnish.'

'And I've brought a knock-'em-dead outfit,' said Alyssa, following in her friend's wake. 'It's makeover time for you. And absolutely no arguments. We're like Gok Wan, Maxine, only female!'

Maxine did not look best pleased. 'And what's she doing here?' she demanded; her eyes narrowed as Laney followed Alyssa.

'Come on, Maxine, give her a break. How many times does Vince have to tell you? *It wasn't Laney's fault*,' said Isla. 'He got drunk, felt like nobody appreciated him, and when she was kind, he kissed her. It doesn't mean anything.'

Maxine's eyes filled with tears and her bottom lip trembled. 'It meant something to me.'

Laney couldn't bear it. Before she could think, she put her arms around her friend and hugged her tightly. 'Vince adores you,' she told her. 'And he is so sorry for being such an idiot. And I'm sorry for not telling you straight away. I should have done. I know that now.'

Maxine swallowed. And then both of them were crying and hugging and gasping out even more apologies.

'It's not your fault,' Maxine said. 'You were in a horrible situation. I'm sorry too.'

Laney felt quite faint with relief. She'd hated falling out with Maxine and had really missed her friend.

'Enough of all this soppy stuff,' said Alyssa finally, passing them a wad of kitchen roll. 'We can't go clubbing with red eyes.'

'I can't go clubbing anyway. I've got the children to look after,' hiccupped Maxine.

'Wrong. I've already asked Nancy to come over and hold the fort until Vince gets back from the environment committee, so no excuses!' cried Isla triumphantly.

'Jump in the shower, shave your legs and wash your hair,' Alyssa ordered, propelling a protesting Maxine up the stairs. 'We won't take no for an answer. There's been far too much sitting around feeling sorry for yourself. Tonight you are getting the full Alyssa Woodward makeover.'

Maxine grimaced.

'Don't look so worried,' Laney said. 'This is going to be fun.'

'You haven't seen Alyssa out on the town, have you?' said Maxine. 'She looks like the love child of *TOWIE* and *My Big Fat Gypsy Wedding*.'

Alyssa shrugged. 'If you've got it, flaunt it. Now, get up those stairs and get ready, Maxine Swinnerton.' She brandished her straighteners. 'We've got work to do!'

*

Vince's mouth fell open when, after returning home early, he caught a glimpse of his wife.

'You look . . . uh, you are . . . Wow!' he spluttered as she twirled around the sitting room to the delight of the twins.

Maxine tossed her now-glossy straightened hair back from her flawlessly made-up face. 'I know,' she said.

The twins shrieked with laughter at this idea, but Vince didn't look as though he thought it at all funny. The truth of the matter was that Maxine did look amazing. Once the three girls had worked their magic she was transformed from a sad housewife into a drop-dead-gorgeous woman. With some Fake Bake, her hair curled and pinned up onto the crown of her head and her face beautifully made up by Isla, she wouldn't have looked out of place in the smartest of London clubs. Armed with a pair of trusty Spanx, Maxine had then been poured into a kingfisher-blue bustier, skin-tight Armani jeans and knee-length spike-heeled boots, all courtesy of Alyssa. The girls hadn't been joking about her wardrobe taste.

Laney had dressed up too, but kept her look low-key. She'd plumped for a white angel-sleeved top and skinny jeans teamed with her favourite L.K. Bennett strappy heels. Her hair had been straightened by Isla – who was wasted running a gift shop and really should open the first St Pontian hair-

and-beauty salon – and fell past her shoulders in a glossy golden sheet. As for Isla and Alyssa, they had really pulled out all the stops. With their micro-miniskirts, hot pants and massive false eyelashes, they looked like WAGs on tour.

No wonder Vince was looking worried.

'Where are you going?' he asked nervously as his wife sauntered past him to the taxi that was tooting its horn outside. 'Will you be late?'

'No idea,' Maxine said airily, over her shoulder.

And with this passing shot she hopped into the taxi, leaving her stunned husband standing at the front door looking very shocked.

'When was the last time you dressed up and went clubbing without him?' demanded Isla as the taxi sped off towards Tetbury.

Maxine thought hard. 'I don't think I ever have. No, in all the years I've been married, I've never gone out partying on my own.'

Poor Vince, no wonder he looked so taken aback. This worm hadn't just turned – it was doing a break-dance.

Alyssa, busily applying yet another layer of lip gloss, was horrified.

Maxine shook her head. 'No, you don't get it. I never wanted to go anywhere without Vince. I like being with him. When you find your other half, your soulmate, you don't want to be apart.'

Laney understood exactly what Maxine meant. If she could have been with Toby – if things had worked out differently – she wouldn't have wanted to be parted from him, either. Alyssa and Isla just rolled their eyes and made vomiting noises. They were well and truly in the mood to party.

⁂

'If I stay in with Steve I want to throttle myself,' said Alyssa, referring to her farmer boyfriend. 'He's up so early with his dairy herd that he's asleep by nine in the evening.'

Laney didn't like to say that when she wasn't working late, by attending a party or an opening, her idea of bliss had always been to get into her PJs and be in bed by nine. Maybe this was where she'd been going wrong? She should have gone clubbing more.

The cab pulled up in the High Street, where Isla wanted to begin with a visit to a smart wine bar she knew. It was down a side street, so the girls had to walk for a while, which was easier said than done because the cobbles weren't designed with heels in mind. It was also really cold, and in her thin top Laney was shivering. She never thought it would come to this, but she was actually missing her red Puffa coat and her warm boots.

'Not much further,' Isla promised, pointing at the small wine bar and bistro just ahead. It spilled a dim light into the darkness and the scent of garlic and tomatoes filled the air. 'This is it, Ravello's.'

She was just about to open the door when Alyssa pulled her back.

'Maybe not such a good idea, babes. Look who's already there.' She pointed her red-nailed hand at the pretty bay window, where Toby was eating dinner. With Anna.

Laney's bones crumbled. With their heads bent so close that their eyelashes were practically touching, they were so deep in conversation that they were oblivious to the rest of the world. Even their plates of food were untouched.

'Oops!' Isla pulled a face. 'Toby always did like it here.'

'Shall we go straight to the club?' wondered Maxine. In her skimpy top she was shivering like a whippet.

'What is he thinking?' Alyssa was still staring. 'I thought he hated Anna, after everything she did to him. Shall I go in and drown that bitch in her soup?'

The others laughed, but Laney felt as though she'd been punched in the stomach. There was no mistaking this. It was the perfect setting for an intimate dinner for two, exactly the right place to rekindle a romance. It was obviously no coincidence that Anna had decided to find Tana a place to stay in St Pontian. She'd been determined from the start that she would win Toby back. And judging by the way he was held rapt by her every word, that was not going to prove a very difficult task. Swallowing the tight knot of misery that had risen in her throat, she turned away.

As she followed the other girls towards the club Laney knew with fatalistic certainty that she had fallen head over heels in love with Toby Woodward. Never mind fireworks. It was as if a nuclear bomb had detonated in her brain.

28

Laney woke up to a herd of elephants tap-dancing in her skull. Even though her eyes were still shut, she could sense slices of daylight sneaking in through the blinds, ready to stab her in the eyeballs. Her stomach was churning like a washing machine on the spin cycle.

Oh God! She was obviously getting too old to be out drinking into the small hours.

She sat up, wincing when her brain swivelled inside her skull and the sunlight poked her in the iris. Staggering to the mirror, she groaned aloud at the bleary-eyed, mascara-smeared monstrosity that peered back at her. Just how much *had* she had to drink last night? She was (just about) living proof that attempting to drink your sorrows away really didn't work. Now she just felt broken-hearted *and* hungover.

After spotting Toby and Anna enjoying their romantic dinner, Laney's evening had swiftly gone downhill. The club Isla chose was hip and funky and undeniably cool, but it was packed to the gills and Laney had been elbowed and shoved so many times that her sides were black and blue. The music had been so loud it had practically made her ears bleed, and she hadn't recognized any of it, which made her feel ancient. Her only consolation had been that Maxine seemed to be having a wonderful time: rebuffing advances, strutting her stuff on the dance floor, and getting off her trolley on Bacardi Breezers. Figuring that if you can't beat them, then join them, Laney had got stuck into the half-price cocktails and eventually found herself jigging about to some very loud rap music. *The more I drink, the less I'll think about Toby, surely?* Laney had thought hopefully, but in reality the opposite was true. It seemed that no matter what she did, she just couldn't put him from her mind.

Pulling on her dressing gown, Laney padded downstairs to fetch a glass of water and a couple of aspirin. The scent of cooked breakfast made her stomach turn and for a moment she had to stand very still and pray she wasn't about to be sick. She was twenty-nine, not nineteen.

'Morning, Laney,' trilled Janet from her position bent over the cooker. 'I'm just doing a big full English for that lovely Tana. I've never known a boy with such an appetite. Would you like me to pop a couple of eggs in for you?'

Just the thought of this was enough to make Laney's stomach lurch.

'Just dry toast for me,' she said quickly.

'Oh dear. Has somebody got a sore head?' Janet teased. 'Sit down, love. I'll make you a cuppa.'

Laney filled a pint glass with water and did as she was told. The kitchen floor was rocking alarmingly and she took a few deep breaths. She was never, ever drinking again.

'It looks like you had a good night last night,' Janet remarked, once she'd taken Tana his mountain of sausages, eggs and bacon. Untying her flowery pinny, she took the seat next to Laney and poured tea from the large blue teapot. Wrapping her hands around her mug she added, slyly, 'Did you and Martin have a lovely time? I hope he isn't in a similar state to you. He's got to be in chambers today.'

Eh? Confused, Laney blinked at Janet, before painfully slowly her alcohol-blurred brain caught up. Of course! She was supposed to have been on a date with Martin last night. Goodness knows what Janet must be thinking.

'I had a fun evening,' she said carefully. There, that wasn't a lie, was it?

'Lovely.' Janet beamed at her. She couldn't have looked more thrilled if Laney had announced that she and Martin were about to get married and produce a tribe of chubby-cheeked grandchildren. Oh dear, whoever Martin was hiding from his mother, she hoped he'd come clean soon. Laney was hopeless at fibbing. How people ever managed to have affairs she had no idea. You'd need a mind fit for Mensa.

'I'll get dressed in a second and give you a hand with changing the beds,' Laney said. The combination of warm tea and aspirin was starting to make her feel more human.

Now if only there was a pill she could take to help her to get over Toby Woodward, she'd be back to normal . . .

'Oh, don't worry yourself about that, love. There's no beds to change,' Janet said cheerfully. 'Anna and Tana both stayed elsewhere last night. He only popped back because he wanted his breakfast, bless him, but that other one won't be putting in an appearance. She doesn't eat a thing – not from what I've seen anyway.'

Laney's blood ran cold. So Anna *had* spent the night with Toby. Suddenly she felt quite nauseous again.

'I wondered why I'd had Tetbury Manor on the phone this morning,' Janet continued, helping herself to a slice of toast. 'This will make you laugh, Laney: Ms Snooty has been up to no good. The hotel manager called looking for her. They'd found a pair of men's briefs in her suite and had been given this number as her contact. Did we want the briefs forwarded to us?'

Laney wasn't laughing. Instead her stomach curdled.

'I'm sorry,' she said faintly. 'I think I'm going to be sick.'

A pair of men's pants left in the bedroom suite of a luxury hotel? Now she knew for sure: Toby and Anna had spent the night together.

After a hot shower and another pint of water Laney's hangover was receding. Her heart was still aching, but unfortunately this was nothing to do with drinking cheap cocktails, and way beyond the help of tea and toast. Dressed in her comfy Juicy Couture tracksuit bottoms, soft pink hoody and trusty Uggs, she felt ready to face the world; or the Barwell kitchen at any rate.

'You've got a visitor,' Janet announced when Laney rejoined her. Sure enough Martin was sitting at the table, his socked feet up on the surface, tucking into toast and looking very pleased with himself. Her heart sank, not because Martin was there, but because he'd brought with him the most enormous bouquet of pink and cream roses she'd ever seen. Bollocks! Janet was going to get *totally* the wrong idea.

'Hello!' carolled Martin through a mouthful of toast and Marmite. 'Isn't it a beautiful morning?'

Laney glanced out of the window. The bright sunshine of earlier had given up, bullied into retreat by low and leaden clouds. A spatter of drizzle hit the pane. It was the opposite of a lovely day. WTF? Was Martin on something?

'You should be ashamed of yourself, letting Laney get in such a state,' Martin's mother chided him. 'You should at least have made sure she didn't drink on an empty stomach. What was it you had? Oysters and champagne?'

He smiled, a secret smile to himself. 'Yes, actually.'

'Well, next time you take her out for dinner, make sure it's somewhere they give you a good feed.' She paused as a thought occurred. 'You can't beat those eat-all-you-like buffets at Pizza Hut.'

'Thanks, Mum, I'll remember that,' said Martin kindly.

'Make sure you do.' Janet was pulling on her coat. 'Now, I'm off to the church, it's my brass-cleaning morning, so I'll leave you two young things to it, shall I? Give you some time alone?'

And with this parting comment, and what looked suspiciously like a wink to Martin, Janet let herself out.

'Martin,' said Laney despairingly, 'you utter, utter muppet.'

'What? What have I done?'

Men. They really were clueless. It was a miracle that patriarchy had ever worked at all.

'Your mother thinks we spent last night together, remember?' Laney said. 'I'm hungover to high heaven, you're all twinkly-eyed and waxing lyrical about the wonders of nature and, just in case she hasn't got totally the wrong idea, you turn up with flowers.'

'What's wrong with the flowers?' Martin looked perplexed.

'Martin, that has to be the most over-the-top and romantic bouquet ever. I was with my ex, Giles, for sixteen months and he never once bought me anything like that.'

Martin gave her a horrified look. 'Then the man was an idiot.'

'No, he wasn't. He just wasn't very romantic,' Laney said. 'However, women are, and your mother will have got totally the wrong idea. I bet she hasn't gone to clean the brass at all; she's probably booking the church.'

'You may be right.' He laughed, seemingly unfazed by this. 'But the flowers are for you as a "thank you" for covering for me.'

'It'll take more than flowers to get yourself out of this one,' Laney said darkly. Picking them up, she filled the sink and plunged the stems into cold water. Maybe she'd divide them up and put them in the guest rooms? If any of her guests ever deigned to spend the night there, that was. 'Was your date worth it?'

The slow smile that spread across his face said it all. Oh, Lord, Martin Rolls had it bad. Whoever the mystery woman was, she must be something special.

'Just don't leave it too long before you tell the truth,' she urged. 'These things have a nasty habit of coming back to bite you on the bum.'

'Believe me, I'd love to come clean, but it's really complicated.'

Laney fixed him with a stern look. 'Tell me exactly: how is it complicated?'

Martin looked as though he was just about to say something, but infuriatingly at this point there was a knock on the door and Maxine arrived, looking far too fresh-faced and perky for a girl with Bacardi Breezer for blood.

'Morning! How are we all today?' she sang, perching on the edge of the table.

'Suffering,' said Laney. 'Why aren't you?'

'I feel like I've been rebooted,' said Maxine. 'I can't believe I've left it so long since I went dancing. I loved the things you guys did to my hair and make-up – I'm really going to keep at it. I'm going shopping in Oxford this morning for a whole new wardrobe. No more tatty joggers and baggy hoodies.'

'No, indeed,' said Martin. 'Laney has cornered the market in that look.'

'Don't pick on me,' pleaded Laney. 'I'm weak. I can't keep up with the Bacardi Queen here.'

'Last night was a total revelation,' declared Maxine, ignoring her. 'It's made me realize that I've wasted far too much time running around after Vince. I'm going to put myself first. No more Mrs Nice Maxine.'

Uh-oh. That wasn't supposed to be the way this went. Maxine was meant to rediscover her youth, feel good about herself and remember why she fell in love with Vince in the first place. She wasn't supposed to become St Pontian's answer to *Cougar Town*.

'What about Vince?' Laney wanted to know. 'Surely he liked your new look?'

Maxine grinned. 'Of course he did. And he wasn't the only one, either. The builders working on the pub roof whistled at me when I just went past. The twins were scandalized.'

Worse and worse. Maxine was supposed to fall back into Vince's arms, not start looking at other guys. Maybe this idea of hers wasn't quite so good after all?

'Where's that hot new guest of yours?' Maxine asked, helping herself to piece of Martin's toast. 'The rugby guy? Tana Whatshisname?' Maxine started fluttering her eyelashes.

'Tana's gone training,' Martin told her. 'He left while Laney was in the shower, but not before my mother had weighed him down with some Eccles cakes.'

'He'll get us into trouble if he keeps on eating like that,' Laney said. 'Anna's got him on a strict diet.'

'He can't be expected to live on rabbit food,' said Martin. 'He's seriously fed up with Anna's food regime.'

Laney stared at him. 'How on earth do you know that?'

'We chatted in the kitchen,' said Martin. 'More toast anyone?'

Was he changing the subject? Laney hoped Martin wasn't encouraging Tana to break his diet. She wouldn't put it past Anna to try and sue the B&B for poor performance, if her client put on weight.

'I saw him coming out of your office yesterday afternoon,' Maxine remarked. 'I hope that wasn't a secret bun-eating session?'

Martin grinned. 'Hardly. No, it was nothing as much fun as that, I'm afraid. I'm doing the conveyancing for him on the house he's decided to buy.'

'Ooh!' Maxine leaned forward. 'Is he buying a house in the village?'

'He hopes to.' Martin looked smug about being on the inside of this celeb gossip. 'And before you ask, I'm not telling you which one. Client confidentiality.'

Laney was taken aback. This was a sudden decision. Tana must really like the village to have made up his mind to buy here in such a short space of time.

'Who's he moving in with?' Maxine wanted to know, her eyes big circles of excitement. 'His girlfriend?'

Martin shook his head. 'Tana doesn't have a girlfriend.'

'He's single?' Maxine let out a whistle. 'How is that possible? Surely somebody with a body like that must be taken? I bet he's got a lingerie-model girlfriend somewhere. Or maybe a pop star?'

'Not as far as I'm aware,' Martin said patiently.

'My God! The ladies in the village will go wild.' Maxine jumped to her feet. 'I'd love to stay and chat, guys, but I think I need to get to Oxford on the double. That new wardrobe of mine is definitely in order now. Tana Heretini is moving to St Ponty! Oh, my God! Wait till I tell Nancy.'

And with that exciting thought Maxine tore out of the kitchen in a blur of ringlets and high-heeled boots. Stunned, Laney and Martin stared after her. Was this really the same

Maxine who only twenty-four hours ago had been practically mainlining chocolate and sobbing into her pillow?

Martin exhaled slowly.

'Laney Barwell,' he said, with a disbelieving shake of his head, 'I fear you may have created a monster.'

29

Once Martin had gone, Laney wandered into the sitting room with a pot of black coffee and her mobile phone. She was more upset about Toby and Anna than she liked to admit, and it had taken a Herculean effort to keep chatting light-heartedly with her friends while it felt as though somebody was dragging her insides through barbed wire. Now that they had gone, she was free to crumple into a heap if she wanted to and howl like an extra from a werewolf movie.

When life decided to flick her a V-sign there was only one thing for it: she had to talk to Catherine. Her best friend always had a sage word for every occasion and, as a professional matchmaker, she was the most qualified person to talk to. Taking a swig of bitter Costa Rican blend and wincing, Laney curled up on the sofa and hit the speed-dial key.

'Catherine Wheeler dating agency, where your happy ending is just beginning,' trilled Catherine when she picked up.

'I could probably have you there under the Trade Descriptions Act,' said Laney darkly.

'Hello, babes, I was just thinking about you.' Catherine

sounded delighted to hear from her. 'Have you seen today's *Femail*? Julian Matlock's in it, making toad-in-the-hole, and he's recommended Middlehaye Farm's produce. Isn't that great?'

Yep. Flipping wonderful! Yet another blot in her already very blotted copybook with Toby. Honestly, what was it with PR? This was the sort of campaign and publicity that she used to dream about, yet Laney didn't feel at all excited. Maybe she just wasn't cut out for it any more? Perhaps she'd lived in the country for too long?

'That's probably the last thing Toby wants to hear,' Laney said gloomily. 'I'm hardly his favourite person at the moment anyway.'

'Not all that Vince-stuff? Didn't Toby understand when you explained?'

Laney swallowed. A lump the size of one of Tana's rugby balls had bounced into her throat. 'I haven't seen him since bonfire night.'

'You haven't seen him since he kissed you and then mistakenly thought you're a serial flirt? Are you telling me that you haven't been up to the farm to try and put things right? In five days?'

When Catherine put it like that, it didn't sound great.

'Yes,' she said in a small voice.

'Laney,' said Catherine sternly, 'you are a great big cowardy-custard.'

Laney thought she was probably such a big cowardy-custard that you could serve her with Christmas pudding and mince pies.

'I know, I know. And now something even worse has

happened.' Her voice started to tremble. 'Oh, Cat, I think there's somebody else.'

'Babes, don't get upset. Hold on a sec.'

There was a pause, followed by the sound of Catherine's heels clacking across the office floor and the click of a door shutting.

'Right,' she said. 'I'm all yours. Tell me everything.'

So Laney did, and when she finished she was tearful, snotty and very relieved not to have to keep her feelings cooped up any more.

'When he kissed me, I really did feel those fireworks,' she finished sadly, 'and I thought he felt them too. But I was wrong. He's already back with Anna. It must all have been in my imagination.'

'It sounds to me like the pair of you need your heads banging together!' Catherine said briskly. 'I know this is probably a wild and crazy solution, but have you tried talking to him? I generally find that communication helps. Especially in relationships.'

'That's easy for you to say. You and Patrick have *the* perfect relationship.'

'We do not.' Catherine sounded surprised. 'We row and we have days when we hate each other, and days when we drive each other nuts – just like everyone else – but we work at it, and when there's a problem we talk it through. Just like you need to go and talk things through with this Toby.'

Laney thought she'd rather chew her arm off. 'I can't. It's too hard.'

Catherine sounded exasperated. 'Laney, please shove all the romantic stuff out of the way for a moment, will you?

Love *is* bloody hard! Once the fireworks are over and the sparklers have fizzled out, you have to work at what it is that holds you together.'

'But—'

'Get off *your* butt, stop moaning, and go and talk to him.'

'When did you get so bossy?' Laney grumbled.

'It's called *tough love.* Oprah used to do it all the time. Of course, if I was Jeremy Kyle, I could get Toby to do a lie-detector test. Then we'd know one way or another if he'd really spent the night with this Anna.'

'She's his ex-fiancée. He must have loved her enough once to propose. What if his feelings haven't changed?' she wondered miserably. Anna was slim, successful, clever – what wasn't there to want?

'So he has a past? Big deal. Find me anyone at our age who hasn't.' Catherine was getting cross now. 'No one is perfect. If you love him like I think you love him, then bloody well go and get him.'

'I don't know.' Laney started to chew her thumbnail nervously, an old habit she thought she'd beaten. 'I don't think I can.'

'Well, then you'll never know. He could be the love of your life and you've thrown him away because you're a clucking chicken,' said Catherine briskly. 'Still, up to you, I suppose.'

Laney felt as if she was being told off by a teacher.

'Look, I'm throwing a big Singles' Ball next week.' Catherine seemed to be softening. 'There'll be oodles of really gorgeous guys. Why don't you come up to that? You're bound to meet somebody who'll sweep you off your feet and make you forget your broken heart.'

Laney thought about it. The idea of returning to London, to the familiar routines, friends and places, was very attractive. Her bank balance was starting to dwindle, and it might be an opportune time to see if she could meet some of her contacts and pick up some more work. Promising to think about it, she rang off, with Catherine's words about talking and *getting off her butt* ringing in her ears. By lunchtime she'd stewed over this so much that she'd made serious inroads into her poor thumbnail and was starting to wish she'd never given up smoking. If she didn't do something fairly soon, she'd be so wound up she'd start to chime.

There was nothing else for it. She had to talk to Toby.

⁂

Tana's penchant for sausages meant that the B&B's supplies were running dangerously low. A trip to the farm shop to restock – if Julian Matlock hadn't totally decimated supplies – wasn't just an excuse to see Toby, but a necessity. At least this was what Laney kept telling herself as she walked the two miles to Middlehaye Farm.

The rain had stopped now and a watery winter sun was trickling through low clouds, tipping the pie-crust ploughed fields with gold and making Laney feel a bit more optimistic. Everything was going to be fine, she told herself firmly as she walked up the drive to the farm. She was going to be casual and polite when she saw Toby – there was no way that she'd be in danger of making a fool of herself. She was dressed in her country uniform of jeans, wellies and scarlet Puffa and had only applied minimal make-up, so there was no way he'd think she was trying to impress. She planned to be friendly when she saw him, but to wait and see what his reaction was before she broached the subject of *that kiss*. If it didn't mean anything to him, then it wasn't going to mean anything to her, OK? They were adults and could be civilized about all this.

'Laney. Hello.' Alyssa was serving in the farm shop and looked delighted to see her. 'Oh! You look a bit peaky. Just how many of those cheap cocktails did you have?'

'Far too many.' Laney's stomach lurched at the memory, or at least she thought it did, but the sinking sensation could be because Toby wasn't anywhere to be seen.

'It was a great night, though, wasn't it? Maxine looked fab, didn't she? We must do it again,' enthused Alyssa, firing off a volley of questions without waiting for an answer. She looked as fresh as a daisy, all sparkling wet-peat eyes and bouncing curls. Laney must be out of practice.

'Maxine looked amazing,' she agreed, placing her basket on the counter and trying not to look as though she was peering too obviously into the storeroom. Was Toby there?

'Maxine always could scrub up a treat,' nodded Alyssa. 'And Vince wasn't too much of a minger once, either, believe it or not. I think marriage and kids just took a toll.' She shuddered. 'And Steve wonders why I keep turning his proposals down?'

Laney laughed. Steve, Alyssa's adoring farmer boyfriend, was a sweetheart, but she couldn't imagine that her lively new friend was quite ready to settle down to a life of Labradors, babies and Saturday-night TV just yet. A small, cold hand squeezed her heart because that picture actually appealed hugely to her, but seemed a million miles away now.

'Is Toby about?' she asked as casually as possible, not wanting Alyssa to think she was pursuing him.

'Somewhere in the yard, I think,' said Alyssa. 'He's in a really weird mood, though. I think he had a late night.'

Laney was *sure* he'd had a late night, but she wasn't going to discuss this with his sister. Instead she bought some sausages, then wandered into the yard with her wicker basket on the crook of her arm.

Toby was in the sand-school lunging an enormous black horse. Guinness, Laney recalled, Isla's show jumper. For a moment she stood far back and watched in awe, controlling her fear as best she could. The powerful animal cantered in circles around Toby, every kick of its muscled quarters throwing sand into the air, and loud snorts punctuating the stillness. Toby barely moved, but his eyes were trained on the horse. There was something about the skilful way in which he controlled all that energy and power with just a click of his tongue and flick of the lunge-line. It took Laney's breath away. She stood by the gate and watched him for a while, until he worked the horse back down through the paces and then slipped the cavesson off, to let the hot animal stretch and have a roll. Only then did he seem to notice her leaning against the railings and an expression of surprise crossed his face. Then he gathered himself together and his mouth set into its familiar sardonic line.

'Laney.' He crossed the school, coiling the lunge-line expertly. 'What is this? Aversion therapy?'

She smiled. 'I can be quite brave when they're behind a solid fence.'

Sound normal! Sound normal! shouted a voice in her head, but when it came to Toby Woodward she had absolutely no idea what normal was any more. All the rules and certainties went out the window and she could think of nothing more than how much she wanted him to kiss her again. Swallowing hard, she tore her eyes away from those strong arms corded with sinew and muscle, which had just controlled a ton of horse with such ease, and which she knew would feel heavenly wrapped around her.

There was silence. Oh dear, that had obviously killed the conversation.

'Isn't it a lovely day?' she said brightly.

'Very nice,' he replied.

Silence grew and swelled between them like a living creature. *Oh, sod it!* Laney thought, *life is too short to waste time on small talk.*

'Look, Toby, I know that the other night was awkward—' she began, feeling almost sick with nerves at broaching the dreaded subject.

'Awkward?' he interrupted. A frown furrowed his brow, then he exhaled and nodded. 'Right.'

She looked away from his searching dark gaze. 'You need to know that nothing ever happened with Vince. It was all a big misunderstanding.'

'So I've heard.'

Laney stared at him. 'You've *heard*? Who told you?'

He shrugged those broad shoulders. 'About eighteen people in the village.'

Laney felt hot and cold with mortification at the thought of the entire village gossiping about her, and to Toby, of all people. If a big crater had opened up and swallowed her right there and then, it would have been a happy release.

Toby looked as though he was on the verge of saying something else, but luckily for Laney at this point a huge van emblazoned with the legend *Julian Matlock* had drawn up at the gate.

'Oh, Christ!' he said despairingly. 'Not again. They'll clear us out. Look, lovely to chat, Laney, but I'd better go and deal with this. I'll catch you another time.'

Leaving Guinness nibbling the long grass that edged the school, Toby vaulted the gate with ease and strode across the yard to let the van in. Laney watched him and her stomach constricted with a cocktail of longing and regret – far more lethal than anything she'd drunk the night before. Clearly that kiss meant nothing to him after all, although there was no way she could pretend it meant nothing to her.

Then, with a sigh, she trailed away with her heavy basket of sausages and an even heavier heart.

30

When she returned to the B&B Vince was at the kitchen table drinking tea and eating Janet's biscuits. Laney's heart plummeted. *What now?*

'Hello, love,' said Nate, looking up almost guiltily when she walked in on them. 'I didn't think you'd be back this soon. Vince and I were just discussing the business.'

'What?' Laney couldn't believe it. After all she'd said to Vince about not stressing her dad out, he'd still come back to try again? Suddenly she didn't feel quite so sorry for Vince any more. 'You've got a nerve—'

'It's not what you think.' Vince looked quite upset. 'This was his idea, not mine.'

She slammed her basket down on the table and glowered at him.

'Darling, it's true. I called Vince.' Nate looked really upset, which was no good at all for his blood pressure. To Vince he said, 'I'm sorry, I should have spoken to Laney first. Can we discuss all this in a bit? Maybe in about ten minutes?'

'Of course, Nate. Whenever you're ready.' Vince stood

up and shot Laney an injured look. 'Whatever I do, you'll always think the worst of me, won't you?'

She ignored him. With Vince it was now a case of *guilty until proven innocent* as far as she was concerned. Once he had left, with much heavy sighing and a sad face, she turned to her father. 'What was all that about?'

Nate said, 'Sweetheart, I need to level with you. Please sit down. You're making me nervous, standing there brandishing sausages like Boudicca.'

Laney bunged the sausages in the fridge and slammed the door.

'Right,' she said as she sat down and faced him across the table. 'What's going on? I'm out for one hour, and in that time Vince-bloody-Swinnerton has moved in on the business again. It makes me furious.'

Nate shook his head. 'No, Laney, I invited Vince over.' He sighed wearily and gave her a sad smile. 'The B&B was always your mother's dream, wasn't it? She adored St Pontian, and it's my biggest regret that I never came here with her. I should have put our dreams first. If I'd only known just how little time she actually had . . .'

His voice tailed off. Laney reached across the table and squeezed his hand. 'It's not your fault, Dad. How were you to know?'

He shrugged and suddenly she was struck – shockingly struck – by just how old he seemed.

'Well, I did it in the end, didn't I? I fulfilled Mum's dream, even if she never got to see it.' He blinked back the tears. 'But now it feels like it's time to move on.'

What?

'You're right, love. I'm not in the best of health, and running the B&B does feel like hard work some days.'

'Dad! I'm happy to help out for as long as you need me.'

He smiled. 'I know, love, but I think it's almost gone beyond that point now. I have to be honest with myself. It's time I took it easy and retired.'

Laney said nothing, but her eyes filled with tears.

'I just need to work out what I want to do next,' Nate continued, staring thoughtfully into his teacup as though the answer might be there. 'I can't say I have a clue at the moment.'

Nate had never been the kind of man who liked to talk about his feelings; he'd always been rather old-fashioned in that respect. Mum had dealt with the emotional things, the cuddles and wiping away of tears, and Dad had helped with homework and mended stuff. When her mum died there'd been a yawning chasm left for both of them, a deep void where unvoiced fears and emotions swirled. For the first time since then Laney felt as though she and Nate had built a bridge across it.

'You deserve to move on, Dad,' she said. 'Whatever you decide, I'll support you.'

⁂

Vince had been waiting in the garden. When Laney went out he was sitting on a bench, staring morosely at the river as it danced and chuckled beneath the little bridge. He looked so sad.

'Vince, I'm sorry,' she said, sitting down beside him. 'I jumped to the wrong conclusion.'

He looked at her and his eyes were bleak with misery. 'I can't say I blame you. I haven't exactly given you the best impression, have I? I don't blame you for hating me.'

'I don't hate you.' If she told Vince he'd lost her the love of her life, he'd probably try to hurl himself in the river, so Laney said nothing about it.

'Maxine's asked me to move out,' he said.

Laney was shocked.

'She's decided that it's over and that she wants to have fun.' He clutched his thinning hair in despair. 'What am I supposed to do now? I'm going to lose her and the girls. I just want my family back, but that's never going to happen now, is it? Your plan didn't work, Laney. You girls have put too many ideas into her head and she'll probably run off with some toy boy by the weekend. Why did you have to interfere?'

'Because she was bloody miserable,' Laney shot back. 'Honestly, Vince, have you any idea just how selfish you can be? Don't you want Maxine to feel good about herself again, to be the best version of herself that she can be?'

'Of course I do. I hate the thought that I've made her so unhappy. It breaks my heart.'

Laney could have screamed. It always came down to what Vince was feeling, didn't it? 'You haven't made her unhappy,' she said through gritted teeth. 'She just lost touch with herself for a while. She's forgotten what it was like to be Maxine. That can happen when a woman is flat out being a wife and a mum.'

'I thought she felt good about looking after our family,' he said sadly. 'I thought that was enough. First she's telling me she's getting a job in the gift shop and wants to go out during the week. Then she tells me she needs space and says I need to move back in with my mum. She was so angry! I don't know her any more.'

'Nonsense,' said Laney briskly. 'Of course you do. She's still the same girl you fell in love with all those years ago. You just have to find a way of winning her back.'

He hung his head. 'I don't know if I can.'

'Of course you can. You did it once and you can do it again. We'll think of something, you'll see.' She patted his shoulder. 'Now it's freezing out here, and I can't have you dying of hypothermia and haunting this place. I'll get the kettle on, and you go back in and chat to Dad. I think he's got a proposition for you.'

He shook his head. 'The B&B was supposed to be for us. I only wanted to buy it so that we could spend more time together.'

'And you will do. Just have a little faith in your wife.' Laney gave him a shove. 'Go on, go and talk to Dad and sort out your future. I promise I'll talk to Maxine.' She crossed her fingers behind her back. 'It's all going to be fine.'

Vince looked doubtful, but shuffled off as instructed, a sad shadow of his former bumptious self, and Laney watched him thoughtfully. Had she inadvertently helped to destroy a solid marriage? Had she been wrong to encourage Maxine to feel better about herself? Laney didn't think so. She'd only wanted her friend to discover the fireworks again – but with her husband, not with anyone else.

She took a deep breath of cold, wood-smoky air. It wasn't too late to sort things out between Maxine and Vince. She was sure that underneath the misunderstandings they still loved one another very much indeed. Now all she needed was to come up with a plan. And this time it had to be a really good one.

31

If Maxine was working in the gift shop, that seemed like the ideal place to see her. She'd be behind the counter and unable to go very far, which meant that she wouldn't have any choice but to listen to what Laney had to say. Quite what this would be she had yet to figure out, but with any luck by the time she'd passed the church and crossed the street she was bound to have thought of something. Wasn't she?

Laney was just pondering all this as she passed the famous village noticeboard (which now had a sign promoting the book group *inside* the glass), when she spotted Toby leaving the gift shop. He was wearing a dark-red coat and indigo jeans rather than his usual overalls or Barbour. Maybe he was on his way to see Anna and had just popped into the shop to buy her a present? This thought was not a happy one and Laney gave herself a mental shake. She had to stop torturing herself like this. It was high time that she got a grip and moved on from the bonfire-night kiss. Toby obviously had.

Toby sensed her gaze and, looking across the street, smiled and waved. Her poor heart somersaulted. God, he had a lovely smile! It was deep and warm, and she loved the way that faint laughter-lines spider-webbed from the corners of his eyes. Her own lips curved upwards in reply, and she was just plucking up the courage to cross over and say hello when Martin came out of the village shop and made a beeline for her.

'Laney, glad I've bumped into you,' he declared, kissing her cheek warmly. 'I need to ask you an enormous favour.'

Laney kissed him back, standing on tiptoe as she tried to see what Toby was doing. There was no sign of him. He must have seen her kiss Martin and gone on his way, probably back to another luxury hotel suite where Anna was waiting for him, wearing just a squirt of perfume and a predatory smile. Oh God! What was the matter with her? She had to stop thinking like this.

'So will you?' Martin was asking, looking down at her questioningly. He'd been asking her something, Laney realized with a jolt. She'd been so busy thinking about Toby that she hadn't heard a word.

'Sorry, Martin, I didn't quite catch that. What did you need me to do?'

'I was just wondering if you'd be able to cover for me again? Tomorrow night? It would only be for a few hours. Could you tell my mother that we've gone to the cinema? I'll even pay for you to go, if you like, and throw in a giant bucket of popcorn? What do you say?'

Laney stared at him. 'You're bribing me with Butterkist?'

His pale face flushed. 'No! No, of course not! God, when you put it like that, it sounds awful. I just thought I could pay you back for helping me.'

Laney was seriously cheesed off. Not only because Martin

was embroiling her in whatever secretive things he was up to, but because he had stopped her from talking to Toby. She was shocked by just how badly she wanted to see him, even for a few minutes.

'Martin, why don't you just come clean with your mum,' she suggested wearily.

He shook his head. 'I can't. There's no way.'

'Come on, of course there is. Janet's a reasonable person. She just wants to see you happy, and whoever this mysterious woman is, she clearly makes you very happy indeed. So what's the problem?'

'You wouldn't understand.'

Laney had just about had enough of this. It was all getting quite ridiculous.

'You've already told me that she isn't married, so what's to stop you?' Then a thought occurred. Her hand flew to her mouth. 'Oh, my God! You're not dating a pole-dancer, are you?'

Martin laughed. 'No. I am *not* dating a pole-dancer.'

She folded her arms across her chest and gave him a stern look. 'So stop worrying. Just be honest. Whoever it is, you like them, and they make you happy. Of course Janet will approve.'

Leaning down, Martin whispered into her ear, 'Even if it's a man?'

Laney's bottom jaw dropped. For a second she just goggled at him, before all the pieces of the jigsaw started to rearrange themselves. Martin was gay. Of course he was! No wonder there hadn't been the slightest spark between them. Her *gaydar* was wonky.

'Now do you understand?' said Martin when she didn't respond.

Laney did a bit, but not totally. This was, after all, the twenty-first century, and things had surely moved on since poor old Oscar Wilde had been sent to Reading Gaol? Janet was a lovely person, so warm and generous. She would love her son, no matter what.

'Of course she would,' Martin replied impatiently when Laney said this. 'That isn't the point. Mum is *desperate* for me to get married. She wants one of those huge white dos that would make the royal wedding look half-hearted. Lord knows, she practically frogmarched you up the aisle the day you arrived. And then she wants grandchildren – oodles of them. How can I let her down? It's all she's dreamed of for years.'

Laney said gently, 'You can't run your life according to your mum.'

'I know all that, in theory,' said Martin sadly, 'but believe me, it feels very different in practice.'

They stood in silence for a while. The only sounds were the clip-clopping of metal-shod hooves on tarmac as Isla hacked Guinness through the village, and the distant rumble of a tractor. Country sounds – St Pontian sounds – now as familiar to Laney as London's rush of traffic.

Then another thought occurred. It was so clear and so obvious that she couldn't believe she hadn't realized sooner.

'It's Tana, isn't it?'

Martin smiled, a smile of such sweet tenderness it took her breath away.

'Yes. We met when I was looking for a celebrity to start

the fireworks display. Do you remember the meeting where we talked about it?'

She nodded. That dire meeting would be etched on her memory forever. It would probably take years of therapy to remove the damage caused by it.

'We met up in London and we really hit it off,' Martin recalled. 'Things have happened very fast since then, but as you can imagine, it's pretty complicated. Especially as he's got his image of being a macho-man.'

Laney thought of Tana with his muscle-bound body, legs like tree trunks and rippling Maori tattoos. With his mole's-pelt hair and merry smile, there was no doubting that he was a good-looking guy.

'You can't keep running around in secret,' she told him. 'Take it from me: these things have a horrible habit of coming out.'

'That's an unfortunate way of putting it,' said Martin wryly.

Laney chuckled. 'Sorry about that. Tana's a celebrity, and hugely in the public eye. The press would go crazy for a story like this, and then imagine the fallout – and not only for him. Janet would be heartbroken to learn the truth from a tabloid.'

He nodded. 'I know. Don't think I haven't been through all this a thousand times. I just have to wait until I think the time is right. Will you promise to keep it to yourself until then?'

What else could Laney do? It wasn't her secret to tell. 'Of course I will. But I can't keep covering for you. It wouldn't be right.'

Martin gave her a hug. 'I know. Thanks for doing that,

even just the once. It was wonderful to be able to spend some time alone. Even if it never happens again, I'll always treasure that memory.'

Laney's eyes filled at the tenderness in his voice. 'You really love him, don't you?'

He blushed. 'I guess I must do. It happens to us all eventually, I suppose.'

Not to me, thought Laney bleakly, after kissing him goodbye.

She walked into Isla's gift shop. With the success rate of her love life, she was more likely to win the Lottery than find Mr Right. Maybe she should have listened to Catherine and settled for Mr Nearly Right? There was a very good reason why fireworks always came with a health-and-safety warning.

'I saw you hugging and kissing Martin Rolls. And in full view of the entire village, you hussy!' teased Maxine when Laney entered the gift shop. 'Do I detect that romance is in the air?'

Oh God! Now she was going to become even more embroiled in this mess, if she wasn't careful.

'No, we're just good friends,' Laney said firmly. Then, to change the subject, 'I love the new top. I take it you had fun in Oxford?'

'Didn't have time to go. Isla collared me into working the afternoon shift so that she could go riding. I found this top in Tetbury.' Maxine did a little pirouette and the delicate green-and-pink chiffon fabric floated out behind her. With her hair piled onto her head in glossy curls and a pair of tight white jeans teamed with high-heeled boots, she looked fantastic and a world away from the crying wreck who'd answered the door to the girls only yesterday.

'You look amazing,' Laney told her and then, partly because she'd promised to and partly because she felt guilty, 'I spoke to Vince earlier. He was in pieces.'

A strange expression flitted over Maxine's face. It looked a little like sadness. 'It's his own doing. He lied to me, Laney, and he cheated on me. Don't look at me like that – I know nothing happened, and that it wasn't your fault. The fact remains, though, that in his head Vince was willing to risk everything just to boost his own pathetic ego.'

Laney said gently, 'I think he probably felt exactly the same way you did. Wouldn't it be better just to go and talk to him, rather than throwing yourself into the party scene? He obviously loves you to pieces, and he's devastated that you've asked him to move out.'

Maxine bit her lip. 'I don't know, Laney. It's too soon. I think I just need some space to think about what *I* need, for once.'

It was a fair enough point and, sensing that her friend's mind was made up, Laney changed the subject. Pretending to be fascinated by a range of hand-painted eggcups, she said nonchalantly, 'Was that Toby Woodward I saw leaving here just now?'

Maxine nodded. 'Yep.'

Laney moved on to some cloth rabbits with sad eyes and waistcoats. They reminded her a bit of Martin.

'What was he doing here? Looking for Isla?'

'No, he came in to buy a gift.'

Laney knew it. OK, so he had been in the gift shop, so she hardly needed the brainpower of Stephen Hawking to work that out. Hadn't Anna mentioned that she had a birthday coming up? And that she wanted a gluten-free cake? Had Toby popped in to buy something special for her? She was suddenly consumed by a terrible devouring curiosity. She simply *had* to know what he'd bought.

'What did he get?' she demanded.

Maxine looked at her pityingly. 'Maybe you should forget about him? Toby Woodward is gorgeous – undeniably – but he's really damaged. That Anna has done a bloody good job on him. He's never got over her, if you ask me.'

Laney *wasn't* asking Maxine. The last thing she wanted to hear was that Toby still carried a torch for his ex-fiancée.

'Just tell me what he bought!' she cried.

Maxine pulled a face. 'OK, OK, keep your hair on. I think we've got another one somewhere, but I'll have to unlock it from the jewellery display cabinet.'

Jewellery display? Laney's eyes widened. Surely he hadn't bought Anna a ring? When he'd kissed her there had been so much passion, such depth of feeling, that it had to have meant something to him too! She simply couldn't believe that it was one-sided. He'd felt the fireworks too – she knew he had.

Maxine was fiddling with some keys. 'This place is worse than flipping Fort Knox,' she grumbled as she struggled to fit the right one. 'Aha. Got it! What do you think?'

What did she think? Laney couldn't speak. It wasn't a ring, but it might as well have been. In the palm of Maxine's hand was the most exquisite glass rose, perfect in every detail, from the thorns of the stem to a delicate dewdrop on one crimson petal.

Toby had bought Anna a red rose. Its meaning could not have been any clearer.

Laney curled her hands into her palms, fighting the urge to howl. That was it then. All her hopes were dashed. Toby still loved Anna, that was obvious.

She couldn't stay and see them together. It would kill her. There was nothing else for it: she would have to go back to London.

32

Music followed Laney as she wandered into the large, orange-blossom-filled ballroom of Lullington House, the lavish fairytale venue that Catherine had booked for the Singles' Ball. The sounds of laughter, light chatter and the tinkle of glasses filled her ears, but Laney didn't think she'd ever felt less like a party or like looking for romance. She'd been back in London for several days now, but felt no closer to moving on from the events of Guy Fawkes Night.

No matter what diversions she found for herself, and there were loads – from shopping in the West End to catching up with friends and visiting the gym – nothing seemed to soothe the ache in her heart whenever she thought about Toby. He was probably with Anna at this very moment, holding her close and pressing kisses onto her glossy mouth. The very thought was enough to make her insides curdle. As she stood in the hot ballroom, breathing in the mingled scent of exotic flowers and expensive perfume, she could have been right back in St Pontian, wrapped in Toby's arms again, while a million fireworks exploded overhead. Would she ever be able to get over the magic of that night? It was so unfair. To have got so close to heaven, only to be snatched away, was worse than never having had a glimpse at all. At least beforehand she hadn't really known what she was missing.

As she watched the chatting couples, all beautifully dressed and sparkling like champagne beneath the chandeliers, Laney wished she could enter into the spirit of the evening. She had spent hours perfecting her hair and make-up, and an absolute fortune on a beautiful deep rose-hued ballgown that pulled her waist to a hand-span, but none of this made her feel excited as it would have done six months ago. The men in the room were all successful, articulate professionals whom Catherine assured her would be wonderful to date, but no matter how hard she tried, Laney just couldn't summon the enthusiasm required to chat and dance. Instead she was polite to the men who did approach her, but rebuffed their overtures, preferring to stand by a potted palm sipping her champagne and watching the happily dancing couples. She was trying very hard not to think about Toby Woodward. Her feelings for him would have to remain a deeply buried secret.

'What are you doing skulking behind a plant?' Catherine appeared at Laney's elbow. She looked fantastic in her full-skirted lime-green Karen Millen dress, and even though she was clearly not on the market – her sparkling wedding band telling a message all its own – she was still attracting lots of admiring glances. Her hair, dyed red to compliment the dress, tumbled down her back in a riot of snaky curls, and Laney made a mental note to try that look herself. After all, wasn't she living proof that blondes really didn't have more fun?

'I'm not skulking, Cat, I'm watching,' she said mildly. 'To

be honest, I can't really get into this at all. Everyone seems so shallow and boastful. If I hear any more bragging about six-figure salaries and supercharged Range Rovers, I think I'll scream. Why on earth would anyone need a Range Rover in London anyway? There's no mud or off-roading.'

Toby had been right. Life in the city could be superficial. She hadn't minded that once, hadn't even noticed it, but now she did and it was seriously irritating. The problem was that, now that her eyes had been opened to it, Laney wasn't convinced she could ignore it.

Catherine studied her through narrowed amber eyes. 'Nothing's changed here, babes. You used to find this kind of thing great fun. Why don't you let me introduce you to Alex Willowby Smyth? See him over there, by the ice-sculpture? He's really interesting. Works for Goldman's.'

Laney followed her friend's subtle indication and saw a fairly tall man with pale hair. He looked nice enough, she supposed, and was well dressed, but he didn't make her knees turn to overcooked pasta. Maybe nobody ever would again? She sighed.

'Come on, Laney, do try and give it a go,' said Catherine despairingly when Laney made non-committal noises. 'You can't expect to meet anyone if you don't put yourself out there.'

Laney supposed she had a point. As Catherine left to circulate and make sure that all her customers were having a wonderful evening, she drained her champagne and braced herself for the ordeal ahead. Project *Get Over Toby* was go.

'Laney! I can't believe you're here. What a lovely surprise.'

The delighted and familiar voice behind her caused her to spin round. It was Giles, her ex-boyfriend. Laney's heart filled with joy. Any negative feelings she had had were replaced with affection.

She hugged him tight. 'Giles! What are you doing here?'

He laughed. 'Same as you, I suspect! Looking for love, and wondering why on earth I thought I'd find it in a crowded ballroom. I think that kind of thing only ever happens in Jane Austen novels.'

It had been one of their shared guilty pleasures to curl up in front of their *Pride and Prejudice* box set on a rainy Sunday afternoon. He'd always joked that he didn't understand what women saw in Darcy, with all his cold aloofness. In Giles's opinion, Bingley, who was friendly and open, was a far better option. Laney used to argue back that all the passion lurking beneath that haughty surface was very attractive. Now, bearing in mind all that had happened with Toby, she was starting to wonder.

Giles might not have been the most obviously romantic guy, and his obsession with planning had been annoying at times, but at least he cared for her. He was open and there were certainly no deep and brooding passions running beneath the surface. Maybe there was something to be said for that, though? There might not have been any of the fireworks she'd dreamed of, but maybe she'd just been kidding herself?

With a smile she tucked her arm through his. 'Shall we take a turn around the room?'

He smiled, and at once slipped into the old familiar banter. 'Delighted, Miss Barwell. And your father? He is well?'

'Most recovered, I thank you,' Laney said. And just that easily they were chatting away as though their break-up had never happened.

The evening passed pleasantly enough, now that she had Giles to keep her company. It was lovely to catch up with him and to talk about old times. It was also very easy to remember why she'd fallen for him. He was charming, articulate and intelligent. Maybe she had been too hasty when she'd broken up with him? After all, he was only trying to plan a secure future for them both.

'What on earth's going on?' Catherine hissed in Laney's ear when Giles went to the bar.

'I'm talking to Giles,' said Laney, smiling at him across the dance floor. His DJ was loose; he'd lost weight since they'd broken up. Maybe she could wean him out of his cords and his Rutland checked shirts and take him shopping for some new clothes.

'Hello! Earth to Laney? Are you receiving me?' Catherine waved her hand in front of Laney's face. 'This is Giles – your ex, remember? The man you dumped because you said he couldn't even go to the toilet without checking his itinerary.'

Had she said that? Laney felt a stab of guilt. That was harsh.

'He's not so bad,' she said defensively. 'He's quite sweet really, he just likes to be organized.'

'*Not bad*,' said Catherine in disbelief. 'Laney – he drove you insane!'

'Maybe I was being too picky?' said Laney.

Catherine gawped at her. 'What happened to the fireworks, and not settling until you found them?'

She looked away. In her memory she felt Toby's lips on hers and saw again the rockets exploding above their heads in myriad crimson, gold and silver stars, felt her heart blossom. But this was all it could ever be. A memory. She closed her eyes wearily.

'I don't believe in fireworks any more.'

'Bollocks!' snapped Catherine. 'They're worth holding out for, aren't they?'

'You've changed your tune.' Laney was surprised. Only a few months ago Catherine had been telling her to be more realistic and to give people a chance.

She shrugged her bare shoulders. 'I think you should follow your heart, not your head, that's all.'

'That didn't get me very far, did it?'

'Giles wasn't right for you before, so what makes you think he would be now?' asked Catherine.

'Maybe I've changed,' Laney said slowly. 'Grown up a bit.'

'Are you sure it's Giles you want?' asked Catherine, biting her lip. 'If it is, I'll back off now.' She looked so worried. It was quite endearing for Laney to see her friend's concern for her.

Over Catherine's shoulder, Laney could see Giles returning with two glasses brimming with champagne.

'You can back off now, thanks, Cat,' said Laney.

Catherine gave a sad smile that Laney couldn't understand. She made polite excuses and disappeared back into the throng, where she would probably spend the rest of the evening socializing flat out with her guests and generally being matchmaker extraordinaire.

Honestly, there's no pleasing some people, Laney thought. Catherine had been on at her for ages to be less romantic and more practical when it came to matters of the heart, and now she'd finally taken her friend's advice. Smiling up at Giles, she was determined to have a good evening. If she thought several times that she saw Toby in the crowd, his dark gaze fixed on her intently, then it was just her imagination playing tricks. Toby hated the city with a passion; there was no way he would make the journey all the way from the Cotswolds to London. And he certainly wouldn't be at a Singles' Ball. Not when he was home and dry with Anna.

Feeling sick with disappointment and longing, she focused on Giles, laying her hand on his arm and looking as though she was listening intently to his every word.

'Are you all right?' asked Giles, all concern. 'You've gone very pale.'

'It's so hot in here.' She fanned her face. 'I think maybe I need to go and get some air.'

Giles glanced at his Tag Heuer watch. Laney was jolted to see it there, chunky and solid on his wrist. She'd bought it for his thirtieth birthday and was touched to see that he was still wearing it.

'I don't know about you, but I could do with getting out of here,' he said. 'It's way too crowded, and to be honest there's nobody I'd rather talk to than you. What do you say to calling a cab and going for dinner?'

For a moment she dithered. A chance meeting was one thing, going for dinner something else. In spite of herself she glanced around the ballroom one more time, just in case she could see that gorgeous tousled dark head. But there was no sign of him.

The time had come to leave Toby Woodward well and truly in the past. This was the way it had to be from now on, or else she would drive herself insane. Tucking her arm through Giles's, she took a deep breath, smiled brightly up at him and nodded.

33

The ringing of her mobile phone dredged Laney back through the heavy sludge of sleep into wakefulness. Without even opening her eyes, she reached for her mobile. As she peeled open her reluctant eyelids, her alarm clock told her it was only eight a.m.

On a Saturday. Surely there ought to be some kind of law against this.

Laney hadn't had a desperately late night – she and Giles had enjoyed a meal at a cheap and cheerful pizza place – and then, ever the gentleman, he had dropped her back in Shoreditch. He hadn't even asked if he could come in for a coffee. Laney had to admit she'd been relieved. Tempting though it was to soothe her bruised ego by falling into his arms, she didn't want to rush into anything.

Janet Mobile read the screen of her phone, and Laney's heart went into freefall. Suddenly wide awake, she sat bolt upright, her thumb stabbing at the *Answer call* button. An early call from Janet meant only one thing: something had happened to Nate.

'Janet! What's wrong?' she asked frantically, her heart

crashing beneath her ribs. Already she feared the worst, and her panic was not eased by the sound of Janet's sobs.

'Janet, please. Speak to me!'

Sick with worry, Laney leapt out of bed and started to pace the worn carpet of her room. 'What's happened?'

There was a loud hiccup and a gasp from the end of the line. 'Oh, love, I'm so sorry,' wept Janet. 'It's your dad.'

The blood froze in her veins. 'He isn't—'

'He is in a really bad way.'

Laney started pulling on her socks and jeans.

'He's had another stroke. The doctors say it's much worse this time.' Janet broke into harsh, racking sobs. 'Could you come to the Radcliffe as soon as possible? He really needs you.'

'I'm coming now.' Wild horses wouldn't have kept her away – a saying that really had value for a girl with a horse phobia. Tucking the telephone between her chin and her shoulder as she hopped into her jeans, she said, 'Can you tell me what happened?'

Breathe, she told herself sternly as Janet choked out the details of how Nate had been found collapsed on the village green. Paramedics had been called and he'd been rushed to the Radcliffe, where he was currently in intensive care and undergoing tests. Janet was in the visitors' room waiting to hear more.

'He's holding on,' she assured Laney. 'He's a tough customer is your dad. The doctors say he's stable now, but he's given us all such a dreadful scare.'

Too right he had. Laney thought she could probably date her first grey hairs to Nate's TIA, and the rest that followed would probably be down to this latest incident. She was trembling like a whippet left out in the rain.

'I'll get a taxi,' she said as she scooped up some loose change and her credit cards from her dressing table.

'Would you be able to go to the house first? Nate hasn't got any of his bits and pieces with him.' Janet was sounding pretty stressed herself. She wasn't a spring chicken either, and the last thing Laney wanted was for Janet to get herself into a state. Reassured that Nate was stable, and making Janet swear faithfully to call her the minute there was any kind of change, Laney promised her that she would pick up everything that Nate felt he needed.

Laney sent a quick text to Giles cancelling their plans to meet for lunch and explaining what had happened. Then she stuffed a change of clothes into a bag, grabbed her purse and tore out of the house. There was a taxi rank on the corner of the road and it would be quicker to hail one there than to call and wait. What the cost of a cab to the Cotswolds was didn't bear thinking about, but Laney didn't care.

Slamming the door of the shared flat behind her, she tore down the stairs and shot into the pallid November sunshine like a ball-bearing in a pinball machine. There wasn't a minute to waste. She had to get to her father.

By the time she reached the B&B it was nearly eleven and her fingernails were nibbled almost to the quick. She didn't think she'd ever been so happy to arrive anywhere in her entire life. The journey seemed to take forever, and weaving their slow way through the counterflow on the M40 had been absolute torture. She'd wanted to wallop the cabbie over the head with her rucksack and hijack the car, zooming through the traffic and zigzagging through the cones like a villain from *Police, Camera, Action!* Or a more modestly clad Daisy Duke. Instead, she'd been forced to endure endless delays and diversions while remaining glued to her mobile. Janet texted once to say that Nate was going for a CT scan, and there was one sweet message from Catherine, but apart from these the phone was silent. Laney was glad; she didn't think her nerves could take it if there had been a constant barrage of message alerts. Quite possibly she would have gnawed all the way up to her elbows by now.

Laney paid the cabbie a figure so high that he probably required oxygen even to look at it, before trekking over the bridge to the house. The B&B was picturesque, but it was very inconvenient. It was also very large, and the bills on it had to be quite a worry. As she paused on the doorstep, fishing her keys out of her bag, Laney decided that the business really did have to go. Nate had made the right decision. From now on he would have zero stress in his life, and achieving that was now her personal mission. Maybe Nate could come and live in London with her?

Musing on all sorts of possibilities, and refusing to entertain the thought that Nate might be a lot more poorly than Janet had let on, Laney threw her keys into the glass bowl by the door and marched into the kitchen to make a packed lunch. She nearly leapt into orbit when she saw Anna sitting at the table with her head in her hands.

'God, you made me jump!' Heart hammering, Laney leaned on the doorframe for support.

Hang on, what was Anna still doing here? She'd said she was leaving for New York a few days ago.

Was it her imagination, or was Anna crying?

The usually glossy hair was lank, the make-up missing and the sharp power-suit replaced by a dressing gown. Either she was in fancy dress or Anna Marsh was in a bad way.

Anna looked up and her eyes were red with weeping. She dashed the back of her hand across them. 'Sorry. I'll get out of your way. You're in a hurry to get to Nate.'

This was true, but Laney's soft heart hated to see anyone in distress, even the woman who was responsible for dashing her own hopes and dreams. She glanced at the kitchen clock. Ten past eleven. Nate was due to have a CT scan at half-past and that would take an hour, according to Janet. She'd take his car, which meant that she could be at the hospital within twenty minutes.

'I've got a moment,' she said gently. 'Would you like a coffee?'

Anna nodded, tears pooling in her eyes. 'Yes, please.'

It was strange to be back in Nate's kitchen, moving about in the familiar way and opening the same cupboards. Although she'd only been gone a short while, it felt like a lifetime. In terms of emotion, Laney supposed it had been an enormous journey. She'd left with her heart in pieces, but now it was starting to heal slowly. Maybe by extending the hand of friendship to Anna she would move herself even further along the road to recovery. Some day soon would she look back on her feelings for Toby with fondness?

Hmm, she doubted it, but a girl could live in hope, couldn't she?

'So,' she said, placing a mug in front of Anna, 'what's happened?'

A tear trickled down Anna's cheek. 'I've been trying so hard to make him understand. He never sees things from my viewpoint. Talk about a stiff-assed Brit.'

'Who?'

'Toby-bloody-Woodward. Who'd ya think?' The words were practically spat out onto the table and it took all of Laney's self-control not to recoil. 'I made a few mistakes, but I'm human, right? Everybody fucks up sometimes, right? But not him. Oh no. Toby Woodward never makes mistakes.'

He did when he kissed me, thought Laney. Aloud she said, 'What's happened?'

Anna wrapped her hands around the mug as though seeking comfort from the warmth. 'When I met Toby I was engaged to another guy, Emile, and things had gotten kinda stale between us. Toby was different from Emile in every way, and he just blew me away. I couldn't get enough of him, and he certainly seemed to feel the same.' Her face grew dreamy just with the recollection. 'My God, that man is dynamite in the sack.'

Laney actually didn't want to hear this, but sticking her fingers in her ears and singing la-la-la very loudly might have looked at bit rude.

'I had no idea what to do. Toby's *way* cute, but he lives in this godforsaken place, and I didn't want to lose Emile and then discover that I'd made the wrong choice.' Anna shrugged. 'So I did what anyone would do: I decided to see which guy suited me the best.'

Laney stared at her, shocked that Anna believed everybody else thought like her. 'You didn't tell Toby about Emile, did you?'

Anna shook her blonde head. 'How could I? I was torn.' Anna made patterns with her forefinger in the crumbs on the tabletop. 'I loved my life in New York, but I loved Toby too. I didn't think I could live here. I mean, look at the place! It's dead.'

Laney felt quite indignant to hear St Pontian described in such a manner. Granted it didn't have a Starbucks, and heaven only knew where the nearest Waitrose was, but the village had so much more going for it than she had ever dreamed. Where else would Nate have been so well cared for? The friends she'd made here and the community spirit were worth far more than trendy shops and wine bars.

Anna clearly didn't see it that way. 'Anyway, Emile wound up coming over to surprise me. Toby was mad. He broke off our engagement straight away.'

Laney was hardly surprised. 'Can you blame him?'

'I hoped he'd be a bit more understanding.' Anna's eyes filled again. 'It was a huge thing for me to break off a good potential and leave my life in the States on a whim. I'd been with Emile since high school. The thing with Toby was a whirlwind romance and, although I adored him, I was scared. I mean, can you really see me as a farmer's wife?'

'Not really,' Laney admitted, allowing herself a wry smile, which Anna returned. Part of her sympathized with Anna, for it must have been hard. On the other hand, she knew beyond all doubt that if Toby had been in love with her, she would have left the city in a heartbeat to be with him. 'What happened to Emile?'

Anna shrugged her slender shoulders. 'It didn't work out.'

Laney said nothing and just poured Anna some more coffee.

'I always checked in on this little place from afar. And when I heard about the Bonfire-Night Bonanza, and the need for a celebrity, I got my assistant to call and offer Tana's service.'

So that's how she turned up again.

Anna took a sip and sighed. 'Thank Christ for caffeine. Anyway, I wanted to meet up with Toby and explain. I guess part of me hoped that he might still love me after all and that we could start over.'

Bracing herself for an answer that she knew she mightn't like, Laney asked, 'And did he?'

'We met for a meal in Tetbury.' Tears pooled again in her eyes. Tears of regret or self-pity? Laney wasn't sure. 'Toby said he was cool with everything now, and that he'd come to terms with what had happened. He even said he forgave me for what I'd done.'

Laney's heart sank. Did Toby still love Anna?

'I told him I'd booked a room in a nearby hotel. I offered it to him on a plate . . . but he turned me down.'

What?

'What a fucking embarrassment!'

Laney's heart stopped in mid-freefall, grew wings and began to flutter back upwards.

'He said he was in love with someone else.' Anna pulled a face. 'Kinda divine justice, huh?'

Toby was in love with someone else? Laney's pulse quickened. Could she – dare she – hope that maybe it was *her*?

Could it be possible that he had felt those fireworks too? That he felt *exactly* the same way? She was just about to let herself have the teeniest, tiniest slither of hope when she remembered the phone call that Janet had taken about the mystery underpants. Was Anna telling the truth?

'I have no idea,' said Anna, when Laney mentioned men's underwear. Her cool blue eyes never even flickered. 'How droll. Maybe somebody sneaked in after I checked out? In any case, why are we talking goddamn *boxers*? I'm in pieces here!'

Laney's sympathy was fading fast. The woman was more self-absorbed than a sponge. Toby had had a lucky escape, in her opinion. And, more to the point, he didn't want Anna back because he was in love with somebody else.

Did she dare to hope that somebody was *her*?

34

Laney couldn't think about Toby right now – she was too busy worrying about her dad. Leaving Anna still slumped at the kitchen table, she grabbed the keys to Nate's Golf and set off to the Radcliffe.

'Laney, thank goodness!' Janet was sitting on a plastic seat outside the nurses' station and jumped to her feet when she saw Laney. Her usually merry face was pale and etched with lines of stress. 'I'm so glad you're here.'

Laney hugged her. 'Thank God for you, Janet. What was I thinking, leaving him?'

'Now don't you dare go blaming yourself,' said Janet sternly. 'You know your father – he's not one to take it easy.'

This was certainly true. Laney was pretty sure that following her departure from St Pontian, Nate had been up to all his old tricks and running himself ragged. He'd probably been joining Tana in his daily sausage-eating marathon.

'How is he?' she asked as Janet led her towards a side room. Already the smell of antiseptic and the squeak of rubber soles on polished floors were conjuring up a whole host of unpleasant memories. A knot of panic tightened in her stomach and Laney tried to push it away.

'The doctors won't say much to me because I'm not his next of kin,' Janet told her. 'However, they seem a little more optimistic. Why don't you go in and see him?'

The side room was darkened, with heavy blinds pulled down to shut away the world outside, and still except for the rhythmic beep of a heart monitor. As her eyes grew accustomed to the gloom, Laney could make out the inert form of her father fast asleep on the raised hospital bed. Her hand flew to her mouth and a cry of dismay shrivelled on her lips. He was cast adrift on the starched white sheet in a sea of monitors, tubes and wires, and looked so frail that it broke her heart.

'Oh, Dad,' she whispered and the room blurred. Somehow she managed to find her way to the seat beside the bed and crumpled into it. Taking Nate's hand in hers, she was shocked by the papery thinness of the flesh. When had he suddenly become so old?

As Laney sat next to her father she didn't think she had ever felt so lonely in her entire life. Nate was the only family she had. There were no grandparents, no cousins, no siblings and no mum. He was all she had in the world. Surely she wasn't going to lose him too? The last time she had sat next to a parent's hospital bed the outcome had been bleaker than she could ever have imagined. Tears fell thick and fast, dripping from her chin and splashing onto the regulation blanket. Suddenly all her angst over Toby seemed like a distant memory. *Please God*, she prayed, *if you make my father better, I promise I'll never moan about Toby Woodward – or anything else – ever again.*

'Miss Barwell?' A hand rested on her shoulder as a nurse leaned across to check one of the monitors. 'Your father is very unwell. A fifteen-minute visit is all he's up to at the moment.'

Fifteen minutes had passed? Seriously? Laney shook her head in disbelief. Nate had been asleep the entire time.

'But I never got to tell him how much I love him,' she choked, wiping her eyes with the back of her hand.

'He knows, darling,' the nurse said kindly. 'He knows.'

Laney gazed down at Nate, his face as white as the bed sheet. 'I hope so.'

The nurse wrote something on a clipboard before gently ushering her from the room. 'Wait here a moment. I'll ask one of the consultants to come and have a word with you.'

'Thank you,' whispered Laney. Once outside the room, she took a tissue from Janet and tried to compose herself while she waited for the doctor. Going to pieces wasn't going to help Nate.

'Miss Barwell? I'm Dr Leavingson, your father's clinical consultant.' A tall man with salt-and-pepper hair joined Laney and Janet. 'If you would be so kind as to accompany me to the visitors' room, I'll explain your father's prognosis and subsequent treatment regime.'

Laney stared at him. The words didn't make any sense, and suddenly the corridor felt as though it was spinning.

'Laney, love?' Janet looked concerned and put her arm around Laney's shoulder. It was solid and comforting and, she realized with a half-sob, motherly. To the consultant Janet said, 'This has been the most dreadful shock for her. May I come with her?'

'Janet is family,' said Laney, when he looked as though he was about to refuse. This was true enough, wasn't it? During the time that she'd lived in St Pontian Laney had noticed Janet and Nate growing closer. If Janet wasn't *officially* family just yet, Laney had a strong feeling that, God willing, she might be some day.

Dr Leavingson nodded and ushered them into a small room painted in muted shades of cream and beige. Posters on the wall warned of the perils of smoking; children's toys were piled higgledy-piggledy in a corner; and some sad-looking flowers wilted on the coffee table. Indicating that they should join him on a selection of sagging armchairs, the consultant opened a folder of notes, at which he gazed for a moment before steepling his fingers and regarding them thoughtfully.

'Your father's been extremely lucky,' he said. 'We've had the results of his CT scan back, and that confirmed that he has had an ischaemic stroke. That means he had a blood clot in his artery, which made its way to his brain and blocked the flow of blood. I suspect this clot was caused by hardening of his arteries due to excess fatty tissue.'

And this was *lucky?*

'Your father was found by people who did exactly the right thing: they knew that time is of the essence and acted quickly, and we've been able to treat him by injecting Alteplase directly into his vein,' he continued.

'What does that mean, Doctor?' asked Janet, looking worried.

'It's a clot-busting medicine that will directly dissolve the clot and hopefully limit any further damage,' he explained.

'Damage?' An icy claw scraped at Laney's heart. She'd been so relieved to learn that Nate was not in immediate danger that she hadn't even stopped to contemplate the consequences of a stroke. Would he be able to talk? Or walk? Or feed himself?

'So far he seems weakened on his left side, but the areas that control speech don't seem affected,' the consultant reassured Laney and Janet. 'We'll know more once we've run another set of tests. Until then, please try not to think the worst. Of those people who survive a stroke, about three in ten are fully independent within three weeks. This rises to about five in ten within six months. If it hadn't been for that couple who brought him in so quickly, the outlook could have been very different indeed.'

Leaving them a little more reassured, the consultant promised that as soon as he knew more he would speak to them again, and gently suggested that they left Nate to rest.

'I blame myself,' Janet said as they made their way through the hospital and out into the car park. 'I should have stopped him from joining Tana in all those fry-ups.'

Laney shook her head. 'Dad's a big boy, Janet, and made his own decision.'

Just as Toby had made his decision about her, she thought, and just as she was making the decision to move on.

Then, as though thinking about him had conjured him from thin air, Toby Woodward was walking straight towards them. His hair was a mass of curls and his long legs ate up the distance of the long corridor. Laney's mouth dried. No matter what she decided, the fact remained that he was still the most attractive man she thought she'd ever laid eyes on. Her head might be telling her to move on, but every other cell of her being was longing to be close to him.

Breathe, she told herself sternly, *or they'll be taking you into ICU next.*

'Laney! I am so sorry,' Toby said, his dark eyes brimming with regret. 'How's Nate doing?'

She took a deep breath. 'He's stable. We'll know more later.'

He inclined his head. 'Of course. We came to check on him. We've brought some flowers.'

We? For one awful minute Laney thought Anna was about to materialize. It was almost a relief when Isla joined them, complaining breathlessly about car-parking prices. They looked very cosy together, Isla threading her arm through Toby's, and in their matching Barbours and Dubarry boots looked like a glamorous couple from *Country Life Style* magazine. They had so much in common, not to mention their history, and with a jolt Laney realized that Isla was probably the person Toby was in love with. And why not? Isla was pretty, St Pontian-born and bred, and she shared his passion. It all made perfect sense now. Just as Martin's feelings for Tana had been shielded by Laney's own preconceptions, so the same was probably true here. Maybe they had both decided that common ground was enough to make the relationship work? Rather as she was thinking of Giles.

She smiled, even though inside it felt as if a razor blade were slicing through her heart. She wished them well.

'It's kind of you to come and visit,' she said.

'Kind?' Toby looked puzzled. 'I've been worried sick.'

'Oh!' Janet turned to Laney apologetically. 'I meant to tell you, but I got so caught up in everything. It was Toby who found your dad.'

Toby? Laney's eyes widened. He was the person whose quick thinking had probably saved Nate's life?

'He was amazing,' gushed Isla.

Toby looked embarrassed. 'I just did what anyone would have done.'

'I owe you more than I can say,' Laney said softly. 'If you hadn't acted so swiftly, Dad could have been so much worse.'

He turned pink. 'I just called an ambulance.'

'He's too modest,' said Isla, laying her auburn head against his shoulder and smiling up at Toby adoringly. 'I was impressed. He's a total hero.'

Toby cleared his throat awkwardly.

'Well, I certainly owe you,' said Laney. She smiled at him and for a moment their eyes locked. Then she dragged hers away. There was no way she was doing this any more. It was like self-harm to the soul.

'I hate to hassle you, Tobes, but can we get going? I've got to work at three,' said Isla.

Toby seemed to have to pull himself back to the present.

'Of course. Take care, Janet. And you too, Laney,' he said. And then he stepped forward and dropped a kiss onto her cheek. 'I hope you'll be really happy with your new man,' he whispered in her ear. 'He's more fortunate than he'll ever know.'

Laney stared after him, hardly able to breathe. Her hand rose to her face. Where his lips had brushed it, her skin burnt as though his touch had been a branding iron.

New man? What on earth did he mean?

35

It was late afternoon when Laney arrived back at the B&B. The light was fading from the sky, and shadows pooled across the path as she crossed the bridge, and she cried out in alarm when a figure stepped out of them, calling her name.

'Giles!' Her hand flew to her heart, where it thudded painfully beneath her ribs. 'You scared me to death.'

'God! Sorry.' Giles looked horrified. 'I got your text and I drove straight here. I've been calling and calling you.'

'I've been at the hospital. I had my phone switched off.'

'How's Nate?' Giles was all concern.

She shrugged. 'Tired and very poorly. I'll know more tomorrow.'

'I'm so sorry. I wish you'd called me. I would have driven you. I hate to think of you going through all this on your own.'

His eyes met hers and they brimmed with kindness. A lump rose to her throat. How wonderful would it have been to share today with somebody? Giles was such a gentleman and would have been a marvellous support.

'That's really sweet of you, Giles.' Laney unlocked the

front door. The joy of being with someone for sixteen months meant that she didn't have to pretend with him. She really wanted to crash for a couple of hours, and she knew Giles would understand.

'Laney, I'd do anything for you. Not a day's gone by since we've broken up that I haven't missed you. When I got your text, all I could think about was getting here to be with you and to help you.'

Laney smiled gratefully. Appearing on her doorstep unannounced, and after having driven miles, was the sort of spontaneous and romantic gesture that she used to long for Giles to make.

'You don't need to ask. I want to be there for you.' He stepped forward and took her hands in his. 'Laney, let me help. Please. You need to let people help.'

This plea struck a chord. Hadn't Nate said something similar about her mother? She exhaled slowly. Giles was a lovely man. He might not be the most romantic sort, or make rockets and jumping jacks explode in her heart, but he was kind and honest. There was a lot to be said for this. Maybe it was time she gave him another chance?

Pushing open the door, she smiled at him. 'Shall I put the kettle on then?'

A wide answering beam spread across his face like sunshine. 'I can't think of anything I'd like more.'

⁂

The next week flew by in a flurry of hospital visits and appointments with doctors and rehabilitation nurses. Laney lost count of the times she and Janet drove to the Radcliffe –

so many that they could probably drive there in their sleep. Giles took the week off work so that he could help out. Although Nate was a lot brighter, his speech was a little slurred and he was left feeling absolutely exhausted. It would be a long time before he was up to running the business again. Dr Leavingson was pleased with his progress, but warned them that the road to recovery was going to be slow. There would be speech therapy and physiotherapy to contend with, and under no circumstances was Nate to place himself under any stress.

'I'll have to take over,' Laney said to Giles one evening as they ate in the pub. 'There's no way Janet can be expected to do it. I can't ask you, and Martin can't help out indefinitely.'

Giles looked thoughtful. 'There's a lot to be said for living in the countryside. Martin was telling me about a legal practice in Banbury that he knows is looking to take on a senior partner.' He reached out and took her hand. 'What do you think?'

What did she think? The honest answer was that Laney really didn't know. Giles had been very sweet and he'd helped out enormously. She was fond of him, and having him around was lovely – so easy. But to have him here permanently? She wasn't so sure.

'You know how I feel,' Giles said, his voice lowering. 'I want us to try again. I think we stand a really good chance of making it work. If you put it down on paper, the odds are more than stacked in our favour.'

There he went again. Laney's heart plummeted. Although she knew this was just a figure of speech, she wouldn't have been surprised if somewhere Giles really had jotted down all the pros and cons of getting back together with her. The idea left her cold.

'I can't think about anything like that at the moment,' she said gently, slipping her hand away, but not before Alyssa had seen the gesture from the bar and raised a quizzical eyebrow.

'I understand. You have a lot on your plate right now.'

That was Giles all over: reasonable, considerate and rather lacklustre at times, she thought guiltily. If he did have any violent passions, he certainly hid them deeply, that was for sure. Feeling bad, she smiled at him gratefully. 'Things have been hectic. Thank goodness there's the Winter Ball to look forward to.'

Giles nodded his sandy head. 'Yes, I'm so pleased to have been invited. I almost feel like a local.'

'I wish I could have done more,' sighed Laney. 'It was my idea really, but I've been so flat out with Dad that I haven't had a minute to help. Thank goodness for Maxine and Alyssa. They've been brilliant.'

'Ah yes, Maxine.' Giles took a sip of his port. 'Is it still over with her husband?'

Laney sighed. Vince and Maxine's shattered marriage was something that played on her mind quite a lot. Vince had moved out, as directed, and Maxine had been very busy shopping and revamping her image. But on the last two occasions that Laney had seen her, Maxine had seemed rather low. Single life wasn't quite the endless round of partying she'd thought it would be, she'd said sadly, and sometimes she even missed Vince. Not enough to forgive him – heaven forbid! But all the same . . .

'Here she is now,' Giles said, as Maxine came in to sell more Winter Ball tickets. He waved and smiled. 'Hello!'

Maxine waved back. 'Drinks?'

'I'm fine, thanks,' said Giles and Laney nodded. She'd just had a really good idea and she needed her wits about her if she was to stand a chance of pulling it off. Pink-wine brain was a definite no-no.

'Budge up.' Maxine squeezed in next to Laney and placed her collecting tin and notebook on the table. 'I've sold loads. The place will be packed.'

'That's great.' Laney smiled at her. 'You ought to be a party planner. You'd be brilliant.'

Maxine's eyes sparkled. 'Wow! Yes, that would be fantastic! In fact, how about a wedding planner? That would be even better: spending other people's cash on frocks and flowers. I loved planning my wedding . . .' Her voice tailed off and the sparkle in her eyes dimmed. 'I wonder if Vince will be coming to the Winter Ball?'

'Babes, I thought you were moving on?' said Laney briskly. 'Isn't it time you started thinking about finding somebody new?'

Giles looked at her in shock. 'Laney, I don't think—' he began and then yelped when she kicked him hard on the ankle.

Maxine's mouth quivered. 'I'm not sure.'

'Come on. I thought you were all for discovering who you really are?' Laney gave Maxine a stern look. 'My best friend Catherine runs a really successful dating agency: she's always saying that if the fireworks aren't there, then he's not your guy. Why don't you let her set you up? Imagine turning up at the Winter Ball with a new date on your arm.'

Maxine bit her lip. 'I'm not sure. Isn't it a bit too soon?'

'It's just a date! Nobody is expecting you to marry the guy.' Laney picked up her mobile and made a big show of texting Catherine. 'Come on, it's just a bit of fun.'

Giles was staring at Laney open-mouthed. Putting her hand beneath his jaw, she shut it with a click.

'You will need to follow a few rules, though,' Laney said, hoping she didn't sound like a teacher.

Maxine laughed nervously. 'Oh God, really? I'm so out of practice.'

'Nothing scary,' Laney promised. 'It's just that Catherine insists on blind dates being very mysterious. She thinks it's far more romantic that way.' Laney started ticking the rules off on her fingers. 'You can't speak to him before you meet. You'll meet your man on the night, in the sports pavilion, by the tables. You need to wear a purple flower in your hair. He'll carry a white rose.'

'Bloody hell,' Maxine shook her head. 'Is it always this complicated?'

'No arguing,' Laney told her.

'OK,' said Maxine. 'Why not? I'm a free agent.' She finished her drink and shot them a bright smile. 'Right. Onwards and upwards. I need to sell the rest of these tickets.'

She wandered off and started hassling people at the back of the pub, thrusting tickets in their faces.

'What on earth,' said Giles once Maxine was out of earshot, 'was that all about? Since when has Catherine insisted on mystery? I thought you wanted Maxine and her husband to sort things out?'

'O ye of little faith.' Laney grinned.

'Laney Barwell, what are you up to?'

She tapped the side of her nose. 'You'll just have to wait until the Winter Ball to find out, I'm afraid.'

A knot of excitement tightened inside her chest. This was a good idea, she just knew it. Or at least it would be, once she'd managed to have a little chat with Vince.

The next morning saw Laney returning to Middlehaye Farm on yet another sausage run. Tana really ought to buy shares in Toby's company, she thought, when Alyssa informed her that they had sold out yet again. The amount he ate must make a fortune and was a great advert for the quality of the produce. Hey, now that was an idea – maybe she could ask Tana if he'd consider doing an advert for her? He was so popular, and rarely out of the papers these days. Everything he touched seemed to turn to gold. Anna might be a rather inadequate human being, but as a sports agent there was no denying that she was good.

Laney was just crossing the farmyard, thinking about when she first arrived there and about how things had changed, when she heard a soft voice chatting away.

'Now listen, Rosie. I can't have you bullying Bumper like that. Do you hear me? She's very near her time, and the last thing she needs before a farrowing is you hassling her out.' There was a pause as though the speaker was listening. 'Really? Well, I don't think her being in the trough at all hours is an issue. There's enough food for all of you girls, and when your babies arrive there'll be plenty for them too.'

The voice was coming from the barn where the pig pens were. Intrigued, Laney stepped closer. For a moment her eyes struggled to adjust to the dimly lit interior, before she made out a solitary figure leaning over a stall. It was Toby, and he was chatting away to the pigs as though they were people. There was something really sweet about this unexpectedly sentimental relationship with his animals.

'Who's there?' Toby called, his face in silhouette. 'You can come in.'

She stepped forward. 'It's only me. I'm sorry; I didn't mean to disturb you. I came to buy some more sausages.'

At the sight of him her heart squeezed. Toby Woodward – the one who got away.

He inclined his head towards the pigs. 'Still cooking, as you can see. Your PR job has just been far too effective.'

She couldn't find anything to say. Just being this close to him snatched her words away. Longing coiled around her heart. At last she found her voice.

'It's all going well?'

He chuckled. 'You could say that. I can't keep up with it.'

'I'm glad.' She paused for a minute, unsure of what to say next. 'I'm glad that I was able to make a difference.'

'You have certainly done that,' he answered quietly. 'All the difference in the world.'

Silence. An awkward look passed between them.

'I heard you just now, you know?' she said, plastering on a cheeky smile. 'Chatting to your pigs.'

'I don't know what you're talking about,' Toby replied,

feigning ignorance. 'This lot are like products on a factory line to me.'

She laughed. Then more silence. The atmosphere was concrete-heavy. Not a sound except for the snuffling of the pigs and her own drumming heart. She almost stepped forward to stand beside him, drawn to touch him as a moth is to the flame, but then Toby seemed to stir himself out of a reverie.

'I'm so sorry, I never asked after Nate.' He turned and gave her a smile, but it was a polite smile that never touched his eyes. The atmosphere shattered. 'How's he doing?'

Small talk. Laney was appalled at how bitterly disappointed she was. *I have to get over this man*, she thought desperately.

Biting back her misery, she gave him a cheerful smile. 'Much better, thanks. He's making progress. Janet's been amazing; she's there every day. In fact everyone's been brilliant. Martin, Tana and most of the sports committee have been to visit.'

'And Giles, of course,' said Toby. His face was impassive as he spoke.

She nodded. 'Yes. He's been fantastic too.'

There was another pause. And they stared at one another. He took a step closer and she felt weak just being near him. For a moment Toby looked as though he was about to say something. Then he shook his head as if he'd thought better of it.

'I'd better get on – this place doesn't run itself. Nice to see you, Laney. Give Nate my best.'

Laney swallowed hard. He was as out of reach as the

sliver of moon that still hung in the darkening sky. With a heavy heart she retraced her steps home to the B&B, where Giles was waiting, a good man who loved her. And she could love him too, if she tried. With his sweet smile, kind heart and loyal nature he was the kind of man that any woman would be proud to love. She loved a lot about him already.

So why then did she struggle to picture his face, and see another's stamped over his features? Laney feared that Toby's kiss would haunt her forever.

36

Laney's hands flew to her mouth as she stared at the sports pavilion in amazement. 'It looks spectacular! Is this really the same place?'

Gone was the familiar utilitarian hut, and instead there was a winter wonderland. White fairy lights were looped from the trees and swung gently back and forth. They had been strung around the eaves, and icicle lights hung from the porch, filling the inky night with silvery starlight. White streamers were draped across bushes and somebody had even rigged up a bubble machine to throw soapy kisses into the darkness. A jazz band was playing, light chatter rose and fell, and glamorous couples in evening dress strolled up the steps and into the warmth beyond.

'Not bad, huh?' Alyssa said, looking proud. She pulled her pashmina a little closer against the December chill. 'Everyone really pulled together to get this off the ground in such a short time.'

'You've all been brilliant.' The Winter Ball mightn't have the glitz and gloss of a London gathering, and they were drinking cava rather than Cristal, but Laney wouldn't have traded places for the world. Everything here had been done with love and generosity. And that was what St Pontian was all about.

She reached into her vintage beaded evening bag and pulled out a white rose. 'Can you give this to Vince?'

Alyssa raised a dark eyebrow. 'I thought that was all a big misunderstanding? Only kidding,' she added hastily when Laney gave her a look. 'Of course I will. It might cheer him up. He's got a face like a wet weekend.'

'Not for much longer, with any luck,' Laney said fervently, while crossing her fingers. Surely something had to go right at last?

Leaving Alyssa to find Vince, she handed her ticket to one of the Swinnerton twins, who took great delight in stamping her hand with a red heart. Inside, the pavilion had been transformed even further. A mirror-ball twirled from the beamed roof and every wall had been covered in silver-and-white paper. Black and white was the dress code, and all the dancing and chatting villagers only added to the surreal sensation that she'd walked into a scene from Narnia.

'It's great, isn't it?' Martin joined her, looking very suave in his tuxedo. He kissed her on the cheek and handed her a glass of cava. 'Well done you, for having such a fantastic idea. I can't believe we haven't celebrated St Pontian's Day before. Mind you, it is a bit of a grisly tale.'

Laney sipped her drink. 'Why? What happened to him?'

'Got sent to work in some hideous mine, and was then martyred by being beaten to death, I think.' He grimaced. 'Kind of puts my moaning into perspective.'

'And mine,' said Laney.

'Ah yes, the dashing Mr Woodward.' Martin paused. 'I need to tell you something, but you must absolutely promise not to let on that I told you, OK? Alyssa would kill me.'

Laney was intrigued. 'What?'

'Not until you promise, cross your heart and hope to die. Say it, girlfriend!'

She laughed. Martin really was getting camper by the day.

'Cross my heart.' She drew a cross over her chest. 'Satisfied?'

Martin leaned forward until he was whispering into her ear. 'Toby followed you to London. To that Singles' Ball.'

Laney stared at him. 'What? Why?'

Martin slapped his hand against his forehead. 'Doh! He was following you. He had a glass rose that he wanted to give you? Alyssa found it smashed in the bottom of the waste-paper bin in the farm shop.'

Laney was stunned. The rose had been meant for her? She was totally perplexed. He'd come all the way to London. How on earth could Toby have known about the Singles' Ball? Then the penny dropped: Catherine. No wonder her friend had been so desperate to keep her away from Giles. Ever the matchmaker, Catherine must have taken the bull by the horns and contacted Toby. But why would he go?

Unless . . . unless he felt the same way she did?

'But why didn't he say?' she whispered. Then she realized exactly why. She hadn't imagined that she'd seen Toby at the ball. He really had been there – and when he'd seen her with Giles, he'd thought they were a couple. After Catherine had asked Laney whether Giles was the one she wanted, Catherine would have told Toby her response. That was what Toby had meant when he'd mentioned her 'new man'. She felt hot with heartache. Giles had been staying at the B&B too, and even though absolutely nothing had happened between them, it probably looked to everyone else as though they were an item.

She felt sick.

'Hello, you two! What are you whispering about?' Janet asked. Poured into a tight ballgown with a puffball skirt, and with her hair piled high on her head, she looked like a refugee from the Eighties.

'Nothing,' said Martin.

Janet had looked so hopeful that her son was whispering sweet nothings, Laney decided that she'd had enough. All these secrets were starting to make her feel exhausted.

'Martin's got something to tell you,' she said.

'Have you?' Janet looked baffled.

Martin shot Laney a warning look. 'No.'

'Martin,' said Laney, 'she's your mum. She loves you. She'd be delighted to meet the person you're in love with.'

Janet's eyes widened. 'Of course I would, love. Anyone who makes you happy makes me happy.' Then she frowned. 'It isn't you, Laney?'

Laney shook her head.

'Well, who then?' She glanced around the room, looking confused.

'Who what?' said Vince, joining them. He'd had his hair cut in a trendy ruffled style, which although it didn't quite work was a very brave effort. He'd lost a bit of weight too, which suited him, and in his DJ he actually looked quite dashing. The white rose was in his buttonhole, Laney noted with satisfaction. Top marks to Alyssa.

'Martin's new partner,' Janet explained. 'He was just about to tell us who she is.'

There was a pause.

'Martin,' urged Laney.

He shook his head. 'I guess I have to break the news at some point. Tana! Can you come here a minute?'

The rugby ace turned round and gave Martin a smile of such sweetness that it would have melted the hardest of hearts. Crossing the room in two strides of his massive legs, he was soon at Martin's side, where he beamed delightedly at them all.

'Isn't this a great party?'

'Tana,' said Martin, 'you know my mum, Janet, already, don't you?'

'Hello, pet.' Janet reached up on tiptoe to kiss Tana's cheek. 'Of course I do. We see each other at breakfast daily.'

Martin's Adam's apple bobbed nervously. 'Mum, Tana's my partner.'

'How lovely!' said Janet, while Vince turned puce and made gasping sounds. Everybody stared at her.

'Lovely?' echoed Martin. 'Is that it? Do you understand what I'm saying? I'm gay, and Tana is my boyfriend.'

'What do you want me say, Marty?' His mother put her hands on her hips and gave him an arch look. 'It's hardly a surprise, is it, dear? Your house hasn't exactly been like the Playboy Mansion.'

'But aren't you shocked? Disappointed? Upset that I won't give you grandchildren?' he spluttered.

Janet rolled her eyes. 'Honestly, Marty. What century are you living in? I've had my suspicions for ages. That's why I was so amazed when you started hanging out with Laney. I was pleased, because I liked *her* so much and you seemed so happy – but not because she was a girl. I'd like anyone who made you happy. As for grandchildren, gay people do have children these days, you know.'

'But . . . how come I didn't know?' Vince had finally regained the powers of speech and was no longer opening and shutting his mouth like a cod.

'Because it never came up,' said Martin gently.

Vince looked as if he was trying to work out a very hard maths sum in his head. Then a thought occurred. 'Hey, Tana! How about some tickets to your next game?'

While they talked and laughed, with Martin looking as though about ten tons of concrete had fallen off his shoulders, Laney spotted Maxine standing shyly at the back of the hall. As instructed, she was hovering by the tables, pretending to be fascinated by the big cake Nancy had made, and was wearing a purple silk flower. *Yes! Game on!*

'Isn't there something you need to do?' she said to Vince.

He blanched. 'I'm not so sure, Laney. It sounded like a good idea the other night, but what if she sees me and is disappointed?'

'Don't be such a wet lettuce.' She gave him a shove in the small of his back. 'Go.'

Looking as though he was off to his execution rather than to woo back his wife, Vince set off across the pavilion, rose in hand. Maxine's eyes widened when she saw him and she really did a double-take when she noticed the rose. Was she melting a bit or was that just wishful thinking?

Vince handed her the rose in his hand. Laney could see the tears in Maxine's eyes from here. Stepping onto the podium, Laney switched on the mike.

'Ladies and gentlemen, if you would, please clear the floor,' she said. 'Mr Vince Swinnerton has something he would like to say.'

Right on cue, Isla pressed a button on the pavilion's ancient PA system and Boyzone's 'Love Me For a Reason' began to play.

'Our song!' gasped Maxine, her hand flying to her mouth.

Vince walked away from Maxine and towards the podium. Laney stepped down and handed the mike to Vince and started to pray. He mustn't mess this up. Far too much depended on it now.

'Maxine,' said Vince, his voice quavering into the microphone. 'I've been an idiot. I was scared that I was getting old, and that we were starting to drift apart. I did some stupid things and I made some huge mistakes, because I didn't think I deserved you. I still don't think I deserve you, but I promise that if you give me another chance I will love you every day for the rest of our lives. Wherever you go, whatever you do, I will be right here waiting for you. You're the best thing that has ever happened to me, and I can't bear to be apart from you for another minute.'

A chorus of *Aaahs* rippled around the crowd at this. It was pure Cheddar, but Laney knew the sentiment was one hundred per cent sincere and her eyes filled.

'I'm so sorry,' said Vince. 'Maxine, I love you and I want you back. I want our life back. What do you think?'

Everybody in the place seemed to hold their breath as their eyes turned to Maxine. She was standing very still and tears streamed down her face.

'I'll think about it,' she said.

And Maxine thought about it for a millisecond, before racing across the dance floor and hurling herself into Vince's arms. The pavilion erupted into cheers and claps and, as Maxine and Vince kissed, oblivious to everyone except themselves, the dance floor began to fill with swaying couples. The mood of romance was contagious, and Laney smiled to see Alyssa and Steve join in, as well as a shy Tana and Martin.

'Would you like to dance?' Giles asked, holding out his hand.

Laney was taken aback. He'd not been there a few minutes ago.

'I'm sorry I'm late. The M40 was hell,' he continued. He smiled his sweet smile at her and her heart twisted. He was lovely, but he wasn't for her. He never had been and never would be. 'Will you join me?'

She was just trying to find the right words to tell him things were never going to go any further when Isla bounded up and said, 'Laney! Will you please stop hogging all the fit blokes around here. Let some of us have a chance.' Catching the stunned Giles's hand, she tugged him onto the dance floor. Then she turned and mouthed over her shoulder, 'Go and find Toby. It's *you* he loves.'

For a moment Laney stood transfixed as the words sunk in. Isla was telling her that it was her – Laney Barwell –

whom Toby was in love with. As the truth hit her like a sucker punch to the stomach, she couldn't stand there any longer. She had to find him and tell him how she felt.

She couldn't bear to waste another second.

37

There was no sign of Toby inside the pavilion. Although the dance floor was now crowded and the queue for the bar six deep, Laney would have known in a heartbeat if he were present; every fibre of her being would have told her. He must still be on his way. Unable to wait a moment longer to tell him how she felt, she wrapped her pashmina around her bare shoulders and set off in the direction of Middlehaye Farm.

It was one of those beautiful clear wintry nights and the velvet sky was sprinkled with stars. As she walked across the field, her ballet pumps crunching on the frozen grass beneath, the merriment of the Winter Ball faded into the distance. Soon all she could hear was the trembling hoot of an owl and her own rasping breathing as the cold air hit her lungs. Her breath rose heavenwards like incense, and Laney found herself hoping that her dearest wishes would float up there with it. Maybe somebody would hear, and then they would come true?

She was just trying to open the heavy gate that led to the first of Toby's fields, all Cadbury's Flake ploughed land at the moment, when a piercing snort made her almost jump out of her pumps. With a cry of fear Laney leapt back, and not a moment too soon either, for looming out of the darkness was a horse, eyes rolling and nostrils flared. White foam like whipped egg-white frothed from the bit, sweat flecked its neck and, as the rider tried to pull it up, the horse pranced and shied as though possessed. Feeling sick with terror, Laney flattened herself against the gate.

'Whoa, you stupid animal!' the rider cried, or rather tried to, because she was so drunk that the words were little more than a jumbled slurring of syllables. 'Belle! I said stop!'

Belle? This plunging creature was the gentle, velvet-nosed Belle? The injured show jumper that Toby had been nursing back to health? Surely not? This frenzied creature was nothing like her. Whoever was on Belle had reduced the normally sweet-natured mare to a quivering wreck.

'Christ, another goddamn gate! What is it in this miserable country?' Sawing at Belle's mouth, the rider managed to pull the horse up, all but tumbling to the ground in the process.

Laney's eyes widened. Even in the darkness and with no more light than that thrown down by the stars, there was no mistaking that voice and slim body: Anna. And judging by the swaying and the slurring, she was totally and utterly wasted. Drunk in charge of a horse? There had to be some kind of law against this, surely? And what about poor Belle? Toby said that she couldn't be ridden.

Fury at seeing an animal so abused and mistreated suddenly drove away all fear and recollection of her phobia. This was Belle – who loved pats and carrots – reduced to a shuddering sweating mess, and all Laney could think about was calming the petrified mare. Stepping forward and taking a long shaky breath, she reached out and grabbed Belle's reins in one hand, soothing the hot neck with her other.

'Ssh, Belle, ssh,' she murmured. 'It's all going to be fine.'

Laney's heart was racing, but she tried to calm it by controlling her breathing.

Anna lurched forward. Her hair, tumbling down from a chignon, was straggling over her face. As she pushed it back, Laney saw that she must have been crying because her mascara had streaked her face in sooty rivers.

'Eh? What the hell?' Her eyes, crossed with drink, tried desperately to focus. 'Oh, it's you. What are you doing out in the dark?'

'Never mind me!' hissed Laney, absolutely incensed. 'What on earth are you doing? This horse is injured. Get down!'

'No,' Anna said, sounding like a toddler. 'I'm looking for Toby.' She clutched Belle's mane for support as she listed in the saddle. She was so drunk that it was a miracle she'd managed to get on the horse in the first place, let alone ride Belle bareback almost all the way to the village.

'Toby isn't at the party,' said Laney. And he obviously wasn't at the farm, either. Where was he?

'He isn't? But I need to see him. I need to tell him that I'm sorry.' Anna's bottom lip wobbled dangerously. 'He won't listen to me. I thought if I rode a horse all the way to find him, he'd believe me. He'll see that I've changed. I've even taken up horse riding because I love him. He'll fall in love with me all over again.'

Quite frankly, Laney thought that if Toby saw the state of Belle he was more likely to want to drown Anna in a water trough than fall in love with her.

'Please get off,' she said, tugging at Anna's leg. 'Belle really shouldn't carry anyone.'

Anna was too drunk to either listen or care. Instead she wound her fingers into Belle's silvery mane and started to cry. 'Toby won't forgive me for still being with Emile when we met. Emmy made it ten times worse, when he let it slip that we were still sleeping together. Toby wanted to be exclusive, but nobody in New York is ever exclusive until they're sure. He's so goddamn provincial.'

Laney shook her head. She was totally out of sympathy with this selfish woman. 'This is St Pontian, Anna, not *Sex and the City*. Of course Toby was upset. He thought you were engaged to him.'

Anna didn't seem to hear a word Laney was saying. Instead she just wanted to carry on sobbing out what she obviously thought was a tale of woe.

'I saw Toby in *Country Life Style* a few weeks ago. He looked so hot, and I thought that maybe he was changing? Becoming a bit more urbane?' She leaned forward and clutched Laney's shoulder. Sour breath hit Laney full in the face, and she flinched from the smell. 'You understand, don't you? We're alike, us city girls.'

'We are *not* alike. Now get down from the horse,' Laney ordered.

For a second Anna deliberated, torn between the conflicting desire to try and prove herself to Toby and the exhaustion of attempting to keep her balance. Eventually gravity won and she slithered to the floor. Heaving a sigh of relief, Laney reached over to the leading collar and took the reins. Miraculously her breathing had calmed, she didn't feel faint, and neither was she breaking out into a cold sweat at the sheer terror of being this close to a horse. All she wanted to do now was get Belle back to the farm and wrapped up in a rug, so that the mare didn't catch a chill. If anything happened to this horse, Toby would be devastated.

'Just tell me something,' she said to the swaying American woman. 'The night you stayed in the luxury hotel, the night when Toby wouldn't join you, whose underpants were they?'

Anna giggled shrilly. 'Emile was in this country on business. It would have been a waste of a lovely suite not to have invited *somebody* to share it with me.'

Laney stared at her, appalled. The needle on Anna's moral compass was well and truly broken.

'I'm going to the party,' Anna slurred.

Her dress was torn and muddy and her make-up ruined. Her glossy red pout was smeared across her chin as though she'd been snogging Edward Cullen.

'It's cold – you need to get warm,' Laney told her. No matter what she thought of Anna, she couldn't leave her outside this drunk. If she passed out, Anna could get hypothermia. On the other hand, Belle was starting to shiver. 'I need to walk Belle home. Let's go back to the farm.'

Anna shook her head. 'No way. I'm going to party.'

And with this passing shot, she hurled herself over the gate and lurched into the darkness. *Fan-flipping-tastic*, thought Laney. Reaching into her beaded evening bag, which was looped about her wrist, she pulled out her phone and dialled Alyssa. The call went to answer phone, so Laney left a message explaining what had a happened and asking her to come and hunt for Anna. There wasn't much more she could do. She didn't have Toby's number, and Isla's phone was switched off.

Laney patted Belle's neck. 'I guess it's you and me now,' she said.

Belle whickered softly and blew sweet, oaty breath against Laney's neck.

'You're cold, aren't you, girl?' From those long-ago golden days – the days when Mummy had still been healthy, and Laney had loved nothing more than to read about and dream of horses – she remembered that if a horse caught a chill it could get colic. Horses could die of colic, couldn't they? She had to get Belle back. This was no time to be afraid or dither in the hope that back-up might arrive. The time for phobias was over.

'I'm cold too,' Laney told Belle as they set off across the ploughed field in the direction of the farm. Actually, *cold* was putting it mildly. She was freezing. Her Fifties-style prom dress was very pretty, with its beaded boned bodice and ankle-length tulle skirt, but it was designed for balmy Alabama nights, not frosty English winters. Her teeth were starting to chatter. *I have to get moving*, she thought worriedly, *before we both catch our death*.

'Come on, Belle, let's go home.' She tugged at the reins and Belle picked up some speed, even though her foreleg seemed to be causing her some trouble. Laney kept talking and scratching the horse's neck, which seemed to calm Belle.

Hearing her own voice in the still darkness was reassuring too, and as they walked together she told her patient mare all about her feelings for Toby and her fear that maybe she had left it too late.

'I love him, Belle,' she murmured as they turned through the gate that led down the lane to the farm. 'I'm pretty sure I've loved him since the first time I saw him. I can only hope he feels the same way, or I don't know what I'll do.'

Belle blew gently on her neck. She was a good listener, and Laney was pretty certain that she would keep all of the secrets she had heard this night. All that Laney had to say to Toby had to come from her own lips.

At last she reached the stables, almost weeping with relief when she saw the warm light shining into the darkness. Her feet were numb in the thin ballet pumps, and her fingers so stiff and frozen that she thought she would never move them again. Somehow, though, she managed to coax Belle into a stable and find a rug to throw over the shivering mare. Then she slumped against the wall. She didn't think she'd ever been so cold or so exhausted. She backed out of the stable and bolted the door, then rested her head against the wood – the adrenalin caused by the fear escaping from her was making her feel shaky.

'Laney! Laney! Thank God you're safe.'

That voice! If she'd only heard one syllable, she would know it anywhere – it had haunted her for so long now. She opened her eyes, almost unable to believe that she wasn't dreaming, as Toby stepped from the shadows and into the light of the stable. She took a shaky step towards him and would have fallen into the straw if he hadn't caught her in his arms.

'Toby,' Laney gasped. 'Anna was riding Belle. She was drunk, and poor Belle was so frightened. I got her home.'

'I know, I know.' Toby pulled her close and wrapped her in his arms. 'That was so brave of you. Thank you.' Releasing her for a moment, he shrugged off his tuxedo and draped it around her shoulders. The fabric held the delicious warmth of his body and, when he pulled her close, she felt the heat of his skin against her cheek. Suddenly she didn't feel quite so chilly. In fact her blood was catching fire. A tidal wave of emotion swept over her and she closed her eyes. There was nothing she wanted more than to be here, right now, with Toby holding her. Everything else faded into total insignificance.

'You are something else!' he whispered into the top of her head. 'I know how scared you are of horses.'

She tilted her head back to gaze up at him. Staring into that strong face, those intense dark eyes, was enough to make her feel quite weak again.

'I'm not so scared of her any more,' she said. 'Besides, I didn't want Belle to get hurt.'

He nodded. 'It won't have done that pedal-bone injury any favours, that's for certain.' Releasing her for a moment, he opened Belle's stable and, crouching down by the horse, ran an experienced and tender hand down her leg. Belle looked at Laney and she could swear that the horse was gloating again.

'She'll be fine,' Toby said. 'Thanks to you. And well done

for cooling her off with the rug too. I couldn't have asked for more.'

For a moment Laney basked in the warm glow of his admiration. Then a thought occurred, and with a jolt her hand flew to her mouth.

'Toby, Anna's out there in the freezing cold.'

'Don't panic. Anna's absolutely fine,' Toby reassured her. 'Alyssa caught up with her and was drip-feeding her coffee, the last I saw. The worst that will happen to Anna is having a very sore head tomorrow.'

And an even sorer ego, Laney thought.

Toby was shaking his head. 'What on earth was she thinking of? Anna doesn't even ride.'

'She was thinking of winning you back,' Laney said gently.

He crossed his arms and regarded her thoughtfully through narrowed eyes. 'Believe me, that was never going to happen. Rekindling old relationships is never a very good idea. If the past was so good, it wouldn't be the past, would it?'

She flushed. Was he referring to Giles? It was time to make everything clear. 'Who exactly are you talking about?'

Now it was his turn to colour. 'I mean, for me. For other people it could be different . . .'

'I'm not back with Giles,' she told him quickly. 'He's a sweet guy and a good friend, but he isn't anything more than that. When you saw us together at the Singles' Ball we were just chatting.'

Toby groaned. 'You saw me?'

Laney nodded. 'I thought I was imagining it, though. You must admit that was the last place I'd ever expect to see you.'

He buried his face in his hands. 'Oh dear; you're right, of course. Talk about busted. You must think I'm weird.'

She stepped forward and peeled his hands away from his face. 'So tell me – Mr *I-Hate-the-City* Woodward – what *were* you doing there exactly?'

'Looking for somebody,' Toby said softly. He pulled her into his arms and his voice was husky with intensity. 'Somebody who is brave enough to face her phobias, kind enough to give up a life that she loved for her father, and so sweet that she gives piglets names like Applesauce.'

Laney hung her head at this. 'I suppose you must think I'm a really stupid city girl.'

'I think you're a great city girl. I never thought you were stupid. I thought you were beautiful and clever, and so far out of my league it was impossible even to hope that you might look at me.'

Laney couldn't speak. He thought she was beautiful? And clever? And out of his league? Really?

'I'm just a country boy at heart,' Toby said quietly, his hand skimming the soft skin of her shoulder, 'and I know I'm far from perfect, but I'd like to try to be.'

This was it. Time for the truth. There would be no more hiding from her feelings. When it came to Toby, she couldn't hide them, even if she wanted to.

'You *are* perfect,' she said, and her hands stole upwards to clasp his neck. Her fingers buried themselves in the curls at the nape of his neck, and they felt so right beneath her touch that she could have wept. 'Perfect for me.'

There was no further need for words. When Toby's mouth brushed hers, sparklers of pure happiness flamed through Laney, moving her almost to tears. And as a million fireworks exploded above their heads she knew beyond all doubt that Toby heard them too. His kisses told her so.

From now on, every day was going to be November the fifth.

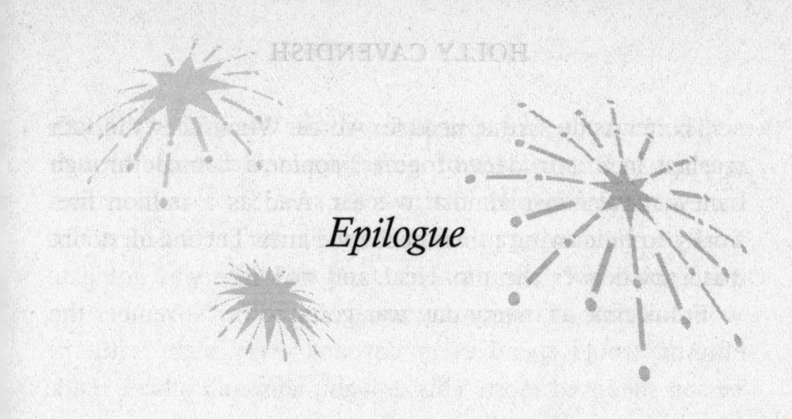

Epilogue

November the fifth, one year later

'I'm glad I'm not part of the Bonfire-Night Bonanza committee this year,' Toby said to Laney. Wrapping his arms around her, he pulled her to rest with her back against his chest. His lips grazing the tender skin of her throat, he whispered, 'I've got much better things to do.'

Laney turned her head and kissed him. She'd been kissing Toby for a year now, give or take those few odd weeks after last year's disastrous November the fifth, but she didn't think she'd ever get used to it. The fireworks were still there, but were even more colourful and vibrant now.

'We'd better watch the display first,' she told him, slapping a mock-severe expression onto her face.

'I'd much rather watch my girlfriend unpacking her things into our house,' grumbled Toby, pretending to be offended. 'And I'm so tired from lugging all the boxes down from her third-floor flat that I need to lie down on the bed. Preferably with her.'

His lips strayed to her earlobe, sending shivers of longing

across her body like a lit fuse. All the November the fifth displays in Britain added together couldn't compare to their own magical fireworks, that was for sure. She was so excited finally to be moving to Middlehaye Farm. The business had quadrupled over the past year and now she was going to work full-time as marketing manager.

And would spend every day and every night with the person she loved most. This thought, above all others, made her want to combust like a rocket with pure joy.

'Toby and Laney! Focus on the fireworks. Martin will be really offended otherwise.' Maxine joined them, waddling slightly over the uneven ground. Seven months pregnant, she and Vince were still slightly shell-shocked, but also deliriously happy. Vince was strutting around proudly, the twins were desperate to name the new baby after all the members of One Direction, and Maxine was glowing. She also had Vince running around after her so much that he'd lost at least another stone. Or maybe this was from all the hard work that came with running the B&B? Since he'd bought it from Nate, Vince said he'd never been so busy. Nate, recovering from his stroke thanks to Janet's TLC, was happily ensconced in a gorgeous Cotswold stone cottage just a short walk from his beloved river.

'At least it isn't raining this year,' said Martin with relief when he joined them. Wrapped up in his bobble hat and scarf against the cold, he beamed at Tana, who was also snuggled up in matching gear. Laney recognized Janet's handiwork. 'Let's hope this year's display is less eventful,' he added.

'Oh, I don't know,' said Toby thoughtfully, pulling Laney close. 'I quite like eventful.'

'Mum was hinting like crazy about Tana and me having a wedding on November the fifth,' said Martin. 'Is that eventful enough? Is St Pontian ready?'

Laney glanced across the green to where Nate and Janet were standing arm-in-arm watching the bonfire. Her heart lifted because Nate looked so much better. He was walking with just one stick now and had fully regained his speech. Their faces were blushed with firelight and happiness.

'I don't think it'll be long before Dad and Janet have their own announcement to make,' she said. 'How many weddings can one village take?'

'How about one more?' said Toby, and without warning he suddenly stepped into the display zone. 'OK, Martin?'

Martin nodded.

Laney looked from one to the other. *What's going on?* Now Toby was holding a taper and crouching down to light a fuse. She'd thought Tana was starting the display again this year.

There was a whoosh and a whizz of sound, and then one by one letters on a wire wall of fireworks started to go off in myriad pinks and purples and golds.

Laney, they read.

She couldn't believe that Toby had set all this up for her.

will you

Laney could guess what was coming next; she looked at Toby and he beamed back.

marry me?

Laney gasped. This was everything she had ever wanted. Fireworks were exploding all around her, literally and metaphorically.

'I thought country boys weren't into big displays of affection?' she teased.

Toby, on one knee now, and slightly muddy, looked up at her and gave her a smile of such pure love that her heart turned a somersault.

'They are when they find the right girl,' he answered.

The entire village seemed to be holding its collective breath, but for Laney there was only one person that she could see. There had only ever been one person for her – one man who lit her fuse. And there was only one answer too, wasn't there?

'Yes!' she half-laughed, half-sobbed. 'Yes. Of course I'll marry you!'

As the gathered crowd burst into cheers, Toby jumped to his feet and pulled Laney into his arms, raining down onto her upturned face kisses that were every bit as explosive as the fireworks behind them.

And as she kissed him back, Laney knew beyond all doubt that this was one fireworks display that was going to last for the rest of her life.